The Device Trial

Tom Breen

PEGASUS BOOKS

Pegasus Books
3338 San Marino Ave
San Jose, CA 95127
www.pegasusbooks.net

First Edition: May 2016

Published in North America by Pegasus Books. For information, please contact Pegasus Books c/o Christopher Moebs, 3338 San Marino Ave, San Jose, CA 95127.

Library of Congress Cataloguing-In-Publication Data
Tom Breen
The Device Trial/Tom Breen 1st ed
p. cm.
Library of Congress Control Number: [2010943502]
ISBN – 978-1-941859-47-6

1. FICTION / Thrillers / Legal. 2. LAW / Insurance. 3. LAW / Ethics & Professional Responsibility. 4. FICTION / Legal. 5. MEDICAL / Health Care Delivery. 6. MEDICAL / Practice Management & Reimbursement.

10 9 8 7 6 5 4 3 2 1

Comments about *The Device Trial* and requests for additional copies, book club rates and author speaking appearances may be addressed to Tom Breen or Pegasus Books c/o Christopher Moebs, 3338 San Marino Ave, San Jose, CA, 95127, or you can send your comments and requests via e-mail to cmoebs@pegasusbooks.net.

Also available as an eBook from Internet retailers and from Pegasus Books

Printed in the United States of America

This book is dedicated to my father and mother, Frank and Joan Breen, may they rest together in the peace of God. Their guidance and selflessness was the foundation upon which five children learned to confront the challenges of life by realizing the strength that's found within.

I have also dedicated this novel to Erin and Siobhán, the children of my marriage with Deidre. They have accomplished more than we ever imagined, while bringing warmth and a smile to those fortunate enough to be part of their lives.

Acknowledgement

Nothing would have been accomplished without the indispensable input, insight and editing of my wife of thirty-seven years, Deidre E. Breen, the love of my life.

I would also like to mention a note of appreciation to New England School of Law in Boston. Over forty years ago, I was admitted to the law school, then located at 126 Newbury Street, and graduated in 1976. New England Law has received national acclaim and recognition for the excellent legal skills imparted to its students. I will always be grateful for its emphasis on practicing the law, not just reading the law.

Once again, a special thanks to Jean Burke, on Fulton Street in NYC. She found errors and omissions obvious to her and completely overlooked by me.

New York attorney Brian Bradford was severely injured and hospitalized after the violent confrontation at the end of the first novel, ***The Complaint.*** Having not learned his lesson from the first litigation against ZeiiMed, he decides upon his return to work to commence a second lawsuit against the billion dollar health insurance company. He agreed to file the suit after meeting the elderly Martha Dudley and learning that she was dying from a defective hip replacement device manufactured by a subsidiary of ZeiiMed.

To obtain evidence that ZeiiMed knew of the defects, Brian must engage in illegal and unethical conduct that once again results in a life and death struggle with John Edison, the CEO of ZeiiMed.

In preparing for trial against ZeiiMed, Brian realizes he has little chance of success without the invaluable assistance of his colleague Mary and his dear friend Meadhbh. Together they form a team that will hopefully bring ZeiiMed to its knees in a high profile trial in lower Manhattan.

A creative plan of sexual diversion is implemented to provide Brian with critical inculpatory documents hidden by ZeiiMed in a masterful deception.

ZeiiMed, of course, refuses to accept defeat at trial and unleashes a storm of violence on Brian and the women he cherishes. It's up to Brian to win both inside and outside the Courtroom, despite ZeiiMed's best efforts to destroy anyone in its path to victory.

THE DEVICE TRIAL

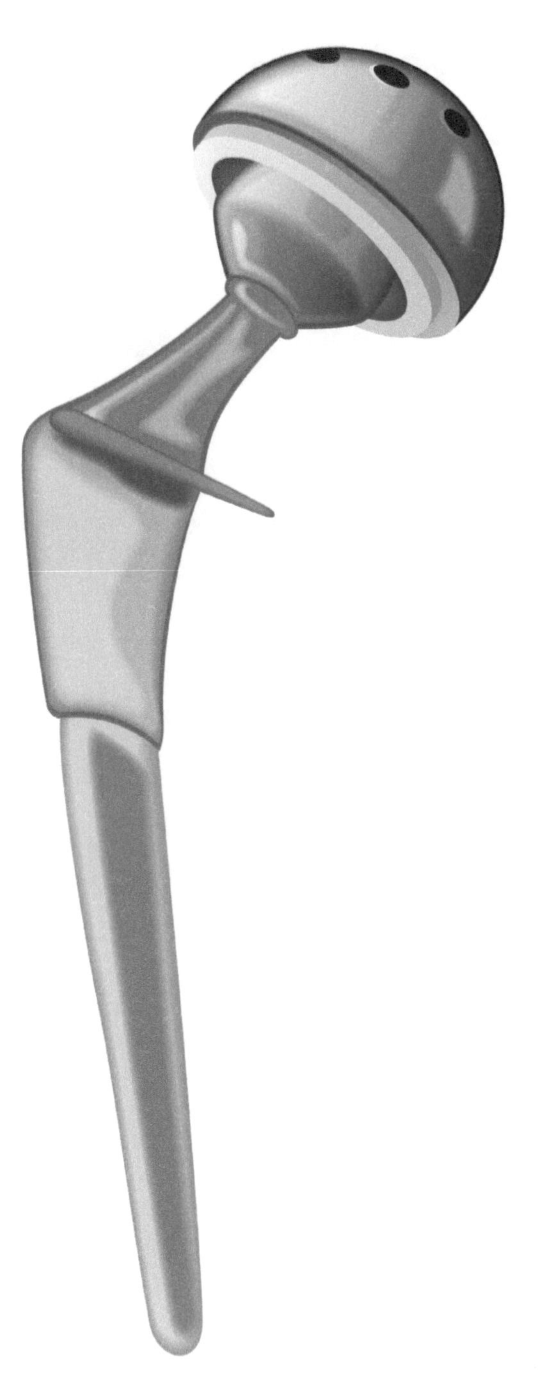

PROLOGUE

New York Press. Page 5, April 22, 2010:

RUMBLE IN THE RAMBLE

What could possibly be the reason that a downtown lawyer and the Chief Executive Officer of the largest health insurance corporation in the world decided to settle their differences by hand-to-hand combat with knives and clubs in an isolated, wooded section of Central Park late at night? According to the police, the answer is not known. But, enough is known to conclude that these two idiots aren't bright enough to let the Courts decide whatever dispute they may have.

The police reported that John Edison, the boss at ZeiiMed, everyone's favorite insurance company, was found in the Ramble with a foot wound that bled excessively from a knife that ripped through his foot. Although close to death, Mr. Edison was resuscitated and rushed to the hospital. After receiving treatment, he told the hospital staff that Attorney Brian Bradford had assaulted him with a knife and a billy club in a surprise attack while on an evening walk in the Park. It has been confirmed that Mr. Bradford recently commenced a massive lawsuit against ZeiiMed and then settled the case for $1 billion several months ago. We can only guess that Mr. Bradford was very disappointed in the fee he received in the settlement with ZeiiMed, although no one knows for sure.

Mr. Edison's face will be surgically repaired and reconstructed, with his foot requiring several operations. Mr. Bradford's injuries are unknown. Hopefully, this incident is not reflective of a new trend by lawyers to beat up their adversaries not only in the courtroom, but also in the streets and parks of the City. It is not known when Mr. Bradford will be questioned by police.

-1-

How could I have possibly thought that the practice of law in downtown New York was the height of boredom which increased in intensity as each piece of paper was slowly pushed from one side of the desk to the other each long day? I've now learned how utterly wrong I was in making that assessment. Lying immobilized in a hospital bed is, without question, the ultimate trip to the extremes of boredom.

It's April 23, 2010 and I'm a patient at the Nicholas Institute of Sports Medicine and Athletic Trauma at Lenox Hill Hospital on 100 East 77th Street. But my injuries have nothing to do with recreational sports. Ironically, I was beaten into this state of disrepair in a face-to-face fight with an enemy I had intended to ambush while in an isolated section of the Ramble in Central Park one evening. I know, it doesn't sound very sane and it probably wasn't a very good plan in retrospect. But, the guy I was fighting–his name is John Edison–had instructed his thugs to seriously injure a dear friend of mine, which caused me to obsess with evening the score.

Truth be told, despite my wounds, I did succeed in seriously injuring Edison. Although my recall remains hazy due to the brutal beating he likewise inflicted on me, I know for sure that I stabbed my razor knife completely through his foot and then smashed his face with a billy club for good measure. I left him in the woods to suffer as his blood slowly drained from his wounds. I was eventually able to find help and get an ambulance. The ambulance was for me, not Edison.

I thought Edison would bleed to death, but the New York newspapers said he was eventually rescued. While my actions and attitude towards Edison may seem unmerciful, there are reasons for my uncompromising hatred of the man.

In addition to the horrendous beating of my friend, he was responsible for the attempted killing of my wife, the murder of a New York City detective and a lawyer who worked at a prominent midtown firm. He also made numerous threats of violence against people working with me at my law firm. I had just cause. And, now I get to enjoy thinking about how much Edison must be suffering.

As my wife Kim would certainly remind me, lawyers are not trained for physical confrontation and will usually lose in rather severe fashion. Since I am still alive, my opinion is that I didn't lose my encounter with Edison in the Ramble. It was Edison who was left bleeding in an isolated corner of Central Park. I am, nonetheless, in extreme pain and confined to the four corners of this small, rock-hard bed, with my only activity being the flexing of my toes as they dangle over the end of the mattress.

My injuries were caused by two violent blows with a metal pipe delivered by Edison as he stood over me after I tripped on a dirt pathway in the Ramble. I thought I was approaching Edison undetected when, in fact, he was purposefully luring me to a place advantageous for his unforeseen assault on me. Lawyers often lack common sense and reasonable judgment, in addition to having poor combat skills.

The metal pipe first struck me on the left elbow with bone-crushing force. The doctors called it a radial head fracture, which is essentially a breakage of the round disc that controls all the movement of the elbow, the lower arm and fingers. During surgery, the doctors removed the broken pieces of bone, reconstructed the radial head and fixed it in place with screws and pins. There was soft tissue damage as well. My arm is currently encased in a fiberglass tube, which runs from my shoulder to my wrist, with the elbow bent at a 90 degree angle. I'm stuck with this club arm for the next several weeks.

The second blow from the metal pipe was just below my knee. I was lucky. No bones were broken, although muscles were bruised, the tissue torn and substantial subdural bleeding. It will take more time to heal than the elbow, with a cane or crutches necessary once the leg no longer needs to be elevated 24 hours a day.

It's difficult to read in the hospital bed because balancing a book and turning the pages with one hand is challenging. There is a television, but there are huge gaps of unfulfilled hours between major sports events such as the Mets and the Yankees. I've only been here two days, but my constant struggle with the pain and lack of stimulation is mental agony. In fact, the only bright spot in my day is the vision of feminine pulchritude known as Registered Nurse Brenda Norman.

As usual, Nurse Brenda was all business as she entered my hospital room.

"Good afternoon, Mr. Bradford. How are you feeling? Has the pain in your arm gotten better? Is the swelling in your leg reduced?" she asked, as she prepared to take my blood pressure.

"Do you want me to lie and say how great I feel or tell the truth about how miserable I am?"

"Typical lawyer, you never give a straight answer. Tell me anything you want because I've already learned to ignore most of what you say, even though we hardly know each other."

"That sounds very much like something my wife would tell me," I responded.

"Then maybe you aren't as hopeless as I thought. You were bright enough to marry a very smart woman."

Brenda was now squeezing the rubber air pressure bulb and evaluating my rising numbers on the blood pressure gauge as I observed her. Her dark complexion was radiant. Her elongated brown eyes seemed to stretch to the side of her face, with the upper and lower rows of exotic lashes accentuated by thick black eyeliner that came to a point at the edge of her temples. Her long dark hair was pinned up and contrasted nicely with her white jacket and skirt. Under the jacket, she wore a light blue blouse, but it was the white stockings that really made my day.

"The more you stare at me, the higher your pressure rises. Maybe you should just look at the wall or think about the saints while I'm checking your vitals."

“It won’t work. You’re stored in my memory bank,” I commented.

“Look, we have a lot to do today, so let’s try our best to maintain professional decorum. But before we proceed, I want to mention that I read a very interesting newspaper article about your encounter in the Ramble. I didn’t know you were such a celebrity. The article also implied that the police will eventually interview you. It should be fun when the police get here. Do you mind if I stay?” Brenda asked.

“Very funny. That article only tells half the story. How do you think I got in this condition? That guy Edison beat the hell out of me with a metal pipe while I lay helplessly on the ground. I had tripped on a dirt pathway in the dark. If he had gotten off one more blow, he probably would have killed me. But the article was informative because I learned that Edison was alive. I thought he bled to death in the Ramble after I put a knife through his foot and crushed his face.”

“I understand. But that doesn’t explain how you and he ended up in a physical confrontation in a secluded section of the Park.”

“I admit I was following him with evil intent, but he had a history of violent behavior, attacking me, my wife, a police detective, and a young woman who is currently being treated uptown for severe brain damage.”

“I’m so sorry. It sounds like you have been living this nightmare for a while. I guess you decided to just end it once and for all with this Edison character. Unfortunately, however, whatever your motive, the police will certainly be paying you a visit. But, today’s your lucky day. You’re scheduled for a sponge bath. I’m sure you want to look your best for the visitors.”

“A sponge bath? What does that mean exactly?” I asked.

“You don’t need to do a thing. I use a wet sponge and you just lie still while I do my job.”

“You’re kidding, right?”

“No, I am not. First, I’m going to pull this curtain around your bed and then we’ll get started.”

“Are you sure no one can see around the curtain?”

"Yes, I'm sure. I'm surprised you asked that. You don't seem like the shy type. Now, lie still. Next, I'm going to pull down your bed covers and put a plastic sheet under you."

"I feel like a sandwich about to be covered in Saran Wrap."

"You're doing fine. I'm now going to open your hospital gown from the front. If you will please lean forward a little. I'll pull the gown over your good shoulder, and then over the cast. Good. We're ready to begin your bath."

"I feel rather exposed lying here naked."

"Other than your injuries, you look very healthy and fit. There is nothing to be ashamed of. I do this every day and have seen hundreds of naked men of all ages, even men your age."

"I'm only in my fifties."

"Don't be so sensitive, I enjoy the company of older men with or without clothes."

The warm, moist sponge on my chest did feel soothing and pleasant. I closed my eyes and tried my best to concentrate on the Holy Ghost, but it was clearly a losing battle. My mind fixated on the thought of Brenda's eyes focusing on the task before her.

I heard the metal rings supporting the curtain slide along the curtain rod. I opened my eyes.

"I would certainly recognize that body anywhere," Kim said. "You look in peak condition for a sick person. I should know better than to leave you alone."

Kim, my wife of many years, had pulled the curtain open and now stood next to Brenda.

I tried to pull my gown across my body with my one good arm. I wasn't very successful.

"Don't cover up on my account. I'm your wife, remember? I've seen it all before and rather enjoyed it on occasion," commented Kim, as she continued with her comedy routine.

"Kim, this is my very able and professional nurse, Brenda. She's been a life saver," I said, hoping to change the subject.

"I can see. You do seem to be savoring life quite a bit at the moment, my dear husband."

Kim shook hands with Brenda.

"Hi, Brenda. Nice to meet you. All kidding aside, thanks for your hard work. It's rare I have such a prime opportunity to make fun of Brian, so I hope you don't mind."

"Not at all. I understand. I'll finish up later. I'm sure you two want to be alone. Your husband is quite a character, but so far he hasn't yet stepped out of line," Brenda mentioned to Kim.

"Ladies, ladies. I'm sure you're enjoying your chat, but could someone please cover me with something?"

"Brenda, I'll take care of him. I'm sure your skills are better utilized on truly sick patients who don't talk back. Thanks again for all your help."

"See you later, Mr. Bradford. You're due for more medication in about an hour. Mrs. Bradford, very nice meeting you and I'm quite happy to transfer his supervision to you."

Brenda pulled the curtain fully around the bed as she left. Kim took a folded blanket from the end of the bed and covered me from neck to toes.

"Thank you. That's comfortable. I'm so glad to see you," I said sincerely.

"I guess you *are* badly injured. Normally, you would insist on me taking care of business before I covered you up. I guess I'll be a little more sensitive to your painful condition."

"Yes, you're right. I am seriously injured and a little sympathy would be appropriate," I responded. "By the way, thanks for stopping by and leaving the 'Get Well' card when I was in a post-surgery dream world. When I'm feeling better, I think we should discuss your note about reevaluating life."

"Well, if you must know, I am still very upset from the call two nights ago informing me you were about to have emergency surgery. I knew you were meeting again with that creep Edison because of what was done to Meadhbh

O'Shea, but I didn't know you were planning on having a fight to the death."

"I hadn't planned on it either. I wanted to punish Edison for the injuries to Meadhbh, but I had no idea that he would end up breaking my arm with a metal pipe."

Meadhbh, pronounced M-a-y-v, is a recent acquaintance who became a very dear friend. She is the bartender at the restaurant *Très Bien* on East 84th Street. I first spoke to her at the bar while trying to figure out a way to have a face-to-face meeting with John Edison. That was well before our "Rumble in the Ramble" as the *New York Press* coined it.

The first time I met Meadhbh, I already knew that Edison lived in an apartment above Très Bien with the same street address as the restaurant. What I didn't know was that Meadhbh would prove very helpful in assisting me in confronting Edison on two occasions prior to the Ramble: Once in his apartment where I appeared uninvited and unwanted and a later occasion at a table in the restaurant. Unfortunately, her assistance was noticed by either Edison or some other goon at ZeiiMed, a billion-dollar managed health care company with Edison as its Chief Executive Officer. As a result, one night she was beaten viciously by a couple of assailants outside her apartment. She is now receiving medical treatment for traumatic brain injury.

"I'm still upset you showed such poor judgment, but so thankful you're alive," said Kim. "It's just mind-boggling that your lawsuit against ZeiiMed to recover millions of dollars of unpaid fees owed to hundreds of thankless doctors would catapult into a murderous scheme that resulted in the death of your two doctors, however evil they may have been, a police detective and a ZeiiMed lawyer. And, let's not forget ZeiiMed's vigorous attempts to physically injure or kill both of us. It's just too much to comprehend."

"I know. It's all beyond belief. I'm sorry I ever got involved with ZeiiMed because the eventual consequences were so grave to so many. As for the other night, you're right. I should have been smart enough not to end up in some desolate area of Central Park with that lunatic. But, the good news is that it's over. Edison is so badly injured he may never get out of bed. I put him as close to death as possible without the Grim Reaper getting his soul. My lawsuit against ZeiiMed is settled and doctors all across the country have finally been paid the money wrongfully withheld from them. I'm now done with my personal pursuit of both Edison and ZeiiMed. That part of my life is now closed forever," I said with a sincere, yet unrealistic, belief in the truth of my words. "I want to return to our uncomplicated, mundane, predictable lifestyle that we both found rewarding and comfortable."

Truthfully, I really didn't know how my battle with ZeiiMed would finally play out. But, I knew the extreme injuries I inflicted on Edison would hold everything in abeyance for a while. As a result, my present goal was to keep Kim calm and relaxed and, most importantly, not apprehensive of physical harm to either of us.

"I sure hope you're right, but I'm not totally convinced. After publication of that article in the *New York Press,* I know for sure the police don't consider their investigation to be over. Plus, if Edison was really out of the picture because of his injuries, I'm sure he'll just be replaced by someone else at ZeiiMed. There will be an interim CEO appointed and who knows what his or her agenda will be," Kim stated, apparently understanding that my unconvincing effort to assuage her fears lacked any credibility.

I couldn't help but stare at Kim's natural beauty. Her bangs flowed slightly down her forehead, with the rest of her straight, dark hair touching her shoulders. Her tan face and toned body made her appear ready to run the New York Marathon at a moment's notice. Yet, her look was sensuous, as well as athletic. In addition to her large brown eyes, her full upper lip curved gently upward to form two distinctive peaks above her brilliantly white front teeth. The combination created an irresistible feminine allure.

Kim and I have lived for many years in the Village of Port Jefferson on the North Shore of Long Island. Our house is a short walk from Port Jefferson harbor, which protects the Village from Long Island Sound. For many years, Kim taught high school in the Village. She retired a few years ago and now works for the Bridgeport and Port Jefferson Steamboat Company. The Company operates three large ferries, which run from the pier in the Village across the Sound to Connecticut, with each ferry capable of carrying at least ninety cars. On the pier, the ferry company has a building with an administrative office, a customer waiting room and an information booth. Kim is part of the office staff and enjoys working there Monday through Friday. She meets many new people, walks to work and has an office facing the water. Maybe one day I'll smarten up and apply for a job there.

"So, let's take it one day at a time," I said. "I can handle the police and steer clear of Edison, although I will keep an eye on ZeiiMed's reaction to his current unavailability to function as the CEO. Edison won't be up and running for a while, so I don't think we have to worry about him for the foreseeable future. Now, help me put on this hospital gown so I'm decent when the police arrive."

"My pleasure. While the curtain's drawn, don't you want me to cuddle up with you on the bed?" Kim asked flirtatiously.

"Thanks, as always I find you irresistible, but I must restrain myself. I am convinced the authorities will arrive any moment. Let's make a date for tomorrow morning," I answered, as she helped me look presentable.

"I'll be on my way. Call me if you need anything, but I won't be available tonight. I've got something to do, but I'll be by tomorrow as planned."

We kissed.

We hugged.

Kim opened the curtain.

"You won't be available? I finally asked. "What does that mean? What will you be doing? Are you referring to the note in your card–something about another person to turn to for comfort?"

"I can't tell you about it just now," Kim responded. "We do need to talk, but it can wait until you feel better. I'll explain everything when the time is right."

Kim kissed me again, this time on the cheek.

She left the room.

Where was Kim going tonight? Why was she "unavailable?" Something is happening and I need to find some answers quickly. I must do everything possible to speed up my recovery and expedite my discharge so I can find out what's going on.

Once home, I will have a long chat with Kim about why she was unavailable to me, yet apparently available to someone else. Maybe I'm assuming the worst but, as we all know, anything can happen when it comes to the most complex and unpredictable relationship of all–marriage.

-2-

As I anticipated, an hour after Kim left the hospital, two NYC police officers knocked on the open door before entering my hospital room.

"Are you Brian Bradford, the lawyer who works on Wall Street and resides in Port Jefferson, Long Island?"

"Yes, I am. And who do I have the pleasure of meeting?" I asked.

"I'm Sergeant Melissa Black and this is Officer Mark Miller. As a result of an incident in Central Park a couple of evenings ago, we have a few questions to ask as part of our investigation."

I immediately knew this conversation with the Sergeant was not going to go smoothly. She had a thin face and deep set eyes that created a look of sternness. Her thick, brown hair had blond streaks, most of which were somehow stuffed into her navy blue uniform cap. The cap was pulled down almost to her eyebrows. Her crisp police uniform looked sharp and seemed to enhance her stiff demeanor. The navy blue, long-sleeve shirt had a collar and covered pockets, with a matching tie. There were decorations and a badge above the left pocket and the NYC police patch on her arm in the shape of a curved triangle pointed downward.

Officer Miller had the same uniform, without the Sergeant's rank. He had broad shoulders, hair shaven to the skull and a round face with thin lips. They both had chosen the Glock 19 as their 9mm semiautomatic service pistol.

"Okay. Proceed with your questions. I'll answer to the best of my ability. But before we start, I have just two inquiries. Am I under arrest and should I have my lawyer present?" I asked, to put them a little on the defensive.

"No, you are not under arrest at the present time and it's totally up to you whether to have your lawyer present," the Sergeant responded, with the slightest hint of a smile. Maybe I was softening her up. Then again, probably not.

"I'll tell you what. As long as you keep smiling while we talk, I won't call a lawyer. As soon as your smile vanishes, that will be my signal to get an attorney."

"Don't be such a wise guy. We don't need your smart aleck comments," Officer Miller said aggressively.

I ignored Officer Miller.

"Proceed, Sergeant, I'm all yours. Please pardon my attire. This the best they have to offer here. And, in case you're interested, I am in a lot of pain and have a morphine drip I dispense manually at my discretion. If I don't like a question, I'll take an extra dose before answering."

I think Officer Miller was ready to smack me, but the Sergeant gave him some kind of barely detectable signal to restrain himself.

"You really are quite a clown, Mr. Bradford. I will remind you that this is not a laughing matter and needs to be taken seriously," the Sergeant admonished.

"Like I said, please proceed. I don't know what you have on your mind so I don't know if it's serious or not."

I guess that was a lie, but the Sergeant didn't take out her handcuffs.

"Do you know a Mr. John Edison?" the Sergeant asked.

"I know him in the sense that I have talked with him on several occasions and I filed a legal Complaint against his company, ZeiiMed, the largest health insurance company in the world."

"Did you see Mr. Edison leave his apartment building on East 84th Street after dark a couple of nights ago?"

"Yes, I did."

"Did you follow Mr. Edison as he proceeded to walk toward Central Park?"

"Yes, I did."

"Prior to that occasion, had you been observing Mr. Edison's apartment house both day and night?"

"Yes, periodically."

"Did you continue to follow Mr. Edison as he entered Central Park on his evening walk?"

"Yes, I did. Would you like to know why?"

"Yes, but Mr. Edison has already explained the reason. Mr. Edison said that you blamed him for the mugging of a young woman who works as a bartender at *Très Bien*, the French restaurant on the ground floor of Mr. Edison's apartment building. Mr. Edison said he had nothing to do with her injuries. In fact, he dines at *Très Bien* and enjoys speaking to her on occasion."

"Meadhbh. Her name is Meadhbh. She is a lovely woman of Irish descent and a dear friend of mine. Edison either specifically authorized her brutal beating or somehow communicated to his staff by words or actions that he would be pleased to see her injured. Yes, I followed him and I intended to let him know there will be consequences," I stated, unfortunately letting my emotions shape my response.

I forced myself to recover my composure.

"Did you also intend to inflict physical injury on him as revenge for Meadhbh?"

"No, that was not my intention." I lied once again.

"Mr. Edison told us that you attacked him as he walked in the Ramble. As part of your attack, you put a knife through his foot and then crushed his facial bones with a billy club. Do you deny Mr. Edison's statement?"

"I don't deny that I inflicted those injuries, but my actions were completely in self-defense. Take a look at me. He beat me senseless with a metal pipe while I was on the ground, defenseless. If I hadn't stopped him from hitting me, I'd be dead right now and Edison would be wanted for murder."

"It's your word against his and I believe Mr. Edison to be truthful," Officer Miller interrupted.

"I don't care and it doesn't matter anyway. I'll bet Edison hasn't sworn out a criminal complaint against me," I mentioned.

"No, he didn't. In fact, he said he wouldn't appear at the criminal trial if we charged you with a crime. But that doesn't mean the District Attorney will not bring the case," the Sergeant clarified.

"I'll tell you why Edison said he won't cooperate with you. It's because he is a ruthless monster who gave orders to kill a number of people. I'm also convinced that ZeiiMed authorized the death of a good friend of mine, Detective Jack Jarret. Jack was assigned to protect me after ZeiiMed tried to kill me on two separate occasions. He was murdered at JFK Airport while watching out for my safety as I was leaving for vacation. Although the guy who actually killed Jack claimed he did it on his own, I personally believe ZeiiMed approved his death because Jack's surveillance impeded ZeiiMed's plan to end my life."

"You're accusing Edison and ZeiiMed of intentionally arranging the murder of a New York City Police detective?" asked Officer Miller, incredulously.

"Yes, but you won't find any record of it downtown. The guy who actually strangled Detective Jack to death was also killed by ZeiiMed shortly thereafter. The NYPD never looked into the fact that Jack's killer was a ZeiiMed henchman. His name was Dr. Stanley Hyman and he was my client, a plaintiff in my lawsuit against ZeiiMed. For the record, I'm the one who turned Hyman over to the authorities after he confessed to killing Jack. Off the record, I tortured Hyman until he confessed–but, at least I got the truth. It turns out that I was set up–Hyman really worked for ZeiiMed. But, because Hyman failed to kill Jack, he was eventually murdered by ZeiiMed in a hospital while in police custody. I know this sounds insane, but it's the truth. I've told the same story to the New York Attorney General and the Department of Justice, but no one was able to nail Edison or ZeiiMed."

"Your story is beyond belief, but I will look into the records on the detective's death. If it turns out to be consistent with your story, then we can probably call your altercation with Edison self-defense," the Sergeant stated as her evaluation of the matter. "However, Edison seems to have a lot of influence downtown, so I can't guarantee anything."

"I don't care who he knows. It was self-defense and there is no way in hell that Edison wants to face me in a criminal trial. It's too much publicity for him, too much trouble for

ZeiiMed. And, by the way, I want to swear out a criminal complaint against Edison for putting me in the hospital."

"It ain't happening," the Sergeant stated. "Like I said, this guy Edison knows people. I'm not getting involved. You want to swear out a complaint, you'll have to go down to the precinct yourself and talk to the desk sergeant. But from the look of your injuries, it doesn't seem you'll be walking to the precinct anytime soon."

"That's right. It's best you just mind your own business and hope we consider this little incident a wash and forget about it." Officer Miller added, apparently summarizing in local vernacular the position of the New York City Police Department.

It was now clear this interview with the authorities was going nowhere.

"So, here I am, nearly beaten to death by Edison and you tell me he has friends at Headquarters so nothing is going to happen to him. Plus, I'm lucky I haven't been arrested for attacking him. Well, I think you two should be ashamed of yourselves. But, I do hear what you're saying. Even if I swear out a complaint, the case will never go to trial and Edison will never face jail time. I'll bet ZeiiMed gives a ton of money every year to the NYPD Widows' and Orphans' Fund."

"You better shut up right now or I'll make sure you're arrested as soon as you can get in a wheelchair," Officer Miller threatened, as he stepped closer to the bed.

"What are you going to do, handcuff my one good arm? I think our little chat is over. The Manhattan District Attorney won't prosecute Edison and Edison doesn't want to be any part of a criminal prosecution against me. So, we'll all just close our files and walk away, except I'm not yet capable of walking."

"Like I said, a wash," Officer Miller repeated.

"Yes, I get it. Nice seeing you, Sergeant Black and Officer Miller. I'm hoping we don't meet again. And, be sure to look at the file on Detective Jack--it will confirm everything I've told you, including the fact I restrained Hyman on an airplane, physically forced him to admit to suffocating Jack and then turned him over to the police. I'll handle things on my own from here on out."

"Goodbye, Mr. Bradford. I suggest you don't cause any trouble for Mr. Edison or you'll see us again," Sergeant Black said, as she turned to leave the room.

"Goodbye, Bradford. I'm sure you're in a lot of pain, but it probably won't last longer than a couple of months," Officer Miller said with a nasty grin.

That didn't go well.

I really should learn to behave better when meeting with New York's finest.

-3-

While Brian Bradford was languishing in self-pity and pain at Lenox Hill Hospital, John Edison was likewise unhappily confined to a hospital bed on 168th Street. A patient at New York Presbyterian Hospital at Columbia Medical Center, he was being treated for serious injury to the skull bones that support his facial features.

In their encounter in the Ramble, Brian Bradford had used a billy club to collapse Edison's face inside his skull. The repair and stabilization of the fractured bones required extensive craniofacial surgery to reconstruct the skull and attempt to correct the complex facial deformity. Bone grafting and the insertion of natural and man-made polymeric materials were used to address his extreme facial trauma.

John Edison was motionless as he tried to sleep. It was practically impossible without drugs. Not only was the pain intense, but the extremely uncomfortable bandages covered his entire face as they wrapped around his skull from the bottom of his chin to the top of his head, with narrow slits for his eyes, ears and nose. Only the bald spot on the very top of his head was left uncovered. He didn't know what he looked like under the bandages, but he was certain he would never look like himself again.

The plastic surgeon had numerous photos to guide them in recreating his image. But they could only do so much. The doctors restored his face, but they were unable to duplicate his looks. The damage was too extensive. The doctors had told him as much before the first of several operations.

His foot was badly damaged to the point of possible amputation. Bradford had forced his knife completely through Edison's foot and increased the depth and width of the wound by moving the knife back and forth as the penetration increased. It was a miracle he hadn't bled to death before being found on a remote dirt path deep in the Ramble.

"That bastard Bradford left me to die in the woods," Edison mumbled loudly to himself in a sweaty frenzy of hatred, his eyes closed and no one around but medical staff more concerned with their coffee breaks than his ranting.

The painkillers finally started to relax him, although his obsessive fixation on Bradford continued to dominate his diminishing consciousness. Edison's mind was now speaking to him as if someone in the room was narrating a tale of the events in the Ramble, as if the story had occurred to someone else.

> *Bradford knew that Edison wouldn't be found that night in the Ramble. Bradford could have told whoever eventually assisted him that there was another injured person not far away, but he didn't. Edison's only hope was to be spotted the next day after sun-up, having spent the night in a pool of his own blood, with the anguished torment of knowing his face was a pulverized mass of indistinguishable flesh. Edison was eventually found the next morning. Edison had been forced by Bradford to fight for his life during the course of an entire night, the approaching death relentlessly trying to consume him.*

The imaginary voice reading to Edison suddenly stopped as he fell asleep. Edison's body and mind were starting to recover, although he knew some of his injuries would never be restored to normal. Edison's recovery was driven by the depth of his animosity and disgust for Bradford. Edison's soul was consumed with the singular goal of inflicting unspeakable horror and pain on the life and being of Bradford.

But, physical injury to the body of Bradford would not be enough. Bradford must also endure the mental anguish of knowing that others close to him had also been punished because of him. Edison's sole source of strength was his commitment to achieve health in order to inflict havoc. He would not know peace or contentment until his goal, his only goal, was achieved and Bradford was extinguished in unbearable agony along with his wife and allies. Edison would not stop until his mission was accomplished.

Edison woke from his sleep and once again faced the reality of his physical misery and forced confinement. He struggled to reconstruct the events that led to his injuries several days earlier. Edison was able to visualize what had occurred, as if he was viewing himself from above as he watched the moments unfold. In the haze created by the drugs, Edison's mind again seemed to be reading him a tale that relived the events leading to the encounter in the Ramble.

> *Bradford had been staking out Edison's apartment building on East 84th Street on a regular basis each evening from a coffee house across the street. Edison was sure that Bradford was pursuing him in order to eventually confront him about the mugging of the female bartender at Très Bien, the French restaurant on the ground floor of Edison's building. Prior to the mugging, Bradford had confronted Edison one evening in the restaurant demanding that ZeiiMed stop harassing him and his family in retaliation for a lawsuit against ZeiiMed. Bradford had sued ZeiiMed alleging that ZeiiMed underpaid the medical profession by programming its computers with old, out-of-date billing data that reduced or depressed the payments to the doctors.*
>
> *Bradford had vigorously prosecuted his lawsuit against ZeiiMed and wouldn't relent. That's when ZeiiMed decided to send him a message by threatening his life and well-being. Events spiraled out of control and Edison's staff decided to attack the bartender, Meadhbh O'Shea, to teach Bradford a lesson.*

Bradford started staking out Edison's apartment building right after Meadhbh suffered severe head injuries in the assault.

Knowing that Bradford would not back down from his pursuit of revenge, Edison decided on a plan to turn the tables on him. Although Edison's staff at ZeiiMed wanted to quickly terminate Bradford while he slept at his home in Port Jefferson, Edison wanted to personally administer a brutal punishment on Bradford.

Edison eventually settled on a plan. He would make sure that Bradford saw him entering his building each evening and occasionally walking next store for dinner at Très Bien, but always with his security force. Then one rainy night, Edison implemented his plan to leave his building without any security sometime after 9 p.m. Since it was wet out, Bradford didn't suspect that Edison's full-length unopened umbrella had been modified to contain an easily accessible metal pipe.

Sure enough, Bradford followed at a presumably safe distance as Edison walked towards Central Park without his bodyguards. Entering the Park at 72nd Street, Edison headed toward the Boathouse Restaurant for a cold beer at the bar. Edison knew Bradford was lurking not far behind. At the Boathouse, Edison tried to relax before the big finish. Edison was relishing the anticipation of the encounter, to be quickly followed by Bradford's demise.

Edison needed a secluded location so there would be no chance of detection by others. It was a particularly dark night when Edison continued his walk, leaving the Boathouse Restaurant and heading to the most remote section of the Park called the Ramble. Again, Bradford followed behind as Edison walked deeper into a heavily wooded section with trees and bushes on both sides of the asphalt paths. Edison quickly turned off the walkway onto a narrow, isolated dirt path with overlapping trees forming an impenetrable wall of dense foliage.

Bradford followed onto the dirt path and suddenly startled Edison by moving quickly towards him, closing the gap between them. However, just a few yards from Edison, Bradford fell to the ground having somehow lost his balance on the dark, uneven dirt path. It was now Edison's opportunity. He slid the pipe out of the umbrella and approached the fallen Bradford. Bradford was still on the ground when Edison struck him twice, first on the upper body and then on his leg. Edison then prepared to deliver a final blow to Bradford's head. However, Bradford unexpectedly lunged forward from the prone position and plunged a knife through Edison's foot, pinning it to the ground. As Edison bent over to free his anchored foot, Bradford released the knife from his hand, quickly grabbed a small billy club he had previously dropped close by and delivered a devastating blow to Edison's head. It shattered his skull and collapsed his face like a ripe melon struck with a baseball bat.

Edison's mind ended its narrative. The story was over. He remembered nothing more about the Ramble, other than briefly waking during the long, agonizing night, unable to see because his swollen face was in a patch of dirt saturated with his own blood. Each breath seemed to contain the taste of his lacerated flesh.

As Edison started to regain consciousness from his hospitable bed, he bellowed like a deranged mental patient, loud enough to echo down the hall, but to the attention of no one.

"With all my soul, I devote my continued existence to the termination of Bradford's life in unrelenting misery and pain. Nothing else matters and nothing will stop me, I swear to God and all."

-4-

I've been in Lenox Hill Hospital for four unbearably long days now. Kim visits each day and, luckily, Nurse Brenda comes by three times a day. Brenda hasn't mentioned another sponge bath. In fact, when I asked if I was scheduled for another one, she said never again and suggested I should crawl down the hall on my one good hand and one good leg to use the group shower. I guess I won't bring up the subject again.

Being away from the office for so long was starting to worry me. Checking emails on my smartphone was no substitute for being at my desk. I was about to contact some of my long-time clients, when the hospital phone next to my bed rang. It was a message from the front desk. A visitor was on her way up to see me. It wasn't hard to figure out who it was.

I knew there was a hand-held mirror somewhere around the hospital room. I found it in the drawer of the small nightstand next to the bed. Okay, I don't look too bad considering all the trauma I've been through. My black hair hasn't turned any more grey and it still has its wavy, unkempt look as it dangles down my forehead and over the top half of my ears. My eyes looked tired and a little red. Fortunately, the long, curly eyelashes that cover the top of my pupils remained both unchanged and unusual. I don't know anyone in my family who has the same feature. When I was young, the lashes seemed an undesirable feminine attribute. As I matured and grew tall, I found that the positive female reactions to my eyelashes offset the negative comments from macho males buzzed out on five-hour energy drinks.

I pulled the bedcovers all the way up to my neck to hide the drab hospital gown. My injured arm and part of my leg protruded from the covers. The curtain surrounding my bed was pulled back so I could see Mary as soon as she entered the room.

She looked delightful. Her thick blond hair rose about two inches above her forehead and then flowed haphazardly to the back of her head and down to her shoulder blades. Her thin eyebrows arched upward on a milky smooth face that narrowed to a sculptured point at her chin. The two-piece gray suit with the hemline just above the knee looked very professional, and distracting.

"Nice to see you, Brian. Work is pretty uninteresting without you getting into life and death struggles at the office," she stated, as she approached the bed.

"Well, nice to see you, Mary Douglas. I was just thinking about how much I missed the daily grind at the law firm."

"You better get back to work soon. I'm swamped, while you're enjoying the early summer on your soft hospital bed with three meals a day," Mary continued in an unsympathetic fashion.

Mary is a young associate at Alfonso and Ryan, the law firm on Wall Street where I work as a partner. She drafted the Complaint we filed against ZeiiMed. However, that's only a small part of her contribution. She also saved my life. It's a long story. During discovery in the lawsuit, I obtained a series of emails that established a systematic and continuous underpayment of doctors as a result of ZeiiMed's programming of its computers with outdated payment schedules that depressed the amounts paid, otherwise known as the Depressor Data. It doesn't sound like a big deal–just another Defendant who was caught because of emails that never should have been sent. However, the case quickly turned into a very big deal that forever changed both our lives.

After I discovered the inculpatory emails, the plot thickened because ZeiiMed attempted to kill my wife and me by blowing up our condominium in Baiting Hollow on the North Fork. Kim and I were in the condo when I discovered the explosive device moments before detonation. Luckily, we escaped injury.

Later that same day, I traveled to my office at 40 Wall Street. This is where Mary performed her heroic deed. The office was dark and deserted since it was a Saturday afternoon. I went to the office to urgently prepare an email report to the New York State Attorney General regarding ZeiiMed's Depressor Data. Quite beyond belief, I was sitting at my desk when Dr. Martin Brown, my client, suddenly appeared in the doorway of my office. He had a gun, which he threatened to use unless I remained quiet and let him inject me with an untraceable drug to induce a heart attack. The absurdity of the scene was enhanced by the fact that Dr. Brown was not only a trusted client, but also a named plaintiff in my lawsuit against ZeiiMed. I guess you can't trust doctors any more than you can lawyers.

But, getting back to the confrontation in my office, it was Mary who rescued me. She quietly snuck up behind Dr. Brown and split his head open with a glass globe about the size of a softball. The globe was a gift from my wife that is always displayed on the top of the credenza next to the entrance to my office. Mary had been in the office that Saturday because she was leaving on vacation and decided to catch-up on some work before her departure.

"As you well know," I responded to Mary, "I am forever grateful and eternally in your debt for your selfless act of saving your helpless boss from a painful execution. That being said, I think you should restart the conversation with a long, rambling monologue about how sorry you are that I am injured. Also, feel free to mention the great void in your life now that I'm not at work with you. Finally, I suggest you make a sincere offer to do whatever is necessary to make me feel better."

"Oh, yes, Mr. Bradford, of course, you're right. How are you feeling? Can I do anything to make you feel better?' Mary asked sarcastically.

"Why are you calling me, Mr. Bradford? I thought we got beyond that a long time ago."

"You wanted me to act predictable and phony, so there you are," Mary answered. "If you want normal adult discourse, then don't place restrictions or limitations on me. You did that once before and it didn't work out."

"Okay. Okay. I'm glad you stopped by. I am feeling better and hope to get back to work as soon as possible. How are you handling both your caseload and all my work?"

"It's been slow. We need you back to get some new clients and new lawsuits. We've devoted so much time to that crazy lawsuit against ZeiiMed that new business pursuits haven't received sufficient time and attention, which brings me to my next point. What were you thinking when you decided it was a good idea to engage in hand-to-hand combat with the CEO of ZeiiMed in the Ramble?"

"I've been hearing that a lot lately. Looking back now, it certainly wasn't a rational course of action, but it did go a long way in bringing some measure of revenge for the attack on Meadhbh."

"Yes, I heard about the brain injury she suffered and I guess it was noble of you to attempt to even the score. But look where we are now. Meadhbh's still in the hospital, you're in the hospital and that creep Edison is also in the hospital. That doesn't sound like a favorable ending for anyone. How does this all go away?"

"I don't know," was all I could say. "Hopefully, it ends right now and ZeiiMed is never again a factor in our lives."

"I have a strong suspicion that won't turn out to be true," Mary responded.

"I know. What can I say? Let's hope for the best. Now, is there anything going on at work I should be aware of?"

"A number of things, but I can handle most of them. As I said, I think we need to focus on new business opportunities. Your new-found fame from the ZeiiMed lawsuit should be our calling card. Doctors all over the country now know who you are and they, in turn, are telling their friends and patients about the huge settlement that put lots of money in their pockets."

"Yes, we talked about these opportunities and how we can leverage them to grow our business and keep the public aware of ZeiiMed's dirty tricks at the same time. Since I'm stuck in this hospital, I need you to start on this in my absence. Any ideas?"

"Actually, I do have a thought," Mary said. "It may turn out to be nothing, but a couple of months ago, in the second week of March, there was an article in the *New York Times* stating that a hip implant device was being withdrawn by the manufacturer. The implant essentially had two main components: a hollow, circular metal cup that is attached to the hip and a metal ball that is inserted into the cup. The metal ball has a metal extension in the shape of a spike that is connected to the leg. So, once the operation is completed, the hip and the upper leg are joined by the metal cup, with the ball inside the cup."

"Interesting, what is the exact name of the device?"

"It's called the HID, that's H-I-D. It stands for the metal-on-metal Hip Implant Device. But let me get to the point. Although the newspaper article mentioned that the HID had an early failure rate that seemed high, the manufacturer said it was being phased out because of decreasing sales, not safety concerns. Well, you know me, that raised a lot of questions in my mind and I started doing some research. It turns out that some medical studies conducted outside the United States confirmed the early failure rate of the HID and the subsequent need for repeat surgery. I determined that there are issues about the design and proper positioning of the cup itself, as well as a more serious problem also. The cup and ball are made of various metals, including cobalt, chromium and stainless steel. The metal-on-metal friction of the ball inside the cup may cause poisoning by the release of metal particles in the blood."

"Sounds like you may be on to something. I certainly trust your instincts. The first thing we need to do is find a client with the HID so we can check the medical records and history to see if we have a possible case. We also need to set up a new page on the firm's website stating that we are investigating a possible lawsuit based on the defective HID. We should provide a brief summary of what we know to date about the HID and ask anyone who had HID surgery to call us to determine whether they have a claim."

"No problem, I can set that up," Mary stated. "And by the time our first potential HID client makes an appointment, you will, hopefully, be back at work."

"God willing, I certainly hope so."

"Well, let's get to the most important point. Aren't you going to ask me who manufactures the HID?" Mary asked.

"Yes, of course. How silly of me. What is the name of this very unlucky company that will soon have its stock price drop dramatically once our lawsuit is filed?"

"It's an old friend... ZeiiMed," Mary responded. "Actually, a subsidiary of ZeiiMed that makes medical devices called MendMed, but it's all the same thing. Edison has full control over the subsidiary."

"Don't you mean fiend, rather than friend? I should have known. Nothing surprises me when it comes to ZeiiMed. I really don't want anything more to do with that company, but let's see where this leads us. I wanted to get as far away as possible from ZeiiMed, but we can't ignore this if ZeiiMed injured a lot of people with the HID. Since we will be dealing with ZeiiMed once more, assume the worst. The odds are that ZeiiMed's press releases on the HID are false and some kind of a cover up is already in the works. It's really funny that ZeiiMed would call one of its medical devices by the name HID, when we both know evidence will be found that ZeiiMed 'hid' the medical studies with negative test results regarding the Device's performance."

"I know. It is ironic. I also would be happy to never have any contact with ZeiiMed or its lawyers ever again. But, I will look into the HID and prepare a new web page for your review. Between you and me, I hope there's nothing there so we don't have to go anywhere near ZeiiMed," Mary said.

"Amen to that. But you know it's not going to happen that way," I commented.

"I guess you're right. There's no avoiding our fate. ZeiiMed will continue to haunt us for a long time. So, you better get a timetable for returning to work soon. I need you."

"Yes, I will. Thanks for coming. Say hello to everyone at the office," I said, as Mary started to leave.

Mary then stopped, turned and quickly leaned over to bestow a departing kiss on my cheek. I didn't move my head and didn't look directly into her eyes. Personal relationship management in a business context is getting more difficult by the day. Even more so when the boss is in the hospital and physically unable to either deflect or return the offer of affection.

"Bye, Brian"

"So long, Mary. Always nice to see you."

It all seemed such familiar territory. Another looming showdown with ZeiiMed and more personal complications with women I trust and cherish, including both Kim and Mary.

I really need to work on both my business skills and personal relationship skills. Maybe NYU offers night classes that can help. Then again, I don't want to interfere with my beer drinking time after work. Forget the whole self-help thing. I'll worry about it later. Right now, my sole priority is getting better and getting out of this hospital. I need two healthy legs and two functional arms to face the forthcoming challenges with ZeiiMed.

-5-

After a few more days in the hospital, I was finally discharged. My arm remained in a hard cast, but my leg was much better. I walked with a cane, but not very well and only for short periods of time. The day before, Kim dropped off a button-down shirt and slacks, with one pant leg cut off above the knee.

My doctor told me the improvement in my leg was remarkable as he signed the discharge papers.

I called Kim and left a message on her cell phone. I knew she was at her job with the Port Jeff Ferry, but would probably retrieve my message at lunch. Kim has said many times how she enjoys the solitude of having lunch on a park bench near the water when the weather is nice.

Next to the ferry terminal in Port Jefferson Village is Danford's Inn, located on the waterfront. A parking lot in the rear of the Inn extends from the Inn itself to the wooden pillars that support the pier and the waterside walkway adjoining the pier. It is a short walk from the ferry terminal to Danford's parking lot. On the east side of the parking lot, there is an entrance to the 5.1 acre Harborfront Park. The Harborfront Park has several benches along a shoreline promenade that provide a relaxing, hypnotic view of the harbor beach and water. It is the first bench just beyond the entrance that Kim considers her spot for relaxation and lunch.

I arrived home at about 2:30 p.m. and hobbled into the house with my cane. The law firm was very gracious in making a private car available to transfer me from the hospital to home. Brenda had taken me by wheelchair from my hospital bed to the curb in front of the hospital. I thanked her a million times for all her help and professionalism. I also mentioned that I will miss her services because such thorough treatment will not be available at home. I think she misunderstood my remark because she made some comment about how happy she was to transfer my care to Kim.

Kim wasn't home yet. I had assumed she would get out of work early for my homecoming. Then again, I'm sure she's doing the best she can.

I was reading in the living room when Kim arrived home about an hour later.

"Darling, I'm so glad you're home from the hospital. Sorry, I couldn't be here to meet you when you arrived."

I remained seated. Kim leaned down and gave me a big hug and a lip touch that lasted a nanosecond.

"Well, I'm darn glad to be here also and ready to start the rest of my life. By the way, you look very nice. Thanks for dressing up for me."

In fact, Kim did look very attractive and smelled very enticing. Her tight, yellow linen dress hugged her naturally athletic body and barely managed to cover her upper legs. The scent of her perfume seemed to carry us to a secluded open field with hundreds of flowers blossoming simultaneously.

"Didn't the doctor order you to stay in bed? I'll be quite happy to play the role of your nurse at home. I don't have all the professional skills of Brenda, but I did buy a cute nurse's outfit that I'm sure will help create the fantasy."

"That sounds like quite a proposition, but I can get around with the help of this cane and I really hate staying in bed all day. But, I could use some assistance in getting dressed because it's really difficult using only one hand."

"As you know, I'm very adept at dressing and undressing so I don't think we'll have a problem there," Kim said. "But, that's later. Right now, I have an idea. How about if I drive us to the Steam Room for steamed lobsters and beer? We'll celebrate your homecoming. Plus, I have a few things to talk to you about."

"Sounds great to me, but I'll need your help getting in and out of the car."

"No problem. Let's go."

The Steam Room is directly across the street from the ferry terminal. We could have easily walked there from the house, if not for my injuries. It has good seafood in a glass-enclosed room, with an umbrella above each table and a retractable roof. It provides a perfect view of the ferries as they dock at the water's edge, with the vehicles loading and unloading from the hull of the ferries. Kim ordered our food and drinks at the counter, then picked up the order on trays when it was completed.

I had just taken a large gulp of beer when Kim began her story. "This is fun, but I do have something we need to discuss."

"No time like the present. I can't imagine that you have any major issues to discuss, other than the discomfort of not having slept with your husband for several nights," I said.

"Actually, this is no time for jokes. I believe you'll find the topic to be fairly serious."

"Okay, then. No more interruptions. Please proceed."

"It's very casual at the present time, but I want you to know I've met someone."

I gagged on the beer in my mouth and almost spit it out. I'm sure the expression on my face was alarming to other patrons at the restaurant, but it was late afternoon and the usual large dinner crowd hadn't arrived yet.

"Don't stop now. You're on a roll. I'm ready for the details, I think."

"There really isn't much to tell. He's a doctor who works at Mather Hospital up the hill. He likes to have lunch at Harborfront Park. About a month or so ago, on a particularly nice spring day with lots of people around, we found ourselves sitting on the same park bench with sandwiches on our laps."

"How cute! Sounds like a scene from a low-budget movie."

"Please, let me go on. After I explain the situation, I also have a proposed plan for how we may be able to proceed from here."

"Fine, go on. I haven't finished my beer. You have some time," I said, although I actually felt like walking out. Unfortunately, at the present time I don't walk very well, so I decided to stay.

"So, I meet my doctor friend about three times a week for lunch, either in the park or at a restaurant. We get along very well. His wife has been dead for a couple of years now. He's mostly bald, with a heavy beard that is slightly greying. I say that because it's not some overpowering sexual attraction. He is more of a safe harbor–a comfort from the violence and mayhem that ZeiiMed brought into our lives."

"A beard? No, please don't tell me he has a beard. Doesn't that scratch your face? Now I'll be looking all the time for red blotches on your cheeks."

"You know, you really aren't funny, but it does lead me into my next point."

"There's a 'next point'? Hopefully, it doesn't match the bombshell you just dropped," I commented.

"You will be happy to know that we haven't done anything sexual, and that includes kissing, so you don't need to inspect me for red blotches."

"Great! I'm supposed to be relieved? Should I quit work so I can supervise your lunchtime activities?" I asked.

"No, but I like him. His name is Joe and I don't intend to stop seeing him."

"Joe? His name is Joe? That can't be right. Medical school won't accept you if your name is Joe. The American Medical Association strictly prohibits any doctor being called 'Doctor Joe.'"

"As I was saying, I enjoy his company, just as I have always enjoyed your company."

"So, what's supposed to happen here?" I interrupted. "We just continue into the future–you, me and Dr. Joe until death do us part? I'm not agreeing to that unless I get a big discount on office visits."

"The answer to your first question may be 'yes,' but the truth is I really don't know because I don't know what the future holds. Your second question doesn't deserve an answer."

"So, I just continue to come home from work each evening, but now we chat over cocktails about how your involvement with Dr. Joe progressed that day. Maybe I can prepare a chart like a baseball score card. I can hear your comments now: 'Honey, I only got to first base today, but I feel really good at the plate and I hope to do better tomorrow.' I don't think I can live like that."

"First of all, as I said, nothing has gone on between us and maybe nothing ever will. I love you and my level of love for you hasn't lessened in the slightest as a result of Joe. What has happened is that my capacity to love has grown. I still love you as much as always, but now I also have the ability to feel great affection for Joe also. At this point, I need you both in my life."

"What happens when your affection for Joe turns into action? We're only human and things happen between boys and girls when the chemistry is right."

"It wouldn't mean I love you any less. I've developed a greater capacity for love that now extends to more than one person. I don't know how my ability to love increased so dramatically, and I didn't even know I had such a capability."

"You've got to be kidding," I said, as my level of exasperation increased exponentially. "How am I to react when your dispensing of love reaches the point where you are having sexual relations with Dr. Joe and your husband at the same time? Not to be crude, but how do you expect us to have dinner and a movie after you spent the afternoon with Dr. Joe in a room at Danford's Inn? Not to carry on, but what happens when I suggest we have relations? You might answer, 'No thanks, I had plenty of sex today with Dr. Joe and now I have a headache.' Don't you think that sounds totally unmanageable, if not completely insane?"

"Stop. Now. It hasn't happened and maybe it will never happen. I love you and felt you deserved to know everything that is happening in my life. Please, let's take it slowly, one day at a time."

"That's what you should be telling Dr. Joe. I meant the part about going slowly, not the part about being in love."

"I know. I am going slowly with Joe. But, you deserve full disclosure. Let's go home now. I'll help you into bed so you can rest. We'll continue this conversation tomorrow."

"Only if you agree to put on your new nurse outfit."

This talk about Dr. Joe suddenly created a wave of elevated affection towards Kim. Jealousy? Maybe. Probably.

It makes little sense. I should be angry, but all I wanted now was to be alone with my wife. Kind of like a wolf marking his territory.

"I think that can be arranged. A little fantasy can really spice things up."

"Forget a little fantasy," I responded. "I'm talking full-fledged hallucination. Kind of like an LSD trip from the '60s, but with booze and imagination providing the high."

"I'm game. Let's go now. I can't wait."

"Just promise me you won't be thinking about Dr. Joe and I'll promise I won't be thinking about my old girlfriend."

"You have a deal. By the way, I didn't know you had an old girlfriend."

"No comment, I don't want to ruin the moment. We can discuss it another time."

"That's fine, but don't forget. After all our years together, I'd love to hear about some of your lost loves."

"Right now, you're the only love I want to concentrate on."

We headed home as quickly as we could. My injured leg seemed to be working remarkably well. It's amazing how the proper motivation leads to enhanced performance.

-6-

I woke up early the next day. My wife was beside me in the bed. The covers were still on the bed, but our clothes were strewn all over the floor. How I managed with a broken arm and injured leg, I'll never know.

I went downstairs for coffee and thought. I slumped at the kitchen table.

Kim's revelation about Dr. Joe made my stomach churn. It might eventually all work out with Kim, but maybe it won't. I don't want to lose her, but I can't control her or limit her life. She is going to do what she is going to do and I will be left to react to each change. I just want my life back as it was. I was foolish in failing to fully enjoy and appreciate the comforts and pleasures of everyday life with Kim before our twosome became a threesome.

My goal, my only goal, is to return to our former life with a new enthusiasm and purpose. Not to change it, but to relish it. That's what I failed to do the first time around.

If I only could go back in time, I would relive every day of life with a new and deep understanding of the preciousness of each moment.

As is my habit, I started to write down my thoughts. The creation of words sometimes provides answers to the puzzle of reality.

THE ANSWER

How do you restore what was before?
How do you return to moments that were?
How do you resume a way of life that can't
be lived again?
The questions are clear, but clarity seems
beyond our grasp;
The goal is known, but embracing the end
is elusive;
The desire is consuming, but cannot alone
reverse the reality;

The answers may be unavailable, but does
not mean they are unattainable;
The solutions are unseen, but does not
mean they are unachievable;
The vision is limited, but the light of hope
is not lost;

Devote each minute towards reaching a
resolution;
Don't be discouraged when disappointment
delays;
Resolve is the key to reaching the Answer,
with the when and the waiting left to their
own, unable to be known.

* * * * * * * * *

Alright then. Resolve it is. I will dedicate myself to the goal of fixing whatever was broken between us.

It was interesting that Kim didn't say any particular action or behavior on my part caused her to be receptive to new companionship. She didn't say that I ignored repeated requests to change something that constantly annoyed her. She didn't mention specific behavioral patterns that she consistently demanded to be different. Rather, Kim confirmed she loved me and that her love for me hasn't changed. She has simply learned that her capacity for love isn't limited, so there is now plenty of room for both Dr. Joe and me in her life. I don't know how she does it. I feel cramped already and I just learned of Dr. Joe.

Whatever the reasons and whatever the explanation, the reality is that Dr. Joe is on the scene and must be addressed before their companionship progresses into an intimate relationship. Dr. Joe may be happy with just lunch at the present time, but knowing the nature of males, he will quickly look to pick up the pace.

Of course, I have great difficulty with the idea of sharing my wife with another man. Then again, maybe I have to change with the times and expand my horizons. If I leave Kim because of Dr. Joe, all I would be doing is providing Dr. Joe one hundred percent of Kim's life and one hundred percent of her time. How is that a happy ending? If I give up Kim because of Dr. Joe, then he gets Kim because I let her go. That seems stupid.

Kim didn't say she was leaving me and doesn't seem to have any intention of doing so in the future. She is agreeable to being with me as my wife, provided I am agreeable to her concurrent relationship with Dr. Joe. So, I will take life one day at a time and do everything in my power to convince Kim that her greatest happiness in life will be on an exclusive basis with her current husband. It sounds like an uphill battle, but it's the challenge I'm presented with. I accept the challenge and will do my best to return to the life Kim and I shared for so many years, if that is humanly possible.

Also, last night, Kim discussed with me another significant ramification of her lunches with Dr. Joe. She no longer wants to move into the City. Before I had my "Rumble in the Ramble" with Edison, we had decided to move into New York City near to where Edison lives. In fact, we were planning on living in the apartment building next to his. The idea was to demonstrate to Edison that I was always watching and always close by, so he would not even think about having ZeiiMed once again harm or intimidate us. The plan, however feeble, was to hopefully discourage any future altercations.

Well, now that Dr. Joe is around, Kim no longer wants to move into the City. She didn't say Dr. Joe was the reason, but I know it is. I agreed with her decision not to move. I told her I also don't want to move because I might be shortly involved in a big lawsuit regarding a defective HID.

Since we have mutually agreed not to move, Kim can stay in close proximity to Dr. Joe and I get to immerse myself in a new case at work.

This really doesn't sound like a plan for a happy marriage.

-7-

I continued to rest at home for the next several days. Kim was at work during the week, but off on weekends. She didn't mention Dr. Joe. Of course, neither did I. Eventually, I will ask about him because my possessive nature wants to know whether I've lost my exclusive. I need to know if we are now in a sharing cycle. But, that's for another day. I don't need a complicated confrontation right now. It's best to let a little time pass before I revisit the issue.

Also, I made plans to return to the office next week. But, before I start work, I have decided to pay a visit to John Edison at Columbia Medical Center. I understand that any rational being would consider this decision to be irrational. Regardless, I intend to do so. Maybe this new three-way relationship thing has me thinking a little crazy. I don't know.

Finding him wasn't hard. All I did was start calling the major hospitals in the City. I located him on the third call. The hospital operator was quite happy to volunteer the information.

His room is on the 9th floor of the McKeen Pavilion in the Milstein Hospital Building of New York-Presbyterian's Columbia University Medical Center. Visitors are allowed around the clock. The McKeen Pavillion is known for its private rooms with accommodations similar to a luxury hotel, without the usual hospital activities and routines. That should prove helpful in lessening any distractions or interruptions while I'm with Edison. Also, I intend to visit him at a time when the hospital staff will be at a minimum.

I decided midnight would be good. Of course, I was sure there would be security of some sort around the clock because of Edison's elevated position and notoriety. Edison had recently been nominated by the President to the position of National Administrator of the Centers for Medicare and Medicaid Services. According to the newspapers, his nomination would shortly be approved by Congress. Plus, he still held his job as the Chief Executive Officer of ZeiiMed. He had publicly stated that he was going to take a leave of absence from ZeiiMed to assume the position of National Administrator, but had not yet done so.

Edison is seriously injured and incapable of doing much of anything. I may complain about the injury to my leg and the cast on my arm, but the injuries I inflicted on Edison's face and foot have caused much greater pain and harm to him. I really don't think he'll be glad to see me. It should be interesting.

I arrived at the hospital at 630 West 168th Street just before midnight. The subway was a bit unsettling as a very strange cast of characters entered and exited the subway car upon entering the Bronx. I had my razor knife for protection, but I'm sure I looked like an easy target with my wounded arm and cane. Plus, my short-sleeve button down shirt and solid yellow tie accentuated my out-of-place presence.

I walked through the front door of the hospital and approached the security desk. I showed my ID and said I was Edison's brother-in-law. I was gambling that security would not call Edison's room and announce my visit. I was told Edison's room number and pointed in the right direction. I simply don't understand how hospitals manage to ignore the need for heightened security in a post 9/11 world. It totally baffles me.

I reached the 9th floor and walked down the hall towards Edison's room. There was a large, bulky man with a sweaty face in a loose fitting suit sitting hunched over on a stool in front of the door to Edison's room. No one else was in the corridor. The noise of my shoes on the linoleum announced my arrival. The man looked up from his newspaper and saw me approaching. His right hand reached into his suit coat. How could this be? Was he about to shoot me? When was the last time someone was gunned down in a deluxe, state-of-the-art, private hospital in New York City? I stopped. The man withdrew his right hand, holding only a white handkerchief. He wiped his forehead, stood and moved his stool away from the entrance to the room. I continued walking, now five feet from the man.

"Go ahead in. I know who you are," was all the man said.

It was a large hospital room with a cluttered assortment of monitors, gauges and IV tubes attached to the patient sitting up in the bed. To my great surprise, there were no bandages around his face or skull, but the skin was badly bruised in an assortment of shades of black, blue and green. Yet, the most shocking realization was that Edison no longer had the same face, other than the piercing ice blue eyes that I immediately recognized.

His plump, round cheeks were replaced by a thin, sunken facial structure that seemed to indent into his skull just below his eyes. The shape of his nose seemed the same, except it appeared to extend grotesquely from his face now that his cheeks had shrunken in size. His bushy hair was still combed back on the sides of his head by use of a thick grease of some sort. The large bald area on the top of his head was shiny with sweat. Edison's uninviting appearance seemed to radiate a formidable sense of menace. It was extraordinary that he was able to manifest such a threatening aura of dread without moving or speaking.

"You left me face down in a pool of blood in the Ramble, unable to move and choking on my own fluids," were Edison's first words.

"I was pretty banged up myself. As I recall, you came darn close to killing me before I crushed your face like an empty beer can."

"You should have made sure the job was finished," Edison snarled. "Now I swear my revenge each morning as I look in the mirror. Of course, I would have left you to bleed to death if our roles had been reversed. I would greatly enjoy thinking of you engulfed in agony, hoping to be found before the last precious drops of blood seeped from your wounds."

"You're lucky I have the cast on my arm or I just might punch what remains of your ugly face. But, I don't need to do it now. As I once said to you, I can get to you anytime. As I recall, once I actually put a gun to your head while you were asleep in bed and then injected you with my drug of choice."

"We can leave such matters to another day," Edison stated. "Rest assured, my feelings are reciprocal. But, I have no time to deal with a punk attorney like you. You are an aggravating nuisance that my colleagues at ZeiiMed have convinced me to ignore. I am now the head of a massive federal agency and can no longer let a two-bit lawyer like you get under my skin. But, you came here for a reason. The guard let you in because we anticipated your arrival. ZeiiMed knows exactly where you are at all times. Let me hear what you have to say and then get the hell out."

"It's interesting you mentioned that because I do have a topic I want to discuss with you. In early March, there was a newspaper article discussing one of ZeiiMed's medical products, the metal-on-metal Hip Implant Device, referred to as the HID. As reported in the newspapers, ZeiiMed made a public statement that it was continuing to phase out its manufacture of the HID and emphasized that the phase-out was due solely to commercial reasons and not safety issues. However, independent medical studies found that the HID appeared to have a high rate of early failure, requiring further surgery and treatment. Several doctors who installed the HID stated on the record that they believed the HID to be unsafe due to both defective design and improper positioning of the cup inside the hip," I explained.

"Yes, of course, I'm aware of this. ZeiiMed is exploring new hip replacement technologies and we're moving away from the metal-on-metal HID. The world is changing fast and ZeiiMed has to keep pace. The change had nothing to do with safety," Edison responded.

"I'm sick of your crap. You and I both know that is a bunch of garbage. The HID was and is defective. I can't prove it yet, but knowing how ZeiiMed does business, it certainly wouldn't be surprising that ZeiiMed has a ton of documents confirming that the HID was faulty and confirming that injury was sure to follow."

"No medical device is perfect," Edison said. "There are hundreds, if not thousands of doctors across the nation who successfully installed the HID each day and confirmed the patient's ability to eventually walk, run, swim and exercise with full mobility and no pain. Talk to the doctors. Talk to the Food and Drug Administration. Do a little digging and you'll see I'm right."

"You can't possibly believe I'm foolish enough to believe one word of what you are saying. The chatter in the medical blogs is that ZeiiMed made major monetary grants to doctors that use the HID and also provided them with highly desirable speaking, teaching and writing opportunities with generous compensation. Of course, these money-grubbing physicians rubber-stamped the merits of the HID. Do you have any idea of the extreme pain and injury the HID is inflicting because the metal-on-metal design simply doesn't work, with metallosis resulting from severe cobalt and chromium blood poisoning as metal particles are released by the grinding of the metal ball inside the metal cup? The tissue in the hip is destroyed, mobility is lost, as well as possible deafness, blindness and organ failure."

"You have no proof of anything. You're making it up and hoping I'll make some kind of admission that you can use against ZeiiMed. I knew you would come looking for me as soon as that newspaper article appeared in March. Once you learned that ZeiiMed produced the HID, I was sure we would have another face-to-face confrontation, preferably without knives and other weapons. What do you expect me to say? Admit that ZeiiMed did bad things and write you a check from my hospital bed? You are a fool. You think you are on a great crusade for the poor and suffering masses. You're convinced they will all be relieved of their pain once the great advocate, Brian Bradford, takes over their cases. Just get out of here. You have confirmed to me your predictability and stupidity. I am through with you."

"All right, Mr. Edison. I am leaving. I came here because the lawsuit hasn't yet been filed and ZeiiMed hasn't yet retained counsel to defend the HID lawsuit. As such, the rules of professional conduct permit me to speak directly to you without a ZeiiMed attorney present. I was hoping you would agree to produce documents proving that ZeiiMed didn't know of the dangers of the HID. If you did, I'd forget about a lawsuit. Since you will not do so, I'll assume you're guilty as charged and my lawsuit will follow shortly."

"Rules of professional conduct? Since when do you follow them? You have to be joking. How many times did you confront me during the first case and physically attack me to the point of death? You have no ethics. You make it up as you go along and break the rules because you think your cause justifies it. Like I said, get out of here! You are a sanctimonious windbag shyster who has no idea what you're talking about."

Edison touched a button on the side of the bed. The door to the hospital room opened quickly. The light from the corridor brightened the room. I turned to see the security guard entering the room. "Mr. Edison wants you out of here," the guard growled, as he approached me.

The guard was now standing next to me at the foot of Edison's bed. He reached for my shoulder to forcefully escort me out of the room. I ducked below his extended arm and lunged forward. My shoulder drove into his soft, bulging belly. The guard fell backwards and crashed into a series of medical monitors and computer tables that toppled on him after he hit the floor. The IV tubes tore from Edison's body and also fell to the floor, as the supporting poles holding the medications tumbled in succession like a house of cards. Edison tried to get out of his bed, but his badly injured foot wouldn't support his weight. He fell on top of the guard and other debris on the floor. Edison screamed in pain as he cut his head on one of the broken monitors. I punched the guard on the side of his head with my one good hand so he wouldn't pursue me. I resisted the temptation to punch Edison also. Actually, he was too grotesque to touch even with a closed fist. Plus, he was not physically able to stand up, no less follow me out of the room. However, it was the last time I would ever show an ounce of restraint in dealing with Edison.

"Isn't this funny? The last time I left you in the Ramble, you were likewise on the ground and bleeding. Now, I'm again leaving you in the same condition. This is a habit I'm starting to enjoy. Goodbye. The next time we meet, I hope to have uncovered all of ZeiiMed's hidden secrets regarding the

HID. Maybe this time around I'll be successful in bringing down not only you, but all of ZeiiMed."

I left the hospital room and closed the door behind me. As I boarded the elevator down the hall, a nurse asked if I enjoyed my visit.

"Yes, it was great to see to Mr. Edison again. He got pretty tired at the end and is sleeping now, so he probably shouldn't be disturbed for a while."

The elevator doors closed and I descended to street level.

-8-

It was the first week of June 2010. I had just entered my office building to finally return to work at the law firm. My plaster cast had been removed and my arm was in a black cotton spandex sling that wrapped around my neck. My arm didn't hurt, so I intended to ditch the sling in a couple of days. As far as I was concerned, my recovery was complete.

Kim hadn't mentioned Dr. Joe in the last two weeks, although I guessed she was still seeing him at lunch during the work week. Our physical relationship had not lessened and, in fact, probably picked up a bit while I was home each day convalescing. I'm guessing that Kim and Dr. Joe were not yet engaging in heavy physical contact. Kim hadn't left the house at night for a date with Dr. Joe and didn't seem to get calls from him in the evening. Plus, Kim wouldn't be carrying on two adult relationships at the same time. At least, I didn't think so.

As I mentioned before, I don't plan to leave Kim because then she becomes available to Dr. Joe all day and all night. If I leave, I'm gone forever and Joe is free to sleep in my bed. I can't live with that, so I'm going nowhere at the present time.

It appears this love triangle is going to last for a while. There's not much I can do to change that, so I just have to adjust to it and react reasonably as the daily events of life unfold.

Of course, that's assuming my Irish temper doesn't flare up and I punch Dr. Joe in front of his staff at the hospital.

-9-

My office at Alfonso and Ryan is on the 45th floor of 40 Wall Street, now known as the Trump Building. It felt very comfortable to once again sit at my desk anticipating the challenge of reviewing legal decisions and drafting legal documents for filing in court.

There is no question I was once fed up and bored by what I believed to be mundane, lifeless and repetitive legal work. However, after commencing my class action suit against ZeiiMed and experiencing the life-threatening situations that followed, I eagerly looked forward to a long life of predictable events and established routines.

Actually, my first order of business was to decide which pending case to work on first. My desk was filled with stacks of white paper that could not be put into the filing cabinets until reviewed and responded to. I turned my desktop computer on. The number of emails that needed replies seemed overwhelming. I had opened and reviewed most of the emails on my smartphone while at home, but now I needed to answer and print each one.

As I was thinking about how I could use some assistance in organizing my work, I looked up from my desk to see Mary Douglas entering my office with a pleasant smile and her consistent comeliness.

"Well, look who has finally shown up for work. Welcome back, Brian. You were certainly missed," Mary said.

"Thank you. It's good to be back."

Mary continued walking towards me. She stepped around my desk, extended her arms and gave me a tight hug as I remained seated. I didn't move. I couldn't return the hug with only one arm. Her thick blond hair brushed across my face. Her body scent surrounded me. I just sat there. I counted to myself, "One Mississippi, two Mississippi, three Mississippi." She released the embrace and returned to the other side of my desk. I needed a cigarette.

I'm sure I was blushing. I don't know the appropriate post-hug conversation.

"That was nice, but I think the firm's employee manual discourages any physical contact at the office," were regrettably the first words out of my mouth.

"Brian, let's not go down that road again. You know my feelings on the subject, and I'm not changing. Just in case you forgot due to your injuries, I will quickly review past events. I saved your life right here in this very office. The blood of the villainous Doctor Martin Brown dripped all over your rug after I split his skull open with the glass globe from your credenza. As a result of my quick actions, you avoided death by lethal injection and/or gunshot wound. As I recall, Dr. Brown had made either option available to you. As a result, I can do whatever I please with regard to us. Every second of time you have on this earth is due to me. You are all mine and please don't forget it."

"Enough said. I am grateful. I hereby confirm that you are free to forever interact with me in any manner you desire unless, of course, there are other people around. I will keep my conservative Catholic upbringing in check and never again resist or discourage your advances, Okay?" I responded, mostly in jest, but Mary just proceeded as if we were having a normal, everyday conversation.

"That's fine, I won't make you put it in writing, provided you don't break your promise."

"Thank you. I would be uncomfortable with a signed document describing the limits, or the lack thereof, to our 'relationship,' if that is the right word," I stated, hopefully ending this ridiculous banter.

"Good enough. I'll sit down and we can talk about work," Mary said.

Thank goodness, was my first thought.

Now that I could take a deep breath and get back to non-provocative legal discourse, I noticed that Mary was dressed very fashionably. She was wearing a creme, cable knit Alexander McQueen dress. There were parallel lines of blue trim at the waist, wrist and short hemline. The folded collar extended down the front until it formed a dangling thin scarf that knotted just below a low-cut neckline. She appeared more suited for a yacht club than the office, but the firm's employee manual prohibits comments about a person's choice of clothing. The last thing I wanted to mention was how she looked in her dress.

"As we discussed in the hospital, I have been working on a sales pitch to put on our firm's website to hopefully attract some clients who suffered injury from a metal-on-metal Hip Implant Device. It's only a couple of paragraphs," Mary said. "I'll read it to you.

> 'We urge anyone who has a metal-on-metal Hip Implant Device and experienced post-surgery pain, swelling, difficulty walking and/or a constant clicking noise, to consult a doctor immediately. Then, consult our firm about a possible lawsuit. We strongly encourage people not to stay at home and suffer. Rather, we suggest potential clients call us and consult with one of our lawyers about your rights and your possible entitlement to compensation, as well as the payment of all medical bills. There is, of course, no charge for the consultation. Even if no pain is currently felt post-surgery, the constant grind of the metal cup and ball produces cobalt and chromium flakes that may be circulating in the bloodstream. This contamination may slowly cause a poisoning that can cause organ damage, deafness and/or blindness, if left untreated. We are here to help.'"

"That sounds good. Of course, we can't mention that we specialize in personal injury lawsuits, because we don't," I commented. "In fact, I don't think our firm has ever filed a personal injury lawsuit. But, so what? We've already done battle with the multi-billion dollar health care behemoth,

ZeiiMed, and won. We have the settlement papers and the newspaper articles to prove it. That's our sales pitch."

"Also, I've done a little more investigating while you were out. The big gossip in the medical world is that ZeiiMed received patient post-surgery reports that were so bad that ZeiiMed will announce a complete recall of the HID in August. That should help to get us a few clients."

"Good work, Mary. It seems beyond belief, but hardly out of character for ZeiiMed. ZeiiMed first announces a phasing out of the HID for reasons having nothing to do with safety, then issues a complete recall due to disastrous medical results several months later. You and I both know what that means."

"Exactly," Mary said. "The medical reports and patient evaluations regarding the HID were so negative that not even ZeiiMed could ignore them or hide them."

"So, what do we know for certain?" I asked. "We know that ZeiiMed has documents in its computers that are extremely critical of the performance of the HID. Also, we know that there are so many such documents that ZeiiMed can't possible destroy them all or pretend they don't exist. The documents exist and ZeiiMed has them. All we have to do is find them."

"I can smell blood in the water already," Mary commented.

"Yes, but we know from experience to expect the unexpected from ZeiiMed. Edison will come up with surprises we never imagined and throw us to the ground when we least expect it. If we try to corner ZeiiMed, the reaction will be ruthless and violent. The infliction of physical torment and even death is part of ZeiiMed's way of doing business. But the good news is we're better prepared this time because we know what to anticipate and we know to be ready. What do you think?"

"I'm ready if you are. All we need now are some HID clients," Mary responded.

"I'm sure they'll come eventually. Remember, I'm not just another run-of-the-mill lawyer. I'm now a well-known, class-action attorney who obtained a billion dollar settlement from ZeiiMed," I said, not really believing my own hype. Well, maybe I believed a little of it.

"I understand that," Mary responded. "And, remember, we had no idea what we were doing in our first go around with ZeiiMed. We were flying by the seat of our pants. If we hadn't been extremely lucky in discovering the incriminating emails camouflaged in a ton of cyberspace junk, we would have been thrown out of court. But now, we know what to expect and how to prepare for the unexpected. Also, let's not forget that you are darn fortunate to still be alive after all the attempts on your life, once by Dr. Brown in your office, once by Dr. Hyman in an airplane and once by a gang of ZeiiMed bad guys who destroyed your vacation condo. And, of course, the grand finish being the well-publicized 'Rumble in the Ramble.' But, we've learned from these experiences and we're stronger now because of them."

"Well, we don't need to bring up any of that at the HID client meetings. Let's emphasize our good points and bury the bad ones forever."

"Isn't that what all lawyers do?" Mary inquired.

"Of course. If the public knew us as we really are, no one would ever hire an attorney."

"Some world we live in."

"I know. But we didn't create it. We just do our best to live within it, and bend a few rules when necessary," I said.

"Bend a few rules? Who are you kidding?" Mary asked. "What do you call breaking into Edison's apartment armed with a gun and a syringe, then stabbing his foot and crushing his face in Central Park? I'd say you threw the rule book out the window long ago."

"Sometimes the moral urgency of a situation mandates the breaking of laws to achieve the desired outcome. And, for the record, I haven't been arrested or charged with a crime. So, that must mean no law has been broken."

"Although we both know the truth is to the contrary," Mary pointed out.

"Yes, we do. But who cares? Anything else I should know about the HID?" I asked, hoping to move the discussion along.

"There is a ton of information you need to know. There are approximately 250,000 installed each year, but there doesn't seem to be an accurate count as to how many of those are metal-on-metal. There is also a ceramic HID that contains a layer of polyurethane on the cup and ball, and has proven to be much safer. There have been reports that the metal-on-metal HID has been found to fail within five years of installation in almost fifty percent of the patients, although we would need to verify the accuracy of that statistic. At first, the problems were attributed to a cup design that was allegedly too shallow, so the cup didn't fit into the hip socket properly. The shallow cup also caused the ball to pop out once inserted in the cup, causing dislocation. Then the real problem was exposed—metal grinding against metal. The metal-on-metal HID exposes the patient to metal poisoning. But as we discussed, the statistics are incomplete because many of the doctors who installed the Device have lucrative consulting contracts with ZeiiMed for thousands of dollars each month."

"It's really quite shocking. With regard to metallosis, what can be done, if anything?" I asked.

"The patient can be given chelation therapy. It involves the intravenous infusion of ethylenediaminetetraacetic acid. This chelating agent binds with the cobalt and chromium ions in the blood and then allows the combined mass to be absorbed through the intestines and naturally removed. If you wait too long, the therapy may not be effective because metallosis has already caused organ damage to the kidneys, liver or brain. Plus, no scientist or doctor has produced a conclusive study to demonstrate that chelation therapy is positively safe for people over 65. There can be an adverse reaction to the therapy for some people."

"Thanks for all your work. It looks like you have a pretty good handle on this mess. Let's get the promotional material on our website and we'll see what happens. All we need are a handful of clients to enable us to file the Complaint as a class action. Of course, we will have to allege that the class members all suffered the same types of injuries, but we can fudge it a bit until we hire an expert doctor to testify that the

HID deteriorates in the same manner for each patient and causes generally the same physical ailments, along with metallosis."

"Maybe this time we can litigate against ZeiiMed without all the bloodshed and violence. I said I'm ready to do this, but you know how I'll react if people start getting hurt again," Mary said. "It happened once before and I will be unable to cope if it happens again."

"No, I don't believe history will repeat itself. ZeiiMed has learned through experience that we can't be intimidated or bullied. Also, Edison knows that any injury inflicted on us will be avenged against the actual decision-makers at ZeiiMed. So don't be concerned and don't give it another thought."

Of course, I forgot to mention my recent altercation with Edison and his security guard in Edison's hospital room. Why create needless worry? I'm sure I can handle whatever comes up. Then again, maybe not.

-10-

Returning to work was satisfying, but my life remained incomplete. I needed to see Meadhbh. I needed to see her now. She was the reason I took revenge against Edison in the Ramble. Injuries were inflicted, lives were changed. We had much to talk about.

Before my confrontation with Edison in Central Park, ZeiiMed's thugs had viciously attacked Meadhbh outside her apartment as pay back for assisting me in getting access to Edison on two earlier occasions. On the first occasion, she had helped me break into the lobby of Edison's building so I could confront him as he slept in his apartment. On the second occasion, she helped me arrange an uninvited meeting with Edison at a table in *Très Bien*, the restaurant where she worked as a bartender. Edison's apartment is located in the building directly above the restaurant. I mistakenly thought the encounters would be helpful in convincing Edison to cease all efforts to injure or kill either myself or those close to me.

Meadhbh sustained serious head injuries as a result of the beating she received. She needed specialized treatment and was admitted to the Neurological Institute of Columbia University. It's been months since the assault, so I assumed Meadhbh was no longer at the hospital. When she was first injured, one of her co-workers, a woman named Judy, called to inform me that Meadhbh had been injured and taken to a hospital. I visited Meadhbh in the hospital several times, but I haven't been there in a while as a result of my own injuries.

I called *Très Bien* and asked for Judy. Luckily, there wasn't more than one Judy because I don't know her last name.

"Hello, this is Judy. My tables are backed up and the bar is packed, so get to the point."

"Hi, Judy. You don't know me, but we talked once before. I'm a friend of Meadhbh and you had called me a couple of days after she had been attacked. My name is Brian Bradford."

"Yes, I remember now," said Judy. "Sorry about my abruptness. Sometimes I get customers calling here asking for a date when I'm trying to work. Plus, it's been especially rough without Meadhbh to handle the bar. But, hopefully, she will be back soon."

"I know you're busy, so I'll be quick. I called to get Meadhbh's address. I'm sure she's been discharged from the hospital by now, but she never told me exactly where she lives, although I think it's somewhere in Brooklyn. I'd like to visit her."

"She would love to see you. You're right, she has an apartment in the Borough Hall section of Brooklyn, right across the street from the Appellate Division Courthouse on Monroe Place. A lovely tree-lined street. But she isn't there now."

"OK. Where is she then? I'd like to drop by and see her tomorrow."

"I know this sounds a little far-fetched, but she is staying at the Ritz-Carlton in Battery Park. Don't ask me to explain, I'm sure she will give you the details when you see her."

"Thanks for the information. I can walk to the Ritz from my law firm downtown. I really appreciate your help. See you at *Très Bien* soon. Bye."

The next day at about 4 p.m., I left my law firm and walked down Broadway towards the Alexander Hamilton Custom House, which is now occupied by the United States Bankruptcy Court and the American Indian Museum. Turning onto Battery Place, I walked towards the Hudson River until I reached Two West Street and arrived at the Ritz-Carlton. It's a 38-floor tower, a prominent part of the downtown cityscape. The hotel is located across the street from Battery Park at the southern tip of the island of Manhattan. There are exceptional views of the New York Harbor and the Statue of Liberty.

In front of the Ritz-Carlton, there are carved granite slabs with gently cascading water flowing along the surface. I entered the lobby. The reception desk was directly in front of me. Of course, I had to ask for Meadhbh's room number, but I also knew the receptionist would call her to get permission before giving it to me. The thought crossed my mind that Meadhbh might not want me dropping by and might not agree to provide her room number. I hoped I wouldn't have to deal with that embarrassment.

As it turned out, Meadhbh answered her phone and told the receptionist that I could come up. I faintly heard Meadhbh's voice on the phone and I don't think she used any profanity in response to my unanticipated arrival. I took that as a good sign.

Meadhbh's room was on the twentieth floor. I admired the beautiful decor of the lobby as I walked to the elevator bank. Light wood wall panels, high ceilings, large flower vases on polished antique tables; and, a tasteful multi-colored rug with pink and red highlights. All combined to project an image of quiet wealth.

I knocked twice on the door to Meadhbh's room. I was perspiring. The last thing I needed was for sweat to start dripping down my forehead. The door opened. She looked up at me. Her green eyes dazzled with such intensity I was momentarily frozen by the familiar pleasure of being in her presence.

"Are you going to speak or just stand there and nervously blink at me with those cute curvy eyelashes?" she asked.

The little voice in my head screamed at me to snap out of it and say something.

"Meadhbh, it's so good to see you. Sorry, I didn't call before coming over. I just thought I'd take a chance on you being home."

"I'm way ahead of you. Judy called and said you would be coming by. You think I get this dressed up just to sit on the couch all day by myself? Come on in, I'm very happy you came by."

She was attractively dressed in a short, light green bubble skirt with a tight, white silk top. Her black Dolce Vita flats had shiny silver tips. Her hair was only about two inches long following her surgery, with a side part that revealed some stitch marks in her skull. The strawberry brown color accentuated her freckles.

She closed the door behind me. I kissed her on the cheek as we embraced. “I thought we were beyond cheek kisses, but maybe the time apart has set us back a couple of steps,” Meadhbh said, in her usual blunt style.

“It takes me a while to warm up,” I said, but had no idea what I meant by the comment.

As usual, Meadhbh already had me off-balance. I took that as a sign she was recovering well.

“Take a seat on the couch. I’ll get you a beer.”

Her accommodations were spacious and tasteful. A gold velvet couch and matching arm chair were in the first room, with a dark wood table in the middle and a large, flat-screen television directly across from the couch. The picture window behind the couch provided a remarkable water view of Ellis Island, Liberty Island and Governor’s Island. The double French doors leading to the bedroom were open, revealing a queen-size bed with a gold spread in front of a mirror that extended the length of the wall. Not a Vegas-type ceiling mirror, but it seemed to serve the same purpose.

Meadhbh sat next to me on the couch. She handed me the beer and poured some bottled water for herself.

“This room is lovely. How did you end up here rather than your apartment in Brooklyn?” I asked.

“It’s all my father’s doing. I think I mentioned him when we talked at the hospital. He’s kind of a strong personality. He likes the best of everything and he likes to pay cash. You can’t get very far trying to disagree with him or change his mind. He insisted I stay here after I was released from the hospital. He didn’t want me to do anything but rest and not worry about groceries or water or dusting or cleaning. He was right about that—they do everything for you here with a smile and a friendly hello. But, the fun is almost over. I’m checking out next week and returning to Brooklyn before going back to my job at the bar at *Très Bien*.”

“I’m so glad to hear that. So, you really are feeling a lot better?”

"Yes, I really am much better. I still stammer once in a while and I have headaches occasionally, but the doctors said that is to be expected based on the severity of my head injuries."

"I agree. Your injuries were very serious. It tore me apart when I saw you suffering so extensively at the hospital."

"I heard about your silly effort at revenge against Edison. Maybe it made you feel better, but it wasn't what I wanted. You could have been killed in the Ramble. I read in the papers that Edison almost beat you to death."

"Well, that's true. I ended up in the hospital, but the good news is that Edison was also hospitalized and came a lot closer to death than I did. The funny thing is that Edison claims he didn't tell his thugs to hurt you. He contends that some of his deputies took it upon themselves to initiate the attack."

"Like I said, I didn't want you to jeopardize your life, but I guess it shows your feelings for me. Maybe I can live with it on that level."

"I did it for you. Just for you. Only for you," I said.

"That's very special. It makes all my pain seem a little more bearable. I will always remember your words and never forget your valiant intentions. But, it still was stupid and ill-conceived to almost die trying to beat up Edison."

"I admit it might not have been the right thing to do or the smartest thing to do. But, what's done is done. Now we have to get back to our everyday lives as best we can."

"How's Kim doing?"

"Well, she's doing well. But as a couple, we aren't doing good at all."

"I'm sorry to hear that. Do you mind telling me what happened?"

"She met a doctor from one of the local hospitals in Port Jefferson. As far as I know, they have lunch together during the week. Kim says she doesn't love me any less, but her capacity to love increased as her affection for Dr. Joe grew."

"That's the doctor's name? Dr. Joe? Are you sure? I never heard of a doctor named Joe. Also, I hope you don't really buy her story about an increased capacity to love.

You couldn't possibly believe that fairy tale, right?" Meadhbh asked.

"I know. I found the whole thing a little hard to swallow myself."

"So, you and Kim are still together at this point, or not?"

"Yes, we are. I don't intend to leave and she hasn't said she wants me to leave."

"If anything changes, I'm here to grab you on the rebound."

"Thanks for the support."

"I guess this also means that you're not moving into an apartment near *Très Bien*."

"No, that's on hold," I responded. "Kim isn't interested in relocating anymore."

"I guess not, since Dr. Joe is around."

"Very funny."

"Sorry, I was joking around. I learned that from you," Meadhbh said.

Meadhbh leaned toward me on the couch until our shoulders lightly touched. Her face was inches from mine. I was a bit overwhelmed from the fragrance of her skin and the closeness of her physical presence.

"Like I said, I'm here for you. If your wife has a boyfriend, why can't you have a girlfriend? Fair is fair. You and Kim can compare notes," Meadhbh said, with a grin.

"Another joke? You know, I'm not good at taking my own medicine," I mentioned. "I think we need some fresh air, let's take a walk. Do you feel well enough to walk to the North Cove in front of the World Financial Center for a burger and beer at P.J. Clarke's?"

"Sounds good. The summer air will serve as our cold shower. I'm ready to go."

"I agree. We'll just end up in trouble if we hang out here much longer," I commented.

"This is the first time we've been alone together, other than your visits to the hospital. I'm not putting any pressure on you because I'm not fully healed yet. But, I want you to know you'd be in big trouble if I was feeling a hundred percent," Meadhbh candidly stated.

I stood and opened the door to her hotel room just to make sure we didn't change our minds about the walk.

We left the hotel and turned right on Battery Place, heading towards the Hudson River and the Museum of Jewish Heritage that borders the river. The Museum has a unique and diverse collection of magnificent flowers and blooming bushes that provide an impressive array of colors. The benches in front of the Museum are next to a line of trees that provide a canopy of shade conducive to introspective thought.

Just north of the Museum is a half circle of large, majestic evergreen trees that surround the South Cove, a small inlet of water. The South Cove has an elevated walkway above the water that provides an uninhibited view across the Hudson to New Jersey. The trees surrounding the South Cove create a small forest of tranquility that is unique to New York.

After passing the South Cove, we exited the tree-lined area and continued north on South End Avenue.

After walking several blocks, we approached the World Financial Center, which consists of four granite and glass office towers. The World Financial Center is located next to the esplanade that surrounds the North Cove of the Hudson River. Inside the World Financial Center is the Winter Garden Atrium, a 10-story structure with a marble floor, a wall of glass facing the water and a glass semicircular ceiling. The Winter Garden contains sixteen palm trees, each over 40 feet in height. The glass was destroyed and the palm trees harmed when the Twin Towers of the World Trade Center collapsed on 9/11, but everything was expeditiously rebuilt and opened once again in September of 2002.

I noticed that P.J. Clarke's had outdoor tables on the north side of the North Cove. But before going to the restaurant, I wanted to show Meadhbh the on-going construction of the 9/11 Memorial on the east side of the World Financial Center, right across the West Side Highway.

"Meadhbh, before we get something to eat, let's take a look at the World Trade Center site and the 9/11 Memorial directly on the former location of the destroyed Twin Towers."

"Yes, I would like that," Meadhbh responded, as we walked from South End Avenue to the east side of the World Financial Center.

"Straight ahead of us is the unfinished North Memorial Pool and the South Memorial Pool. When completed, water will flow over the edges of the four black granite walls of each pool. As you can see, the pools are massive, with each wall about 200 feet long and 30 feet deep so the water will flow downward from street level. I heard that about 52,000 gallons of water a minute will pour over the walls of both pools."

"Truly amazing."

"Once fully operational, the wind will carry some of the cascading water into the air, creating an inspirational floating mist that will appear mystical, yet reverent to those who perished. When the sun shines directly on the falling water, a rainbow will magically appear."

"What is being built in the middle of each of the pools?" Meadhbh asked.

"Those are smaller square pools being built into the base of both the North Memorial Pool and the South Memorial Pool. The smaller pools represent the footprints of the original Twin Towers. The names of the victims of both 9/11 and the 1993 World Trade Center bombing will be engraved on bronze plates to be placed at the top of each wall of both pools."

"That is magnificent. So fitting an honor to those who perished."

"And right next to the Memorial Pools is the Freedom Tower, now known as One World Trade Center. Notice that there is a concrete base that extends upward for about 185 feet, with the office floors constructed on top of the base. The base was designed to protect against street-level bomb impact. You can also see the steel beams outlining the upper floors. When finished, it will rise 104 floors and stand 1776 feet tall, with a transparent glass facade that will reflect the sun and surrounding images during the day."

"I can't wait to go to the top someday. Hopefully, they will build a bar on the observation deck," Meadhbh said.

"Speaking of bars, you are looking at the former location of a great bar once called the Tall Ships Bar and Grill. It was inside the Vista International Hotel, later known as the Marriott World Trade Center. The hotel was connected to both the North and South Towers, so you could walk to either Tower. Tall sailing ships were etched into the windows of the bar and engraved on the beer glasses. Images of maritime vessels and nautical decor were everywhere. It was, of course, destroyed when the Towers collapsed, along with the brave firemen who were using the hotel lobby as a safe haven to fight the fires. I've heard that the Tall Ships Bar had a door which opened onto Liberty Street and was important in the evacuation of the hotel before it was destroyed."

"So much misery and death was experienced by so many that September morning. The 9/11 Memorial will honor their deaths and forever pay tribute to many who died helping others survive," Meadhbh commented, her voice cracked with emotion.

"So true," was all I could manage to say.

We then walked in silence back to the World Financial Center and sat at an outdoor table at P.J. Clarke's on the North Cove.

"This is a lovely spot. The yachts docked in the Cove are very impressive. The sky is blue and the sunshine of the setting sun is warm."

"I agree. Perfect beer-drinking weather," I said. "Also, the cheeseburger is referred to as the 'Cadillac of Burgers.' Being of fine Irish heritage, I'm sure you know the history of P.J. Clarke's."

"I do. The original red brick building at 55th Street and Third Avenue has been serving drinks since 1884. I think it was about 1912 when it first got its name from a bartender-turned-owner named Patrick J. Clarke."

"That's right. You do know your local history."

"I'm in the bar business. I need such tidbits of knowledge to divert the conversation when middle-aged men make sexist comments while I'm bartending."

"Men do that to attractive bartenders? I'm shocked to hear that such things go on. I apologize on behalf of the entire male population of New York," I said in jest.

"The apology is not accepted because it is worthless. Boys will forever continue to be boys and the comments will go on whenever alcohol is served. So long as the tips are good, I consider it all part of the job."

We ordered cheeseburgers and draft beers.

"Turning to a more serious topic, I think I mentioned that Edison claims he did not order the attack on you. His men did it, of course, thinking that Edison would be happy with the result. It really was my fault because Edison's security detail saw us talking together at the bar and caused them to assume you were assisting me. I am very, very sorry."

"We've been over this. Don't be sorry. ZeiiMed and Edison inflicted a lot of pain and suffering on people you love. I was happy to help in trying to get it stopped. But, I didn't want you injured in the process. You did that on your own and I would have stopped you, had I known beforehand," Meadhbh responded.

"What's done is done. I did what I thought was necessary. Changing subjects, I want to tell you about a new fight I'm about to pick with ZeiiMed. I don't have a client yet, but I intend to sue ZeiiMed over the manufacture of a defective metal-on-metal Hip Implant Device. I refer to the Device as the HID. The HID didn't work as advertised and I'm convinced ZeiiMed knew this all along. In addition to pain and suffering experienced by patients post-surgery, there is always a danger of blood poisoning due to metal fragments detaching from the HID and entering the blood stream."

"I can't believe you are taking on ZeiiMed again. You're lucky you escaped with your life the first time around. Can't you find clients who have injuries caused by a company other than ZeiiMed?" Meadhbh asked.

"That's a good question. I agree it's crazy to cross swords with ZeiiMed once again. But, I didn't start out intending to repeat my pursuit of ZeiiMed. Our research led us to ZeiiMed and I'm going to pursue it, once I get a client or two with an HID problem."

"I understand, I guess," Meadhbh said. "I don't want you to get hurt again so I'm volunteering my services to assist you one more time, if you need me. I hate that bastard, Edison, with all my soul. But, I plan to return to work and I will continue to smile and chat with him when he comes in the restaurant. He will not have any idea of how much I despise him. Hopefully, that will put me in a position to help you screw him one last time. How's that for a plan?"

"Thank you, Meadhbh, but I will not involve you in future battles with Edison. During our so-called Rumble, I made it clear to Edison that I would kill him if ZeiiMed ever came near you again. Hopefully, you are now off limits and I want nothing to change that."

"I understand, but keep my offer in mind. It would help heal my physical and mental wounds to know that I played a part in the final downfall of Edison."

"I will," I responded, although I sincerely believed I would never accept her offer.

After consuming our cheeseburgers and a few more beers, we headed back to the Ritz-Carlton in a cab.

"I'll have the driver drop you off at your hotel and then I'll head to Penn Station for the train home."

"You're going to get home late. Doesn't Kim wonder where you are?" Meadhbh inquired.

"No, I think she has other things on her mind, but I really don't want to talk about Dr. Joe anymore."

"Actually, you're lucky that you don't have to make a big decision tonight."

"Meadhbh, I don't know what you're talking about."

"I'll tell you. If I was feeling better, I would invite you up to my room. But since I'm tired from the walking and drinking and healing, not necessarily in that order, I'm not going to ask you up. As a result, you don't have to make a major decision about our future."

"So, I should be happy that you didn't ask me up?"

"Exactly."

"But what if I wanted to be asked?"

"Since you know I am on the 'physically unable to perform' list, you shouldn't care that I didn't invite you."

"Okay," I said, though I wasn't sure what I was agreeing to.

The cab pulled up to the front of her hotel.

I gave her a quick kiss that lacked any message of affection.

"You know, Brian, I've taught you how to do that correctly so you really should give it more thought the next time the impulse hits you."

"I'll see you at *Très Bien* in a couple of weeks. Good luck with your return to work," I said, dodging the topic of kissing technique.

"I will email you my address in Brooklyn, with my cell phone number. By the way, I don't think it would break any laws for us to get together somewhere other than *Très Bien*."

"That depends on what you mean by 'get together'."

"You don't understand what those words mean?" Meadhbh asked. "I thought you were a lawyer."

"If you mean we should start spending time together on real dates, I think there are a number of laws we might be in danger of breaking," I countered. "The authorities don't prosecute such violations, but the laws are still there."

"Why do attorneys make everything such a long story? Just say you will call," Meadhbh replied.

"I'll call," I responded, unsure if I sounded sufficiently enthusiastic.

"Thanks for lunch and thanks for stopping by," she continued, while stepping out of the cab.

"You're welcome. Talk to you soon."

"You better," was her last remark.

-11-

August in Manhattan. The heat and humidity were unbearable.

Of course, it doesn't help that I continue to wear a suit and tie each day to work. I just don't feel like a lawyer if I'm not dressed to look like one. I'm comfortable playing the role of a well-dressed attorney ready to meet potential new clients on a moment's notice. The problem is that I've been waiting weeks for a new client to show up. But, you never know when your luck can change. On this particularly steamy day in the City, it was Mary who brought me the good news.

She entered my office with a grin of satisfaction.

"I finally got a response to our new website. I received a voice mail from an elderly gentleman who said his wife has a metal-on-metal HID that has become a real nightmare. She's in a wheelchair, experiences horrible muscle pain and seems to have little chance of ever walking again. She is too ill to have a ceramic replacement HID inserted. His name is Fred Dudley and he wants to meet at his wife's nursing home in Brooklyn."

"Good work. It sounds like a start. Call Mr. Dudley and tell him we will meet him at the nursing home at 3:00 p.m. tomorrow."

"Perfect. I'll set up the meeting. By the way, I forgot to tell you. As we anticipated, ZeiiMed has announced an official recall of the HID based on reports showing consistent premature failures at alarmingly high rates. The failure data must have revealed overwhelming evidence of a defective design of the HID or ZeiiMed would never have taken the drastic step of recalling the product."

"I agree. So, as of now, everyone knows the HID is junk that can cripple and possibly cause death. The key to our case will be to establish that ZeiiMed knew of this before the sale of the first HID years ago."

"ZeiiMed probably knew it didn't work properly in the early planning and design stage–before the first sale," Mary added.

"Yes, and it will be our job to find the documents that prove it. So, let's sign up our first HID client tomorrow and be ready to do battle with ZeiiMed. I'd love to see the look on Edison's face when he realizes our signatures are on a new Complaint. That's assuming, of course, that he is able to make facial expressions at all with his new, surgically manufactured face."

"I have an idea about how we can get the documents we need from ZeiiMed," Mary stated.

"OK, let's hear it," I said.

"All we need to do is get a 'Google Street View' car from 'Google Maps.' The Google car can then gather all the unencrypted electronic data from ZeiiMed's headquarters in the Grace Building."

"What are you talking about?" I asked.

"I can't believe you don't know about this," Mary responded. "Earlier in the year, Google was criticized for collecting emails, text messages, social network postings, passwords and other personal communications from households that they filmed from the street. Google claims that the purpose of the digital filming was to collect images of neighborhoods worldwide for Google Maps and Google Earth. The Google Street View car has a large roof-mounted antenna that looks like the extended periscope of a submarine. At the top of the antenna are cameras and complex computer accessories that capture and store electronic communications and data as the Google car is driven slowly past each house."

"You're kidding. Our personal information from the privacy of our homes was gobbled up and stored by Google without our permission?" I asked.

"Essentially, yes. Google takes a digital image of your house and also gets access to all the sweet nothings you email to your wife."

"Or that my wife emails to her new boyfriend. Maybe I should call Google and see if I can get her electronic love letters. Hopefully, they are in an alphabetic files so it's easy to look under 'J' for Joe."

"Joe? That's the name of your wife's new boyfriend? I hope you're joking."

"Yes, of course I am," I lied. There is no way I'm fully disclosing my marital problems at work. I have enough difficulty balancing the overlapping relationships in my life without further aggravating the problem.

"Getting back to my point, I suggest that we ask Google to lend us the Google Street View car so we can park it outside ZeiiMed all day and night to collect the HID payload data from their unencrypted WiFi hot spots."

"I'm going to assume this is your idea of humor. Clearly, I need to remind you that we are dealing with a serious legal matter here. Google isn't going to help us illegally eavesdrop on our adversary. I'm sure Google is doing everything possible to reach an agreeable resolution with the regulators and governmental agencies that are reviewing the unauthorized personal data collection. We are supposed to be committed to conducting the litigation in accordance with the rules of the Courts. And that is exactly what we are going to do. Follow the rules and play by the rules," I instructed, as if I was lecturing colleagues in a large auditorium at the annual convention of the American Bar Association.

"I understand fully, even though your track record with ZeiiMed doesn't reflect your consistent compliance with such a high code of honor and conduct. But, that's another story."

"It certainly is and I'd rather not get into it now," I responded.

"Then let's talk about Joe. How did your wife meet him? Is it serious?" Mary asked.

"No, I am not talking about Joe either. In fact, this conversation is over. Tomorrow we will go to see the Dudleys. Hopefully, we'll be able to obtain compensation for Mrs. Dudley's injuries and do some financial damage to ZeiiMed. But, we will do so by following the letter of the law and the rules of the courts. End of story."

"Yes, Mr. Bradford. You know I always do what you ask. I'll go call Mr. Dudley right now."

“Thank you very much,” I responded to her feigned formal compliance with my directive.

“You know, you definitely are in a bad mood. Your wife’s new boyfriend must really be getting to you,” Mary continued.

“Please close my door on the way out. I usually enjoy a little sarcasm, but not today. Email me when Mr. Dudley confirms tomorrow. See you later. Thanks for your help.”

Life is funny. The one person I want more involved in my life, my wife Kim, seems to be slowly creating space between us. Whereas, Mary and Meadhbh seem to want more involvement in my private affairs while I’m resisting their efforts at increased personal intimacy.

I’m not sure where this is all heading, but I know for sure the road into the future will be bumpy and unpredictable. Then again, there might be some fun in unforeseen roadside pit stops here and there along the journey. For now, the plan is to wake each new day with a smile, ready to navigate the twists and turns of an unknown fate.

-12-

Mrs. Dudley was a patient at an "affordable" assisted living facility in Brooklyn called "Pleasant Pastime."

Mary and I got on the Canarsie "L" train at the station located at 6th Avenue and 14th Street. We got off in Brooklyn at the stop for 105th Street and Farragut Road. As we exited the subway, the building was across the street.

Pleasant Pastime needed a lot of maintenance work. The five-story brick building had several broken windows, missing or dislodged shutters and concrete steps that were cracked and crumbling.

Upon entering the premises, the smell of putrefaction was nauseating. The staff attempted to cover the vile odors with antiseptic sprays which I could taste. The floor was a checkered linoleum littered with black scuff marks. Mounds of dry dust gathered in slightly moving balls that lined the edges of the floor.

Mary and I walked up to a small reception desk in the middle of a large empty room that reminded me of a vacant high school gymnasium. Every sound seemed amplified, especially the noise of our footsteps. Also, it was uncomfortably hot. There was no air conditioning and the windows were shut.

The receptionist was an elderly lady with silver hair and thick glasses. She quietly stated that Mrs. Dudley's room was on the third floor, Room 328. She didn't ask us our business and did not inquire about identification. Her nametag identified her as "Donna."

In fact, the only thing that Donna did mention was Mrs. Dudley's floor and room number in response to my inquiry. Not even "Hello" or "Have a nice day."

Donna immediately returned to her paperback book after providing the location information. I guess Donna doesn't get many opportunities to speak with human beings, so she was out of practice. I whispered, "Thank you." She didn't look up from her reading.

Mary and I walked around the reception desk and headed to the rear of the building where the elevator bank was clearly identified. Despite our attempts to walk as softly as possible, the noise of our heels tapping on the floor echoed throughout the room.

The elevator opened on the third floor. We stepped into the hall and started looking for 328. Wheelchairs cluttered the corridor. In each wheelchair was a feeble and seemingly disoriented patient.

The wheelchairs started slowly heading towards us in a haphazard fashion as each patient turned the wheels by hand. Some could not hold their heads up straight. Some had their tongues dangling from their mouths. All were elderly and all were mumbling mostly incoherent words. It seemed they were desperate to speak with us, yet physically unable to do so. As the wheelchairs surrounded us, we said, "Hello," but quickly and gently moved a few to the side to make a pathway. Their misery was palpable, but there was little we could do to help.

We arrived at Room 328. There was a bed, a chest of drawers and a wheelchair next to the bed. A small lamp on the windowsill provided the only illumination. An elderly woman was asleep in the wheelchair. Next to her, sitting on the bed, was a short, stocky man in Bermuda shorts with a baseball cap that said "NAVY" across the front. His feet dangled above the floor.

I approached the bed.

"Mr. Dudley? Mr. Fred Dudley?" I asked.

"Yes, I am," he said, as he hopped off the bed.

"I'm Brian Bradford and this is my colleague Mary Douglas. We are lawyers. You asked us here today."

"Thanks for coming," Mr. Dudley said as we shook hands.

"I spoke with you on the phone yesterday regarding our appointment for today," Mary mentioned.

"Of course. Nice to meet you both. I appreciate that you made the trip to see us," Mr. Dudley responded.

The woman in the wheelchair started to move. She slowly opened her eyes.

"I would like you to meet my wife, Mrs. Dudley," as he motioned towards the wheelchair.

Mrs. Dudley's eyes suddenly popped wide open. She seemed attentive and aware.

"Don't be so formal, Fred. Hi. My name is Martha and I'm pleased to meet you. I've got a case any lawyer would drool over. Maybe we can make litigation history together. I can't walk because of this lousy hip gadget that was put in me, but that doesn't mean I'm not ready to do battle. Ask me anything you want and I'll tell you everything I know. Don't be shy. Speak right up."

Although Martha appeared to be over sixty, her skin was smooth and tight, with jet-black hair pulled back to form a bun in the back of her head. It was a very practical hairstyle to accommodate the heat. Her makeup had been carefully applied and the blush on her cheeks gave her an attractive coloring. Despite the temperature and lack of a breeze, she seemed comfortable in a white, button-down sweater with a pin made of colored rhinestones in the shape of the Scales of Justice. She clearly didn't fit in with the dreary surroundings. She was larger in size than her husband, and was clearly ready, willing and able to test the legal waters and confront whatever and whoever caused her harm.

But, the "Scales of Justice" pin worried me a little. It's difficult to please a client with the high expectations and unrealistic goal of overcoming the injustices of society. All I do as a lawyer for a plaintiff is recover money, if I'm lucky. If money doesn't make your day, then my services usually aren't what you need. If your objective is to keep the Scales of Justice in equal balance, you probably should consult with a priest, a social worker, a newspaper reporter, or a psychiatrist, in whatever order you desire.

"Your enthusiasm is appreciated. Why don't you tell us your story, starting with the first time you felt any pain, the doctors you consulted and the medical treatment you received," I said.

"It's going to be a long story. I'll get some extra chairs from another room," Mr. Dudley offered.

Once we were all comfortable, Martha began.

"Starting around three years ago, I developed a pain that occurred periodically in my left hip. I was also having trouble sitting down and then more trouble trying to stand up. The pain was intense and it felt like there was no cushioning tissue in my hip. The area was very brittle and made grinding noises. Of course, I consulted with a surgeon and was told I needed a hip replacement. The surgeon explained in great detail how the new metal-on-metal Hip Implant Device was vastly superior to the ceramic or plastic models. The metal-on-metal Device lasted longer and could withstand much greater stress from extreme movement or exercise. Plus, a shallow, thicker cup created better mobility."

"All the doctors we consulted said essentially the same thing. The metal-on-metal Device was simply a better mouse trap," Mr. Dudley added.

"Such propaganda was part of the problem," Mary explained. "Many of the surgeons who were recommending the Device were undisclosed paid consultants to the companies that manufactured the HID, as we call the Device. The largest manufacturer is a company called MendMed, a subsidiary totally controlled by its parent, ZeiiMed."

"I know about that," Martha said. "I'll explain. Many of the elderly patients here at the not so lovely Pleasant Pastime have dementia or Alzheimer's disease. They also developed problems walking as they got older. The next thing you know the nursing home's resident physician recommends a metal-on-metal HID made by MendMed. I did some research and reached the same conclusion you did–that MendMed is a puppet of ZeiiMed. Many here had the surgery. All are now in wheelchairs. I'm sure there was a pay-off to the physician in residence. In fact, I'll bet ZeiiMed pays consulting fees to resident physicians all across the country because nursing home patients rely on their in-house medical advise."

"My investigation turned up much the same information," Mary noted. "It's been speculated that ZeiiMed focuses on mentally limited patients in nursing homes because they can be easily persuaded by the nursing home physician to undergo the surgery. No one listens to their complaints when the HID fails. The elderly are sitting ducks targeted by ZeiiMed because when the ducks start to quack, it's attributed to mental illness and not blood poisoning caused by the HID. ZeiiMed is happy because another HID was sold and the guinea pigs remain locked in a nursing home. Any cries of pain are merely the random rants of an unbalanced mind."

"That's important background information. We'll use it in our lawsuit. Mrs. Dudley, please continue with your story. The surgeon you consulted recommended the metal-on-metal HID. What happened next?" I asked.

"I did what the doctors told me. I had the HID surgically implanted on the left side in 2007. I had no choice, really. I could no longer live with the constant pain. I was told the surgery went well. No complications. The doctors seemed comforting and competent. The hospital staff assured me I would be walking pain free in no time. Obviously, it didn't work out as planned."

Martha seemed close to tears.

"At first, it seemed her recovery was going well," Mr. Dudley added. "She was close to walking and feeling only slight discomfort. Then the hip started making clicking and grinding sounds. The pain followed. It grew stronger and more constant. The doctor gave her painkillers, but it persisted. She couldn't walk, couldn't sit and sleep was difficult."

"Finally, I switched my orthopedic surgeon," Martha said. "Apparently, I got lucky and found one who wasn't getting a kickback from the manufacturer of the HID. I was told the metal ball was popping in and out of the surgically implanted cup. But that wasn't the worst of it. When the ball remained in the cup, the friction of the metal parts rubbing against each other caused metal particles to be released into my blood stream and eventually broke down into toxic ions. In addition to poisoning the blood with cobalt and chromium, the ions killed the tissue around the hip until there was nothing left but a blackened mass of dead and decaying flesh. Now I have headaches, memory loss, balance issues and blurred vision, as well as possible heart and kidney damage."

"Of course, the HID must be surgically removed or else her condition will just continue to deteriorate," Mr. Dudley mentioned. "She can no longer walk, she can't dress herself and can't even get out of bed without special assistance. That's why she is a resident here at Pleasant Pastime. We managed at home for as long as we could, but it eventually got to the point that full-time assistance was needed. Unfortunately, we don't have the money for a better place. We're doing the best we can here at Pleasant Pastime."

"I'm so sorry for all your misery," Mary commented. "No one should have to endure such damage and pain because of the gross negligence of ZeiiMed and the doctors it pays to peddle the HID. Has your new doctor recommended a replacement of the defective HID?"

"I'm not healthy enough to survive a second operation," Martha responded. "The HID is not only killing me slowly, it's also made me too sick to remove it. It's a horrible Catch-22. Meanwhile, the soft tissue continues to break down and the poison continues to spread inside me."

"If you agree to retain us, I promise we will do everything possible to prevent this from happening to others, in addition to recovering money to compensate for your pain and suffering. The first step is to obtain a sample Device so a medical expert can test it and testify in court about its defects," I said, knowing I wasn't much comfort to Martha since she knew her medical condition probably would not change. I realize that Martha wanted to help others, although she could not help herself.

"I have a sample HID," Mr. Dudley said.

"Excuse me, did you say you have a ZeiiMed manufactured metal-on-metal HID?" I quickly asked.

"Yes, I do," he responded, as he reached into a shopping bag on the floor. "Here is the shiny metal cup and here is the ball and attached stem. Our new doctor gave this to me. He said to keep it until we consulted a lawyer. The doctor said that ZeiiMed instructed all orthopedic surgeons to destroy each HID as it was removed from complaining patients. Also, all new but unused Devices were to be returned immediately to ZeiiMed for a full refund. Basically, a cover up of the evidence, but this one wasn't destroyed because Martha's doctor knew there was something wrong with it."

Dudley handed me the HID.

I closely examined the design of the metal cup.

"The edge of the cup is very sharp. You could easily cut your finger by running it along the edge."

"Yes, that's true," Mr. Dudley agreed. "That's what happened. With each movement, the ball grinds against the edge of the cup and caused the metal flaking, just like you were sharpening a knife against a grindstone. There's also a groove inside the cup."

"That's also part of the problem," Mary noted. "The groove was placed inside the cup to assist the doctor with the correct insertion and placement of the HID during surgery. The groove makes it easier to maneuver the cup during insertion. An instrument is inserted into the groove, like a marshmallow on a stick. Of course, the groove created additional edges in the cup that enhanced the grinding effect while walking."

"A remarkably horrible story. I hope you believe me when I promise to pursue ZeiiMed zealously and not relent until all is revealed," I commented.

"Absolutely, I believe you," Martha responded. "I need your help and I will do whatever is necessary to win the case so others won't go through this hell."

"Fred, are you on board with this?" Martha asked. "It's my decision to make and I've made it, but I hope you will go along. Has a cat got your tongue? Now is the time to say 'yes' or 'no' or forever hold your peace."

"Martha, you know I'm with you one hundred percent," Mr. Dudley said.

Of course, I couldn't help but think she would jump out of the wheelchair and beat him to a pulp if he disagreed.

"That's settled," I said. "Mary will prepare the retainer agreement and explain all its terms to you. The standard fee is thirty-three percent of any recovery, but I'm reducing it to twenty percent for this case. My job is to bring ZeiiMed to its knees and I'll do my best to accomplish that. But, remember, ZeiiMed is a formidable opponent with unlimited resources and ruthless management. The Company won't think twice about inflicting injury and even death to achieve its goals."

"I don't care," Martha interrupted. "I'm already in pain and already facing death. What else can they do to me?"

"I like your spirit. From now on we are a team. Welcome to the war against ZeiiMed," I said enthusiastically. "After the retention agreement is signed, the firm will start the lawsuit against ZeiiMed and hire an expert medical witness to testify about the defective and harmful design of the HID. We will focus on obtaining documents from ZeiiMed that reveal knowledge of the dangerous design before the first HID was sold. There is no guarantee we can obtain such inculpatory documents, but ZeiiMed's devious track record speaks for itself. ZeiiMed does bad things and then tries to hide the evidence under the rug. But, we are going to find it, God willing."

I kissed Martha on the cheek and hugged her husband. Mary kissed both of them. I think Martha was tearing up again. We promised to be in touch shortly.

Mary and I left Pleasant Pastime. As soon as we were on the street, I persuaded Mary to join me at a local pub. I needed at least a couple of drinks. I guess I don't handle emotional situations well. At least that's what Kim tells me.

I've always found it easy to persuade clients that I can successfully handle their cases. The difficult part is the realization that they have placed all of their trust in me based on a sincere belief that I can accomplish the unrealistic goals I promised. The clients are depending totally on my ability to succeed, when I'm not sure there is a reasonable chance that I can succeed. The need to attract new business fuels my dilemma. The clients' expectations are a result of my inflated promises of success, but I would never have been hired without the exaggeration and overstatement.

Maybe next year I'll make it my New Year's resolution not to lie to my clients anymore. I would probably be out of business by the 4th of July. Nobody wants to hear the truth, especially not from their lawyer.

-13-

It's late September and I should have the new lawsuit filed soon. Mary prepared the draft Complaint and provided a copy for my review.

The law firm of Alfonso and Ryan consists of ten partners and fifteen associates. Most of my work at the firm is mundane and repetitive insurance or banking matters, although a couple of years ago my first suit against ZeiiMed was filed. It was successful because it ultimately resulted in a settlement of one billion dollars. On the negative side, the case got a little too personal and little too emotional. That's really not accurate. The case got extremely personal and very emotional.

My bloody combat with John Edison in Central Park was the final climax. We both ended up in the hospital, although I still contend I won because his injuries were worse.

Regardless, it was stupid and achieved no purpose. I did it out of misplaced revenge for the beating that ZeiiMed's thugs inflicted on Meadhbh, but she didn't approve of either the risk that was taken or the injuries that were inflicted.

Like my wife Kim, Meadhbh felt it was an unnecessary, unwarranted and unsolicited confrontation that caused needless injuries and almost caused a loss of life. (It was Edison who almost bled to death, not me, so I don't completely see their point.)

Based on the collective wisdom of women whose opinions I trust, the point appears to be that I'm wrong, once again. I see a pattern starting to form here. Maybe, I should stop asking them what they think.

Mary walked into my office and sat in one of the armchairs in front of my desk. I am not going to ask her opinion on anything. I'm keeping the conversation to work-related topics.

"Hi. What did you think of the draft Complaint?" Mary asked. "I tried to keep it simple. I alleged that Mrs. Dudley had left hip replacement surgery that involved the HID designed and sold by MendMed, a subsidiary controlled by ZeiiMed. Both ZeiiMed and MendMed are listed as defendants. I then added a paragraph that the HID was defectively designed and ZeiiMed was aware of it, but withheld the critical information from Mrs. Dudley. So far, so good?"

"Yes, it does summarize our case in a short and direct manner," I responded. "You correctly included a cause of action for negligence in the manufacture of the HID, along with the contention that MendMed and ZeiiMed failed to warn of its risks and dangers. The HID was unfit for its intended purpose and ZeiiMed should have disclosed this to the public. That is exactly what we want to allege."

"Don't forget the claim for punitive damages," Mary said. "That's the best part. We contend that because of ZeiiMed's willful, wanton, and malicious acts and omissions, Mrs. Dudley and other plaintiffs similarly situated are entitled to receive a generous portion of ZeiiMed's net worth as punitive damages to punish the harmful behavior and prevent others from doing the same. We're talking billions here."

"That's the key to a big payday and the only way to really inflict financial damage on ZeiiMed," I emphasized. "To recover punitive damages, the jury must be convinced that ZeiiMed knew of the dangers and risks of the HID, but intentionally did nothing other than continue to push sales worldwide with an army of paid physicians singing the virtues of the HID. I don't know exactly when ZeiiMed first learned of the defects, but I damn well know ZeiiMed shouldn't have hidden the information."

I continued to review the Complaint, and noted to Mary, "You correctly drafted the Complaint for filing in the Supreme Court of the State of New York, County of New York, since we allege state law causes of action, rather than violations of federal law. The lawsuit will move slower in state court, so we will need to keep pushing for a trial date. But, it's always a thrill to climb the steps to the venerable Courthouse at 60 Centre Street."

"Actually," Mary said, "I've never been to that Courthouse before. I'm looking forward to the opportunity."

"I recently attended a dinner inside the Courthouse sponsored by the State Bar Association. I learned a few points of interest, including the fact that it first opened in 1927 and there are 32 steps from street level to the entrance, with each step 100 feet long. At the top of the steps, facing the street, are ten granite Corinthian columns that hold up a triangular section of the roof called a pediment. The area within the pediment contains, in capital letters spanning the front of the building, the phrase: 'THE TRUE ADMINISTRATION OF JUSTICE IS THE FIRMEST PILLAR OF GOOD GOVERNMENT.'"

"Thanks for the history lesson," responded Mary, with a hint of boredom. "Since I had to listen to you ramble on about some old Courthouse, I think it appropriate for you to listen to a point of interest I would like to discuss."

"Proceed," was my only comment, knowing there was no way to avoid the verbal barrage to come.

"Two days ago, President Obama held a town hall meeting with ordinary people supposedly representing the workers of America, the middle class, as well as students and people living on pensions. The event took place at the Newseum in Washington, DC, a museum that memorializes journalism and free press. The conversations with the President were televised live. *The New York Post* reported that one middle-class woman told the President she was 'exhausted from defending you, defending your administration, defending the mantle of change that I voted for.' She also mentioned that she voted for a man who said he was going to change things in a meaningful way for the middle class, and then noted that she is still waiting."

"I know. I heard it on the news. The middle class that overwhelmingly voted for the President truly believed him when he said he would change their lives."

"I guess that's my point," Mary continued. "Obama promised the middle class change they could believe in. He created an image that each member of the middle class will have a mailbox full of social entitlement checks. Of course, no president is capable of that, but the fiction was created and repeated."

"So what happens when his first four years are up and he hasn't delivered as promised?" I asked, immediately breaking my promise not to ask for opinions from the significant women in my life.

"It's not hard to figure out," Mary answered. "The re-election campaign will have the President pleading for four more years to finish the job he started. He will state to the American people that his job is not yet done, change doesn't happen overnight and four more years are needed to complete his promises. He will succeed in getting re-elected and will serve the second term. But he will never tell the middle class the true reality that a President cannot single-handedly elevate your quality of life; cannot deliver better food to your tables; cannot provide a better car and home; and, cannot deliver the change of life promised again and again."

"But, if you asked the President," I noted, "he will say he did deliver. He got healthcare reform passed; signed legislation that created regulations to govern banks and Wall Street; and, set a timetable for an end to the war in Afghanistan."

"I know, but that wasn't the change the middle class believed the President was speaking about. The middle class thought he was talking about elevating their day-to-day lives, not national reforms or foreign policy. And that's the shame of it. After eight years in office, the American people will look back and realize the dream wasn't attained and the promises undelivered. America will be left heartbroken by the false hope that their lives would be changed significantly. It was all a big con job."

"Look on the bright side," I said. "One day there will be new presidential candidates of both parties saying they will provide the promised land that the current president failed to deliver."

"And life goes on, the same as ever, repeating itself time and time again."

"Yes, Mary, that's how it works," I responded. "None of this should be a surprise to you. Someone my age has seen the same pattern repeat itself decade after decade. It's up to the American people to read, learn and not forget."

"That's a point we can both agree on," Mary stated.

"I have another point we can agree on, " I noted. "The North Korean government is on track to cause havoc in the world for the foreseeable future. A day or so ago, North Korea's dictator Kim Jong-il made his twenty-seven-year-old son a four-star general. The kid, Kim Jong-un, has no military experience, except he possibly attended a few years at a military school. How many four-star generals do you know who were never in the military?"

"What's your point. Why do you care if daddy gives his son a fancy uniform with a lot of ribbons and gold?" Mary asked.

"Because daddy is not in good health. He had a stroke a couple of years ago. So, two years from now the father could be dead and Kim Jong-un will be the new leader of North Korea. North Korea has already conducted two tests of a nuclear weapon. By 2016 or 2017, Kim Jong-un may have as many as a dozen nuclear weapons. Regardless of the economic sanctions imposed on North Korea by the free world, the father and presumably the son will continue to refuse to disarm or halt the nuclear program, while also refusing the U.N. inspections of the nuclear facilities. Kim Jung-un will use the threat of nuclear war as leverage to obtain the economic aid and worldwide trading rights he has demanded. Bottom line, the world will be stuck with a very young leader with no experience, in charge of an arsenal of nuclear weapons that are his only bargaining chip to get essential supplies and aid to his country. And it's going to get worse. North Korea has already developed a missile capable of reaching South Korea. All that's left is for North Korea's scientists to figure out how to reduce the size of a nuclear weapon to fit on a missile head."

"What are the possible solutions to this developing world crisis?" Mary inquired. "Israeli and American jets dropping bombs on North Korea's nuclear facilities? I don't think China would react well to that."

"I know," I answered. "It appears to be a problem without a reasonable solution."

"That happens in life," Mary commented. "All we can do is deal with the problems we have before us and hope matters outside our control somehow work themselves out. Right now, our number one priority is getting the lawsuit against ZeiiMed filed and served. I'll get it done by next week. I suggest we put current events on the back burner."

"I get it. When you want to talk about world events, I'm supposed to give you my full attention. But, when I have something to add, you couldn't care less. Whatever. Get the Dudleys to approve the Complaint and then serve ZeiiMed by having our process server bring the Complaint to the Grace Building," I instructed.

"Consider it done," Mary responded. "Our next exciting adventure with ZeiiMed is about the begin. Hopefully, with no loss of life or limb, or other physical harm, this time around."

"Maybe we'll get lucky and that's how it will play out. But, don't count on it and be ready for anything. We do seem to bring the worst out in ZeiiMed," I said.

"I've noticed," Mary agreed.

"And I have the scars to prove it," I added.

-14-

Within a week, Martha Dudley had read the class action Complaint and consented to its filing.

The lawsuit was commenced by the filing of the Summons and Complaint with the Clerk of the Court in the basement of the Courthouse at 60 Centre Street. Upon payment of the filing fee, the Clerk stamped an index number on the first page of the Complaint and the litigation was entered in the Court's computers that supervise and control new lawsuits filed in the Supreme Court of the State of New York, County of New York. A judge was randomly assigned from the Commercial Part of the Supreme Court. The Commercial Part of the Supreme Court consists of a number of judges who handle only complicated commercial disputes involving complex legal issues and significant damages.

The New York Civil Practice Law and Rules (CPLR) set forth all the statutory obligations and deadlines that control the content and pace of the litigation. Essentially, it's the playbook of the New York litigation game.

The CPLR dictates the mandatory time period for service of the Summons and Complaint and describes the manner in which service must be made. I served ZeiiMed by two of the methods permitted by the CPLR. One was personal service by a process server at ZeiiMed's headquarters in New York City. The CPLR requires that personal service be made upon an officer, director, managing agent or person authorized by the company to accept service. I hired a process server to take the Complaint to the Grace Building and effectuate service. Unfortunately, there were some difficulties encountered, as I learned from Mary later in the day.

The process server arrived at the Grace Building but, of course, the security detail did not permit the process server to proceed past the security desk immediately inside the front revolving door. Security called upstairs requesting a

ZeiiMed person come down to accept the Summons and Complaint from the process server.

Shortly thereafter, a very young woman eventually disembarked from the elevator and walked into the lobby. She described herself as an administrative assistant to the supervisor of the duplications department at ZeiiMed. She smiled, took possession of the Summons and Complaint and immediately returned to wherever she belonged within the bowels of ZeiiMed.

"Based on her aloof attitude," Mary said, "She probably placed the Complaint in her supervisor's in-box, where it will remain for days while the duplication department decides what to do with it. Once the Complaint finally reaches the desk of someone in the legal department, I'm sure all hell will break loose and the duplication department will have a lot of explaining to do about the delay. Eventually, however, some unfortunate soul at the legal department will be required to deliver the Summons and Complaint to CEO John Edison at his hospital bed or wherever he is currently recovering from the 'Rumble in the Ramble' as the local newspaper called it."

I imagined with great satisfaction the anger on Edison's face as he paged through the Complaint and saw my signature on the last page, immediately above the clause demanding billions of dollars in punitive damages.

To address the possibility that the administrative assistant to the duplication department placed the Complaint in her desk drawer and totally ignored its importance, I also served the Secretary of State in Albany, New York. A corporation operating in New York State is required to agree to service on the Secretary of State as an additional method of service on a domestic corporation. One way or another, Edison will eventually be presented with the Summons and Complaint.

Two weeks after service upon the Secretary of State, I received both electronically and in the mail the Answer of ZeiiMed. An "Answer" is the legally required response to the Complaint. ZeiiMed's Answer denied all the allegations and listed numerous Affirmative Defenses. Affirmative Defenses are legal arguments as to why ZeiiMed did nothing wrong and is not required to pay damages. ZeiiMed argued in its Affirmative Defenses that the HID was not defectively designed and that ZeiiMed had no knowledge of any risk of injury that it failed to disclose to the buying public. No surprise there. It was standard operating procedure for a Defendant to take a posture of complete denial early in a litigation.

More problematic, ZeiiMed also contended in another of its Affirmative Defenses that Mrs. Dudley does not meet the obligatory legal prerequisites to proceed as a class plaintiff in a class action. This will be a critical issue in the case. If Mrs. Dudley can sue only on her own behalf, and not on behalf of a class of all patients with a defective metal-on-metal HID, then our billion dollar claim won't get to first base because we can only recover for the injury to Mrs. Dudley and not for the collective injuries to all patients with the HID.

Pursuant to the CPLR, I am legally required to demonstrate that Mrs. Dudley is qualified to proceed as a proper representative of a class of all people injured by the HID. That is, it is my legal burden to prove to the Court that there are common questions of law or fact "which predominate over any questions affecting only individual members." Also, Mrs. Dudley's claims must be "typical of the class." This will require me to establish to the Court that the other members of the class suffered the same or similar injuries from the metal-on-metal HID and that the damages sought by Mrs. Dudley are typical of the damages suffered by each class member. This issue will quickly come before the Court because I am required to file a Motion for Class Certification early in the litigation. The Motion will request an Order permitting the suit to proceed as a class.

The Motion will contend that Mrs. Dudley's situation is similar to thousands of other patients who had the metal-on-metal HID placed in their bodies. I will argue that ZeiiMed, through its manufacturing subsidiary MendMed, advertised that the HID was safe and assured the public it had no safety risks while enhancing movement. When, in reality, ZeiiMed designed the HID so that its sharp metal edges caused poisonous metals to be absorbed into the blood of everyone who had the surgery. The simple common fact is that every person who received the metal-on-metal HID did so because a medial professional said it would help them get better and walk normally. ZeiiMed sent the same message to everyone. ZeiiMed inflicted the same injury on all based on the same broken promise.

Although I believe the case is meritorious and warrants class certification, it will be difficult to convince the Court that I am right and the ZeiiMed litigation machine is wrong. ZeiiMed will strenuously contend that the HID is safe and there is no proof that ZeiiMed caused the same injury to a class of people with the same medical history as Mrs. Dudley. Nonetheless, we will give it our best shot and hope the Judge gives us an opportunity to obtain the evidence needed to proceed as a class.

The CPLR requires that the Motion requesting the Court to permit the suit to proceed as a class be filed within sixty days of receipt of ZeiiMed's Answer. As a result, Mary and I immediately prepared the Motion for Class Certification and filed it with the Court thirty days after receiving ZeiiMed's Answer.

The Motion was then scheduled for a Hearing in Court on November 15, 2010.

-15-

On November 15, 2010, Mary and I arrived at the Supreme Court Building in downtown New York City. We were early for the 10 a.m. start time of the Hearing on my Motion for Class Certification.

We carefully ascended the 32 concrete steps in the front of the Courthouse and entered through the oversized doors that serve as the entrance to the first floor. The x-ray machine and police security detail were in a great hallway thirty-five feet wide and over seventy-five feet in length. The arched ceiling, two stories high, extended the length of the great hallway. The convex curve of the arched ceiling contained the following words: PROTECTION, SECURITY, TRUTH and ERROR, accompanied by two murals of several women, including one in armor with a sword and another a bare-breasted blonde holding a mirror with a sheer silk garment covering her legs, but not hiding her nudity. An iron chandelier with two rows of lights extended from the ceiling in the middle of the hallway, containing a circle of interlocking metal figurines of the Lady of Justice.

After passing through security, we exited the great hallway. The elevator bank was straight ahead on the periphery of the marble Rotunda, an historical masterpiece of architecture created by a circle of twelve columns and six archways. The Rotunda is over seventy-five feet in diameter, with two columns between each archway. The marble columns are two stories high, with a balcony and ledge above each archway for viewing of the Rotunda from the second floor. The elevated balconies appeared to be miniature versions of the Pope's Balcony at the Vatican in Rome.

Eight stone figures of Pegasus were carved above each set of two columns. The dome of the Rotunda contains a vividly colored, magnificent mural called, "The History of the Law," painted in the 1930s. It depicts the evolution of the law by highlighting important historical events that transformed humanity's concept of justice. Toward the top of the Rotunda are the names and carved faces of Marshall, Moses, Hammurabi, Solon, Justinian and Blackstone, with gold medallions and a circle of gold roping and scrolls adorned above each name. A black chandelier with three sets of lights extends down from the top of the dome, attached to a thick iron chain over thirty feet in length.

The Courtroom was on the second floor. Unlike the Rotunda, the huge square Courtroom was dreary, dull and very humid.

The walls of the Courtroom were thirty feet high, but the first six feet above the floor had wood paneling that surrounded the entire room in a dark intersecting pattern of two-foot wooden squares. The institutional brown linoleum floor, again in a pattern of squares, had a brilliant shine despite the thousands of scuff marks and chips. The five hanging lights and fifteen recessed lights created inadequate illumination.

However, there were some noteworthy aspects of the Courtroom. The Bench stood an imposing five feet tall, made of rare black walnut. On the wall behind the Bench were the words: “IN GOD WE TRUST.” Also, behind the Bench was the American Flag, with a gold eagle at the top of the pole. The flag drooped lifelessly in the still, overheated room.

The Judge’s entrance to the Courtroom was through a dark wood door to the left of the Bench. After entering, there were three steps leading to the Judge’s high-backed leather chair.

To the right of the Bench was the jury box, consisting of twelve wooden seats with leather cushions, with two rows of six seats each. A black walnut railing was directly in front of the first row of six seats. A podium for the lawyers’ presentation pressed against the railing in front of the jury box.

Immediately in front of the Bench was a large wooden table for counsel, twelve feet long and four feet wide. It looked like an old, oversized dining room table that was mistakenly placed in the Courtroom. The deep scratches from the pounding of lawyers’ briefcases were its most distinguishing characteristic.

A dark wood railing three feet high, with fifty carved spokes, extended wall to wall across the middle of the Courtroom, separating the public pews from the judicial area. There were three rows of public pews, with three pews in each row. Each pew was about five feet long and, of course, made of the same black walnut wood.

Mary and I walked through the swing gate in the middle of the railing and proceeded to the table for counsel. It was uncommon to have one large table, rather than the usual two. Each of the eight seats surrounding the table were occupied, presumably by lawyers from Tweed, Fox & Fortune. Tweed, Fox & Fortune is the mammoth legal factory that represents ZeiiMed in its litigation battles, apparently with no restriction on the legal fees generated in the defense of ZeiiMed.

In all my years, I have never seen or heard of a defendant sending eight attorneys to Court for a Hearing. ZeiiMed probably doesn't even review the invoices from its lawyers. It just pays the full amount on the last page of the invoice, no questions asked. How do I get a client like that?

With no room at the counsel table, Mary and I retreated to a pew in the public seating area. I'm sure the lawyers from Tweed, Fox & Fortune found this demotion not only amusing, but also reflective of their elevated status in the legal pecking order. Since the case had just commenced, I didn't want to create a bad impression with the Judge by commanding my adversary to make room at the counsel table. I was also afraid of my pugilistic reaction if no one left the table. I previously had a physical confrontation with one of ZeiiMed's lawyers in my first litigation with ZeiiMed, so I didn't want to go down that road again, at least not at the very start of the case. There will always be other opportunities in the future.

As we sat in the pew, my memory raced backward in time to the previous confrontation with Charles Wadsworth, a partner with Tweed, Fox & Fortune who is now deceased. I referred to Charles as the Count of Confrontation. ZeiiMed killed him for unsuccessfully preventing the public disclosure of incriminating ZeiiMed emails, when he wasn't even responsible for the disclosure and didn't even know the emails existed. ZeiiMed didn't care. Charles was murdered and forgotten and no one at ZeiiMed was ever held responsible. The party line was that he had a heart attack while at ZeiiMed's corporate headquarters preparing company executives for a Hearing. I'm certain he had a heart attack because ZeiiMed somehow gave him a drug that induced it. I admired Charles as a formidable opponent and felt badly about his ugly demise, although I often made fun of his arrogant manipulation of everything and everyone.

I turned towards Mary. "Do you think that any of those Tweed, Fox & Fortune attorneys realize that a former partner, Charles Wadsworth, died under very suspicious circumstances while defending ZeiiMed in the first case we filed against their client?" I asked.

"They know Charles died from a massive heart attack, but not the truth about how it occurred," Mary responded. "Although I'm sure there are plenty of office rumors."

"Actually, I felt a heart attack coming on several times during our last case with ZeiiMed, especially when you were fortunate to save me from the evil Dr. Brown as he was about to take my life."

"You've got it wrong," Mary emphasized. "I wasn't fortunate to save your life. You were fortunate that I smashed Dr. Brown's skull open before he killed you. In fact, I still think you should have shown a bit more gratitude for your new lease on life."

"Well, I'm overflowing with gratitude, but we are getting off my subject. Notice that John Standish Clark is one of the Tweed, Fox & Fortune attorneys at the counsel table. You know, the muscular guy with the crew cut and the flattened nose. He's got the stiff posture of a Marine in dress uniform. Clark was probably with Charles when he had the heart attack because they were working on the case together. Charles was young, active and in his prime. You have to wonder if Clark did any looking around to determine what really caused Charles' heart attack. Then again, maybe he didn't need to. It's possible he already knew it was murder because he understood how ZeiiMed dealt with any form of failure. That reminds me, I should institute the same punishment for associates that don't perform. Imagine how much hard work would get done if you thought your life depended on it."

"Very funny. But it is remarkable to think that someone like John Standish Clark is abundantly aware that he must win the litigation or face dire consequences. He suspects what happened the last time and must devote every breath to making sure it doesn't happen to him," Mary stated.

"It scares the hell out of me to think about what we're up against. Clark is desperate for victory at any cost. It's a matter of life and death."

"It turns my stomach," Mary said.

"We should probably consider another line of work. How many years of study does it take to become a dentist?" I asked.

"Let's change the subject," Mary responded. "Do you think that Clark is now the lead attorney who will address the Court on behalf of ZeiiMed?"

"I don't know, but that would be my guess," I answered. "I don't recognize any other faces at the counsel table. I imagine it's hard to maintain continuity on the legal staff with such a high death rate. Maybe you should apply for a job. I heard the pay is really good, but you must be alive when you pick up your paycheck."

"Maybe we should read our legal papers, rather than talk," Mary said, with obvious exasperation.

There was a loud bang on the door to the side of the Bench. The Judge's clerk entered through the doorway first, followed by the Judge in a long black robe that looked like a graduation gown. As the Judge climbed the three steps to his seat behind the Bench, the clerk stated in a loud, commanding voice:

> Be it remembered that beginning on the 15th day of November 2010, all parties and lawyers came to be heard outside the presence of a jury, in the matter entitled 'Martha Dudley et al. versus ZeiiMed,' with the proceedings before the

Honorable Douglas Horton Horowitz, Judge presiding, in Manhattan, New York County, New York. So help you God.

JUDGE HOROWITZ: Good morning, everyone. This looks like an interesting dispute and I intend to keep a close eye on the litigation as it progresses. For those members of the public sitting in the Courtroom today, I want to point out that no evidence will be heard today and the merits of Mrs. Dudley's allegations will not be ruled upon or decided by a jury or this Court. Mrs. Dudley's lawyers have moved by Motion asking this Court to issue an Order allowing the action to be maintained as a class action. If the Order is issued, Mrs. Dudley will bring her lawsuit seeking damages not only for herself, but for all other persons who have suffered similar injuries proven to be caused by ZeiiMed. I will hear from counsel for Mrs. Dudley first.

I rose from my seat and walked to the podium next to the jury box. I quickly assessed Judge Douglas Horton Horowitz. It was my first appearance before him. About sixty years old, he had brown hair combed back with long strands of hair extending from the top of his thinning forehead to the crown in the back of his head. His beard and mustache were grey, so I guess vanity compelled him to use hair dye. The lenses of his glasses were out-of-date rectangles, held in place by a dark plastic frame. I heard that he considered himself an intellectual, along with an obsessive desire to be entertaining. He indulged his obsession by making humorous comments that caused the lawyers to smile, regardless of whether the Judge's comment was comical.

I stood in front of the podium. The empty jury box was to my right, the counsel table to my left. I was about four or five feet from the Bench. I love being on the stage, everyone listening to my every word regardless of whether they agreed with the content. I looked directly at the Judge and began.

MR. BRADFORD: Good morning, your Honor. My office filed the Motion for Class Certification that you accurately summarized in your opening remarks. As described in the papers submitted to you, Mrs. Dudley is in a wheelchair today, essentially incapacitated and unable to walk after having a hip replacement operation to implant a metal-on-metal hip replacement Device manufactured by MendMed, a subsidiary controlled by its parent, ZeiiMed. The evidence is undisputed that ZeiiMed ran the show and called all the shots.

I will refer to the Hip Implant Device as the HID. The HID was defective from day one and ZeiiMed knew it. ZeiiMed hid from the public the experimental data that revealed the dangerous design of the HID. ZeiiMed didn't care, even though the company's executives knew that many patients would develop serious physical injuries from metal debris released by the HID into the blood.

JUDGE HOROWITZ: Let me stop you right there. I'm aware your allegations make a compelling story, but that's not the issue before us today. The issue is whether Mrs. Dudley's lawsuit can proceed as a class action. Are Mrs. Dudley's claims and injuries typical of the claims and injuries of the class? Isn't it logical to assume that each person who received the HID did so for different reasons and suffered different physical injuries? That does not satisfy the commonality requirement, it seems to me. But, I'm happy to listen to your arguments, especially since you have recently become a prominent prosecutor of claims in the medical field. My wife wanted me to get your autograph. I assured her it would be inappropriate and unethical, but maybe you would provide one after the hearing is over.

MR. BRADFORD: Your Honor is kidding, right?

JUDGE HOROWITZ: Of course, I am. That's my offbeat sense of humor. I guess you haven't been around here much. You'll get the hang of it eventually.

(There were a few rustles of quiet laughter.)

MR. BRADFORD: I find the relaxed atmosphere of your Courtroom refreshing. As my concluding comments, I will just mention that the law does not require each member of the proposed class to have exactly the same claim and exactly the same injuries. There does not have to be unanimity, only a predominance of commonality. That's what we have here. All members of the class had a ZeiiMed metal-on-metal HID inserted in their bodies. All members of the class found that the HID didn't work properly, restricted their mobility and worse, caused their blood to become so tainted by metallosis that severe organ damage occurred or will occur. Mrs. Dudley's medical experience with the HID is typical of the class and she shares the same common facts as the other class members. Quite simply, both her story and the stories of the proposed class members have common, predominating similarities. Thank you for your time.

JUDGE HOROWITZ: I will now hear from counsel for ZeiiMed. Although I see that ZeiiMed has brought many lawyers here today, only one can present the position of ZeiiMed. I assume that everybody drew straws in the corridor before we started. So, whoever got the short straw, please stand and be heard.

I remained at the podium and turned towards the table of ZeiiMed's lawyers, expecting John Standish Clark to stand

and address the Court. To my surprise, a woman attorney rose from the counsel table and walked towards the podium.

She was stunning with short, platinum hair layered by waves of softly curled strands that rose above her forehead in a bouncy, vertical display that contrasted with her tan complexion. Her unique eyebrows were each a different color, one blond and the other dark brown. Our eyes met as she approached the podium, but I was distracted because her pupils didn't move identically. One of her pupils was turned inward, a cross-eyed appearance that caused me to feel a slight touch of compassion.

She approached the podium and, reasonably anticipating that I would move away from the podium to return to my seat, bumped her bare arm against me as I remained stationary. My intense stare now broken, I meekly uttered an apology and walked away.

Mary turned to me as soon as I sat down. "What was that all about? It looked like you had turned into a statue," Mary quietly commented. "Did she put a spell on you?"

"I don't know what happened. She just seemed to catch my attention."

"Catch your attention? You were mesmerized as if in a hypnotic trance. I thought I might need to escort you back to your seat."

"Don't be so dramatic. Men often act that way."

"I don't know what you mean by 'men,' but if you ever looked at me like that, I'd report you to the authorities."

"For staring? When did that become a crime? I think you're making a big deal out of nothing," I said.

"I'll bet you ten dollars that as soon as this Hearing is over, she will quickly leave the Courtroom and get as far away as possible from you. That's what I would do. Your leering is simply not acceptable whether you know the other person or have never met," she stated with emotional emphasis, although in a low voice to avoid attention.

"I'll take your wager because I bet she approaches me after Court."

"You are so arrogant," Mary said, shaking her head.

"I know. It was a learned trait and I studied very hard to master it," I responded in a purposefully irritating manner.

CLERK OF THE COURT: Please refrain from talking. Counsel for ZeiiMed is about to address the Court.

I looked up at the woman at the podium, not caring if I annoyed Mary or not. She wore a sleeveless yellow peplum dress, with a swirling floral design accented by raised flowers. The lack of sleeves or collar created a sensuous, but subtle image. Her leather, Louis Vuitton open-toe heels were highlighted by pink toenail polish. Although probably in her mid-forties, her face appeared youthful with few wrinkles. I noticed for the first time a beauty mark on her right cheek that certainly enhanced her attractiveness.

MS. NUDBELLO: Thank you, your Honor. My name is Suzanna Nudbello. Today, I have the pleasure of addressing the Court on behalf of ZeiiMed. I'm the one who passed the straws in the corridor. I made sure I got the short one. All kidding aside, it's a privilege to be here today and I appreciate the opportunity to participate in these proceedings.

JUDGE HOROWITZ: Welcome. You know the issue. Mr. Bradford wants to proceed with his lawsuit as a class action. What's your position?

MS. NUDBELLO: First and foremost, I would like to clear the air about the HID mentioned by Mr. Bradford. ZeiiMed thoroughly tested the metal-on-metal Device and has the records to prove it. From the time it was first introduced to the public, it has provided a level of mobility and flexibility never before attained by an implant. Of course, ZeiiMed recommended its use, assuming the patient had certain specific impairments and deficiencies with their God-given equipment. Extensive consultation was conducted to make sure the patient had a specific need for the Device and the Device was compatible with the patient. The doctors were paid by ZeiiMed to do this pre-surgical work-up to assure optimal performance after implant.

JUDGE HOROWITZ: We enjoy hearing you fill this entire room with your words of wisdom. However, as I mentioned to your adversary, we are not determining the merits of the controversy, only the Motion for Class Certification.

MS. NUDBELLO: Yes, I will get to that issue now. It is a natural extension of what I just told the Court. As this Court is aware, each patient is unique in his or her medical needs. Each consultation with a doctor about the HID is different because each patient's medical condition is unique. A patient's projected recovery from implant of the Device also varies significantly. As a result, without question, this litigation cannot proceed as a class because each injured plaintiff has incomparable circumstances and special needs that require individualized proof at trial. Plus, the medical advice given and the surgical procedures actually implemented will differ based upon each patient's particular needs and condition. As such, ZeiiMed requests that this Court deny the motion.

JUDGE HOROWITZ: I have considered the arguments of both sides and have read all the papers. Clearly, it is a close question and commonality does not have a precise definition. However, this Court has, by law, the discretion to postpone the determination of whether or not the litigation qualifies for class treatment. Usually, as discovery proceeds, more information will be obtained so a more informed decision can eventually be reached by the Court. Therefore, the parties are ordered to proceed with an exchange of documents and depositions. We will reconvene after the close of discovery and the Court will then reach a decision on class certification before scheduling the trial. Thank you for your time and attention today.

CLERK OF THE COURT: This session of the Supreme Court of the State of New York is completed, with all business before this Court fully considered and adjourned to a date to be provided.

Mary and I remained seated in the Courtroom while everyone emptied into the corridor. I lingered after the proceedings ended because sometimes the Clerk may be available and useful information about the Judge's thoughts may inadvertently be revealed. No such luck today, so Mary and I departed as a police officer proceeded to lock the front door to the Courtroom.

As we walked into the crowded hallway leading to the elevators, I heard my name called. "Mr. Bradford. Mr. Brian Bradford."

I turned.

ZeiiMed's attorney approached me.

"Hi. I was hoping to have the opportunity to meet you. I'm Suzanna Nudbello."

"Really? I'm sorry, I mean, hello. I'm so glad you came over–I was very much looking forward to meeting you also. Actually, I was betting we would meet," I said, as I shook her offered hand.

Ms. Nudbello's unmatched eyebrows arched slightly in response to my comment.

"That didn't come out right—I'm just happy to say hello," I explained.

"I heard so much about you from people around the office. You got a great settlement from my client the first time around, but I hope you understand lightning is not going to strike a second time," Suzanna said.

"From what I saw in the Courtroom today, I'm sure I'll have an uphill battle on my hands. You did very well," I responded.

"From what I'm told, you always do well. We should get to know each other better because soon we will be trying to litigate each other to death. How about lunch in Chinatown?" Suzanna asked.

"I think I'm heading back to the office. You two seem to be getting along perfectly well without me," Mary commented, staring at me and not turning to Suzanna.

"Oh, I forgot. How rude of me. Suzanna, this is Mary Douglas. Mary is working with me on this case."

Mary turned her head quickly to Suzanna and said, "Hello, nice to meet you. Sorry, but I have to go."

"Okay. See you later. Remember, you owe me ten dollars," I said, knowing I was aggravating an already delicate issue.

"I won't forget and don't you forget to return to the office," Mary said, as she turned to walk away.

"Getting back to your question, the answer is yes. I know a particularly good restaurant in Chinatown," I said to Suzanna. "It's only a short walk from here."

Of course, I was asking myself the same questions that I know Mary was thinking.

"*What are you doing and why are you doing it*," the voice inside my head asked. The answer is that I'm not sure. I don't have a definitive answer, but I do have some general thoughts.

First, it can't hurt to develop a professional relationship with the primary counsel for ZeiiMed. Second, any information I learn about Suzanna and her approach to the litigation can possibly be helpful as the case progresses. Then again, maybe it's another, more personal motivation. Kim is lunching regularly with Dr. Joe and has no intention of stopping. She has no remorse over the anguish it causes me. Doesn't that give me the green light to have lunch with an intelligent and attractive adversary who asked me out?

In my selfish and singular view of life and marriage, I have decided the answer is "yes." Then again, what do I know? Working on instinct rather than intellect usually gets me into more trouble than I can handle. I really ought to re-evaluate my priorities.

I'll do that right after lunch.

-16-

Suzanna and I left the Courthouse through the rear of the building, walking east through Columbus Park to the intersection of Mott and Pell Streets. Once on Pell Street, we arrived at Joe's Shanghai Chinatown Restaurant.

The restaurant consisted of a narrow, low-ceiling room with unadorned large, institutional tables and banquet hall chairs. We were fortunate to beat the lunch crowd, so a table for two was still available.

Once it becomes crowded, the custom at Joe's is to seat people next to each other at very large tables; strangers, friends, and lovers all lumped together. It's dim and claustrophobic, with the only natural light through the window in the front door and the windows next to the front door.

The decor, or the lack thereof, does not matter. People come for the soup dumplings and are never disappointed.

The Shanghai soup dumplings are called "Steamed Buns" and consist of a tender dough skin filled with crab or pork, immersed in a hot soup. As soon as we were seated, our waiter, a Chinese-American, arrived and immediately asked if we wanted the soup dumplings.

"Yes, I'll have the soup dumplings with crab meat," Suzanna responded immediately. "Plus, I'd like the crispy jumbo prawns with lime sauce and a glass of white wine. Thank you."

"You make good selections. We like you here. You're very pretty girl," the waiter said, as he nodded his head up and down, agreeing with himself.

"Excuse me, I hate to interrupt, but I'd like the soup dumplings also, with spicy Szechuan sliced beef."

"Yes, sir. Very good, sir. You are pretty, too. Nice looking couple. Very nice looking couple," the waiter added.

"We are not a couple. We just met. We are lawyers," I clarified, not realizing it would only muddy the waters.

"A lawyer couple. Very, very good. We have lots of lawyer couples here from the Courthouse. Talk a lot. Don't say much. Always dress nice," the waiter continued.

"I also need a drink. Please bring me a beer," I said.

"Yes, beer. Nice couple with drinks. More drinks, more lawyer talk between couple. Still don't say anything, but speak lots of words. I will get your order now."

"Thank you. We don't have a lot of time. We need to get back to the office," I mentioned.

"Yes, yes. Lawyer couples always rushing. Drinking, talking, rushing. So glad you are here," the waiter continued and then abruptly left.

"Well, he gave us something to think about. I mean the rushing and drinking comments, not the part about us being a couple," I said.

"I know what you mean, but I thought it was nice that he thought we were an attractive couple," Suzanna commented.

"I don't know for sure, but I think he says that to every man and woman sitting together," I responded.

The cocktails arrived, served by another waiter who was apparently not inclined to impose his thoughts and impressions on us.

"Don't get me wrong," I continued. "I'm not disagreeing with the compliment he gave you about being attractive."

"To get off this now uncomfortable subject, I'd like you to know I reviewed your work in the other case against ZeiiMed. You did a very good job. You found the smoking gun and pressed the damaging evidence against ZeiiMed until you forced a massive settlement for your clients. It was masterful. I know there were violent confrontations with John Edison that caused suffering on both sides. My point is that nothing like that will happen in this case. ZeiiMed has changed. It is a different company. People such as Doctor Hyman and Doctor Brown, may they rest in peace, are no longer affiliated with ZeiiMed. While John Edison was in the hospital, the entire company was overhauled and turned upside down. Mr. Edison's highly regrettable conduct toward you, your family and colleagues will never happen again. No one at ZeiiMed will ever again have the power to authorize physical injury to opponents and adversaries."

"I'll drink to that. I did everything possible to end that hell, but nothing seemed to work. It's nice to hear ZeiiMed may be different, but I want to see it for myself," I said, holding back my initial instinct to tell her she was either very naive or very stupid. She was too pretty to get that aggressive this early in our professional relationship. I'm so shallow. Really.

"You'll see it for yourself. I'm going to demonstrate it to you."

"I'm sorry. Please repeat that. What did you say you are going to show me?" I asked, just because it's sometimes fun to be difficult.

"Let me be clear and to the point," Suzanna answered. "I told several executives at the highest level of ZeiiMed that you are a formidable opponent who knows the law and knows how to handle himself in a Courtroom. I presented a detailed argument in support of an early settlement to avoid a prolonged legal battle with high emotions and bitter confrontations at both depositions and in Court. Believe it or not, ZeiiMed listened and will continue to listen to my recommendations."

"Does that mean that ZeiiMed really did design a defective HID and then covered up knowledge of the defects?" I asked, to see if I could get her to cough up some juicy pieces of information.

"Don't be ridiculous. That's not what I mean," she responded. "ZeiiMed is willing to explore settlement not because it's guilty as charged, but because ZeiiMed knows you are a shrewd and intelligent lawyer who can easily manipulate a very innocent set of facts into a pattern of diabolical deception. You're good and that worries us."

"Thank you, but I think you have it backwards. It was ZeiiMed that was proven to manipulate its corporate records in the last case. I didn't manipulate anything, I merely uncovered the manipulations."

"Does your wife find you this difficult to talk to? Maybe I was confusing. I will try to clarify. ZeiiMed is no longer the company you previously fought against. It is the new ZeiiMed and I am willing to recommend that ZeiiMed make a large settlement offer now rather than later. Not because ZeiiMed did anything wrong, but because it will cost millions to prove our innocence with no guarantee a jury will understand our exculpatory evidence. That's it, short and simple. What do you say to that?"

"The food is here. I'm starved. How about another drink?" I asked.

"That's not the response I was anticipating," Suzanna said. "But, I will have another drink and hope you become more focused."

"All kidding aside, I understand your position," I finally said. "Of course, I am happy to explore settlement and listen to your offer. However, the alcohol, the compliments, your tan arms and lovely dress are all influencing my judgment."

"Okay, I can see I'm not going to get a straight answer today. I guess that's one of your many accomplished legal skills. I will pretend you agreed to conduct early settlement negotiations. I will speak with my contacts at ZeiiMed and get back to you on our settlement proposal," Suzanna stated, with a slight tone of exasperation.

"That's great! Then we can come back here to discuss your proposal. Hopefully, we'll have the same waiter."

"Yes, maybe, but I think we might need a new location to create a slightly more serious business tone. As to the timing, it may take a bit of time before I am ready to present a specific proposal. But you don't need to conduct discovery, file motions or do any investigation while we are in our negotiation phase. You can actually work on other cases that don't involve ZeiiMed," Suzanna said.

"That's a novel idea, but I don't want to work on other cases," I said. "To summarize, you are willing to pay the Dudleys a large sum of money just so I will stop my lawsuit against ZeiiMed, even though ZeiiMed produced only a safe and reliable HID. It sounds like a bribe to me, but I guess that's the system."

"Yes, it is," she responded. "It's the way lawyers do business, not a bribe. Now let's cease all this business talk and enjoy our food. Remember, we're supposed to act like a couple."

"You mean a lawyer couple? I am not sure I know how to do that or what that is. But, I agree. We can always talk about work another day. Let's keep the conversation to weather, recreation and interpersonal relationships," I suggested.

"You have a deal, at least with respect to the first two topics."

Several hours later, I was thinking about the lunch and realized I had a very enjoyable time. I acted like a clown, but I wanted to keep her a little off balance. It's not a good negotiation tactic to appear eager to accept an early settlement. Maybe Suzanna was correct and ZeiiMed was a totally different company. Maybe the days of mayhem and bloodshed were really over. Maybe ZeiiMed now realizes that terrible mistakes were made and the HID was one of them. Maybe ZeiiMed wants to cleanse its past and remedy its evil deeds. If so, I guess I'm willing to take ZeiiMed's money, provided a sufficiently large sum is offered.

I wondered if Kim and Mary would agree with my evaluation. Chances are, if I broke my new rule and asked their opinions, they would say I've lost my mind and remind me that ZeiiMed will never change. Of course, they would probably be right. History is on their side.

-17-

John Edison sat at the end of a conference table on the 35th floor of the downtown offices of Tweed, Fox & Fortune, located at Two World Financial Center. The conference room had a magnificent view of the North Cove and the Hudson River. It was Wednesday, January 19, 2011.

Edison's sunken face was permanently indented with no apparent cheekbones. His face appeared overly long and slender, making his nose and ears appear larger by comparison. His teeth were over-crowded, with each tooth visibly overlapping the next. The sun setting through the window reflected off the top of his bald, wet scalp. The thick hair on the sides of his head was combed back and shiny from some greasy lotion, as usual. He surveyed the room with the cold, ice blue eyes of a Siberian Husky.

With him in the conference room were Suzanna Nudbello and John Standish Clark. Suzanna looked very professional in a navy blue two-piece suit and white blouse. Her Manolo Blahnik snakeskin pumps were hidden from view as she sat at the table.

John Standish Clark was sitting at attention, shoulders back and chest thrown forward. He knew no other posture. Mr. Edison and Mr. Clark were both dressed in suits of unremarkable shades of grey, with ties that likewise drew no attention.

Both Ms. Nudbello and Mr. Clark had looks of dread and intended to say nothing until asked by Edison.

"I called this meeting so we can discuss our strategy with regard to Brian Bradford and his new case against the company. Since I have been sidelined by my injuries, I feel the need to review our priorities and our goals in dealing with our unrelenting adversary. To begin with, Bradford visited me in the hospital and informed me of his plan to sue ZeiiMed over our design and manufacture of the metal-on-metal Device. He was trying to obtain information and the meeting ended very distastefully. As a result, I wasn't surprised when he commenced suit."

Edison continued, "As you know, Bradford is attempting to obtain all our corporate documents dealing with the design and testing of the Device and any information we received regarding possible defects, as well as ZeiiMed's response upon learning of the defects. Since you're ZeiiMed's lawyers, I'll start by telling you there are many damaging documents in the electronic files of ZeiiMed. We designed the Device and released it to the public without adequate testing. Moreover, we eventually received incontrovertible evidence of a defective design and responded by ignoring the information and avoiding public disclosure. Our files contain letters, emails and test results that confirm severe injuries to implant patients and a concerted effort to sell more Devices regardless of the consequences. Any questions or comments before I continue?"

"Yes," Suzanna answered. "First, I would like to welcome you back and hope you return to full health soon."

"Thank you. It's been a very long road back, but my rehabilitation and strength training will eventually have me back stronger than ever, without any excess weight. My mind is the same and my focus on Bradford has actually intensified. Anything else?"

"Yes," Suzanna said. "For my second point, I think it's important to inform you that I have met with Brian Bradford on a couple of occasions. I sweetly manipulated him with compliments. I acknowledged that he was a master litigator who faced almost insurmountable problems, yet succeeded in achieving a massive settlement that is the envy of every attorney. I flattered him until his head was spinning. Then, I convinced him that ZeiiMed was interested in settling because he was such a formidable opponent. He, of course, bought what I was selling and now has his tongue out like a panting dog waiting by the phone for a billion dollar settlement offer. I think the dollar signs floating in front of his eyes have distracted him from a vigorous pursuit of his lawsuit. He really is a buffoon, with a highly inflated view of himself. Plus, his brain cells become fried at the sight of a little female skin."

"Thank you for that report. Later, we will discuss a plan for dealing with Bradford," Mr. Edison said. "But first, I want to discuss my plan for disposing of all our corporate records that have anything to do with the metal-on-metal Device. ZeiiMed has to destroy the documents before anyone outside of ZeiiMed sees them and..."

"You can't just destroy them," Clark said, interrupting Mr. Edison. "They are in electronic form and the deletion leaves a detectable trail, a footprint. Plus, no one in the world would believe ZeiiMed suddenly had no documents, especially not the Judge."

"Just shut up and listen to the plan!" Edison responded. "I know you can't just destroy all the emails. The Judge would punish us by striking our Answer and dismissing our defenses, giving Bradford an unopposed billion-dollar judgment. No, I have a different plan."

"I apologize," Clark stated.

"I said shut up. You damn lawyers just can't refrain from talking. I should have duct-taped your mouths before we began the meeting. The plan is as follows: Last Sunday, you may have read an article in the *New York Times* about a Stuxnet computer worm used by Western intelligence agencies to destroy thousands of nuclear centrifuges in Iran. The gas centrifuges were eight feet tall and contained cylindrical rotors that operated at high speed to enrich uranium for possible use in a nuclear weapon. The centrifuges were infected by the worm and forced to spin beyond their capabilities until they literally ripped themselves apart. But the real beauty of the Stuxnet worm is that it was programmed to avoid detection by sending messages to all monitoring systems that everything was normal, when exactly the contrary was true. The computer feedback to the Iranians was that all operations were normal despite the concurrent destruction of the centrifuges. Do you follow me?" Edison asked.

"Yes, I recall reading about that. Basically, the Stuxnet worm can be coded to attack a specific aspect of a computer system and destroy the targeted area. But, I've only heard of its use in connection with military cyber warfare," Suzanna commented.

"That was correct up to now," Edison answered. "ZeiiMed recently developed its own Stuxnet computer worm programmed to destroy documents, including emails that have been encoded with an invisible marking applied by ZeiiMed. In other words, we are going to program the worm to eat every ZeiiMed document with regard to the metal-on-metal Device. Here's what will happen. We will produce all ZeiiMed's documents to Bradford electronically, then release the worm on its mission to eradicate every one of the documents on both the computers of Bradford's law firm and the computers of ZeiiMed. That is, ZeiiMed will transfer the documents to Bradford directly from its computers, without the involvement of your law firm's computers. In that manner, the worm will only need to be introduced into Bradford's computers and ZeiiMed's computers, with the destruction limited to the documents secretly pre-marked by ZeiiMed. The infection will be released as soon as possible after ZeiiMed sends its documents to Bradford in order to diminish the opportunity for printing any item before being destroyed by the worm."

"You mean we destroy ZeiiMed's own documents on ZeiiMed computers, as well as the documents that ZeiiMed electronically sent to Bradford?" Clark asked.

"Of course. Don't you understand? I thought you were lawyers. We do that to make it look like hackers attacked us both. It's all camouflage so no one can accuse ZeiiMed of intentionally destroying evidence, which is a crime I believe."

"What's to stop Mr. Bradford from moving the documents out of his firm's computers once he notices the worm's activities?" Suzanna asked.

"Good question. A much better inquiry than the stupid comment by Clark. I'm glad I made you the lead attorney for ZeiiMed. As I mentioned, one of the wonderful attributes of the Stuxnet worm is that it doesn't let anyone know what it's doing until its task is completed. It's programmed to create a false reading that everything is fine. That is, it manufactures an image on the monitoring systems and computer screens that all the documents are being maintained in the exact manner they were received. A visual inspection of the documents on Bradford's computer would not reveal that the documents were being destroyed by the worm at that very moment. Upon completion of the worm's magic, the computer-generated images of all the documents will simply go blank, too late to take any corrective measures."

"Astounding," Suzanna responded.

"But how do you get the worm released into Bradford's computers without anyone noticing, if you don't mind me asking," Clark added.

"Finally, an intelligent question from you. I was just getting to that point. It is you, Mr. Clark, who will infect Bradford's computers. The Stuxnet worm will be placed on a USB flash drive no bigger than your thumb and can be concealed in the palm of your hand. The USB flash drive will consist of a circuit board, a memory chip, and a standard metal plug, also called a tongue plate. Your assignment, Mr. Clark, and you shall agree to accept it, is to insert the plug of the USB flash drive into a free USB port in a computer at Mr. Bradford's office. The worm will immediately enter its host's network and the infection cannot be stopped. You will then detach the flash drive and put it in your pocket. While you are doing that, I will simultaneously authorize another USB flash drive with the Stuxnet worm to be attached to ZeiiMed's computer network. All traces of ZeiiMed's files dealing with the metal-on-metal Device will be gone forever and no one will understand what happened. ZeiiMed will report that hackers apparently targeted the healthcare company as part of the political upheaval against Obamacare, even attacking the files ZeiiMed transmitted to its adversary in a pending medical device litigation. We will also imply that maybe the hackers were negatively reacting to the new medical device tax imposed by Obamacare to raise $30 billion to finance the new health care reform law," Mr. Edison concluded, with a slight grin that exposed his heavily stained teeth.

"A remarkable plan. But how do I get into Bradford's law office to get access to a USB port?" Clark asked.

"You will receive your exact instructions when it is time. But, let's suppose you deliver a Stipulation or some other legal document to Bradford's office, with the excuse that his signature is needed before filing with the Court. All you need do is put the USB drive in any USB port. Even the receptionist's computer will work."

"Congratulations on a masterful plan," Suzanna stated, as she started to stand.

"Thank you, but we are not finished yet," Mr. Edison said, as he focused his menacing ice blue eyes on her. "We now come to the fun part–the part I've been anxiously waiting to tell you. After Mr. Clark infects the computers at Bradford's office, he will then have the responsibility of taking Bradford's life the very same day. By sundown, Brian Bradford will be extinct."

"I think it's a splendid finish to the plan," Suzanna commented.

Clark stood and spoke. "Don't get me wrong. I hate the guy and I certainly have the strength and ability to break the wimp in two. But, how do I avoid a murder charge?" he asked aggressively.

"We have a plan to make it look like an accident. We don't yet have all the information we need to confirm his usual routines and habits, so we have not yet been able to orchestrate all aspects of the accident. But, just in case you get cold feet, please understand that ZeiiMed downloaded the contents of your home computer, with all the pictures and files of underage adolescents. You would probably get twenty years. So, I suggest you do exactly as you're told," Mr. Edison warned.

Clark meekly sat down.

"I'm sure Clark will be very successful in completing his assignment. Also, I am happy to assist any way I can. I could possibly be a lure to entice Mr. Bradford to a designated location at a designated time. For example, a hotel room," Suzanna offered.

"That's an appealing suggestion, but I think we need a more public area than a hotel room. A decision hasn't yet been made. We are speaking with our contacts at the National Security Agency to get as much personal information as we can on Bradford to learn what he routinely does and when he does it. As a favor to ZeiiMed, the NSA is using its secret PRISM Program, an Internet surveillance and collection database, to collect Bradford's emails, phone numbers, insurance information, social network posts, bank records, and credit card records. This will enable us to create a complete profile of Bradford and his usual daily activities. Eventually, we will know what he is going to do next before he knows it. In order to keep track of his exact location, a program known as Trilaterization is being used by the NSA to monitor his movements directly from cell phone towers."

"I know it's probably not a major concern to you, but as your lead counsel, I think my firm should investigate the legality of NSA's accumulation of such information without a warrant signed by a Judge," Suzanna noted.

"We just finished discussing our agreed plan to murder Brian Bradford and you're concerned about whether ZeiiMed and the NSA might violate the law by reading his emails?" Mr. Edison responded.

"You're right, silly question," she acknowledged.

"Nonetheless, I do have an answer to your question. The NSA, by law, can implement a surveillance plan only on a foreign target provided it minimizes the acquisition of personal information on Americans, and prohibits the dissemination of non-public information of unconsenting United States persons, according to the fancy language used in the U.S. Code. If the surveillance of the foreign target spills over into a search of the emails and phone messages of an American, the NSA is required under the Foreign Intelligence Surveillance Act, known as the FISA, to obtain a warrant from the United States Foreign Intelligence Surveillance Court, referred to as the FISC. The Judges on the FISC are chosen by John Roberts, the Chief Justice of the United States Supreme Court. It's a 'secret court' in Washington, DC. No transcripts are available, decisions are not publicly disclosed and only attorneys for the US Government appear before it. Obtaining a warrant is easy. Thousands of warrants have been issued by the FISC over the years and only a handful denied. Actually, over 98% of the warrants sought by the NSA are granted by the FISC."

"So, the NSA will request a warrant from the FISC to obtain Bradford's personal information?" Clark inquired.

"No, of course not. The NSA will gather the information we requested on Bradford and provide it to ZeiiMed as a professional courtesy, without the unnecessary involvement of the FISC," Edison responded. "An accommodation between friends. Remember, I was appointed by the President to a federal post as Administrator of the Centers for Medicare and Medicaid Services. Although I took a leave of absence from the position due to my health problems, I still have some influence as a former government official. The NSA simply bypasses the FISC and gets the needed information. Legal or not, no one will ever know so no one will ever care."

"Great," Suzanna said. "To get the plan started, I'll call Brian, I mean Mr. Bradford. I'll tell him that although ZeiiMed is still interested in settlement discussions, ZeiiMed would like to quickly commence disclosure of our documents so he can learn for himself that ZeiiMed has no blame or responsibility for injuries due to the metal-on-metal Device. I'll set a date for ZeiiMed's electronic production of its documents and dates for the deposition of a couple of ZeiiMed's employees involved in the design and sale of the Device. Since our plan is to have the computer worm destroy ZeiiMed's documents once they are transmitted to Mr. Bradford's computers, we will need to focus on getting all our records to him, including all the most damaging documents discussing our faulty design of the Device and our cover-up."

"Coordinate with my staff," Mr. Edison instructed. "It's imperative that the worm is released into both Bradford's computers and ZeiiMed's computers moments after we produce all of ZeiiMed's documents."

"It will be done and done correctly," she said.

"I'm all in 100%," Clark added.

"Good, and don't believe those rumors about ZeiiMed punishing those that fail in their assignments. It's all a big lie. You know how people make things up, right?" asked Edison.

"Yes, of course. I don't believe any of that garbage. ZeiiMed rose to greatness by providing affordable healthcare to millions and takes very seriously its obligation to deal with all Americans fairly and in accordance with the law," Suzanna answered.

"I also don't believe any of that talk about ZeiiMed inflicting injury and death on those that fail to accomplish their missions," Clark added. "That's just crazy."

As soon as Clark finished his statement, he thought about his house being invaded by ZeiiMed and his personal computer records stolen to assure his obedience. Maybe there was some truth to the office gossip about ZeiiMed's punishment for failure. He remembered Charles Wadsworth's concerns about ZeiiMed's ruthlessness and his fear of retribution. Yet, Clark realized he presently had no choice. He decided he would devote every ounce of his being to accomplishing his dual assignment of releasing the worm and eradicating Bradford. However, after that, Clark decided to plan his escape to an untraceable location far from Tweed, Fox & Fortune and the reach of ZeiiMed's ever growing tentacles.

Edison then left the conference room after kissing Suzanna on the cheek and shaking Clark's hand. Suzanna was repulsed by the contact.

As soon as Edison entered the elevator, Clark immediately headed home to inspect the damage to his home and personal property. He knew ZeiiMed would never cease to blackmail him into submission and never cease to give him assignments that involved life and death situations. Sooner or later, he would fail to accomplish one of the tasks, causing the death penalty to be imposed on him by ZeiiMed. However, he now had his own plan in place. He would succeed in killing Bradford at any cost and then simply vanish and hide from ZeiiMed for the rest of his life. If he ran after failing to extinguish Bradford, ZeiiMed would never relent in its pursuit of him. If he accomplished his task and then disappeared, ZeiiMed might lose interest in trying to find him.

It didn't matter to him where he went. The further away, the better. There will always be teenage boys and girls around no matter where he went. The thought pleased him immensely.

-18-

Suzanna called the next day. I picked up on the first ring.

"How are you, Suzanna? I've been waiting for your call. I don't want to do a lot of legal work if we are about to settle. So, where are we on resolving this litigation?" I asked.

"I spoke to my people at ZeiiMed and settlement is definitely an early priority. However, it's going to take some time before an actual offer is made. The ZeiiMed executives I talked with need to make a decision on a number to be offered and then prepare the necessary paperwork to get approval from the Office of the General Counsel and the Chief Executive Officer. We're not talking about a small number. It's large, very large, and cannot be put together in a week or two," Suzanna stated, knowing there wasn't an ounce of truth to anything she said. The key for her was to present a credible story that Brian would accept without raising any concerns as to her truthfulness.

"I was looking forward to our lunch date to celebrate the settlement. Hopefully, the delay won't be too extensive."

"I don't think it will be," Suzanna responded. "But, it won't be overnight. We will need to commence discovery so that the Judge won't get the impression we are dragging our feet. I propose that ZeiiMed electronically produce all it's documents relevant to the metal-on-metal Device within a month, with the first ZeiiMed executive to be deposed three weeks thereafter and a second ZeiiMed witness a week after that."

"That's fine. Your proposal doesn't give me a great deal of time to read and print the important documents you produce, but I can manage it. I do have one concern. You mentioned that any settlement offer by ZeiiMed must be approved by the Chief Executive Officer. I read in the newspaper that John Edison recently returned to the Company as CEO, now that his health has improved. My point is this: John Edison and I are enemies who have done battle on several occasions. As you may know, that includes physical confrontations which inflicted severe personal injuries on each of us. Edison will not approve any settlement involving a significant payment of money to my law firm. Edison's hatred and contempt for me will not allow him to reach any agreement with me. We both have wounds, physical and emotional, that will not heal. As a result, I can't advise my client regarding a realistic chance for an early resolution when the resolution is contingent on Edison's approval," I explained.

"I agree that Mr. Edison has an intense dislike for you," Suzanna responded, accurately for once. "But, he is also a sophisticated businessman who understands the disadvantages of prolonged litigation. I have personally spoken with Mr. Edison and he assured me without any reservations that his priority is to resolve the litigation, without any personal agenda directed at you. I believe him and you should believe me," Suzanna said, with emphasis to stress the truthfulness of her lies. "This is the new ZeiiMed–the old ZeiiMed is gone forever."

"I will give you the chance to prove I'm wrong. I'll agree to the preliminary discovery schedule and I trust your professional judgment that Edison will listen to the advice of his counsel regarding settlement. As I understand it, ZeiiMed will produce all its documents regarding the research, design, manufacture and implantation of the metal-on-metal HID, with all feedback on post-surgical performance provided to ZeiiMed by patients and doctors. I will confirm this in a Notice to Produce served on your office and filed with the Court. Let's set the date of February 23, 2011 for transfer of the documents."

"Agreed. On a personal level, Brian, I look forward to working as adversaries in this litigation. Although we are on opposite sides, I think this case will provide me with a unique opportunity to learn from one of the best. I look forward to it," Suzanna said, rolling her eyes.

"Thank you. Litigation is always challenging, but I think we both realize a fair settlement in the near future is the best course of action. Talk to you soon."

“Bye, Brian. Let’s continue our settlement dialogue as we proceed with discovery.”

“We will. So long.”

Suzanna hung up the phone, pleased with her performance. She had succeeded in her continuing effort to convince Brian that she was a timid and youthful litigator who cannot compare to the accomplished and experienced Mr. Bradford. He bought it. Hook, line and sinker. Such easy prey. The production will be made by ZeiiMed and Mr. Bradford will receive every piece of relevant documentation, including all the corporate research reports discussing the defects and flaws in the HID. But, little did Brian know there would be no time to read any of the HID documents before the Stuxnet worm accomplished its task.

Brian hung up the phone in total disbelief. Edison was back running the show at ZeiiMed and would never agree to a settlement with Alfonso and Ryan, regardless of what Suzanna said. Brian knew Edison’s only objective was to impose as much suffering and injury on him as possible. Edison would not make a multi-million dollar settlement that included a huge fee to Brian’s firm. He did it once and would never do so again. Suzanna was telling one lie after another and was doing so for the singular purpose of distracting him from ZeiiMed’s actual plan. Brian didn’t know what that plan was, but he must be well-prepared for whatever may be coming.

He knew another war with ZeiiMed was about to begin.

He had to be ready.

He survived the first time, but only barely.

He must to do much better this time around.

-19-

John Edison sat at his desk in the corner office at the Grace Building in midtown. It was early February 2011.

Suzanna Nudbello was sitting across the desk from him, her long legs crossed. Her sheer, black silk hosiery was skin tight with no runs or breaks in the fabric. She wore a one-piece black velvet dress that contrasted well with her platinum hair. Edison was aware of her beauty, but it did not affect him on any emotional level. He didn't react to it and couldn't have cared less about it.

"Suzanna, I want to go over the plan one more time."

"I'd be happy too. I want to make absolutely sure that you are comfortable with every element of the proposal."

"Yes, take me through it again, step by step," Edison asked.

"First of all," Suzanna started, "the ZeiiMed documents regarding the metal-on-metal HID will be sent electronically to Alfonso and Ryan. It will consist of approximately 750,00 documents, including e-mails, letters, internal research reports, office memos and all scientific studies conducted by either ZeiiMed or outside medical professionals. It is going to require that we send 10,000 separate emails to Mr. Bradford, each with about 75 pages of attachments. Our stated rationale for doing this is ease of transfer, plus it saves Alfonso and Ryan the expense of converting the documents to electronic form if we had produced only hardcopy paper files."

"Are you sure that everything is being produced?" Edison asked. "I want each and every piece of paper that refers in anyway to the HID to be sent. I also want included every legal report sent by Tweed, Fox & Fortune to ZeiiMed evaluating ZeiiMed's exposure for the defective design of the HID, as well as every document discussing the consequences of our intentional failure to disclose known injuries due to its defective design. As you are aware, we're not worried about a waiver of attorney-client privileged communications because no one is ever going to read the documents anyway, assuming the documents are immediately destroyed as planned."

"I can assure you everything we have will be sent from ZeiiMed's computers to Alfonso and Ryan, including ZeiiMed's most confidential and privileged emails that were once deleted from the ZeiiMed computers due to their sensitivity," Suzanne stated. "The emails have been found, restored and added to the materials being produced. We have missed nothing. Mr. Bradford will receive everything. I guarantee there will also be no opportunity for him to read anything before the worm completes its task. Even if he does open one of the emails, the worm has been programmed to prevent the printing of any document that has been encoded for destruction."

"Good," Edison said.

"The storm of electronic documents and attachments will be emailed at noon on February 23, 2011," Suzanne continued. "Two USB flash drives containing the Stuxnet computer worm have been created and are ready to be used. John Standish Clark will have possession of one flash drive and will call Mr. Bradford at 12:05 p.m. on February 23 from the lobby of 40 Wall Street. He will have with him a Stipulation that needs Mr. Bradford's signature to confirm receipt of the 750,000 documents from ZeiiMed. John will offer some reasonable excuse for appearing in person rather than sending the Stipulation electronically."

"Have you reviewed and integrated the NSA file we received on Bradford into your plan?"

"Yes, I have," Suzanna responded. "To begin with, it's an incredible accumulation of facts about every aspect of his life. We now know his routine for each day of the week–where he goes, who he talks to and the content of what is said, as well as every email sent in the last year and every money transaction. If we wanted to know what goes on in his bedroom, all I need to do is click on the recording in the subfile labeled: 'House Conversations - Main Bedroom.' We have everything–we know more about his life than his guardian angel does."

"How many times did you play the Bedroom recording?" Edison asked.

"I know, the information is so absurdly comprehensive and embarrassingly private, it becomes comical. But to answer your question, only once. Well, maybe twice–it was rather stimulating. However, returning now to the business at hand, the NSA file gave us a complete itemization of his regular and customary schedule each business day. We now know that at 12:30, on February 23rd, he will have lunch at his desk and then head to his gym at 2:00 p.m., as he always does on every Wednesday. Clark will release the worm shortly after 12 noon and then reconnect with Mr. Bradford later."

"The NSA research is extraordinary, to say the least," Edison said. "I heard the NSA is about to secretly tap into Google's and Yahoo's fiber optic cables at the bottom of the Atlantic Ocean. The cables cross the Atlantic and connect to the primary servers of these Internet companies in Europe. The NSA will then have access to unrestricted data on millions of people, maybe even access all those private conversations collected by Google Earth. I offered ZeiiMed's assistance with the project. Last week, I had lunch with the general in charge of NSA and he told me his spies even eavesdropped on the cell phone conversations of the Chancellor of Germany and other European leaders. Wouldn't you love to be on the phone call between the angry Chancellor and President Obama if that top-secret information was ever leaked to the world? Germany's intelligence agency assisted the USA in placing the Stuxnet worm into the Iranian nuclear complex and we repay them by treating Germany's Chancellor like a radical who needs to be monitored."

"I guess there's no expectation of privacy regardless of who you are or where you are," Suzanna noted.

"Except between us. I assure you no one will ever learn of our conversations," Edison responded.

"One last, but equally important, matter is coordinating the placement of the USB flash drive in Bradford's computers with the simultaneous introduction of a second

USB flash drive into ZeiiMed's computers. According to our plan, as soon as Clark inserts the USB flash drive at Alfonso and Ryan, he will immediately telephone a ZeiiMed technician waiting for his call. The technician will then infect the ZeiiMed computers with the worm by use of a second USB flash drive, immediately destroying all the original HID documents," Suzanna explained.

"Sounds like we've covered everything then. If there are problems or difficulties, notify me immediately," Edison instructed. "Of course, you know not to disclose any aspect of this plan. Secrecy is paramount and there can be no loose ends once the plan is accomplished. There can be no possibility of a turncoat or whistle blower."

"You mean the ZeiiMed technician who inserts the USB flash drive in ZeiiMed's computers?" asked Suzanne.

"Yes," Edison responded, "That is exactly what I mean."

"The technician will never have the opportunity to turn against us. Like a kamikaze pilot in World War II, the technician's assistance with our plan will be his last great heroic act in support of our cause, ZeiiMed's cause."

"That's right. The technician should be happy to give his life for ZeiiMed," Edison added.

"I totally agree," Suzanna responded. "Don't worry about a thing. Everything and everybody has been taken care of. The plan will work without a hitch. Then we deny any knowledge of what happened."

"Suzanna, you should be very proud of your hard work for ZeiiMed. On behalf of ZeiiMed, I want you to know I am very grateful for all you have done and all you are about to accomplish. It will not be forgotten and will be generously rewarded, assuming everything succeeds as anticipated," Edison stated, as both a compliment and a warning.

"Everything will succeed as anticipated. This will be ZeiiMed's greatest triumph yet. I am proud to be part of it and thank you for letting me be part of it. Let's get started," Suzanna exuberantly exclaimed.

-20-

At noon on February 23, 2011, Brian Bradford was at his desk looking at his computer screen. The screen suddenly filled with hundreds of emails, each received seconds after the last, each moving the "In-Box" down as the desktop computer continually acknowledged receipt of the newest email with a constant "ping."

Each email with its many attachments was sent directly from ZeiiMed. It was unusual that ZeiiMed's lawyers did not have the documents sent from Tweed, Fox & Fortune. There must be a reason, but Brian couldn't imagine any reasonable explanation for doing so. Suzanna Nudbello better be careful. Her predecessor, Charles Wadsworth, lost control of the documents produced by ZeiiMed and that was the beginning of the end for him.

ZeiiMed was up to something. Brian knew it for sure. He also knew instinctively he didn't have a lot of time to figure it out. However, he was also aware that the vast number of documents being produced practically guaranteed that at least a handful would contain information damaging to ZeiiMed, as well as some emails so carelessly written that any lawyer could distort their meaning into evidence adverse to ZeiiMed. The thought caused him to grin with delight.

A couple of minutes past noon, Brian received a telephone call at his desk. "Hello, Mr. Bradford. This is John Standish Clark of Tweed, Fox & Fortune, counsel to ZeiiMed."

"Yes, of course. I saw you in Court," Brian responded. "In fact, I'm looking at my computer screen as hundreds and hundreds of emails are being received from your client."

"Exactly 10,000 emails, with 75 pages of documents attached to each. That's why I called. I'm in the lobby of your building with a Stipulation I would like you to sign so I can file it with the Court. The Stipulation basically confirms that your law office received the documents produced by ZeiiMed. I could have sent a messenger or emailed it to you, but I had an appointment with another client a block away so I decided to come myself."

"Okay. I'll tell Security to let you through, but I can't sign a Stipulation that confirms I received all the documents because I haven't opened each attachment and reviewed the contents."

"That's fine. We'll talk further when I get up to your floor. I just need you to agree that your firm received the emails. You can confirm the number and size of the attachments at a later time," Clark said, sweating slightly at the possibility that Bradford wouldn't consent to see him.

It was 12:04 p.m. when Clark approached the reception desk of Alfonso and Ryan.

"I am here to see Mr. Brian Bradford," Mr. Clark stated.

"He will be with you shortly," the receptionist responded. "Please wait."

Time was something Clark didn't have. His instructions were to release the worm as soon as the emails were received by Alfonso and Ryan. Bradford cannot be permitted time to attempt to print any of the documents. He would immediately suspect something was amiss once he was unable to do so.

The phone to the left of the receptionist rang and she turned her swivel chair towards the phone to pick up the receiver. Clark realized he had only seconds. The computer tower on the receptionist desk was directly in front of him, now out of the receptionist's line of vision as she had turned away from the computer to answer the phone. Clark had the USB flash drive hidden in his clenched hand. The rear of the computer tower was facing him and no USB port was visible. He quickly realized it was a Hewlett-Packard desktop computer, so the USB port was in the front of the tower. John extended his left arm to reach around to the front of the tower. With his thumb holding the USB flash drive in the palm of his hand, his fingers searched the tower for the port.

"Mr. Clark, how are you?" Brian called out, as he entered the reception area.

Startled, the flash drive fell from Clark's hand and landed on the receptionist's desk. The metal plug made a slight noise as it came into contact with the glass top of the desk. Clark quickly leaned over the receptionist's desk to see where it landed. With his left hand, he picked up both the flash drive and a pen from the desk's glass top. He held the pen with his fingers, the flash drive hidden in his palm, made stationary by his thumb.

Clark turned around to face Brian Bedford. "Hi, I just dropped my pen as I was about to put my name on your sign-in sheet. I couldn't find it for a moment–the eyes just aren't what they used to be."

He shook hands with Brian using his right hand. With his left hand, he reached inside his suit coat and dropped both the pen and the USB flash drive into a pocket in the jacket's lining.

"Let's go into my office to discuss the Stipulation. I was just having some coffee when ZeiiMed engulfed me with emails."

It was 12:07. ZeiiMed expected a call by now confirming release of the worm.

Clark followed Brian to his office. Clark remembered the office gossip about Dr. Martin Brown having his skull split open in Bradford's office. He wondered if there would still be bloodstains on the rug. Dr. Brown had failed in his assignment from ZeiiMed to kill Brian Bradford. Clark would not fail today. Bradford had won the last time, but not this time.

Upon entering the office, Brian Bradford sat at his desk looking at his computer screen. On the other side of the desk, Clark could only observe the back of the computer, but easily recognized it as an iMac with a mounted 27-inch display. It made his job easier. The iMac had four super high-speed USB ports on the back of the display, directly facing him.

"The emails came in seconds apart. As you mentioned, there now appears to be thousands of them, each with an attachment," Brian noted.

"Let me take a look. Okay, if I come around to your side of the desk?" Clark asked, not waiting for an answer.

He came around the desk to view the display. As he bent forward to better see the emails, his left hand intentionally knocked over Brian's paper cup half filled with coffee. The spilled coffee covered the keyboard and dripped off the desk onto Brian's pants.

"My God! The coffee's everywhere!" Brian exclaimed with annoyance as he quickly stood, brushing his pants with his hand. "I'll get some paper towels. The keyboard is soaked. At least, the coffee isn't hot."

"I'm so sorry," Clark responded, as Brian quickly left his office. The distraction worked.

Clark immediately took out the flash drive and reached around to the back of the display, inserting the metal tongue plate of the flash drive into a USB port of the iMac. Using his thumb, he pressed the flash drive firmly in place. It would only take about ten seconds for the Stuxnet worm to be released. Five seconds passed, then ten. Clark then waited for a little more time to pass just to make sure the task was accomplished.

In the hallway, Brian was now only a couple of steps from returning to his office. Clark could hear his footsteps getting louder and closer. He pulled on the exposed part of the flash drive. It was stuck. For better leverage, Clark circled around the desk until he was directly facing the rear of the iMac. He saw the flash drive extending out of the USB port. While stabilizing the iMac with one hand, he grabbed the flash drive between the thumb and fingers of his other hand and used all of his considerable strength to force it from the port. It didn't work.

"What are you doing?" Brian asked, as he entered his office.

Brian was facing Clark's back as he entered the office because Clark was facing Brian's desk. As a result, Brian could not see Clark's hand on the flash drive protruding from the back of the iMac monitor.

"Nothing. I was just looking for the 'off' switch with all this coffee everywhere. Did you get the paper towels?" Clark asked, as he made his last attempt at removing the USB flash drive. It finally released from the port.

"Yes," Brian answered as he walked over to his computer to blot up the liquid on the keyboard. As Brian continued his clean up, Clark quickly placed the USB into his pants' pocket.

"Maybe we got lucky. Everything seems fine. The display still works and all of the emails appear to be here," Brian said, as he scrolled down the emails on the screen. The top of the computer screen indicated 10,000 "unread" emails.

Suddenly, the screen went black as if the electricity had been turned off. "Everything's gone, totally gone!" Brian exclaimed.

"What do you mean? What happened?" Clark asked.

"I don't know, but everything just stopped functioning."

"Maybe it just caught a little bug and will restore itself in a second," Clark said, starting to panic.

Seconds later, the display turned back on by itself. The emails were listed from the top to the bottom of the display just as before. Everything seemed just as it was. Clark knew that the worm was sending a false signal that everything was operating correctly, as it secretly destroyed both the emails and the attachments.

"So, it looks like we're fine now. We were lucky this time," Brian noted.

"We sure were. I'd say very lucky," Clark said, feeling a great sense of relief. "Getting back to the Stipulation, it states that 10,000 emails were received without any description of their contents or an exact count of all documents received as attachments to each email. We can confirm all that at a later time, after you've had a chance to review everything you received."

Brian reviewed the Stipulation and confirmed that his computer showed that 10,000 emails had been sent by ZeiiMed. He signed the Stipulation and returned it to Clark.

"Thanks, Brian. I can find my way out."

They shook hands and Clark left.

As Clark rode the elevator down to the first floor, all he could think about was the worm crawling through every inch of Bradford's computer network eating every ZeiiMed document as if they never existed, yet making the iMac appear to be functioning normally.

Once in the lobby, Clark called ZeiiMed at the special number he had been provided. The technician answered, but said nothing.

"Completed. Repeat. It is completed," Clark stated and hung up.

The technician immediately released the worm into ZeiiMed's computer network by attaching the second USB flash drive provided by Suzanna.

Clark departed 40 Wall Street and started his walk to Whitehall Street to prepare for his encounter with Brian Bedford later that day. It was all part of the plan. He tossed the flash drive into the first sewer drain he passed.

John Edison received a call from the doomed technician confirming that the worm had been successfully released at both locations. Edison chuckled at the thought of Brian Bradford sitting at his computer thinking all was fine as the worm destroyed the ZeiiMed documentation.

Edison was also looking forward to receiving the good news later that day that Brian Bradford had finally been disposed of. Edison liked the plan. Bradford deserved the agony of desperately gasping for air as his lungs filled with water. He will slowly suffocate in a frenzied panic of excruciating distress. How delightful an end for Mr. Bradford.

-21-

The New York Health and Racquet Club is located on Whitehall Street in downtown New York, directly across Water Street from the Staten Island Ferry Terminal. The locker rooms are on the first floor, with the boxing ring, racquetball courts, squash courts and state-of-the-art running machines on the second and third floors. The sixty-foot swimming pool in the basement has four separate lanes for lap swimming, with an additional area for water exercises.

The pool is three feet deep at the shallow end and reaches a depth of eight feet on the other end. Granite tiles form a continuous four-foot perimeter around the pool. The curved ceiling has a vivid, painted image of a bright blue sky.

There is a separate stairway in both the men's locker room and the women's locker room that leads directly down to the basement and a glass entrance door to the pool area. On the other side of the pool, directly across from the entrance door, is a three-foot lifeguard stand. Several feet from the lifeguard stand, on the edge of the four-foot perimeter, is a closed door with a skull and crossbones above the words: "BEWARE—POISONOUS MATERIAL."

I arrived at the Health and Racquet Club at about 2 p.m. on Wednesday, February 23rd, my usual arrival time on Wednesdays. Although unbeknownst to me at the time, the information in the NSA files provided to ZeiiMed was remarkably accurate regarding my daily routine.

I showed my ID at the front desk and walked immediately to the men's locker room. I was surprised not to receive a warm greeting from the long-time locker room attendant, José. He was nowhere to be seen.

I found an empty locker and changed into a loose-fitting orange swimsuit from my gym bag. After grabbing a couple of towels, I walked down the stairs to the pool clothed only in my trunks. The smell of chlorine immediately filled my nostrils as I opened the glass door and stepped onto the pool deck.

It was strangely quiet because no one was either in or around the pool, including the lifeguard. This was rare indeed, but the unusual experience of having the pool entirely to myself felt like a private oasis in a make-believe palace.

As I sampled the water temperature with my toes in the shallow end of the pool, my head turned in disbelief at the sight of John Standish Clark striding through the glass door. Clark, wearing only a skimpy swimsuit, was walking towards me, appearing not the least bit surprised to encounter me.

"Hi, Brian, how are you? A lot of my colleagues that work downtown use this pool. Someone mentioned they had seen you here a couple of times."

Clark had a striking six-pack of pulsating stomach muscles and a "V' shaped torso. His shoulders extended so far from his body that his arms dangled loosely like ripe, curved pods on a Mediterranean carob bean tree. I avoided looking at his very tight, flesh-colored Speedo. Clark's intimidating look and flat-top haircut gave him a striking resemblance to H.R. Haldeman, the arrogant former White House Chief of Staff under Richard Nixon. His flattened nose broadcast a history of many physical altercations.

"Yes, I'm here every week, but it seems more than just a coincidence that our paths crossed twice in a couple of hours," I responded, with a growing sense of dread.

"So, what are your thoughts about the looming government shutdown on March 4th? It's clear the Tea House Party members aren't going to approve a spending bill for the remainder of the fiscal year without significant spending cuts. Apparently, the House Republicans attached a rider to a proposed budget to cut off funding for Obamacare. Sounds like there is going to be quite a battle with the President," Clark stated casually.

I can't believe this guy is talking current events. Here we are, two professional adversaries, standing next to each other poolside, with this clown in his jock strap of a swim suit. I'll play along for a few moments and then politely get the hell away from this idiot.

"I think a budget will eventually get passed for the rest of 2011, but that won't be the end of the story. There will be other budgets in 2012 and 2013, and the House Republicans, especially the Tea Party members, will slowly gain momentum in their threat to send 800,000 federal employees home without pay unless the money for Obamacare is cut off. The House Republicans that pursue this agenda don't care about you or me or anyone. They don't care if the United States government is shut down. All they care about is disemboweling Obamacare permanently," I responded, playing along, although it seemed stupid to be having this conversation with Clark.

"Maybe Obamacare should be put out of its misery," Clark replied. "Let me tell you what I heard. As you may know, the Centers for Medicare and Medicaid were put in charge of creating the federal website for buying insurance under Obamacare. John Edison was appointed the Administrator of the Centers, but then he had that little altercation with you in the Ramble. Mr. Edison was forced to take a leave of absence due to the injuries you inflicted. Without ZeiiMed's assistance, the federal government will never be able to put together an operational federal website for enrollment before the penalty deadline. The whole Obamacare program should probably be trashed as unworkable with Edison now unable to run the show."

"Your opinion of current events may be right. But, you are wrong if you think that Edison didn't deserve everything he got from me. Actually, I should have killed him when I had the chance. I had a very temporary moment of compassion and restraint that won't be repeated. I will not make that mistake again," I said as my anger rose. I stepped closer to him. I wanted to be in striking distance of his ugly nose.

"Funny, you should say that. That's exactly why I am here," Clark growled, as his demeanor turned menacing. "Mr. Edison asked me to be the vehicle of his revenge. He wants you terminated so he never has to worry about you pursuing him again. Welcome to the last day of your life," Clark said, as he lowered his shoulder and rammed his body full steam into my mid-section before I realized what was happening.

I fell backwards into the pool, his heavy body landing on top of mine. Since the water was only three feet deep, Clark planted his feet in the pool locking my body between his legs. His hands grabbed my throat and forced my head underwater. The feeling of suffocation caused extreme panic as my arms and legs were unable to wrestle free of his death grip. I felt an overpowering urge to open my mouth in a desperate attempt to obtain air, despite the knowledge that only water would fill my lungs.

Clark's powerful arms raised my face above the water just before I blacked out. I sucked the precious air into my lungs.

"I want you to know exactly how you are about to die. I'm not going to break your neck or crush your throat. That would leave marks. No, I'm going to submerge you once again and watch as your mouth fills with water and your eyes bulge in horror. There is no escaping your fate. The entrance to the pool has been locked and covered with cardboard. There is no one to help. Enjoy the next few, final moments. I know I will," Clark said, his face inches from mine as his hands seemed to slightly loosen their grip on my neck now that I wasn't fighting to breathe.

It was now or never. Clark's arms stiffened to once again submerge me. I instinctively jerked my lower back towards the bottom of the pool, as I bent my right leg and simultaneously touched my left foot on the bottom of the pool for leverage. I then forcefully thrust my right knee upward into his groin. Clark's body went still for a moment, followed by a loud cry of pain. I tilted my head until my chin touched his slackened hands on my neck. I then lunged upward until the top of my head butted him below his chin, snapping Clark's head back as his mouth violently closed and his teeth pierced his tongue. The blood from his tongue dripped into my eyes.

I quickly resubmerged my upper torso and turned on my side underwater as his legs loosened their vice-like grip. I slid away from Clark with two quick breast strokes. He was bent over as I swam away from him. Turning onto my back, I fully extended my arms underwater until my hands touched the bottom of the pool. Once stabilized, I raised my right leg out the water and smashed Clark's nose with my foot. Clark fell backwards holding his face, as I swam into the deep end of the pool.

I reached the ladder and stepped out of the pool onto the deck. Clark had already composed himself and was also out of the pool, thirty feet away.

Moving towards me, blood streaming down his face, he looked like a zombie stalking his next meal. I wasn't sure what to do next. Physically, he was too strong for me. Not only was the glass door to the pool covered with cardboard, a chain on the outside of the door was visible. Nowhere to run.

Out of the corner of my eye, I noticed that the "skull and crossbones" door near the lifeguard stand was opened a few inches. I immediately ran along the rim of the pool away from Clark and towards the door. I pushed the door open enough to enter the dimly lit room. I stepped inside.

"What are you doing in the pump room? It's off limits," asked a small, mustached, middle-aged man in a green work uniform with a matching cap, holding a wooden tool box.

"There's someone trying to kill me. I need to hide. Who are you?" I asked.

"I'm the repairman for the Stenner peristaltic chlorinator pump. The pump's right next to you on the wall. It's connected by rubber tubing to the thirty-five gallon tank with fifteen percent sodium hypochlorite solution. The tubing broke. I just finished the repair. I've been here for hours," he responded.

The pump room was small, only eight feet long and four feet wide. The tank with the solution was on the floor next to the wall. The Stenner pump, with its connecting tubes, was on an elevated wooden platform several feet above the solution tank.

"There's a dangerous man outside. Hurry, get out of here. Call for help. Use your tools to smash open the glass entrance. It's locked from the outside. Move, now! And keep away from the lunatic by the pool with the Speedo brief and the bloody face," I quickly warned him.

"Okay, I'll go! But this is very unusual," said the alarmed repairman. "Don't touch anything! Like it says on the front door, the liquid chlorine solution is poisonous. Chlorine gas was used in World War II as a chemical weapon. It can destroy lung tissue."

The repairman had taken only one step out the partially opened door when the light from the pool area outlined Clark's imposing body. Clark immediately pushed the door shut with enormous force, trapping the repairman's head between the edge of the door and the doorframe. His ear split open as blood dripped down his uniform. Clark reopened the door about two feet from the frame. The repairman hardly moved as he tried to steady himself from the blow. He dropped his toolbox on the pool deck. Clark suddenly slammed the door a second time, with even greater force, crushing the defenseless man's cheekbone and ripping open his face from temple to chin. Clark released his grip on the door as the repairman fell towards him. He grabbed the collapsing figure with both hands on the back of his green uniform, took one step towards the pool and tossed him into the water.

I was paralyzed with horror as Clark now stood in the doorway facing me, the light from the pool area continuing to illuminate the perimeter of his heaving frame.

Shock from the brutality I had just witnessed was suddenly displaced with rage. I felt a power surge as my cerebral cortex released its buried collection of uncontrollable instincts, suddenly transforming me into an unthinking combatant ready to meet the challenge, without guilt or morality to limit or control my actions and reactions.

In a matter of seconds, I quickly assessed the situation. There was nowhere to go. There was nothing to use as a weapon. I was trapped in the limited space that contained only the elevated Stenner pump, the solution tank on the floor and two long pieces of rubber tubing that looked like black cable wires, each about three feet in length. One cable line carried the sodium hypochlorite, commonly known as chlorine bleach, from the solution tank to the pump and a second cable was a discharge line that pumped the chemical from the pump to a water injection valve connected to the water pipe. I now had a plan. I was ready.

"Okay, so you didn't want to drown to death," Clark said. "Now, I'm forced to beat you to death instead. It's going to hurt a lot more, but it's your choice. I hope the sight of your own blood, doesn't make you faint. It's not much fun punching someone who is unconscious."

Clark stepped into the room. I was only two steps from him as I leaned against the rear wall. He clenched his right fist and aimed his first punch for my left eye. I put my arms in front of my face to lessen the blow. It barely made a difference. As he landed his punch, my eye seemed to recess into my brain as my head pounded into the concrete wall behind me. The eye socket may have cracked. My eyelid wouldn't open. His left arm then delivered a vicious blow to my abdomen.

I bent over from the impact and turned to my left. The Stenner pump was inches from my face. I ripped the discharge tube from the injection valve. Toxic sodium hypochlorite sprayed from the line like a squirt gun. Holding the tube in my left hand, I used my right elbow to jab Clark as hard as I could in the solar plexus. Clark started to bend forward from the pain created by the blow. As he lowered his head, my left hand poked his right eye with the tubing as I sprayed his face with sodium hypochlorite. He staggered backwards. His hands immediately covered his eyes as he screamed in pain. The pungent smell of the clear liquid chemical was nauseating, but I attempted to hold my breath. Clark tilted his head back, his hands still covering his eyes, with his mouth wide open as he bellowed in extreme agony.

I pulled the spray away from his face, cocked my arm and jammed the tube into his open mouth. Now using both my hands, I forced the tube down his throat, ripping his vocal cords and forcing it into his esophagus. The burning in his mouth and larynx caused him to turn ghostly white as the acid destroyed delicate nerves and tissue. Clark vomited on my arms as I continued to extend the tube deep into his esophagus. He was desperately gagging for air as the chemical now impaired the functioning of his lungs. I knew he was near death.

I ripped the tubing from Clark's mouth as his blood soaked tongue dangled from his mouth. I used both hands to push him out of the pump room. He collapsed by the side of the pool. I was about to push him into water, but had second thoughts as I viewed the repairman floating face down. One death was enough. Clark would have killed me, but his punishment was sufficient. I didn't need his death on my hands. Certainly, the police would question how he ended up in the pool after being so viciously injured in the pump room.

I grabbed a hammer from the toolbox and smashed the glass in the pool's entrance door, racing to my locker. I wiped off the vomit with a towel, quickly dressed and left the building.

I knew ZeiiMed, emergency medical personnel and a cleanup crew would arrive very shortly. The incident wouldn't be reported in the newspapers. It never was. All would be quietly and quickly returned to as it was, except for one dead repairman and one permanently speechless ZeiiMed lawyer with an oxygen tank to assist his breathing.

I headed to Penn Station for the train home to Port Jefferson. My eye hurt like hell, but the bleeding around the eye had stopped. I hoped to make it home before losing consciousness. Kim won't be happy when she hears this story and sees my swollen eye socket. Actually, I'm not very happy myself.

I need another line of work.

-22-

Kim was reading in the living room when I opened the front door, hours earlier than usual. Walking was difficult because the extreme swelling covered my left eye and affected my balance.

I entered the living room as Kim looked up. She immediately dropped the book. "What in God's name happened to you? Your eye is shocking. Here, let me help you sit down."

"Thank you," I said, gratefully accepting her assistance in getting to the couch. "But, I was hoping you were going to say it looked fine."

"I'm anticipating a very interesting story about how this happened, but shouldn't we head to the hospital first?" Kim asked.

"You're right. I do need to get this checked out. Let's go to the Emergency Room at Mather Hospital," I responded.

"Give me the abridged version of how you were injured as we get into the car. Lean on me as we go–it will help your balance. Knowing you, I have a very strong suspicion you didn't slip on a banana peel. The last time I carried you to safety, ZeiiMed was involved and I'm starting to see a pattern here," Kim said, in her attempt at very dry humor. I guess she learned it from me.

We were now in the car and on our way to the hospital.

"Yes, of course, it was ZeiiMed and to be precise it was one of ZeiiMed's lawyers who attacked me at the pool, of all places. I guess my HID litigation hit a nerve deep inside ZeiiMed."

"I can't believe two lawyers would engage in mortal combat because of a lawsuit. Then again, maybe it's you. I don't know of any other lawyer who starts a lawsuit and then ends up being literally beaten to a pulp by either the Defendant or the Defendant's lawyer. First, it was Edison in the Ramble and now it's some ZeiiMed lawyer at a pool in downtown New York. My God, the vision in your eye may be permanently damaged. I'm sure you'll be in big demand then."

"Actually, I was thinking about that. Maybe a black eye patch would make me look debonair, with a touch of international charm. I could expand my law practice worldwide."

"You are such an idiot! Anyway, an eye patch will cover those cute eyelashes. You'll lose half of your only appealing quality. Now, please get back to the pool story."

"So, I'm in my bathing suit about to swim laps when John Standish Clark enters the pool area in an obscenely small Speedo," I started.

"I remember him from the Fairness Hearing at the Courthouse in your first case with ZeiiMed. He had a lot of muscles. How did he look in a swimsuit?" Kim asked. She thinks she's funny. I'm in too much pain to tell her she's not.

"I can't tell you, I'm trying to black out the visual of Clark's body. The point is that he is very strong and very big. Getting back to my story, Clark walked over to me and before I knew it, he said John Edison of ZeiiMed wanted me dead. He immediately tackled me as we both fell into the water. I eventually was able to get out of the water unharmed, but moments later we were in hand-to-hand combat in the pump room. That's when he hit me in the eye. I escaped only because I jammed a rubber tube filled with liquid chlorine down his throat, but not before Clark viciously murdered a pool repairman who tried to help. It was a nightmare that will never go away."

"I'm so very sorry. We're at the hospital now. You know, the hospital staff will call the police and you'll have to answer a ton of questions."

"Yes, I know the drill. One thing at a time."

The red brick John T. Mather Memorial Hospital in Port Jefferson is a state-of-the-art, 248-bed facility that first opened on December 29, 1929. Since 1929, the ER has grown from a single bed to the sophisticated Contessa Nadia Farber Emergency Pavilion, with special medical teams for the Chest Pain ER and the Stroke Center. With its original funding from the Will of John Mather, a Port Jefferson shipbuilder, it now has a national reputation for treatment of over 43,000 emergency room patients a year.

We entered the very comfortable, modern waiting room of the Emergency Pavilion. After providing my name to the woman at the front desk, I was immediately asked to sit in a small adjoining office to answer questions regarding my medical condition. A very intense, thirty-something nurse made all the usual intake inquiries, but I found it difficult to respond seriously. Also, I quickly realized there was zero chance I could get her to smile. I guess I enjoy being irritating even when I'm in pain.

"Do you consume alcoholic beverages?"

"Yes."

"How often?"

"Every day."

"How many a day?"

"Depends on how hard a day it was."

"How many on a hard day?"

"Four, five or six beers. Sometimes more, if it was a very hard day."

"How many on a very hard day?"

"As I said, more than five or six, especially if I'm smoking."

"Do you smoke?"

"Occasionally, when I'm anxious or nervous."

"How often is that?"

"It depends on how hard a day it was."

"How many on a hard day?"

"Only one or two, but the number increases exponentially if it was a very hard day, especially if I'm drinking."

"Are you going to keep up the evasive answers to all my questions?"

"I don't know. Why don't you ask me a question about my eye?"

"Okay, when and how did you hurt your eye?"

"Earlier today, I got distracted and bumped into the bedroom door. I thought it was open, but it was closed."

"How come only your left eye is injured and not your nose or other parts of your face?"

"I have a strong nose and a weak eye."

"Are you taking any medication?"

"No, but I hope you'll give me some very soon."

"Thank you for your time, Mr. Bradford. It is clear that you are resisting my efforts to assist in your treatment. I'll let the doctor handle your care from here. Please follow the attendant to one of the beds in the examination area."

The examination room contained many beds, with the headboards against the wall. The beds were separated by several feet, with the usual hospital curtains suspended on a "U" shaped steel rod to permit the entire area around the bed to be enclosed. I sat on my designated bed, leaning my back against the pillows, waiting for the doctor to arrive.

After about thirty minutes, the curtain was pushed open. A bearded man with a stethoscope around his neck entered and closed the curtain behind him.

"Hello, I'm Doctor Joseph Fish. Around here, everyone just calls me, 'Dr. Joe'. I won't ask how you are doing for two reasons. One, I know from the nurse I won't get a straight answer. Two, I can already see you have serious trauma to the eye socket."

"Nice to meet you, Dr. Joe. Doesn't my last name ring a bell to you?" I asked, knowing the answer.

It wasn't the graying, heavy beard and mostly bald head that led me to conclude that he was my wife's boyfriend. It was the incontestable fact that there could only be one physician on Long Island (or the world, for that matter) who goes by the name, "Dr. Joe."

"I know who you are. Is Kim in the waiting room?" Dr. Joe asked.

"Yes, but I believe it's your job to treat my injuries before you continue your courting of my wife."

"You're quite a wise guy. Just like Kim said."

"You and Kim talked about me over lunch?" I asked.

"I don't think our conversations are any of your business," Dr. Joe responded, a little too harshly.

"None of my business? Are you crazy? You're the one dating my wife and breaking up a happy marriage, my marriage."

"You're yelling! This is a hospital. Kim and I are not dating—we are spending quality time together," Dr. Joe corrected me.

"Listen *Joe,* I don't appreciate your verbal gymnastics. You wouldn't be seeing Kim unless you were attracted to her. The only reason nothing significant has happened yet, assuming that is true, is because Kim hasn't given you the green light. You and I both know if she said yes, you'd be all in without a moment's hesitation."

"Well, I think I love her. I just can't walk away. And I don't think she wants me to walk away. She says she still loves you, but that doesn't mean she can't love me also," Dr. Joe explained, however feebly.

"Goddam you! You actually think I'm on my way out? I ought to twist that grubby beard around your neck until your eyes bulge. Remember this, if Kim comes home with red blotches on her face, I'm going to personally rip out that beard, one hair at a time."

"Hello, to my two favorite men!" Kim said, as she pulled back the curtain and unexpectedly joined our conversation. "The nurse mentioned that Joe was on call in the ER, so I came right in to see how you two were getting along."

"Fine," I responded. "Just fine."

"I see. Since tension appears high, I will make two comments. Brian, get control of your temper and behave while the doctor takes care of you. Joe, do what you were trained to do and take care of my husband. He is injured and needs your very fine skills. I will stand here to make sure you both listen to me and do what I say."

"Sounds like you're suggesting a threesome? What happened to all those prohibitions and taboos taught to Catholic school girls by the nuns?" I asked.

"Stop that. I'm serious. Please just stop talking while the doctor examines your eye. Then you can make all the jokes you want," Kim responded.

"Okay, but if Dr. Joe rubs that dirty beard against my face, he'll have a sore eye himself. He probably has lice in there."

"Brian, you heard me!"

"Okay, okay. Proceed with the exam."

"I'm going to examine your eye with the ophthalmoscope to see inside the eye for damage. I will examine the optic nerve, the eye muscles and the orbit, which is the eye socket. I need to determine if the bones that form the eye socket have been cracked. As you can see with your good eye, the ophthalmoscope looks like a black car remote mounted on a silver rod. I need you to open the lid of your eye so I can first put in some drops to dilate the pupil," Dr. Joe instructed.

After the eye drops were inserted, he checked out the entire eye, without the ophthalmoscope or his beard touching any part of my body.

"Everything looks good. No internal damage and no orbital rim fracture. There will be black and blue skin discoloration around the eye, but an ice pack will help. Also, I will prescribe an antibiotic for possible infection. I have one more item to check. I am now opening the eyelid again and please tell me if you experience any double vision," Dr. Joe continued.

"Yes, I do. I see two Kims directly in front of me. This is wonderful! Now, there is a Kim for you and a Kim for me. Everybody's happy," I said to further irritate Dr. Joe.

"That's it! This examination is over. Pick up the prescription at the desk in the waiting room. I'm done with this patient. See an ophthalmologist as soon as possible," Dr. Joe instructed as his parting remark.

Dr. Joe left the area next to my bed and headed out of the emergency room without another word.

"The doctor doesn't have a very good bedside manner. I thought doctors were supposed to have patience with the ill and infirm," I said in a loud voice, so Dr. Joe would hear on his way out the door.

"You really are mean. You did your best to get under his skin and you finally succeeded," Kim said.

"Are you kidding? Before you got here, that creep was telling me how much he loved you and how much you loved him. I'm your husband for Chrissake. How do you expect me to react? I also love you and three is generally a crowd when it comes to matters of the heart."

"We had this conversation. I explained to you my relationship with Joe and told you I am still in love with you also. Everything seemed to be proceeding as normally as possible since then," Kim stated.

"No, it hasn't been normal. I just didn't talk about it. I constantly think about what you two are doing and where you are doing it. But, I suffer silently because I don't want to lose you. Well, I guess the silence ended once I found myself face to bearded face with Dr. Joe," I responded.

"I'm sorry about that. I didn't know he was covering for a colleague in the ER today. Look, please take a cab home. Joe is really upset. I need to see him and apologize to him also."

Kim leaned over the bed and placed a firm, sensuous kiss on my lips. It was so affectionate that the nerve endings in my sore eye started to throb. She lingered and then slightly opened her mouth, my lips following her lead. She pulled away gently.

"I'm going. See you back at the house. The nurse will discharge you," Kim said, as she started to leave.

"You kiss like you love me. Come back, there's plenty of room on the bed."

Kim didn't answer. A nurse heard and gave me a look similar to the one a librarian gives to a teenager talking loudly in the reading room.

I signed a bunch of documents I didn't read and walked out of the hospital through the sliding glass doors in the front of the facility. There was an active hospital access road a few feet from the front entrance, so it seemed the best place to find a cab.

As I stepped outside, directly in front of me was a parked squad car from the Police Department of the City of New York. The window opened on the driver's side as the glass slid down into the body of the vehicle.

"Mr. Bradford? Mr. Brian Bradford? May I speak with you a moment?" the officer in the driver's seat asked.

I approached the car's door.

"I thought I told you not to cause any more trouble," the officer announced.

"Sergeant Melissa Black, what are you doing way out here in the far away seafaring village of Port Jefferson?" I asked with some surprise. "And," I continued, "You didn't tell me to stay out of trouble altogether. Rather, you just warned me not to cause any more trouble for Mr. Edison."

The Sergeant looked appealing. She appeared softer. She wasn't wearing her peaked police cap. Her thick dark brown hair shined brilliantly as the warm glow of the entrance lights seemed to lighten her hair in waves as it flowed down to her shoulders. The thin and shallow shape of her face seemed less apparent with her hair down.

"Your eye looks horrible. You want to tell me what happened at the Health and Racquet Club? My bosses want to know because you seem to leave a trail of dead or incapacitated people all over the City," the Sergeant inquired. "I was sent way out here to get some answers. It wasn't hard to find you–we knew you were in need of medical care."

"I'm happy to tell you all about it–once again it wasn't my fault. I was defending myself. But before we get into that discussion, I have a question. How did you get all lovely hair stuffed into your police cap? It doesn't seem possible, but you had apparently accomplished it the first time we met."

"You make it sound like we met socially. It was an interview, part of a criminal investigation and it really doesn't matter how I wear my cap or my hair. Why don't you get in the car so we can discuss your current problem?" the Sergeant suggested, although I don't think I had a choice.

I walked around the police car and sat in the front seat.

"This is comfortable. My first time in a squad car. It's very exciting. By the way, where is Officer Mark Miller?" I asked.

"I told Officer Miller I could handle the current mess you created."

"That's too bad. I really got along well with him. Maybe next time," I said, not meaning a word.

"There better not be a next time. The repairman at the pool is dead and that lawyer, Mr. Clark, is having convulsions consistent with exposure to poison gas. He can't talk, so we know nothing. Somehow, the bands of muscles that form the voice box inside his larynx were ripped apart. We know you were there, so tell me what happened."

"I'll tell you, but it isn't much different from the first incident with Edison that we talked about. I was at the pool about to swim laps when this lawyer, John Standish Clark, shows up and announces that he is the instrument of Edison's revenge," I started to explain.

"Are you telling me you were physically assaulted by an attorney who you know?"

"Yes, a ZeiiMed lawyer. I've been in Court with him. First, he tried to drown me and I escaped his grip. Then, he tried to beat the life out of me in the pump room after killing the repairman. The poor guy was just in the wrong place at the wrong time. Clark cracked his skull open and then threw him in the pool to drown. I got lucky, I grabbed the rubber tube that injects liquid chlorine in the pool and jammed it down his throat."

"So, you're claiming self-defense, just like your dance with Edison in the Ramble?' Sergeant Black asked.

"Yes, I am. ZeiiMed apparently has a small army of these killers, including Edison himself. I told you about Detective Jack Jarrett. He was my friend and ZeiiMed had him barbarically killed."

"I did ask about the Detective at the precinct, like I said I would. There's no question that ZeiiMed was somehow involved in the Detective's murder. But, ZeiiMed has incredible influence in the Department, so it was never directly connected to the murder on the record."

"And never will be. Jack's killer is also dead and there were no witnesses," I said. "As I told you, Stanley Hyman was the name of the guy who actually murdered Jack by strangulation one morning at JFK Airport. Hyman worked for ZeiiMed and he confessed to the killing once I applied a little physical pain to jog his recollection. But ZeiiMed's involvement will never be established. Hyman claimed he murdered Jack because Jack was watching over me, hindering Hyman's plan to take me out. Hyman wanted me to think he acted as a lone wolf, without ZeiiMed's knowledge. I don't believe that. ZeiiMed wanted me gone and Jack got in the way."

"Don't lose all hope. I'm on your side and there are other cops who also know your story and will pitch in. I'll write this one up as self-defense, as usual with you. Mr. Clark will probably never speak again, but he may still file a criminal complaint against you."

"A criminal complaint against me will never happen. It's not ZeiiMed's way. Zeiimed handles everything on its own terms. Actually, I guarantee it won't be long before Clark suddenly ends up dead, assuming he's still alive as we speak," I said.

"Is there somewhere I can drive you? I want to hear more about what happened."

"Yes, I live about two miles from here, four blocks from the ferry terminal. I'd appreciate a ride. My wife has the car and she needs to stay at the hospital a while."

"Is she injured?"

"No, she needs to speak with a doctor friend about something."

"Her health?"

"No, not her health. It's a personal matter–she's a personal friend of the doctor."

"And you're not?"

"No, I'm not."

"That doesn't sound good," the Sergeant continued.

"No, it doesn't. Did you ever think of becoming a lawyer? I think you have a knack for asking uncomfortable questions."

"Okay, I'll drop it," she said, as she steered the car down the hill towards the ferry terminal at the end of Main Street.

"That's the house right over there," I said.

"That's a cute home. Mind if I come in for a drink before I head back to the City?"

"I thought it was against the law to drink and drive."

"It is, but I'm law enforcement so I can do anything I want."

"Alright, I think a drink or two is a fair price for not being arrested," I said.

"We don't take bribes. The only reason you weren't arrested is because I believed your self-defense story."

"Yes, of course, Sergeant," I said, deciding to keep my stupid jokes to a minimum for the time being. "The real reason I want you to come in the house is so I can write out a criminal complaint against Clark. That son-of-a-bitch brutally murdered that repairman without a moment's hesitation. I want Clark charged with murder and I agree to make myself available to testify against him."

"That's fine. I have the appropriate forms right here."

"Good, let's work at the kitchen table," I said.

We entered the house through the front door and proceeded down the center hall until we reached the kitchen in the rear. She sat at the kitchen table while I got her a scotch neat and myself a beer. I must say there is something very exciting about a woman in uniform, especially the Sergeant's tightly tapered navy blue shirt, cargo pants and tie, with the protruding DeSantis Facilitator holster and Glock service revolver. I quickly reminded myself to focus as best I could on the business at hand. But, I've never been too successful at that when I have female company.

"Shouldn't you put some ice on that eye?"

"Yes, good idea," I responded.

As we sat at the kitchen table, Sergeant Black completed the paperwork necessary for issuance of a Complaint against Clark. I dictated to her much of the necessary information.

"Thanks for the drink," she said, having consumed three ounces of scotch in a couple of gulps. "But there's little chance criminal charges will actually be filed against Clark. As you've taught me, ZeiiMed won't let it happen and ZeiiMed has the connections to prevent it. I'll do the best I can, but don't expect too much."

"No, I won't. Like I said, ZeiiMed will probably take care of Clark for us."

"I'll be on my way now," Sergeant Black said, as she stood.

"Well, thanks for taking the time to talk about it, Sergeant."

"Melissa. Call me Melissa."

"Okay, Melissa, it is. Does that mean I get to take a look at your service revolver?"

"No, not until we know each other a lot better," she responded, clearly becoming more comfortable with my mindless chatter.

"Next time, then," I said.

Before we walked out of the kitchen, she extended her hand. As we shook, her hand pulled my hand towards her body as she stood on her toes and leaned into me, apparently about to bestow a cheek-to-cheek kiss. I somehow pinched my finger on the iron buckle of her utility belt as she guided my hand against her, causing me to pull back in reaction to the pain. She immediately released my hand and pulled away.

"That was awkward. I guess you two don't know each other very well. It takes practice," said Kim, as she entered the kitchen.

"Hi, honey. I didn't hear you come in," I said.

"I know," Kim said, with a grin.

"I'd like you to meet Sergeant Melissa Black. She is investigating my little incident at the Health and Racquet Club.

"Hi, Melissa. Feel free to arrest him. He seems to have too much time on his hands. I can't leave him alone for a moment."

"Hello, Mrs. Bradford. I was just leaving. Your husband was very helpful to our investigation."

"I'm sure he was. Especially when dealing with an attractive woman in uniform."

"Mrs. Bradford, nothing is going on here. I interviewed Brian once before at the hospital in New York City and I sympathized with his struggles against ZeiiMed."

"Yes, I understand. I was just kidding. Please come by anytime if we can assist," Kim said.

Melissa left. Kim didn't mention her again. She also didn't mention Dr. Joe.

The good news is that Kim didn't have any red blotches on her face. I guess she didn't get a cheek-to-cheek kiss either.

-23-

I took several days off to rest my eye. The swelling decreased, although there was a thick ring of black around the eye that made half my face look like a racoon's ugly mug. I returned to work the first week of March 2011.

I sat at my office desk and turned on my computer as I took my first sip of coffee.

Mary Douglas walked into my office before I had time to read my first email.

"Hello, Brian. Welcome back to work. You look terrible, by the way. The office rumor mill is buzzing about how you got beat up once again. You really should stop getting into fights. You don't seem to be very good at defending yourself."

"Please don't start. This is a serious matter. Our esteemed adversary, John Standish Clark, tried to kill me at the pool on Edison's order. I survived, an innocent third party is dead and Clark is seriously injured after I forced him to swallow chlorine, then ripped out his vocal cords. Hopefully, he will be put in jail once he recovers."

"I'm so sorry. This nightmare with ZeiiMed never seems to end. It's incomprehensible that ZeiiMed would instruct one of its lawyers to commit murder. Obviously, we're at war with ZeiiMed again. We knew all along this might happen once we took the HID case, but it's still shocking when it actually happens. Will your eye eventually be okay?"

"Yes, the doctor seems to think so. No damage to the retina or eye socket," I responded.

"Thank goodness. I look forward to you once again batting your long eyelashes at me," Mary commented.

I ignored her comment. I simply didn't feel well enough to get into flirtatious banter with her. Also, I ignored, as best I could, her sparkling blond hair pulled back into a ponytail, with her neck and upper body accentuated by a black, off-the-shoulder sweater. Is this appropriate office dress?

"My only focus is to expeditiously pursue the HID litigation against ZeiiMed," I said. "We now have their documents, so I want a team to review them meticulously so we can immediately proceed with the depositions of the ZeiiMed people who designed and marketed the HID."

"We have a major problem. There are no documents."

"What do you mean? Before I had my little altercation with Clark, I saw the emails we received from ZeiiMed with the documents attached."

"The emails and the documents received from ZeiiMed have all disappeared. Two hours after we supposedly received the documents electronically, I attempted to open and print the materials. All the emails and the attached documents had been deleted as if they never existed. The documents simply were no longer on our computers. I know I should have called you at home with the bad news, but I decided to let you heal before dropping the bombshell."

"So, call ZeiiMed's lawyers and tell them to resend everything."

"I did. I talked to Suzanna Nudbello. She said all the documents at ZeiiMed regarding the HID were also destroyed at the same time our documents were destroyed. Apparently, some kind of a computer worm was released into both our computer systems for the sole purpose of eating every HID document. The documents are gone forever, with no electronic copies anywhere. ZeiiMed is paperless, so there are also no hard copies of the documents."

"A worm? How can that be. No one from the outside had access to our computers," I noted.

"You better be sure of that. Suzanna said she will file an Affidavit with the Court confirming that the ZeiiMed computers were sabotaged and all HID documents were irretrievably lost forever. She also said ZeiiMed is investigating how this happened, but had no answers at the present time. All we know for sure is that the worm was programmed to project a false image that the documents existed while, at the same time, the worm was destroying everything. Once the destruction was completed, both ZeiiMed's computers and our computers finally revealed the eradication by showing a blank screen where the emails had once been. Then the worm self-destructed," Mary explained.

"This is beyond belief. Does ZeiiMed expect us to believe that some unknown hacker did this? ZeiiMed orchestrated this whole thing because ZeiiMed didn't want us to know what the documents revealed," I stated.

"I agree–but I don't know how we prove it. Someone deposited the worm in our network and, so far, there's no way we're able to trace it back to ZeiiMed. We're trying, but I'm told by our computer experts that we have little chance of success," Mary said.

"I'll bet you it was Clark. He had to be the one who infected our computers. He was in my office the day the documents were received. I left him alone for less than a minute, but that would be plenty of time. Of course, there's no way to prove it and Clark isn't talking–literally–so that's a dead end."

"Maybe you shouldn't have ripped out his vocal cords. I'm kidding. Forget I said that. I don't think you're in a humorous mood," Mary commented.

"You're right. I'm not. I'm going to call the Court and schedule a telephone conference with the Judge. If ZeiiMed can't produce the documents, then the Court has the power to strike the defenses of ZeiiMed and grant a judgement in favor of Mrs. Dudley," I stated.

"I agree," Mary noted. "The Court should be made aware of this immediately. But, I'm just not sure that the Court will punish ZeiiMed without proof that ZeiiMed orchestrated the whole thing with Clark's participation as transmitter of the bug, I mean worm."

"I know. It's an uphill battle. If we lose, I guess my only recourse will be to beat up Edison again. I would enjoy that," I mentioned.

"I think it's in your best interest to avoid any more fights. As I said, you don't seem well-suited to a pugilistic lifestyle. Don't take it personally, but men become lawyers because they aren't good with their hands."

"Thanks, I needed that pep talk. By the way, why do women become lawyers?" I asked.

"Because they are very smart and want the challenge of a profession in which they can dominate and subdue male lawyers," Mary answered.

"Okay. I'm cutting off this discussion. I'll provide you with an update once I've spoken with the Court."

"Feel better. I'll see you later," Mary said, as she left my office.

Mrs. Dudley's case was not proceeding well. Without documents confirming defects in the design of the HID, it will be almost impossible to beat ZeiiMed at trial. The witnesses for ZeiiMed will never admit knowledge of a design failure without documents proving they had such knowledge. It's a long shot to think the Court can help in any manner. If ZeiiMed's lawyers swear the documents are gone forever, there is no way to prove the falsity of their position. Even if the Court ordered an independent computer expert to identify and explain what happened, there is still no way to conclusively establish that ZeiiMed released the worm. Clark knows what happened but he's not talking and probably never will. Nonetheless, I am committed to proceeding with the litigation as best I can. I owe that to Mrs. Dudley.

Strange and unforeseen things tend to happen when dealing with ZeiiMed. Maybe, I'll get lucky and something big will break my way. Like I told Mary, if everything does go to hell in a handbasket, I can always hunt down Edison once again and strangle the truth out of him. With each passing moment, this becomes a more and more appealing option, although it will be difficult to explain to Kim, Mary and Melissa how I ended up in hand-to-hand combat with Edison. Again.

I'll think of something to tell the three of them. I always do. I guess that's one of the reasons I became a lawyer. The other reason was a desire to meet female lawyers who are smart and want to dominate and subdue male lawyers.

-24-

I called Suzanna Nudbello the next day.

"It's so good to hear from you. I'm glad you're safe and sound," Suzanna said.

"Well, I'm safe, but I'm not sure how sound I am. Your friend and colleague, John Standish Clark, came darn close to killing me out of revenge for the injuries Edison incurred in the Ramble," I responded.

"Clark's a lunatic. I can't believe he committed such a hideous act. I had no idea he was so unstable," Suzanna replied.

"Are you saying that ZeiiMed and your law firm had no knowledge of what Clark was going to do?" I asked.

"Absolutely. I knew nothing and my client knew nothing. If we had learned of his deranged plans, we would have immediately called the police. As it stands now, he's been fired from the firm and I will cooperate with the authorities in his criminal prosecution by making his files and computers available. I understand there maybe some pictures of sexual abuse of children. Look, he went off the deep end and no one saw it was coming," she continued, pleased that her lies sounded so credible.

"I think Tweed, Fox & Fortune should conduct a special investigation of its attorney staff," I suggested. "In the last year, two of your senior lawyers have been killed or seriously injured while working on ZeiiMed matters. You should be concerned about your own life expectancy now that you are the replacement senior counsel for ZeiiMed," I said, hoping to alarm her about her client's use of physical violence for failure.

"Don't be silly. Clark was both a pervert and a psychotic who went to great lengths to hide his disorders," she responded.

"Okay. I'll drop it. Now let's get to the next subject that you probably also know nothing about. All the documents

ZeiiMed sent have mysteriously vanished into thin air. I want you to resend everything."

"I already talked to Mary Douglas about this. ZeiiMed's documents are gone also. We don't know how or why, except it's clear some sort of computer worm was involved," Suzanna responded.

"You're telling me ZeiiMed has permanently and completely lost every document relevant to the design, manufacture and implant of the HIDs?" I asked incredulously.

"Yes, exactly. We hired computer experts to investigate what happened, but the bottom line is that the documents no longer exist, with no hardcopy version in existence," she explained.

"I want a conference call with the Judge. I've never heard of such a thing. ZeiiMed caused this to happen and I will eventually prove it beyond any reasonable doubt. You know damn well Clark was involved. He was in my office the day ZeiiMed sent the documents. He did something. I don't know what, but I will find out."

"Fine. Set up a conference call with the Judge right now. Cry all you want, but I can't play God and recreate what no longer exists."

Within half an hour, the Honorable Douglas Horton Horowitz agreed to speak with us. It was unusual for the Judge to be so accommodating on such short notice, but I guess the mention of ZeiiMed and its high-priced lawyers commanded some attention.

> THE COURT: Hello, this is Judge Horowitz. It has come to my attention that there is a problem with regard to the HID documents.
>
> MR. BRADFORD: Thank you for taking the time to speak with us. Suzanna Nudbello, counsel for ZeiiMed, is also on the line. The issue is as follows: ZeiiMed electronically produced on February 23, 2011, over 750,000 documents attached to emails. However, by the end of the day, all the documents had magically disappeared from my firm's computers and apparently

also from ZeiiMed's computers. I'm told the documents were irretrievably lost. As a result, I request authorization to make a motion striking the Answer of ZeiiMed, with the Entry of Judgment against ZeiiMed for a failure to produce the documents required by both this Court and New York law.

JUDGE HOROWITZ: Ms. Nudbello, what is your solution to the mystery of the lost documents?

MS. NUDBELLO: Thank you, Your Honor. Unfortunately, I don't have an answer to the mystery of the great document disappearance. Some kind of belligerent computer worm infected both party's computers. I'm not blaming anyone because we don't know how it happened. I will swear to this under oath in an Affidavit to be filed with the Court. My client wants to put this behind them and proceed with the deposition discovery ordered by this Court, without the HID documents.

JUDGE HOROWITZ: I want to emphasize that this is the first time I ever heard of disappearing documents and apparently Jane Marple, otherwise known as Miss Marple, is not available to help. As a result, I want a forensic computer expert, paid by both parties, to conduct an independent investigation of what occurred and submit a report to the Court. Next, I am ordering the depositions to proceed, documents or no documents. Until I review the expert's report, I will not authorize the filing of a Motion against ZeiiMed. I give great credibility to Ms. Nudbello's representation that ZeiiMed did not cause this very unusual situation. That aside, I would like to express my relief that Mr. Bradford is back on his feet after the horrific episode with Mr. Clark that I read about in the newspaper.

Ms. Nudbello, I want to emphasize that you are on notice. If there is any further irrational behavior by one of the attorneys in your firm, I will consider a Motion to Dismiss all ZeiiMed's defenses based on attorney misconduct. Do I make myself clear?

MS. NUDBELLO: Yes, Your Honor. Mr. Clark's actions were reprehensible and do not reflect the very professional conduct of all other attorneys at Tweed, Fox & Fortune. I can't explain why Mr. Clark attacked Mr. Bradford because we simply don't know why and Mr. Clark is physically unable to speak because of his injuries. In fact, Mr. Clark will probably never speak again and will be disabled for life.

MR. BRADFORD: Your Honor, I appreciate your thoughtful comments about my recovery. However, the Court is forcing me to proceed to depositions with both hands tied behind me. How can I conduct a deposition without any documents?

JUDGE HOROWITZ: Come on, Mr. Bradford. You are a famous litigator who has successfully litigated against ZeiiMed in the past. If there is a legally sufficient class of people harmed by ZeiiMed's HID, I'm sure you will be able to prove it. Ms. Nudbello has been very cooperative and I'm confident she will continue to be so. At the last Conference, I granted you an opportunity to conduct discovery rather than have the Court dismiss Mrs. Dudley's Complaint. So, I suggest you proceed as best you can in a professional and diligent fashion.

Ms. Nudbello, I don't want to read about this case in the newspapers again. Both counsel shall act civilly or face my wrath. It was a pleasure speaking to you both. I want the first deposition conducted within thirty days. I look forward to

> presiding over the trial of the case. Goodbye and good day.

The conference call ended. I was out of choices. All I could do was proceed with the depositions of the ZeiiMed representatives and hope for the best.

The next day, I served a legal document on ZeiiMed's lawyers requiring the first deposition to proceed on April 6, 2011.

Here we go again. It always gets my blood flowing to obtain sworn deposition testimony from a ZeiiMed witness. Of course, as a rule, ZeiiMed witnesses never provide a straight story and every other word is a lie. But, my job is to expose the untruths.

Without any documents, it will be difficult, but I intend to fully enjoy my interrogation of ZeiiMed.

-25-

On the morning of April 6, 2011, I appeared at the downtown office of Tweed, Fox & Fortune located on the Hudson River at Two World Financial Center, 30th floor, to conduct the scheduled deposition of a ZeiiMed witness.

The conference room contained a rectangular table with eight dark leather armchairs. Sam Jenkins, the video operator, and Judy Connolly, the stenographer, were already in the room setting up their equipment. I had previously worked with both of them when deposing ZeiiMed on prior occasions in the earlier lawsuit. I had called them again because both were very accommodating.

"Mr. Bradford, good to see you. Thanks for calling us again. Is your eye okay? It looks real sore. I hope that didn't happen during a deposition. There does seem to be a lot of yelling by lawyers whenever a person from ZeiiMed testifies, but I'm hoping it's peaceful today," Sam noted.

"I'm feeling better, thanks. I promise I'll be on my best behavior today. Since the new lawyer for ZeiiMed is a lady, I'm required to act like a gentleman. At least, I'll try."

Sam had on a black muscle tee shirt, which accentuated his bulging upper body. His beard was thicker and longer since I saw him last.

"Hello, Mr. Bradford, it's always a pleasure to work with you," said Judy Connolly.

As usual, her long, straight hair hid a good portion of her narrow face. I can't figure out how she can type with her hair in front of her eyes.

"Nice to see you also. I promise to make your job easy today by not talking at the same time as the witness."

"I appreciate that. I haven't met a stenographer yet that can type everything that is said when two people are speaking simultaneously," Judy responded.

"Hello, everyone," Ms. Nudbello said, as she entered the conference room. She was attractively dressed in a pastel blue blouse and a short white skirt, with a 14k gold, rope chain necklace. I made sure I didn't stare.

Ms. Nudbello continued, "I would like you to meet the ZeiiMed witness who will testify today, Dr. Howard Heeled."

"Good morning, Dr. Heeled. My name is Brian Bradford and I'll be asking the questions today."

"Great, I look forward to it. Let's get cracking," Dr. Heeled responded.

Dr. Heeled made an impressive appearance. His thick gray hair was combed into overlapping waves that extended from the top of his forehead to the back of his head. He had a full face, but thin lips and a smile that showed no teeth. There was a mound of flesh below his left eyebrow that drooped down to cover his eyelid and the top of the eye. It created an impression of curiosity and constant skepticism. His bright gold tie, gold cuff links and dark blue suit projected a sense of professional success. His most unusual feature was a small brown birthmark above each of his eyebrows.

Suzanna was observing my swollen eye and said, "You really did get smashed in the eye. I'm sorry, it looks terribly sore. I can't believe that creep Clark would do such a horrible thing." She started to move closer to me, possibly to kiss me on the cheek. I casually stepped back a little. She proceeded no further. Depositions and kissing don't mix. Then again, maybe I should have made an exception to the rule.

We took seats at the conference table, with Dr. Heeled directly across the table from me. Everyone was ready. The deposition began.

PROCEEDINGS

THE VIDEOGRAPHER: This is the videotape deposition of Dr. Howard Heeled, to be conducted by Brian Bradford, counsel for the Plaintiff Martha Dudley in the litigation pending against ZeiiMed in the Supreme Court of the State of New York, County of New York. This deposition is being held at the downtown offices of Tweed, Fox & Fortune in New York City. My name is Sam Jenkins and I'm the video specialist. The court reporter today is Judy Connolly. We are on the record at 10:05 a.m. on April 6, 2011. The court reporter will proceed to swear in the witness.

THE REPORTER: Raise your right hand, please. Do you solemnly swear that the testimony you are about to give today will be the truth, the whole truth and nothing but the truth, so help you God?

THE WITNESS: I do.

EXAMINATION BY BRIAN BRADFORD

Q: Good morning, Dr. Heeled. How are you?

A: Good morning. I'm doing great. Thanks for asking.

Q: My name is Brian Bradford and I represent the Plaintiff in this lawsuit. I'll be asking you a series of questions. If, at anytime, you don't understand a question, please let me know. We can take a break anytime you wish. However, if there is a pending question, you must answer it before we stop. Is this acceptable to you?

A: Yes, quite.

Q: Are you represented by counsel here today?

A: Yes, my lawyer is the very charming and very capable, Suzanna Nudbello, sitting right next to me.

MS. NUDBELLO: I am appearing here today as counsel for Dr. Heeled. The Court ordered that ZeiiMed be deposed and Dr. Heeled has been selected as ZeiiMed's corporate representative for the deposition. Since we do not have the usual stack of documents for the witness to review, I hope that your questions get right to the point so we can finish by lunch.

MR. BRADFORD: Thank you, Ms. Nudbello. I will continue my questioning now.

Q: Are you currently employed?

A: Yes, I am the Head Orthopedic Surgical Consultant at ZeiiMed and the primary designer of the metal-on-metal hip implant Device manufactured by MendMed, a ZeiiMed subsidiary. My lawyer told me to mention that ZeiiMed takes full responsibility for MendMed and the Device.

Q: For simplicity on the record, I will refer to the metal-on-metal hip implant Device as the HID, H-I-D, short for Hip Implant Device. Is that acceptable?

A: Yes, that's fine.

Q: Did you hold the same position at ZeiiMed when the HID was first released by MendMed in 2003?

A: Yes.

Q: Did ZeiiMed test the HID for performance and safety before making it available for implant in humans?

A: ZeiiMed, through its subsidiary, is the largest seller worldwide of medical devices, including the HID. The research and testing was exhaustive. I should know, because the HID was my baby. I invented it. I designed it and I successfully implanted it in patients many, many times.

Q: Isn't it a fact that ZeiiMed stopped producing the HID in 2010 when the design defects led to a failure rate of 50%?

A: Don't be absurd. We did not cease production for that reason. We did so based on a corporate business decision to focus our resources on the development of other medical devices that could be used by a greater number of people.

Q: So, is it fair to say you weren't making enough money on the HID, so you decided to cease manufacturing it?

A: Yes, not enough people were using the HID to make it sufficiently profitable.

Q: And isn't it true that the reason it wasn't profitable is because doctors wouldn't use it because it was unsafe?

A: No, absolutely not. The HID successfully did what it was intended to do, but there was declining demand due to numerous competing devices on the market that were not completely made of metal.

Q: You are referring to the HID made with plastics and ceramics at points of contact between the cup and the ball?

A: Yes, exactly.

Q: Isn't it a fact that the grinding of the metal parts in the metal-on-metal HID caused a release of toxic ions of cobalt and chromium that are poisonous at certain levels of exposure?

MS. NUDBELLO: Are you asking the question in general or are you asking with regard to Martha Dudley's present conditions? I object unless we get clarification on this.

MR. BRADFORD: Let's start with a general response, then we will address Mrs. Dudley.

Q: Will you please answer the question?

MS. NUDBELLO: Go ahead and respond in general terms.

A: The question is almost impossible to answer in such general terms. When you grind metal against metal, you may get some release of metal micro-particles, but no one is saying they are toxic or poisonous or above a safe level.

Q: With regard to Mrs. Dudley, have you examined the medical records and hospital reports generated by the doctors that implanted the HID and treated her post-surgery?

A: Yes, I have.

MS. NUDBELLO: For the record, I will note that the medical records of Mrs. Dudley were obtained from Mr. Bradford and sent to me in hardcopy form. These documents were not part of the electronic documents produced by ZeiiMed that were the subject of the Great Document Disappearance Mystery.

MR. BRADFORD: Thank you for the clarity and the humor.

Q: Did Mrs. Dudley's medical records indicate levels of cobalt and chromium that were several times higher than what is considered a medically safe level?

A: For cobalt, a safe maximum level in the blood is 2 micrograms per liter. Mrs. Dudley's level was 52.6. Chromium has a normal range up to .4 and Mrs. Dudley registered 24.5. Based on these findings, I would say she had unsafe levels of these micro-particles.

Q: Isn't it a fact that the friction of the metal ball against the thick metal rim of the cup caused the high level of toxic substances in her blood?

A: No, that's simply not true. There are numerous reasons and numerous causes of the toxicity. Mrs. Dudley smoked for over twenty years. For most of her adult life, she worked as the receptionist and bookkeeper at a local auto body shop. The auto body shop was in a small building. No effort was made to prevent or limit the toxic contamination created by the collision repair work from spreading into the public area where Mrs. Dudley worked. It was all one big open area. She was exposed to industrial spray painting, as well as the cutting and sand blasting of metals as repairs were conducted. She was slowly poisoned at work from many hazardous materials, including cobalt and chromium. That is the reason for her kidney failure and tissue damage around the HID that was implanted.

Q: Isn't it a fact that ZeiiMed received reports from the medical profession concluding that the metal fragments released by the HID were due to the faulty design of a cup that was too small and too shallow in comparison to the ball, with a thick rim on the cup and a groove inside the cup that also increased the friction?

A: No, never. If the cup is properly inserted in the hip at a forty-five degree angle, there is no problem. Some doctors were not skilled enough to do so, resulting in a few minor problems. However, through education and medical demonstrations, that problem was solved. The groove inside the cup assisted the doctor in the installation process and was not a design flaw.

Q: Isn't it a fact that ZeiiMed switched to ceramic and plastic components for the HID because doctors worldwide refused to use the metal-on-metal HID and told ZeiiMed exactly that in reports to ZeiiMed?

A: Your question is ridiculous. I would never let ZeiiMed sell a dangerous medical device.

Q: Mrs. Dudley is so ill she cannot survive an operation to remove the metal-on-metal HID. She can't walk, can hardly stand and is in constant pain. In your opinion, the HID didn't contribute to these conditions?

A: No, it did not. Mrs. Dudley's pain is caused by two problems. First, the tissue around the hip is infected. The initial infection may have been caused by lack of a sterile environment during surgery. Second, as you know, the metal cup is inserted into the hip and the metal ball rotates within the cup during movement. Mrs. Dudley's cup was placed at the wrong angle in the hip so the ball is only partially in the cup, causing subluxation, essentially a dislocation of the hip. So, you see, the surgeon who installed the HID may be faulted, but not the Device itself and certainly not ZeiiMed.

Q: It seems you put all the blame on Mrs. Dudley and her doctor, while swearing under oath that your HID did no harm. Is that your position here today?

A: Yes, that is exactly my position.

Q: And you've never read any medical study that found the type of injury and pain suffered by Mrs. Dudley was caused by the metal-on-metal HID?

A: I have not.

Q: You know what? Someday I'm going to make you regret that lie and all your other lies. You understand that?

A: You bastard. How dare you call me a liar. Who do you think you are? Your accusation is outrageous.

Q: I am a lawyer questioning a pathological liar who thinks I'll never find the documents necessary to prove the lie. You are wrong. What do you think of that?

MS. NUDBELLO: Objection. You are harassing the witness. He has truthfully answered all your questions.

A: How dare you talk to me in that manner, Mr. Bradford. You goddam lawyers are all the same. You should be ashamed of yourself.

Q: The real truth is that you are a liar and I promise I'll prove it sooner or later. Then, I will proclaim with a smile, 'Told you so.' Has that gotten through your thick cranium and into your deceitful brain cells?

A: Go to hell.

MS. NUDBELLO: Stop it. This deposition is over, now!

A: You probably deserved that swollen eye, Mr. Bradford. It was probably done by another person you verbally abused. And I'm going to give you another swollen eye to match.

Dr. Heeled immediately lifted his arm from the table, cocked it slightly backwards and then launched a punch with a clenched fist. Luckily, I saw it coming because I knew I had pushed him to the edge. I opened my right hand and grabbed Dr. Heeled's fist with my palm and fingers, surrounding the doctor's closed hand like a baseball glove, stopping its forward progress cold. I then snapped the doctor's clenched fist upward as the bones in his wrist cracked from the force. He screamed in pain. I released my grip and let go. The doctor tucked his injured wrist close to his body.

"That's all on videotape, Dr. Heeled," I stated. "It should play well on the Internet. The police should also find it interesting. You ought to be arrested for assault. This deposition is completed. I'll ask you more questions once I find the documents your employer magically made disappear."

I left the conference room, quickly followed by Suzanna.

"You acted like an idiot. What's wrong with you?" she asked. "I thought we had an agreement to handle this litigation professionally. I admired your skills as a litigator and I thought I liked you personally. Now I'm embarrassed by your behavior."

"That's all very nice. I also enjoyed your company and was challenged by your abilities as a lawyer. But that's all changed. ZeiiMed somehow buried every HID document and you were involved in the scheme. I'm going to figure it out and prove ZeiiMed intentionally destroyed the documents and intentionally lied to the public about the HID," I responded, with my temper once again getting the better of me.

"That's not true! Don't you dare accuse me like that."

"It's too late for your delusions and deceit," I said. "Dr. Heeled is lying and you are lying. I'll make you both regret it one day."

I left the building.

Suzanna walked down the corridor to her office and picked up the phone. She dialed her client.

"He's convinced we destroyed the documents and he's on a crusade to prove it and expose ZeiiMed. He can't be allowed to continue. He has got to be taken out," Suzanna said into the phone.

"I know. I'll take care of it. Consider it done. He can't hide from us and can't avoid the inevitable," Edison replied.

As I walked from Two World Financial Center to my law office on Wall Street, I realized how stupid I had been to show my cards. ZeiiMed and its lawyers were lying, but I shouldn't have told them I knew of their lies. Why tip ZeiiMed off to my plan? Why tell my adversary that I was going to move heaven and earth to find the documents? Why tell a diabolical executive of ZeiiMed that I will do whatever is necessary to recover the documents and reveal his deceit? Big mistake.

The clock was ticking. ZeiiMed will now react by doing anything and everything to stop me from finding the documents and learning the truth. I need to move fast, faster than ZeiiMed.

I have a plan.

To make it work, I needed to see Meadhbh.

-26-

Meadhbh had mentioned she was returning to work at *Très Bien*. I called the restaurant one morning and received confirmation that she was back to her regular shift at the bar.

I didn't want to talk to her on the phone. I wanted to see her. I wanted to see her back to normal, recovered from the serious head injuries inflicted by Edison's stooges.

It was a spring-like evening in mid-April. I took the subway uptown, still dressed in my suit after a long day at the office.

I stood outside *Très Bien* and looked through the window. Meadhbh was there, serving drinks, talking and smiling. The reality of her return to everyday life was elating. Yet, I was nervous, despite knowing full well that being anxious was silly.

I walked in and stood at my usual spot at the end of the bar. I was staring at her, waiting for her to turn.

She turned. I saw the acknowledgment in her eyes.

She smiled and walked down the bar toward me.

Someone asked her for a drink, but she ignored the request.

Her eyes were like two brilliant peridot, her dimples more pronounced as her smile broadened. She wore a simple white blouse and a short plaid skirt. The white apron tied around her waist did not obstruct the view of her long bare legs.

She reached the end of the bar, but didn't stop. She circled around and stood in front of me.

"Hi, Brian. It's so nice to see you. You've been missed," she said, as we stood face to face.

"Hello, Meadhbh. It's good to see you. It's wonderful you're back to work," I said.

She put her hands on my hips and gently moved closer for full frontal contact. Her lips touched mine. As the kiss continued, I tasted her tears. Our lips separated, but our eyes were only inches apart.

"Well, that was a nice welcome. Why the tears?" I asked.

"Why do you think? I'm happy. Happy to see you. Happy to be well. Happy to be back. Happy to have a moment together," she responded.

"I guess I should stay away more often. It seems to increase the celebration once the prodigal friend returns."

"You are impossible. I'm back and I expect you to visit more often. By the way, I think we are more than friends, but you never seem to get it straight."

"It adds to the excitement and the confusion," I responded.

"I know," she said. "It would be nice if someday we reached an understanding about how we felt."

"I think we just did," I said.

"Forget it–we'll discuss our relationship another time. Thanks again for all your prayers. I'm lucky to have recovered and I count every moment as precious."

"Well, you are precious and your recovery is remarkable. God bless."

Meadhbh walked back behind the bar.

"Since we're back to old times together, what can I get you?" she asked.

"A Bud Light would be great."

"Coming right up, and when I return I'd like to hear the short version of the story behind your black eye," she continued.

Meadhbh returned with the beer.

"It's on me. It's the least I can do in view of your misplaced but valiant effort to avenge my injuries. And speaking of injuries, I'm ready to hear what happened to you."

"As unbelievable as it may sound, ZeiiMed sent an assassin to drown me in my gym pool as payback for the injuries I inflicted on Edison in the Ramble."

"Who was he and what happened?"

"A lawyer who does legal work for ZeiiMed. You saw him in Court at the Fairness Hearing in my first lawsuit against ZeiiMed."

“Since when are lawyers trained as paid combatants? Until I met you, I never heard of lawyers punching each other over disagreements. Does the Bar Association approve of this behavior?” she asked.

“Absolutely, we’re encouraged to assault our adversaries–whoever wins gets the verdict,” I responded sarcastically. “Getting back to my story, the ZeiiMed lawyer, John Standish Clark, attacked me and tried to drown me, although I finally succeeded in subduing him. But, not before he landed a punch to my face. Luckily, my eye is much better now. Previously, it was so swollen I couldn’t see. But, I’m sure it will be as good as ever in a couple of weeks.”

“I hope so. And I can see you haven’t damaged those long, sexy eyelashes. They are your best feature.”

“Best feature? How would you know?” I asked.

“I don’t. But, as we explore more of your features in the future, I’ll let you know if another attribute takes over the top spot,” Meadhbh responded.

“I forgot how our conversations sometimes divert into the unpredictable.” I said.

“You enjoy it or you wouldn’t keep coming back. I have some customers down at the other end of the bar who are salivating for alcohol. I’ll get them drinks and be back in a second. I want to hear the reason you showed up today. You always have an agenda.”

“What do you mean? I just came to see how you were doing.”

“Liar. You could have done that three weeks ago when I returned to work. No, you are here today because something is up. See you in a few. I’ll bring you another beer. Don’t worry, I still love you despite your deficiencies.”

Life does have its twists and turns. I spent the day calling ZeiiMed’s lawyer and Dr. Heeled a bunch of liars. Now Meadhbh accuses me of doing the same thing. Doesn’t anyone tell the truth anymore? Now I have to convince Meadhbh that I was being honest, even though I wasn’t. The worst part of telling a fib is having your falsehood discovered. Now I have to convince Meadhbh that I didn’t tell a falsehood and she didn't discover that I told a falsehood.

Meadhbh returned with another beer.

"Okay. Proceed. What can I help you with?" Meadhbh asked.

"I want to again emphasize that it was not my intent to come here tonight just so I could ask a favor," I said.

"Now that you feel better having said that, let's move on. I still don't believe you, but get to the point."

"As I mentioned, I'm convinced Edison has plans to take me out again. He failed in his attempt to have Clark do the job, but we both know it won't end there. As a result, I need to have a discussion with Edison about this sensitive issue of my continued good health," I started to explain.

"Another face to face with Edison? Why bother? You know ZeiiMed won't stop regardless of whatever lies he tells you. I think you are wasting your time there."

"You're probably right. ZeiiMed has a history of not sticking to truces. But, there's another reason I need a private conversation with Edison. It's kind of a long story, but I'll try to keep it short. As I think I mentioned in your hotel room, I've started another lawsuit against ZeiiMed. This one is for damages resulting from the defective metal-on-metal hip implant Device I refer to as the HID."

"Yes, I remember. I also remember I offered to help any way I could. Me and my big mouth," Meadhbh added.

"Somehow, ZeiiMed was able to destroy all its HID documents, probably by use of some kind of undetectable computer worm. So far, ZeiiMed has been able to get away with this. Of course, no documents means I have no chance to succeed in the lawsuit. However, I believe that ZeiiMed still has a copy of the documents somewhere. Of course, ZeiiMed's lawyers deny, deny and deny. So, I need to get the truth out of Edison, one way or the other, about where the HID documents are and how I can get them."

"How nice. More physical violence. I assume you intend to torture Edison until he coughs up the information. You lawyers simply never stop beating each other up."

"I know you're making a joke. But, when it comes to Edison, he deserves whatever comes his way."

"You'll probably end up with another black eye," Meadhbh commented.

"Probably. If I'm lucky that will be all that happens to me."

"Where do you want to meet him?" Meadhbh asked.

"It can't be anywhere in New York. I've got a Sergeant Melissa Black watching my every move. One more bloody incident and I think my luck will run out with her."

"Have you slept with her?"

"What kind of a question is that. I'm serious here."

"So am I. It seems every woman you meet develops some kind of romantic attachment. Kind of like what happened to us."

"That's not true," I insisted.

"What's not true–our romantic attachment or that you're romantic with every woman who crosses your path?" Meadhbh asked, as she continued her interrogation.

"I don't know. I'm not sure I understand the question," I said.

"Wrong answer. You should have said our romantic attachment is definitely true, but the latter comment about every woman who crosses your path is not," Meadhbh explained.

"Can I get back to my story now?" I asked.

"Yes, but you certainly are easy to throw off the track. You were saying you wanted to have your confrontation with Edison outside of New York."

"That's right. And, of course, this will be a surprise meeting. He can't be aware that I'm after him until I'm face to face with him."

"I understand. I'm going to serve a few drinks to my customers and we'll discuss this further," she said.

I drank my beer and watched the flat screen television. Meadhbh was back in less than ten minutes.

"I've solved your problem," Meadhbh said.

"What?" I asked.

"You heard me. I've taken care of everything."

"Go on," I said.

"Edison is taking a vacation in three days to Tortola in the British Virgin Islands. He is staying at a resort called Long Bay. It's a very secluded, very remote hotel right on a beautiful beach with gently breaking waves. I think it's an ideal spot for you to privately approach him."

"I agree. It's perfect. How did you get this information?" I asked.

"As you well know, Edison is a regular here in the dining room. After I returned to work, I was concerned about how we'd interact. On my second evening back at work, he approached me. He said that he was aware that some people blamed ZeiiMed for my injuries. He wanted me to know that he did not know of the assault or approve of it in any way. He mentioned that ZeiiMed investigated the incident to uncover the identities of those involved. He said ZeiiMed likes to administer justice in its own way. ZeiiMed identified the people involved and inflicted severe physical punishment on the perpetrators. The ZeiiMed investigative report, minus the part about the punishment, was provided to the NYPD."

"That's quite a story. Usually I don't believe a word Edison says, but I'll bet ZeiiMed did beat up your assailants. Obviously, it served some purpose for ZeiiMed, if only to warn the world that Edison's favorite bartender isn't to be touched again," I said.

"I hope you don't take the warning," Meadhbh quickly responded.

"I haven't so far. But now I'm worried what might happen if Edison spots me kissing you. Seriously though, he clearly doesn't want any problems at his favorite restaurant."

"There is more to the story," Meadhbh continued. "After our conversation, Edison became very friendly. Each night he dines here, he now stops by the bar for a few minutes of idle chatter. About a week ago, he mentioned his planned vacation to Tortola and the name of the resort. I though he was going to ask me to join him."

"That's unbelievable."

"I know. Are you jealous?" Meadhbh asked.

"No. Well, maybe a little. Then again, maybe a lot. I'm not sure."

"You really do have a problem getting a handle on your emotions," Meadhbh added.

"I will leave that comment alone," I responded.

"Back to business, the information about his trip is just what I needed. As always, you are a great help. I can see why Edison likes you," I said, returning the verbal volley.

"Once again, I'm watching you leave for another encounter with Edison. Your last go around in the Ramble nearly killed you. Even on vacation in Tortola, you know Edison will have bodyguards everywhere. Keep your composure, don't lose your temper and don't take a swing at him. Do we have a deal?" Meadhbh asked.

"Yes, of course. I'm going to be cordial. And, no matter what happens, I won't lay a finger on him or his henchmen," I promised, crossing my fingers.

"I'm going to pretend you're being truthful so I can sleep at night," Meadhbh responded.

"I will call you as soon as I return from Tortola," I promised.

"Call? Are you kidding? Stop by in person at closing so we can go out. Also, don't fight the urge to buy me an exotic little trinket while in the Caribbean."

"Sounds great. I'll get you a coconut, although customs may confiscate it. Seriously, I will be careful and I'll come by when I return."

Meadhbh walked me out the front door. On the sidewalk, we hugged, we kissed, we exchanged affection without words.

My personal life was again becoming terribly complicated while, at the same time, my legal battle with ZeiiMed was escalating into a personal vendetta.

Hopefully, I will overcome both challenges.

-27-

Four days later, I was on a jet out of JFK heading for St. Thomas. I had booked a reservation on a ferry from St. Thomas to the West End of Tortola.

Kim's reaction to my trip was surprising. Normally, I would have anticipated a heartfelt request not to go, coupled with a warning that my prior encounters with Edison resulted in significant blood loss to one or both of us. Not this time. Her basic response was, "Do what you think is best." So much for a romantic departure scene. I assumed this meant Kim's relationship with Dr. Joe was progressing. Maybe she was having the good doctor over for dinner. My God–I hope he's not going to sleep in my bed while I'm gone.

Mary Douglas said I was crazy to have any contact with John Edison.

Mary's reasoning was more legal than emotional. She pointed out that the Disciplinary Rules governing attorney behavior strictly forbade me from speaking with Edison without ZeiiMed's counsel present. I pointed out that maybe one of his bodyguards had a law degree. On a serious note, I also mentioned that ZeiiMed intentionally destroyed over 700,000 documents after presumably creating a hidden electronic depository with duplicates of everything. So, why was I worried about a technical violation of an ethics rule when ZeiiMed commits a fraud on the Court and my client, but doesn't bat an eye?

Mary didn't have an answer, but she repeated that banging heads with Edison wasn't the solution either. She wished me luck and mentioned that injury should be avoided at all cost because the local Peebles Hospital in Roadtown, the capital and financial center of Tortola, may not have the most advanced medical technology available. If I was stabbed, shot or dismembered, Mary recommended Dr. Robin Tattersall, the Director of the Bougainvillea Clinic, in Roadtown. Although once a very prominent reconstruction surgeon and male model, Mary said he is now retired from the operating room, but would be happy to recommend other very competent surgeons at the Clinic. He came to Tortola from England in 1965 and founded the Clinic in 1973.

After landing in St. Thomas, I took a short taxi ride to the ferry terminal and purchased a ticket on a ferry called the Native Sun. The ferry ride was about an hour to Roadtown. I remained on the ferry until it stopped at the West End terminal. The ferry runs at high speed with a constant banging of rough waves against the elevated bow. This nautical disturbance made it difficult to consume my rum punch, heavy on the rum, light on punch. I managed, however. The key is not to gulp. Small sips while on the high seas.

Tortola is only 11.5 miles long, but very mountainous with winding roads that wrap around the peaks to provide spectacular aerial views of beaches unique in nature for their beauty and panorama. It is the largest of 60 British Virgin Islands and is located about 60 miles to the east of Puerto Rico.

I disembarked at the West End ferry terminal on the south side of Tortola. I needed to travel to the north side to reach the Long Bay Resort where Edison was staying. This required a taxi ride over the great and very challenging Zion Hill.

The taxi driver warned me not to be afraid. The road over Zion Hill consisted of an array of consecutive hairpin curves with 180° turns. The curves are so sharp and narrow that it was impossible to see a descending vehicle as we entered the same curve on the ascent. Only one vehicle at a time can negotiate the curve because it not only turns sharply, it also spirals upward as you climb 1,100 feet towards the top. The protocol is to stop and honk before the turn to alert the oncoming and unseen traffic approaching in the opposite direction. Driving on the left side of the road only adds to the complications. There are no guard rails and no break-down lane. Your vehicle is either on the narrow road or in the air free-falling down the side of a steep embankment.

Having survived the climb over Zion Hill, I was now on the north side of the island. In the distance was Bomba's Surfside Shack. The shack and bar were pieced together from driftwood, old mismatched bar furniture and lingerie to create a cozy, local beachfront watering hole. Opened in 1976, it is now famous worldwide for its Full Moon Party that attracts hordes of people for all night dancing and drinking.

The taxi turned left onto the North Coast Road at the Zion Hill Road intersection and proceeded past Sebastian's On the Beach. Sebastian's is an informal and very comfortable European-style, two-story hotel and restaurant that cannot be any closer to the water without falling in. The outdoor bar has a terrace that is only a few feet from the approaching water of Little Apple Bay. The turbulence of the breaking waves propels the water over the sandy beach until it splashes against the stone foundation of the hotel.

The taxi continued through the picturesque village of small shacks called Little Apple Bay and up the quickly elevating road just past the village. At the top of the ridge, there was an unobstructed view of Long Bay Beach, one of the most impressive beachfront areas in all the world. The white sand of Long Bay Beach continues in a straight line for about a mile, with gently breaking waves in a symphony of nature that mixes a continuous stream of white caps with the clear turquoise sea. The stretch of beach ends in the distance as the lush tropical mountain called Belmont Point rises from the water. The white sand beach itself is only about fifteen feet wide, with a dense row of palm trees providing ample shade the full length of this seemingly unending stretch of tropical paradise.

I checked in at the front desk of the Long Bay Beach Resort. I was assigned Room 596, a beachfront deluxe accommodation on the second floor of a two-story lodge at the water's edge. A wooden staircase on the side of the building led to the entrance door of my room. Since my beachfront building was the first in a row of structures to my left, the private balcony in my room provided an unobstructed view of the water and the beach area to the right.

My first problem was finding Edison and confronting him in a private setting before he realizes I'm here. If Edison spots me before I am able to approach him, the whole plan will be off. Edison would either flee the island in a flash or feed me to the sharks. So, I won't be hanging out all day in a lounge chair by the pool.

Assuming I solved the first challenge, the second problem was to decide what I will say to Edison when I confront him. Also, knowing that Edison will be unreceptive to our informal meeting, how will I force Edison to provide the information I want? Do I punch him? Probably not. Besides, his face is already a mess of broken bones from our last go around. Stab him? Probably not. I only have a dull knife from the room's kitchenette that wouldn't do the job. Grab a large tree limb to beat him with? Again, probably not. If Edison starts bleeding, hotel management will certainly want to take him to the hospital and contact the authorities. I don't think it's a good idea to get arrested in a third world country. I can imagine the cinder block jail cell baking in the hot sun without air conditioning. So, the bottom line is that I don't know what I'm doing or how I'm going to do it. Too bad that Kim, Meadhbh and Mary didn't talk me out of this half-baked idea.

The next morning I woke just before dawn. I think it was the roosters. Then again, I probably didn't drink enough rum before going to bed. I stood on the balcony just as first light appeared. To my right, I noticed the figure of a man partially obstructed from view by the leaves of a large sea grape tree. The man was walking along the beach as he tossed food to a group of chickens following him. At first it was hard to tell, but then it became unmistakable. It was John Edison.

I resisted the urge to immediately run down the stairs and confront him. It was a better strategy to observe his activities to make sure I wasn't being lured into an ambush. Edison was dressed in a tee shirt and shorts. He looked remarkably trim and muscular. Gone was the extra weight in his mid-section as well as the swollen, pudgy limbs. He was barefoot and limped slightly, probably from the knife I plunged through his foot in the Ramble.

For an hour Edison just stood at the water's edge, feeding the chickens, talking to the chickens and staring at the water. There were no bodyguards in sight and only one or two people walking casually along the beach. It seemed a perfect spot for my plan. Hopefully, Edison would return tomorrow. It was now too late in the morning to confront him. People were starting to gather on chaise lounges scattered along the beach.

I was up before dawn the next day. I dressed in a navy blue swim suit and yellow tee shirt with the slogan in blue letters on the front: "Give It Your All–The End Of The Line Is Getting Closer." I used it for inspiration.

The sun had just broken the horizon when Edison again appeared through the grove of sea grape trees, feeding the chickens from a plastic bag of crumbs. I didn't waste a second. I quietly but quickly climbed down the stairs on the side of the building. The leaves of the low-lying trees now blocked my view. I walked ten feet through the foliage to the water's edge. I was three feet from Edison. His back was facing me. He didn't sense my presence.

"Mr. John Edison. I would like a few moments of your time."

Edison turned towards me.

"Brian Bradford. You do seem to follow me wherever I go. You don't appear to have a recording device on, so I'll also mention that I have done my best to kill you, but have failed so far, as you are abundantly aware. However, that will change shortly. Your shirt should read: 'The End of the Line Is Very Close.' And it's not just you who is targeted. I'm after everyone near and dear to you as part of my storm of retribution."

Edison's face was a mess. His cheekbones were sunken into his skull, with his over-sized nose swollen and extended. Even so, his laser eyes were still menacing with thick ice-blue rings wrapped around black pupils small as a pin head. I had caused his facial deformity, but felt no remorse. I cannot forget for a second that Edison's prime objective has always been to inflict harm on me and mine.

"I came here for a reason. The sooner I accomplish my goal, the sooner I'll be gone. I don't intend to get into a physical altercation, providing you answer my questions," I stated.

"What do you want, you son-of-a-bitch? Since you are the one close to death, I'll grant a dying man's final question," Edison responded.

"The documents. You somehow released a virus or worm that destroyed the ZeiiMed documents with regard to the Device. But, I'm sure ZeiiMed has a copy of the documents hidden somewhere. Maybe your lawyers don't know where, but you know where. Tell me now and spare yourself the agony of having the information beaten out of you."

"You are such a fool. I'm telling you nothing. One scream and my bodyguards will be here in a flash."

Before Edison could finish his sentence, the rage and anger I was trying to suppress erupted uncontrollably, overtaking my self-control. My arms and legs suddenly became invigorated with a surge of energy that created a strength beyond what I thought possible.

I grabbed Edison's sickly, thin neck with both hands and tossed him into the water. He tried to stand, but fell. His scarred foot couldn't hold his weight. I bent over him in about three feet of water and forced his face under water. His eyes widened and fear spread over his face. After a few moments, his mouth opened as he could no longer hold his breath. I let the water flow down his throat for a couple of seconds before pulling his head out of the water. The noises made by his gasps for air sounded like the agonizing cries of a torture chamber victim.

"Tell me where the documents are hidden."

"Fuck you. You should have drowned in that pool. My mistake," Edison said.

"Well, now it's your turn for a little swim," I answered.

I forced him back under water. His body convulsed, his legs trying to kick me as I loomed over him. My right hand squeezed his throat as I punched his stomach with my clenched left hand. I felt the air being forced from his lungs. I again pulled his face out of the water.

"Okay, okay," he gasped, "The documents are in a Cloud run by a vendor we hired. You should know that. I didn't put them under my bed. But, I don't remember the access code or the password for the Cloud. I don't have the information on me and I don't plan on sending it to you. My lawyers don't have access and don't even know that ZeiiMed uses a Cloud. Go ahead, kill me. You'll never make it off this island alive."

Edison was probably correct. He didn't have the security codes with him and I can't kill him because it would get me nowhere other than jail. Damn you, John Edison.

As I let go of his neck, I punched his ugly nose with enough force to hear it snap and bend into his face. He lost consciousness. I dragged his limp body onto the shore and left him on a chaise lounge with a towel over his face. Maybe it will look like he is resting on the beach, at least until the towel soaked through with his blood.

I returned to my room and quickly packed. I grabbed a cab and was on a ferry back to St. Thomas before ZeiiMed had any chance at retaliation.

Hopefully, it will be hours before Edison regains consciousness and discloses my involvement.

Just another beautiful day in a Caribbean paradise.

Next year, I think I'll go to Europe.

-28-

Within a few days after my return, I scheduled a meeting at the office with Herb and Mary. Herb has a background in computer science, in addition to his law degree. My plan was to develop a strategy to obtain the ZeiiMed documents that Edison said were in a "Cloud."

Herb and Mary took seats in my office. Herb was dressed casually and had a slightly disheveled look, along with thick-framed glasses. He appeared to have gained more weight since I worked with him last year. It seemed such a shame. His unhealthy physical state will certainly cause problems before middle age.

Mary looked radiant, as usual. The sunlight in my office gave her blond hair an attractive, almost regal glow. She was dressed in light tan slacks and a black sweater that seemed a bit tight. I guess she didn't consider my meeting very important because she had on flats, rather than heels.

After the usual pleasantries, I began our discussion with a little background information.

"Last week, I had an opportunity to meet with John Edison. We were both on vacation in Tortola in the British West Indies. I asked him if ZeiiMed had a copy of the HID documents destroyed by the computer worm."

"That's quite a leading question," Mary interrupted. "Essentially, you asked Edison if he had committed a felony by hiding documents, destroying documents and then lying to the Court about both. I wouldn't be surprised if he punched you in the nose after an accusation like that."

"Well, to be totally candid, I punched him in the nose and not the other way around. Plus, I nearly drowned him by forcing his head under the clear Caribbean waters until his eyes almost popped out. But, the good news is that he eventually told me that a copy of all the HID documents were electronically sent to a Cloud storage facility before the worm was released."

Mary looked perplexed and immediately chimed in, "Before we get to the Cloud discussion, I would like a few more details about your altercation with Edison. What exactly did you do to him?"

"I told you. He wouldn't answer my question about whether the HID documents still existed. As a result, I was required to physically persuade him to provide the information."

"I see. You applied water torture techniques to the chief executive of a major corporation that is also a defendant in your lawsuit. Why? Because you're convinced the company's lawyers didn't tell the truth when they told the Court the documents don't exist. Is that about the long and short of it?"

"More or less. But, remember it was ZeiiMed that lied to the Court about the computer worm."

"It doesn't excuse your criminal acts."

"It wasn't a crime because I was in a foreign country that hasn't criminally charged me with anything. No charges, no crime. Besides, what's done is done. Let's concentrate on moving forward."

"I agree, but sooner or later one of your battles with Edison is going to result in his death or yours. Either way you lose. Even if you avoid being killed, you'll end up in jail for killing him. If you don't promise me right now that you will keep away from Edison, I'm finding another job. Look, you know I hate the people at ZeiiMed as much as you and I want them brought to their knees. But, I can't live with all the physical violence between our court appearances."

Mary was clearly upset and in need of assurances. I can't risk losing her, so I had to do what was necessary to keep her on the team. The woman saved my life. Mary showed extraordinary bravery in bashing in my assailant's skull with a glass globe right in my office. I can never repay her. Mary is also an excellent lawyer and professionally indispensable to me. Did I mention that she looks great and always smells nice?

I stared directly at Mary, leaned forward, and said, "Of course, you are absolutely correct. From now on, we will handle the litigation by the book and in accordance with the rules of the Court. I will not meet or talk with Edison again. All communications with ZeiiMed will be through ZeiiMed's lawyers. I promise. Please don't even think about leaving."

"Okay. I believe you. I think," Mary said, apparently trying her best to believe my false promises.

"Can we discuss the Cloud now?" Herb asked.

"Yes, of course," I responded. "Tell me what you know about Cloud storage."

"Let's start at the beginning," Herb responded. "Cloud storage refers to a vendor's infrastructure of remote network servers that permit a client to transfer electronic data to the servers for storage. The transfer goes from the client's computers to the off-premises location of the vendor's Cloud servers. It's like renting a storage room for your stuff, except we're dealing with digital, electronic data."

Herb continued, "For example, there is a company called Cloud Storage for Lawyers. In return for a fee, Cloud Storage will create folders in the computer network of the client law firm. Documents are then transferred to the folders electronically, causing the images to be automatically transferred to the off-premises location of Cloud Storage's massive server complex. That is, the documents are no longer on the law firm's computers–they have been sent to a remote location where Cloud Storage has its server network. The beauty of this arrangement is that the law firm can obtain the documents from Cloud Storage in a second, simply by supplying an appropriate ID number and password. Most important, each lawyer's smartphone is programmed into the Cloud network to permit an instantaneous transfer of documents to and from the Cloud servers via a cell phone. Any questions so far?" Herb asked.

"Yes," I said. "Let's assume ZeiiMed transferred all its HID documents to a remote server of a Cloud vendor such as this company, Cloud Storage for Lawyers. Isn't there an electronic footprint that would show the transfer if a computer expert examined the law firm's desktop computers?"

"There would be evidence of the transfer, usually. However, based on what Mary tells me about the computer worm, ZeiiMed was probably able to get around this problem," Herb stated.

"What do you mean?" I asked.

"It's simple. ZeiiMed takes all its HID documents, thousands if not millions of them, makes a duplicate of everything and then puts one copy into the electronic folders supplied by Cloud Storage or some other Cloud vendor. The HID documents are instantaneously transferred to the Cloud. Then the virus or worm is released purposefully by ZeiiMed into its computers. The worm is programmed to destroy all documents in ZeiiMed's computers that are in any way connected to the HID, even the Cloud Storage folders into which the HID documents had been placed for transfer to the Cloud Storage facility off site. Everything is eradicated, including all evidence of the transfer to the Cloud. The electronic trail or footprint is gone. However, one copy of each HID document remains in the Cloud, without any evidence of the transfer. It's the only way that ZeiiMed would be sure that there was no proof that the documents were sent to the Cloud."

"So how does ZeiiMed get the documents back in the event they were needed for some reason?" I asked.

"Like I said, by use of a smartphone programmed to the Cloud's network. But, ZeiiMed can't take the chance of sending an email from the phone to the Cloud vendor requesting the HID documents. The email would leave an electronic trail. Someone like Edison must call the Cloud vendor from his network phone, give a password and tell the Cloud vendor where to send the documents. The Cloud vendor will not respond unless the phone is linked to the Cloud network and the proper password and identification is provided. This is the only manner to access the documents without detection. Anything else would have exposed the company to the risk of getting caught because there would be an identifiable trail if the Cloud vendor received an email sent from any computer or smartphone in ZeiiMed's workplace."

"Thanks, Herb. That was quite interesting. So, assuming we got hold of a smartphone programmed to ZeiiMed's

Cloud servers, we would still need to know the phone number of the Cloud vendor and the password. Correct?"

"Yes," Herb replied. "But I can solve that. You get a ZeiiMed phone already on the Cloud network, and I'll get you the numbers you need to get the documents from the Cloud vendor."

"How? How is that possible?" Mary asked. "I find that hard to believe."

"I'm not sure I should tell you–it's kind of a geek secret among people considered to be highly accomplished in the tech world. I'm part of a very select IT Club so, I have connections unavailable to the rest of the world."

"Come on, Herb. Everything is confidential here. If we are going to live on the outer limits of the law we need a complete understanding of what we are doing and how we are doing it. Spill the beans," I told Herb.

"There is a software vendor called Mobile Intelligence or MI for short. MI put into all mobile phones, with the knowledge of the wireless carriers, a software that records each time a key is pressed so that all keystrokes can be intercepted, recorded and collected, including all phone numbers, credit card numbers and passwords as they are typed on the keyboard by the cell phone's user. It doesn't matter if the smartphone has a physical keyboard or a touch screen. Actually, there are a number of lawsuits because the placement of this software in our phones wasn't disclosed and, even if a user knew, there is no way to turn it off. All I need to do is call one of my tech buddies in the Club, that also happens to work at MI, and ask for the information. I just need the name of the person we are targeting."

"Is this legal," Mary asked.

"I don't ask those questions and I don't want to know," Herb answered. "If we are going to do this, I can't get bogged down by legality questions. The Club's secrets are never revealed, so no one knows or cares if laws are broken. I can't believe I'm even telling you."

"That's not a very lawyer-like response. Any idiot would know it's illegal. You're stealing the target's personal information to obtain documents you can't otherwise get," Mary said, slightly raising her voice.

"Let's keep perspective here," I responded. "ZeiiMed destroyed the HID documents that the Judge said we were entitled to. We're merely doing whatever is necessary to get the documents back so we can win Mrs. Dudley's lawsuit. I'm all in. Let's do it."

"Mary, it's not such a big deal when compared with the privacy violations going on out there in the real world," Herb stated. "Our Club has people who work at the NSA. As a result, the Club has access to massive amounts of non-public information about how the federal government invades our everyday lives and collects our personal, private communications. The NSA also intercepts the calls of various Heads of State, including the President of Brazil. I guess it will all be exposed someday. Someone will eventually steal the internal NSA documents and store them in a safe haven for disclosure to the world. But, until then, every time a telephone call is made or received in America, the NSA has access to all information concerning the call and collects it as part of the war on terror. This month alone, April 2011, the NSA collected over 194 million text messages and stored them on a database for whatever use they want, including surveillance operations. The data includes the location of the text sender and financial information like credit card numbers, as well as the content of the message itself. This goes on every day and makes our little plan look like child's play next to what the big boys do. I say we proceed. Are you in?" Herb questioned.

"Yes, I'm in," Mary answered.

"Good. The target is John Edison of ZeiiMed. Herb, you'll get me the phone number to ZeiiMed's Cloud vendor and the password. Our ZeiiMed files in the office will tell you everything you need to know about him, such as where he lives and the location of his office. I'll figure out a way to physically obtain Edison's cell phone without his knowledge. It will take some work, but I have a friend that will gladly help."

"I can't believe you're going to get your bartender friend involved in this again. Hasn't she done enough? My goodness, the woman was almost beaten to death by ZeiiMed," Mary commented. "Why don't you leave her alone this time?"

"I know. She has done a lot, but she wants to do more. I will protect her, I promise."

"You can't protect her 24/7. If she is injured again, I don't know how you will live with yourself."

"I said I will take care of her and I will. End of story." It seems I get emotional whenever the topic turns to Meadhbh.

"I'll do what's necessary on my end and get the phone number and password to you as soon as I can," Herb said.

"The trial in Mrs. Dudley's case probably won't commence until early 2012. So we have time. Thank you both for your help. Let's talk at least once a week to upgrade our progress," I concluded.

Herb left my office.

Mary remained.

"You know I'm with you on this, but once again we are breaking the law. If we get caught, we will be disbarred and maybe sent to prison. I'll work the case with you and second chair the trial. But never again. This is it. I will no longer do whatever you want just because ZeiiMed is our opponent. I will never touch another ZeiiMed file again and I'll probably look for other employment opportunities. Let's win, win big at any cost, but never again. Never again will I be a part of your law breaking and violence."

Mary turned and left my office, saying no more.

She was right. No lawyer can consistently break the law and break the rules of Court without eventually being caught and punished. But, I can't retreat now. If our plan succeeds in getting ZeiiMed's HID documents, I'm sure we'll win at trial. The judge will certainly demand an explanation as to how we got the documents, but I will come up with some kind of a credible story. ZeiiMed will be unable to dispute that it hid the documents in the Cloud, so that will help. I probably won't be charged with a crime for stealing documents that ZeiiMed intentionally hid and then lied about. After that, I will follow Mary's lead and never handle another lawsuit against ZeiiMed. I will return to a routine practice of law that doesn't involve murder, deceit and other illegality. Maybe Mary will decide to stay at the firm.

Of course, my plan will be derailed if ZeiiMed attempts physical injury once again. I've already disabled John Standish Clark and bloodied John Edison. Retaliation by ZeiiMed is to be expected. If so, all bets are off, all promises are broken, all plans discarded. The prime directive will be reduced to one objective–the eradication of John Edison, no matter how many bad guys die in the process.

I could easily warm up to the idea.

-29-

I called Meadhbh. We have a date for the first Saturday in May. Anyway, I think it's a date. Then again, maybe it's just a get-together between two people who care for each other. Meadhbh didn't sound surprised by the invitation, just a little frustrated at how long it took for the invitation to be presented. I seem to recall her commenting, "It's about time." However, I'm not absolutely sure. Maybe I misheard.

We agreed to meet at 8:00 p.m. at the "Upstairs," the rooftop bar of the Kimberly Hotel and Suites, located at 145 East 50th Street. The Kimberly has 188 rooms, many of which are spacious and elegantly decorated suites, with Old World touches and private balconies.

The Upstairs has an outdoor bar and adjoining lounge that included soft leather chairs and couches with a brilliant view of the Manhattan skyline, especially the Chrysler Building. The lounge has a glass roof that retracts in pleasant weather, such as a warm Saturday evening in May.

I arrived at the Upstairs early, around 7:30 p.m., to secure seats at the bar. Since it was a very mild, crystal clear evening, the seven or eight stools at the bar were taken. However, about thirty feet from the bar, pushed up against the far side of the lounge, was a black leather, dimpled Chesterfield sofa, with room for three. It was perfect. A private area that afforded a full-length view of the lounge.

I took a seat on the sofa. The waitress arrived immediately for my drink order. I said I would wait until my date arrived.

I saw Meadhbh by the bar. She surveyed the length of the lounge. I raised my arm and waved. Meadhbh walked towards me.

"You certainly picked a very romantic spot. Is there a curtain we can pull around the sofa for privacy?" she said, as her opening comment.

We were off to a fast start.

"Hi. I'm so glad to see you. The bar was packed and this seemed far from the noisy crowd," I noted.

I stood and kissed her on the cheek.

"Are we supposed to both sit on the couch and face each other?"

"Yes, I guess so," I answered.

"Isn't that a little close for you? Usually we have three feet of wooden bar between us."

"We're away from your work now. We can be casual and less inhibited," I responded.

"I don't think you have ever been inhibited, but that's a story for another night."

Meadhbh finally sat on the opposite end of the sofa. "I'm not leading you on, am I?" she asked, as she motioned towards her outfit.

"No, but you do look very nice."

"I'm a little warm," she said.

Meadhbh leaned towards me as she slowly pulled the clinging white linen jacket off her shoulders until her arms were exposed. Her blouse was baby blue and it was abundantly evident from her struggles with the jacket that she had no undergarment on above her waist. Meadhbh's skirt was short and she crossed her legs as she stretched them straight out from the sofa.

"I'm not dressed too revealing, am I?" she asked.

"I don't understand the question. What does 'too revealing' mean?"

"Well, it means I wanted to flash enough flesh to keep your imagination in high gear, but not so much flash that every guy is gawking at me," Meadhbh explained.

"I know exactly what you mean. It's a delicate balance, but you've executed it perfectly," I commented, without the slightest idea of what I meant.

The waitress came. Meadhbh ordered a Cosmopolitan and I requested a Bud Light.

The drinks arrived quickly.

"So, this is a first," she mentioned.

"What is a first? First time at the Kimberly?"

"Yes, it is my first time here, but I meant this is the first time we've had a drink together."

"I always have a drink when I see you."

"Exactly my point. I'm always at work, so you can drink, but I can't."

"So, what does that mean? Should I be worried now that we are both free to enjoy the evils of alcohol?" I asked.

"I'll let you know when to start worrying," Meadhbh responded.

I wondered if all Irish women talk in circles. Then again, maybe my questions are confusing.

"Guess what exciting new thing I did today? Meadhbh quizzed me. "And, I'll give you some clues. It's related to my job, but it has nothing to do with food or drinks. It's very comforting to possess, but you hope to never use it."

"I hope it's not some kind of sexual device."

"No, it's not some kind of sexual device, but men think it's sexy for a lady to have one of these."

"This is getting harder, the more clues you give me. So, it's something on your person as opposed to an activity that you engage in?" I asked.

"It's kind of both."

"How about a portable electric cattle prod suitable for use on unruly patrons and perverts?"

"No, but you're getting closer. I'll tell you. I purchased an FN Five-seven USG semi-automatic pistol, with a 20-round magazine and an additional 5.7 x 28 mm cartridge in the chamber. It's black, with gray controls, easy to handle and light at 1.6 pounds with a loaded magazine. Plus, it's small enough to fit nicely in my purse next to my official gun license from the City of New York."

"Wow! Can I see it?"

"No, it is a concealed weapon under the requirements of my Restricted Business Carry License," Meadhbh responded. "With an emphasis on 'concealed.'"

"What does that mean? I thought New York City had very strict gun control laws, especially with regard to concealed weapons."

"The laws are very tight, but my boss at *Très Bien* submitted a Letter of Necessity stating that I'm required to transport cash receipts late at night, after closing, to a bank depository."

"I didn't know you do that."

"Actually, I don't do that, but I will never again be a sitting duck if someone attacks me on my way home. Luckily, my boss understood and was nice enough to write the required Letter of Necessity."

"Guess what? I'm one of those guys who thinks it's sexy to hang with a woman carrying a loaded pistol. Do you have it with you now?"

"Yes, of course. Technically, I'm not permitted to carry a concealed weapon on casual nights out on the town, but I assume there is little chance of getting caught by the NYPD."

"I'm happy for you. The gun provides peace of mind and confidence that you're ready should evil come your way," I stated.

"Yes, it does. Although it looks like the Austrian Glock 17-shot pistol carried by the New York City police officers, my pistol is Belgian-made and is much more powerful. The cartridges will pierce a Kevlar bulletproof vest. I'm taking no chances. I've got protection and no one will escape my fury, even if you're an experienced killer protected by armor."

"It can't be legal to have a weapon that powerful."

"It isn't. The armor-piercing cartridges are illegal and only a 10-round magazine is permitted with a maximum seven cartridges at a time. I'm breaking the rules, but I have no choice. It's all your fault. You've gotten me involved with some pretty nasty people. That's also the reason I go to target practice every Saturday morning."

"You're a remarkable woman. You never cease to amaze me. And, now that you're carrying, I plan on being much more careful about what I say to you. I can't risk getting you upset, especially when you're drinking. Guns and booze and babes don't mix. By the way, where is our waitress? She better get here fast or I'm going to mention that you have an itchy trigger finger," I said, looking around the lounge.

The waitress arrived without a threat of violence and we enjoyed our second round of drinks.

"This is fun, but let's get down to business. You need my help for something, I can feel it. So, what can I do to assist you once again in your crusade against ZeiiMed?" Meadhbh inquired.

"I think that you have things turned around. I asked you out because I wanted to see you. Coincidentally, I do need your help, but you've said several times you are always happy to assist in my ZeiiMed wars," I replied.

"So, it's not a request, it's a recruitment of a willing candidate with wine and song," Meadhbh said, to further confuse matters.

"Yes, I like that. I'm recruiting you, not requesting you," I said.

"That makes me feel like I'm in the army. You want to enlist me so I'll obey your orders, without question and without hesitation. I could go for that fantasy. Sign me up," Meadhbh continued, without rhyme or reason.

"I think we're sinking into an immaterial and irrelevant area, although your suggestion does have some erotic tingle to it."

"It's not my fault," Meadhbh responded. "You're the one who doesn't get to the point. Lawyers just can't avoid being evasive and ambiguous, and you certainly fall into both categories. I'm just having fun taking your equivocal comments to an absurd extension," Meadhbh said, in what was now clearly a two-cocktail conversation.

"Okay. Here it is. I need to get hold of John Edison's personal cell phone for about five minutes. Of course, he can never discover that I used his phone to make a call. I need your help in getting Edison's phone and then returning it to him before he knows it was ever gone. What do you think?"

"No problem. I believe it can be done while he's at the restaurant one night. Usually, his phone is in plain sight on the table when he's eating. Essentially, I'll divert his attention so he doesn't know his phone is gone. I'm very good at distracting a man. In fact, it is a skill possessed by all women. We know how to distract when we want to. The problem is sometimes we captivate a man's attention when we don't want to. For example, we don't need a man staring at our figures when we're rushing to work from a subway station or parking lot at 8:30 a.m. But, to answer your inquiry, I will do it. I just need some background information as to why I'm doing it."

"We've talked previously about a lawsuit I commenced against ZeiiMed regarding a defective metal-on-metal hip replacement Device."

"Yes, I recall."

"After I filed the Complaint and discovery commenced, all the ZeiiMed HID documents vanished into thin air. Or, to put it more precisely, the documents were eaten by a computer worm that ZeiiMed released into both my computers and their own computers."

"Let me guess. You think that big, bad ZeiiMed hid a second copy of the documents and didn't tell you?' Meadhbh asked.

"You catch on fast," I responded. "Yes, I'm convinced ZeiiMed has the HID documents in a Cloud that probably its own lawyers don't even know about."

"I'm following you. With Edison's phone and the necessary security clearances, you hope to get your hands on the lost documents that really aren't lost, because ZeiiMed knows exactly where it put them in the Cloud."

"You got it. I think you're ready to go."

"When do you want to conduct this little caper?" Meadhbh asked.

"Before we grab his phone, I need time to get the password and ID information to provide access to the Cloud vendor. How about the middle of June? Then, if all goes according to plan, I'll have all the documents with plenty of time to review them before the trial."

"I'll be ready," she responded. "Just give me two days advance warning because Edison doesn't always come in on the same nights each week."

"Good, that's settled. We have a plan! Would you like another Cosmopolitan?"

"No, thanks. Actually, I think I'll head back to Brooklyn. I have a full shift tomorrow. It's my punishment for taking off Saturday night."

"I understand. I'll get you a cab and you'll be home in no time," I said.

"Do you want to come home with me?" Meadhbh asked, as she playfully batted her eyes and tilted her head in a flirtatious manner.

"Are you joking around?"

"No. I'm serious."

"Thanks, but I don't think so."

"Is Dr. Joe still seeing your wife?

"You get right to the point. Yes, as far as I know."

"What's Kim doing tonight?" Meadhbh continued with the questions.

"We didn't discuss it today. I suspect she is either home reading or out with Dr. Joe, if you must know."

"Has Kim ever not come home on a Saturday night?"

"Aren't we getting rather personal?" I commented.

"I think the questions are relevant. Kim's status with Dr. Joe is directly related to your level of comfort with me."

"I'm not sure I see the correlation, but Kim has not slept with Joe."

"Yet."

"Yes, not yet. I can't predict the future," I said, slightly irritated. "Kim says she loves me and that her love will remain unchanged regardless of her affection for Dr. Joe."

"Sounds to me like she may be making plans to stay over soon."

"I know. If it happens, I'll deal with it, although I can't guarantee how I will react. I hope our love as husband and wife will eventually prevail. But, who knows?"

"That's nice. Very romantic. Now, I want to be with you more than ever," Meadhbh responded.

"And I care greatly for you. Maybe someday the time will be right."

"Does that mean we can't fool around in the elevator on the way out?"

Looking into her beautiful green eyes, I said, "Yes, it does mean we can't. But, that doesn't mean I don't want to. We better get going. As usual, our conversations get so complicated I'm not sure what we're promising each other."

We took the elevator down to street level. The elevator was packed, so it was good we were not anxiously anticipating an opportunity for private affection in a public place.

I paid the cab driver and Meadhbh headed to Brooklyn. I then took a second cab to Penn Station to connect with my train for the ride home.

My mind was cluttered. Maybe I should have headed to Brooklyn with Meadhbh, rather than to Port Jefferson where my wife may or may not be home. If Kim jumps the tracks with Dr. Joe, I know I'll eventually forgive her. Doesn't that mean that Kim should forgive me if I take the same leap? I know, it doesn't work that way in marriage.

I have no answers. I'm not sure what is right anymore. Meadhbh cares about me despite the fact I'm married. Kim cares about me despite the fact she has a boyfriend. Mary cares about me despite our complex employee-employer relationship and wants whatever affection remains available after Kim and Meadhbh. This is a lot to think about and too much to comprehend. I wish someone had written a book about these kinds of problems.

I'd run to the library.

-30-

I was at my desk early one morning in the third week of May 2011.

"Do you have time to talk before you run to Court?" Herb asked me from the doorway of my office.

"Please come in. I have time now."

Herb was a bit disheveled and the lenses on his plastic-framed glasses seemed thicker than ever. He should have tucked in his shirt, but I'm sure he thought the style hid a few pounds.

He took a seat across from my desk.

"I've got good news, I think," Herb said.

"You were a big help in the first ZeiiMed litigation, so I was hoping you'd be able to do it again," I responded.

Herb smiled from ear to ear and confidently announced, "I wasn't being very clear. The bottom line is that we hit a home run. I have Edison's ID number and password to give us unlimited access to ZeiiMed's HID documents maintained by ZeiiMed's Cloud vendor. I also have the telephone number that provides ZeiiMed's exclusive access to the Cloud operator. You call the number, give your security information and then request that the HID documents be sent to an email address you designate. Of course, you'll have to doubletalk the Cloud operator because we don't know how ZeiiMed identifies the HID documents in the Cloud. Just wing it and hope for the best. And this whole process will only work if you make the call from Edison's phone because it's an approved access device."

"Wow! That's a lot to take in. I can't believe it. How in the world did you manage to accomplish all this?" I asked.

Herb showed slight dismay and responded, "I told you already. I have a close friend, a Club member who works for a cell phone vendor that installs special software in smartphones that captures each keystroke of the cell phone as the keypad is touched while the owner is making a call or sending a message. Of course, the wireless carriers that permitted the installation of the software contend that it only collects 'diagnostic data,' whatever that means, but those in the Club know differently. So, when Edison recently contacted Cloud Storage for Lawyers on his approved cell phone, my friend was able to collect and store each keystroke as he entered the phone number and his security information. I then double-checked the information with our Club member at the NSA."

"Yes, I remember now. That is remarkable."

"Not to brag, but keystroke collection is only the tip of the iceberg. The NSA has the capability to confiscate every phone call in the United States and every message transmitted over fiber optic cables that connect to the European server networks of several major U.S. Internet companies. More incredibly, my friends at the Club are hacking the computers of foreign countries at the request of American intelligence agencies. But, they aren't doing so voluntarily. They have little choice because the government knows they're responsible for illegally hacking the computers of major American corporations. This is their punishment."

"And," Herb continued to boast without missing a beat, "It's interesting that one of the deepest and darkest secrets of the Club is that Secretary of State Hillary Clinton uses a personal email account for all of her State Department work. Hillary accesses a personal server set up in her home by the Secret Service as part of her husband's office for conducting post-presidential business. Bill doesn't email much, so Hillary has complete control of the Clinton's personal email communications that include both private matters and public governmental work as Secretary of State. I've also heard that Hillary is deleting thousands of emails before her private account becomes public knowledge. It's probably not permitted by federal regulations, but that's not the important point. The Club knows that the bad guys can easily hack into the Clinton's home server, identify Hilary's State Department emails, and use that as an access point to the State Department's computers. That means all the confidential State Department documents, including all communications with our embassies and ambassadors worldwide, are in jeopardy. Again, no one knows about any of this, but I imagine that someday all the NSA shenanigans and Hilary Clinton's private email scandal will be on the front page of the *Washington Post*. It will make for interesting reading. Americans will be shocked."

"I don't think I want to know all this. It seems to me that a lot of laws are being broken. But, back to the problem at hand. Is there any chance that Edison will be able to discover we made a call on his phone after we return the phone to him?"

Herb didn't hesitate a second before answering, "Absolutely not. Edison's phone is equipped with a special application that erases all call histories within moments after each call is made. It's a security device that prevents an unauthorized user from downloading the call history if the phone is stolen or lost. In our situation, it works for us by covering our tracks."

"Good. We need all the help we can get. Herb, if I decided not to pursue this fairly dangerous plan and simply ask the Court to have a computer expert inspect ZeiiMed's computers, is there any chance of finding an electronic trail that would reveal that the HID documents are in the custody of Cloud Storage for Lawyers?"

"Actually, the answer is no. ZeiiMed has done exactly what we anticipated. Every electronic communication with the Cloud vendor and every transfer of documents to the Cloud has been deleted and covered up without a trace. There is simply no electronic trail or footprint connecting the HID document to Cloud Storage for Lawyers. Once my friend from the Club established access to Edison's cell phone, he was able to hack into ZeiiMed's computer operating center, including all its servers. No evidence of any transfers to a Cloud were found anywhere. As a result, our plan is the only way to do what we want to accomplish. That is, get the HID documents from the Cloud without ZeiiMed's knowing we have them and without Edison knowing we used his phone to get them."

"I hope you get a big bonus at year end. You deserve it. Then again, maybe I should hold off on my praise until I plug the ID number and password into Edison's phone and gain access."

"Don't worry. It will work. At least, I'm pretty sure it will. The problem is that passwords and phone numbers are changed periodically to prevent someone from doing exactly what we intend to do. But, don't worry, I'll double check everything before you grab Edison's cell phone," Herb promised.

"That's a good idea. But remember, ZeiiMed is a very dangerous company with tentacles that reach into the smallest of places. If ZeiiMed suspects that it's security wall has been breached, your friends from the Club will eventually be found and the punishment will be secretive and severe. Don't take any chances," I cautioned.

"We'll be careful. My buddies in the Club are the best tech wizards in the world."

"That may be. But if ZeiiMed recruits the NSA to investigate a leak, you won't stand a chance and you'll never know what hit you. Remember, John Edison of ZeiiMed was appointed by the President to be an Administrator in charge of Obamacare. As far as the government is concerned, he runs a federal agency. That status is critical when Edison or ZeiiMed requests access to confidential information from the NSA."

"What a world. The NSA is providing confidential data to ZeiiMed while my Club colleague at the NSA is providing me with confidential data on ZeiiMed's Cloud vendor," Herb commented.

"Let's get to the bottom line. What's the number for Cloud Storage for Lawyers and the necessary security codes?" I asked.

"Okay, here it is. Edison's connected smartphone is a Samsung Galaxy. His personalized number to the Cloud operator is 800-777-1300. His user ID is ZeiiCzar@medmail.com. The password is 11082016. Do you want Edison's tax return also?"

"What? Why would I want his tax return?" I asked.

"Only kidding. The point is that I can get whatever you need from the NSA," said Herb, without a hint of humility.

I wrote down the security information provided by Herb. I stared down at the numbers and exclaimed, "I think I know what Edison is up to. Look at the password—11082016. November 8, 2016 is Election Day. I think Edison plans to run for President after Obama finishes his second term."

"That sounds like a stretch to me," Herb responded.

"No, it isn't. We know Obama will win a second term, but Edison will run after that. ZeiiMed will eventually have at least 33 million people who subscribe to its insurance policies now that the coverage is mandated by law. We all know that premiums are scheduled to skyrocket over the next few years and the available networks will shrink, with the high-end doctors excluded from coverage. Also, there is a good chance that federal subsidies to 7.5 million people will be cut off in the 36 states didn't establish insurance exchanges as required by Obamacare. If subsidies are not available in those states, almost all of them will drop the insurance as premiums increase, leaving only people with serious medical conditions in the insurance market, a situation referred to as the 'death spiral.' All Edison has to do is promise to reduce the premiums for every American and expand the networks. That's 33 million votes right there. Who knows how many more votes he can swing with the help of the NSA investigating the dirty laundry of his opponents. I can't let that happen. I've got to do something. I will do something," I promised.

Mary casually walked into my office.

"What are you going to do?" Mary asked. "I hope it's legal and I hope nobody gets hurt."

"I believe Edison will eventually run for President and that simply can't be allowed to happen," I answered.

"That's a bit far-fetched if you ask me. But let's pretend it's true for a moment. What are you going to do? Shoot him? Who made you the Decision Maker for America?" Mary asked, as she sat down next to Herb.

Mary continued, "Plus, who cares about an election in 2016? Hillary Clinton will probably win it anyway, assuming Bill Clinton's past and future assignations don't interfere. More important, the world has many more pressing issues to solve without worrying about politics in 2016. We have civil wars in Syria, Libya, Egypt and other countries in the Middle East, including escalating violence in Iraq as we withdraw our troops. North Korea is threatening full-scale war against South Korea and continues to develop nuclear missiles. Once again, it's men leading all these governments and all the rebellious forces. Men acting badly is a recurring theme of history that doesn't seem destined to change. What if women were in charge of these countries? Without the male ego and the testosterone rushes, the world would be a tranquil place without civilian massacres and needless violence. Women would never carelessly put a country's young people in a bloody conflict with no guarantee of victory, such as the Vietnam War, the Afghanistan War, or any of the other wars currently being waged around the world."

The room went silent. Neither Herb nor I knew what to say. Mary seemed to be blowing off steam, so there was no point in saying anything, although I agreed with her points.

She looked lovely in a professional and polished sort of way, as usual. Since I'm a sucker for a pretty face, I also decided not to tell her she was rude to change the subject of discussion and rant on about her particular gripes of the day. I took a different approach, a more mature approach.

"Mary, it's always nice to hear the latest news flash and editorial comments, but Herb and I were discussing access to ZeiiMed's Cloud document depository. We would appreciate your input."

"I know what you were discussing. You were thinking about another attack on Edison as a result of his presumed presidential aspirations and you know my aversion to such tactics. But, regardless of that, please proceed as you wish," Mary answered.

"To start again, I'm glad you're here," I continued. "Herb gave me the ID number and password for Cloud access from Edison's networked cell phone. I don't need your help with my plan to get possession of Edison's phone. Meadhbh will take care of all that. However, once the trial begins, I will need your assistance at trial on a daily basis."

"I'm all yours. I will clear my calendar and work only on the ZeiiMed trial," Mary said.

"It's actually more complex than that. I need you ready to take over as lead trial counsel, if something happens to me. I will explain. Once ZeiiMed realizes we have their HID documents, who knows what may happen to me. I need you ready to take over as a trial counsel as my full-time replacement on a moment's notice. You will be required to proceed with the cross-examination of witnesses, closing arguments and jury instructions. You will have to learn fast and think on your feet. I know you can do it."

"Thanks for your faith in me. Herb and I will be there for you and for our client. I enjoy the challenge. Now getting back to the discussion of your early demise, I have a question. If your wake or funeral arrangements conflict with the trial dates, do you mind if I skip the whole mourning scene? I'm sure there will be plenty of other women there crying over your passing."

"I'm not joking here," I said in a serious tone. "Once we've grabbed the documents and ZeiiMed is blindsided with them at trial, all bets are off. You know ZeiiMed's ruthlessness from your own personal confrontations with our adversary. Life holds little value to ZeiiMed, and I will be a primary target. So, as I said, you will need to be ready to proceed as trial counsel without missing a beat. I will let you know as soon as I get my hands on the ZeiiMed documents, so you can start to review them. Hopefully, I will pull off this little caper without Edison or anyone else learning what was done until we reveal the documents at trial."

"If you get captured and tortured by ZeiiMed, please don't disclose Herb's name or my name no matter how much it hurts. Just say you did everything on your own and didn't tell anyone," Mary continued, thinking she was being comical.

"I guess we're not having a serious discussion here today. You seemed to be having a great time making fun of everything I say. This meeting is over. I think you're an indispensable colleague, but for now–please go. I'll keep you posted on my progress."

Once again, I was about to compromise my legal ethics, assuming I had any left, and violate the law to increase my chances of success at trial. I rationalized my actions by telling myself that ZeiiMed had done worse and deserved the worst. Of course, that's not a valid defense for my actions.

But, I'm not going to let ZeiiMed defeat me and defeat my client because my opponent was more sinister and more unremorseful. I cannot beat an enemy as formidable as ZeiiMed without a plan that crosses the line of legality. Either break the rules or Mrs. Dudley is left without a remedy, without compensation and without a just result. I cannot let that happen and my fear of physical harm or arrest cannot hinder or limit me in any manner. The result is all that counts–a result that does justice for Mrs. Dudley and others injured by ZeiiMed's defective HID.

I will not fail.

-31-

In the second week of June, I received a call from Meadhbh at around 6:30 one evening.

"Glad I caught you still at work," Meadhbh said. "How have you been? We haven't talked in a few weeks."

"I'm doing fine. I think about you often."

"Because you need me to get to Edison?"

"No, of course not. Because I care for you on a personal level and because I wish you the best."

"I was hoping you would tell me how desperate you are for my tender touch, but I guess that's asking too much."

"No, it's not really. I think it, but I just didn't say it."

"I'll live with that for now," Meadhbh responded. "I'm calling to update you on the Edison situation. He continues to have dinner at *Très Bien* two or three times a week. We keep a cordial, but distant relationship. If I'm behind the bar when he comes in, I'll say hello. Sometimes the tables are full, so he has a drink at the bar while waiting. Once he is sitting at a table, he always places his Samsung cell phone right on the table. He never seems to keep it on his person. Obviously, that's a great benefit to us. While the phone is idle on the table, the screen shows a standard multi-colored hot air balloon for about ten seconds before the battery saving feature kicks in and the screen goes dark."

"Great, Meadhbh. Very helpful. By the way, Edison doesn't sit in my bar stool at the end of the bar, does he?"

"Yes, he does. And he likes the seat for the same reason you do. He can see behind the bar and stare at my figure as I go back and forth."

"I guess I do have something in common with Edison. At least, he has good taste in women," I mentioned.

"By the way, Edison looks awful," Meadhbh mentioned. "His face seems to be pushed inside his skull and he doesn't appear to have cheekbones. His limp is worse than ever. Sometimes he walks with a cane and tries to avoid putting any pressure on his injured foot. He's hard to look at."

"Well, that's all my handiwork and I'm proud of it. I think he'll have to change his plan to run for elected office, at least until he gets a new face. In our fight in the Ramble, I pushed the knife so deep into his foot, he will never walk properly again. But, don't feel sorry for him. He got what he deserved. He gave a green light to several murders and authorized physical violence on others. I know Edison denies any prior knowledge of the assault on you, but it was certainly the work of his top lieutenants."

"I know. But I have to separate myself from Edison's possible involvement in my injuries or else I can't interact with him and accomplish our goal. Edison thinks I believe his statement that he didn't authorize the assault. I want him to think I believe him. At least, for now," Meadhbh explained.

"Good. So how do we proceed from here?" I asked.

"Edison usually comes in for dinner on Thursday. Tomorrow evening. Let's proceed on the understanding that we are going forward unless you hear from me to the contrary. He will be in by seven. If you get here by eight, he will be at his table with a couple of drinks under his belt. I'll be ready for my performance."

"I still don't know your plan for getting his phone, but I eagerly look forward to hearing the details," I said. "Of course, I will have to stay in the bar area so Edison can't see me. If Edison realizes I'm at the restaurant, he will immediately suspect foul play."

"Yes, I understand. I look forward to seeing you tomorrow night. And remember, our usual rules of conduct apply. No matter what happens, do not punch, stab, shoot or bludgeon Edison. If he panics over something and summons his bodyguards, just run out of the restaurant and don't worry about me. I'll be fine," Meadhbh instructed.

"I agree to the no spillage of blood, his or mine, but I just can't leave you there if things suddenly go awry."

"Yes, you must. You are not Superman and you are not saving me from the jaws of ZeiiMed. I work at *Très Bien* and I want to keep it that way. I will make sure Edison thinks

I'm not involved in any plan to harm him. I'll just blame everything on you."

"Okay, I guess we have an understanding. See you tomorrow for your opening night performance," I stated.

"Make sure you write down the ID number, the password and the telephone number for the Cloud operator. You'll have Edison's phone for maybe sixty seconds at most. There will be no time for wrong numbers or a forgotten password," Meadhbh cautioned.

"Don't worry. You do your part and I'll do mine, assuming Herb's information is correct. Bye, love you and thanks again."

"Love you back, a lot," Meadhbh answered.

As usual, I'm in over my head, both socially and professionally. The plan must work because it's the only plan I have. Without the HID documents, Martha Dudley's case is lost. The question then becomes, how far will I go to win the trial? I guess the answer is "too far."

Once again, I'm about to break the law and commit criminal offenses sufficient to result in disbarment and a prison term. All because I want to win? What's wrong with me? All my common sense and good judgment must have been knocked out of me during the confrontation with Clark at the pool. I'm not only willing to wager my health and professional career, but also the well-being of my closest friends and colleagues in pursuit of my goal.

Maybe it's the Dr. Joe problem that has me so misguided and confused. I have no answers, but I can't retreat now. I'm going to play this out and then re-evaluate. Maybe I'll get professional help. Then again, the easiest solution is to just drink more.

-32-

As I previously mentioned, the front door to *Très Bien* is five feet from the front door of Edison's apartment building at 60 E. 84th Street. *Très Bien* is at street level and the apartments are on the floors above.

Once inside the front door of the restaurant, the bar extends parallel to 84th Street with large picture windows providing a full view of the City's sidewalk hustle and bustle. The dining room is behind the bar. A right turn at the end of the bar leads to the tables in back. Black and white checkerboard tile flooring and red gingham tablecloths create the mood. The dining room cannot be seen from the bar area because floor to ceiling mirrors behind the bar obstruct any view of the tables.

The next day, I arrived exactly on time at 8 p.m. I took my usual stool at the end of the bar. It provided me a view of both the bar room area, and, of course, Meadhbh. Now that she has caught on to my immature and chauvinistic nature, I'll have to be more discreet with my eyeballing techniques. I thought I was a master at inconspicuous gawking, but I guess that's a contradiction in terms.

Meadhbh was behind the bar. She just finished pouring a Bud Light into a pint glass from the freezer. The beer was so cold the glass frosted with a thin coating of ice. Meadhbh smiled as she brought the beer to me.

"I did my best to keep eye contact and not let my vision wander," I said, "and thank you for the beer."

"Today, I want you to check me out. I'm dressed to be a distraction. It's part of my plan. I need to know if it works."

A distraction she was. I couldn't take my eyes off her. She was wearing a white, V-neck short-sleeve tee shirt that tightly clung to her well-defined curves. A sprinkling of freckles extended down from her neck until covered by the cotton fabric that concealed only a small portion of her natural endowment. A short black skirt accentuated her long, muscle-toned legs and suede ankle boots. As we spoke, she quickly finger-combed her strawberry blond hair and pushed her headband in place. It gave her a carefree, schoolgirl look.

"I'm not only distracted, I'm mesmerized. It's like I'm in a trance. I haven't seen such an attractive tee-shirt look since Jacqueline Bisset in 'The Deep'."

"I'm glad you approve. Let's hope it works."

"I guarantee it will work. In fact, you'll have the attention of every man in the dining room. By the way, what are you doing after you get off work?"

"You mean this is how I have to dress to get you to ask me out on a second date?" Meadhbh teased.

"No, but it certainly helps. I'm a man. As a rule, we're very weak and easily distracted."

"Enough clowning around. I'm ready to have the curtain go up on this show. Judy–you remember Judy...?"

"Yes, she called me when you were in the hospital. She's a waitress here. Very thin young girl with short brunette hair and lots of tattoos."

"Correct. She's going to assist me. Once I grab Edison's phone in the dining area, I'll give it to her and she'll bring it directly to you. So, just sit tight at the bar and wait for Judy to bring it to you. There's a bathroom in the back of the dining room and, hopefully, I can get Edison into the men's room while you contact the Cloud operator."

"Got it," I responded, "Good luck and scream if you need help."

"I won't scream and I won't need help. I've got this under control. I'll start by bringing Edison a Bloody Mary. It's not for him to drink, it's to assist me in my diversionary tactics. See you later."

Meadhbh brought the Bloody Mary into the dining room on a small tray. Most of the tables were taken and Edison was sitting at a small square table in the middle of the room. Judy was serving dinners.

Meadhbh approached Edison's table. She saw his Samsung cell phone on the table. The oversized screen on the phone had the manufacturer's image of a multi-colored hot air balloon. Next to the phone was Edison's small, plastic panic button to remotely summon his bodyguards if trouble developed.

"Hi again, Mr. Edison. I made an extra Bloody Mary by accident and thought I'd bring it to one of our best customers," Meadhbh said, as she arrived at his table.

Edison looked up from the table. He didn't smile. His piercing ice-blue eyes focused like laser beams on Meadhbh's face. Slowly, his head lowered as he admired her feminine attributes. He grinned slightly, but stated coarsely, "I don't want a Bloody Mary. I've already had scotch, I don't want vodka."

Meadhbh lowered her tray to nonetheless serve the drink. Edison simultaneously lifted his arm in frustration as he attempted to wave off the cocktail. Meadhbh moved the tray toward his extended hand until contact was made. The tray tipped, the Bloody Mary fell off the tray and spilled on the front of his khaki pants.

Edison jumped up. "You stupid girl! It's all over me!"

Edison grabbed his napkin and started to sop up the liquid, but noticed that the other customers in the room were watching him.

"It needs to be soaked with cold water," Meadhbh stated.

"I'm going to the men's room," Edison snarled.

Edison stepped away from his table and walked past several other tables to a narrow hallway in the rear of the restaurant that led to the men's room. Meadhbh watched intently as he entered the bathroom and the door closed behind him. She quickly picked up Edison's phone from his table and pretended to clean up the tomato juice around where it had been. She then surreptitiously handed the phone off to Judy as she passed by on her way to the bar.

The clock was ticking. Meadhbh continued her cleaning of the table with one eye on the men's room door.

Just as Judy reached the bar, Brian's phone rang. He answered it.

"Brian, this is Herb. My friend at the cell phone software company just called. Edison's password was changed. It could be standard security maintenance or maybe our recording of his keystrokes was detected. ZeiiMed may suspect that we are attempting to access their Cloud documents. I contacted my hacker friend at the NSA, another member of the Club. He intercepted a call Edison made yesterday to Cloud Storage for Lawyers and was able to confirm the password was changed. But we're now unable to obtain the new password by recording his keystrokes, as we previously did. Edison's keystroke selection is somehow being masked."

"Christ, Herb! I'm getting possession of Edison's cell phone right now. What am I supposed to do? The NSA has intercepted the phone calls of the President of Brazil–there has to be a way to get the new password. I'm desperate. I've got less than 45 seconds."

Judy handed Edison's phone to Brian as he continued talking to Herb.

"I know," said Herb. "Unfortunately, we can't seem to override the masking technique. I need time," Herb said.

"You've got time, about 30 seconds at best."

Meadhbh saw the men's room door open. She quickly moved into the narrow hallway outside the bathroom with the towel she used to clean up the spilled tomato juice from the Bloody Mary. Meadhbh intercepted Edison as soon as he left the bathroom.

"Mr. Edison, you still have the tomato juice everywhere," she said.

"It's all right. I'll clean it later."

Meadhbh stood in the middle of the small hallway, preventing Edison from walking to his table.

"I'll help. Stand still," she responded.

Meadhbh lowered herself by bending her knees as she moved into a kneeling position facing Edison's belt buckle. Her upper legs and thighs were now barely covered as her skirt pulled up as she knelt. Edison stood motionless as he stared down. Meadhbh placed one hand behind his upper leg and used her other hand to brush his pants with the soiled towel on the area below his belt. The tomato juice from the towel made the stain larger and more revealing, as Meadhbh had planned. Edison immediately realized what happened as he forced his attention away from Meadhbh's distractions.

"You've made it worse! The whole front is red. I can't go back into the dining room like this," Edison exclaimed with great annoyance.

"I'm so sorry. Go back into the bathroom, take off your pants, soak the stain with water and then dry it with the hand dryer."

"Alright. Let me go. I'll take care of it," Edison answered.

Edison went back into the bathroom. Meadhbh stood and took a deep breath.

Judy entered into the hallway. "What the hell was that? I can't believe what you just did," Judy exclaimed.

"I did what was necessary. I did what I knew would work. Tell Brian he has another 60 seconds," Meadhbh said.

Brian was sitting at the bar with Edison's phone in one hand and his own cell phone in the other. He was waiting for Herb. The phone rang.

"Herb, tell me the good news now!"

"Good news it is," Herb replied. "My hacker friend at the NSA, an elite member of the Club, found an electronic file of all calls by Cloud Storage for Lawyers. Apparently, our national security people have been keeping an eye on the company. Anyway, my friend found a recording of a call to Edison informing him of the password change. The new password is 11032020. I guess Edison's presidential bid just got put off four years."

"Thanks. You saved the day. Gotta go."

"One last thing. Don't tell anyone about the NSA surveillance of the President of Brazil or Hilary Clinton. It's a national security secret."

"Not now, Herb. Good bye!"

On Edison's phone I dialed the 800 number Herb gave me to contact Cloud Storage for Lawyers. I was sweating. My hand was shaking. I could hardly tap the correct numbers on the keypad. My time deadline had to be expired. How could Meadhbh possibly be distracting Edison for this long?

"Hello, this John Edison," I said into the cell phone.

"Yes, we know. Your phone is registered on our security network. This is the Cloud operator. Please type and say aloud your user ID, which is your assigned email address."

"ZeiiCzar@medmail.com is my user ID," I responded.

"Please now type on your keyboard and say aloud your password," the Cloud operator instructed.

My headache felt like I had a hatchet embedded in my forehead. It was now or never. Either the new password works or Mrs. Dudley's lawsuit had no chance of succeeding. Breathe slowly–compose yourself.

"The password is 11032020," I stated slowly and then punched it into the keyboard.

"The password is accepted. Access to your Cloud Account is granted. How can I be of service to you?" the Cloud operator asked.

I was elated, but my pride of accomplishment was tempered by a shortage of time and a complete lack of knowledge as to how ZeiiMed identifies the HID documents in the Cloud. All I could do was follow my lawyering instincts and double talk as much as possible.

"I'm sorry, I didn't catch your name."

"I'm Carol."

"Hi, Carol. Nice to meet you. The people at your organization are always so nice. As you know, I'm John," I said, although Brian instead of John almost slipped out.

"Yes, John. I'm aware you are the CEO of ZeiiMed. We are here to help," Carol responded.

"Carol, I know there was an alert as to a possible security problem earlier, but we were able to head off a breach because you and your colleagues acted quickly to change the passwords and notify everyone. Congratulations on your good work," I said, hoping to be on the right track.

"Thank you, Mr. Edison. We pride ourselves on responding immediately to possible unauthorized access problems. ZeiiMed was concerned about the security of its Hip Replacement Files and we addressed the concern."

"Yes, you did. In fact, I am calling about the Hip Replacement Files. I have made a decision. Please pay close attention. I want you to electronically transfer a complete copy of all the files to the following email address: M.Douglas@AlfonsoRyan.com. Please do so while I remain on the phone," I instructed her.

"One moment, please," Carol responded.

The pain in my head was increasing exponentially. I could barely think. My thoughts were suffocated by constant waves of agony flowing through my brain. *Christ, why doesn't Carol hurry up? What is she doing? Does she suspect something?*

"Mr. Edison?"

"Yes, here."

"This is Carol, again. I can now confirm transfer of the files you requested. They have been received at the provided email address for M. Douglas. Would you like a confirmation number?"

"No, I mean, yes. Please just tell me the number. Do not electronically send the number to me or anyone. Do not send an email confirming the transfer."

"Understood," Carol answered, "The confirmation number is 1311951. Anything else I can help you with?"

"No. Thank you again," I said. "Bye now."

"Have a good day, Mr. Edison. It was a pleasure to be of assistance."

The call ended. The history of the call, with the user ID and password, was all automatically erased by the security software Herb told me about. It was done. I can't believe we were successful. The moment quickly faded. Judy approached me, walking very fast.

"Now! Give me the phone now!" Judy commanded.

I gave her Edison's phone. Judy grabbed it and practically ran around the end of the bar into the dining room.

Edison came out of the men's room. Meadhbh was again standing in the hallway as he exited the bathroom.

"Are you still here? I'm surprised you didn't come in the bathroom and help," Edison said, with a lecherous look on his face.

"I feel so bad about what happened. I just wanted to make sure it worked out all right."

"As you can see, it looks like I got most of the stain out and the dryer made it appear almost good as new."

Out of the corner of her eye, Meadhbh saw Judy pass by Edison's table. She knew the phone had been returned to his table.

"Are you going to get out of my way? I want to order dinner," Edison growled.

"Yes, yes. I'm sorry. I'm blocking the hallway. I better get back to the bar."

"Yes, I think you should. If I need another drink, please have Judy deliver it."

Meadhbh turned and walked through the dining room towards the bar. She saw Edison's phone on his table. Hopefully, mission accomplished. Edison returned to his table.

Meadhbh resumed her bartending duties behind the bar.

She winked at Brian at the end of the bar as she quickly refilled the glasses of her bar patrons. Brian winked back.

Eventually, Meadhbh made her way down to Brian's end of the bar.

"Meadhbh, we did it! I think the extreme stress has given me shingles, but hopefully the sores won't appear on my face until tomorrow. Of course, I couldn't have done it without you. You were great. I don't know how you kept Edison from his phone for so long, but it worked. You didn't kiss him, did you?" I asked.

"Maybe I did, maybe I didn't. I told you I could handle it and I did. The key, as always, is to focus on a male's prurient interests–that causes a temporary regression of brain function to prehistoric levels. I kept his attention on the flesh that I was flashing and the rest was easy, although I did get a little uncomfortable wiping down his trousers."

"You did what? Edison probably thinks he's your new best friend now. Should I be jealous?"

"You have no time to be jealous. Get out of here. You're job is done. If Edison sees you here, he'll suspect he was somehow flimflammed."

"You're right. Gotta go. Your performance was outstanding. Thanks again."

After a short tap of my lips on hers, I quickly left.

The plan had worked well. We achieved our goal. We now had the HID documents and presumably ZeiiMed doesn't know it. I'm convinced that some of the documents will confirm that ZeiiMed knew about the dangers of the HID and purposefully withheld the information. It will take a lot of work to find the few, critical documents containing such information, but all it takes is time. At least the damaging ZeiiMed documents won't be concealed in an undecipherable, encrypted code or buried in a truck load of Internet gibberish because ZeiiMed never expected them to be seen by anyone.

I won't show my hand until trial. I don't want our possession of the HID documents to be revealed until ZeiiMed's witnesses are on the stand telling lie after lie to the jury. The documents will hopefully expose the lies by revealing the false testimony of the witnesses. ZeiiMed's lawyers will cry to the Court that the documents were destroyed and all parties confirmed to the Court they had no copies. I will simply respond that the documents were emailed to my law firm and that's all I know. I will also explain that the documents were originally deleted from the firm's computers shortly after receipt, but somehow were resent months later. I'm anticipating that the Court will never learn that rules were broken and laws violated to get the HID documents from the Cloud. ZeiiMed can't tell the Court of my theft from the Cloud vendor because it was ZeiiMed that hid the documents from everyone in the first place by putting them in the Cloud.

Mrs. Dudley deserves a fair trial and I don't care what's done to achieve that result. It's a code I'm required to live by–at least when dealing with an opponent like ZeiiMed. And, if I end up making a little money by bending the rules to produce a just result, all the better. Mrs. Dudley becomes rich, my law firm has a big payday and ZeiiMed's defective design of the HID is revealed. A win all around.

Of course, ZeiiMed cannot be underestimated. I am terribly concerned about a violent reaction by ZeiiMed once the HID documents are presented in Court. I must be prepared for any nightmare ZeiiMed can create. I am ready to counter with extreme behavior that even ZeiiMed cannot contemplate or avoid. I have the mental and physical ability to inflict severe physical damage on my adversary and no religious or moralistic values to hinder me. I will, at a moment's notice, unleash my darkest and deepest instinct for havoc and harm that even ZeiiMed will find shocking.

I better start getting more sleep.

-33-

In early October 2011, I received notification that a trial date of March 12, 2012 was confirmed by the Court in an Order sent to both parties.

Mary, Herb and myself have spent the last three months on a daily basis reviewing 750,000 pages of documents sent by Cloud Storage for Lawyers to Mary's email address at Alfonso and Ryan. Clearly, ZeiiMed did not catch on to what happened because Tweed, Fox & Fortune would have marched into Court wailing about documents stolen from the Cloud. It didn't happen. Everything was quiet.

Our review of the ZeiiMed HID documents was very successful. As I anticipated, we located several internal ZeiiMed communications that revealed defects in the HID, as well as other communications that confirmed ZeiiMed's decision not to disclose the defects to the public.

In my first litigation against ZeiiMed involving the company's underpayment of doctors, Herb's discovery of inculpatory emails was a "Eureka" moment of surprise and exhilaration. Since then, I've become hardened to the evils of my adversary and fully expected ZeiiMed to have engaged in the most devious and deceptive acts and practices regarding the HID. It's what ZeiiMed does and I am no longer shocked or astounded to find documentary proof confirming a pattern of diabolical behavior.

Based on Mrs. Dudley's description of what occurred after her surgery, there was no doubt in my mind that ZeiiMed produced a knowingly defective Device with an electronic trail confirming intentional avoidance and omission.

The problem was not finding what Herb called the "Critical HID Documents" among the massive collection of paper. The problem was getting the Critical HID Documents admitted into evidence at trial so their damaging contents could be used on the cross-examination of unsuspecting ZeiiMed witnesses.

Of course, ZeiiMed's lawyers will contend that they were unaware of the Critical HID Documents and do not know how I got them. I will submit evidence that the documents were received from Cloud Storage for Lawyers and confirm when the Cloud operator sent them. I anticipate the Court will permit the Critical HID Documents to be admitted into evidence. ZeiiMed can't prove that the documents were stolen because it was ZeiiMed's Cloud operator who sent them. ZeiiMed might consider calling Carol the Cloud operator as a witness, but her testimony that John Edison instructed her to send them via a network phone would only create embarrassment for ZeiiMed.

Of course, ZeiiMed will eventually figure out what happened based on the time and date the documents were sent from the Cloud to Mary Douglas. Edison will recall the dinner at *Très Bien* and the spilled Bloody Mary. How could he forget it? But, it will be too little too late. Edison can't contend I made the call from his cell phone because he doesn't know I was at *Très Bien* that night. Edison knows Meadhbh didn't make the call because she was in close proximity to him the whole time. As far as Edison is concerned, his cell phone was always on the table in front of him, except for his quick trips to the men's room.

Nonetheless, Edison will probably assume I was somehow involved, without any knowledge of how I accomplished the document transfer. The Court will disregard ZeiiMed's accusation that the HID documents were stolen because there is no actual proof from a testifying witness confirming the deception and theft. Meadhbh, Judy and I are the ones who implemented the scheme, and we aren't spilling the beans to anyone, no matter what happens. Our story is that the documents were received from Cloud Storage for Lawyers without any knowledge as to why the Cloud operator sent them.

In the next five months before commencement of the trial in March 2012, I anticipated that ZeiiMed will conduct the depositions of Mr. and Mrs. Dudley. They will both make good witnesses for us. They will tell a compelling story of the events leading up to Mrs. Dudley's surgery, as well as a heart-wrenching account of the crippling pain that she suffered shortly after the HID was implanted. ZeiiMed's lawyers will attempt to demonstrate that Mrs. Dudley's pain and suffering is attributable to environmental and behavioral factors and other ailments unrelated to the HID. They will have some limited success, but ZeiiMed will be unable to cushion the impact of the Critical HID Documents once they are admitted into evidence at trial.

I decided not to conduct any further depositions of ZeiiMed's management. The testimony of Howard Heeled would be mirrored practically word for word if further testimony was taken from other ZeiiMed witnesses. Suzanna Nudbello is an experienced litigator who knows how to train witnesses to tell a consistent story. Until trial, she will continue to believe that we have no documents to impeach her client. As a result, any additional witnesses will deny all knowledge of defects in the design of the metal-on-metal HID and also deny knowledge of harmful blood levels of cobalt and chromium. At trial, Suzanna will call ZeiiMed representatives as witnesses to present her defenses. The ZeiiMed witnesses will consistently tell lie after lie, and then react with shock and dismay once it becomes clear their testimony was false, based on the undisputable Critical HID Documents. That's the plan, anyway.

I've also decided not to proceed with the litigation as a class action. By continuing the lawsuit only on behalf of Mr. and Mrs. Dudley, I will not be required to conduct an extensive Fairness Hearing to demonstrate the fairness of any settlement with the class members. Moreover, I will not be required to present extensive medical testimony that each member of the class was injured in essentially the same manner by the HID and suffered the same injuries as Mrs. Dudley.

The Dudleys' lawsuit will now be considered a "bellwether case." That is, once the jurors decide the amount to be paid to Mrs. Dudley and Mr. Dudley, the jury award will then become the established settlement value for future cases. Once a favorable verdict for the Dudleys becomes publicized, clients who had the same HID surgery will come knocking at the front door of Alfonso and Ryan requesting legal representation in additional lawsuits against ZeiiMed. The dollars will start to flow in because ZeiiMed will decide to settle rather than face more trials and more adverse jury verdicts.

Mary, Herb and I are continuing our preparation full-time as the trial draws nearer each day. The Critical HID Documents are being indexed and summarized; the opening statement prepared and memorized; and, sample cross-examination questions drafted for each ZeiiMed witness. We are set to go.

I can't wait for the show to begin.

-34-

Monday, March 12, 2012, reached record high temperatures. A heat wave in New York City. It was the warmest month of March in decades, with a high of 74 degrees, although it felt like 80 degrees or more based on the heat index. I was sweating and uncomfortable in my wool, three-button, navy blue suit.

The Courtroom of Judge Douglas Horton Horowitz at 60 Centre Street could not adjust to the unusual weather. The heating system continued at full throttle, despite the summer-like humidity. One wall of the square Courtroom had large windows that spanned eight feet high, but did not open. At the base of the large windows were several much smaller windows at eye level. The small windows were opened by the clerk, but the dead still air from the outside just lingered lifelessly in the heat.

Of course, the air conditioning system was not operational because the heating system was still on. The heating system was electronically programmed and, for some unknown reason, can't be turned off until April 30th, no matter what.

Mary and I entered the Courtroom at 9:00 a.m. to begin what lawyers refer to as *voir dire*. *Voir dire* consists of the questioning of potential jurors to determine whether they can be fair and impartial in deciding the facts of the case. The law requires that six jurors hear the case, but a verdict does not have to be unanimous. Agreement of five jurors is sufficient to return a verdict in favor of the Dudleys.

Two alternate jurors are also selected in the event one of the six becomes sick or otherwise unable to carry out the obligations and duties of a juror. The alternate jurors sit through the entire trial and are then discharged at the time the Judge submits the case to the jury for determination.

During *voir dire*, the lawyers for each side direct a series of questions to each juror. The purpose is to learn whether the juror may have a bias, predisposition or inclination that would make it difficult to be fair and impartial. Being prejudiced about a particular topic is not wrong or right–it simply means the juror may not be totally objective if that same topic is part of the case being presented.

For example, if the case involved an injury to a bicycle delivery messenger while weaving through congested midtown traffic, a taxi driver might have difficulty awarding money based on his personal experiences with bicycles in traffic lanes. If the lawyer can get the prospective juror to admit to a bias, the juror is released "for cause." In addition, each party has three peremptory challenges that permits an attorney to discharge a juror without providing a reason, although a peremptory challenge cannot be used to discriminate based on race.

The Clerk of the Court is required to escort each panel of possible jurors to an assigned Courtroom. A panel consists of about forty people selected from the pool of jurors that received a Summons to appear for jury duty. From the panel, eight people will be randomly selected to sit in the jury box and answer questions as required by the *voir dire* process. The judge is not on the Bench during *voir dire*, but is generally available to resolve any disputes that may develop.

Mary and I sat at the Plaintiffs' counsel table directly in front of the Bench. The Courtroom furniture had changed since we were here last. The shared twelve-foot counsel table had been removed and two smaller counsel tables brought in.

Suzanna Nudbello entered the Courtroom at about 9:30 a.m. accompanied by a team of four additional attorneys. Tweed, Fox & Fortune is well known for a law firm culture that fosters the belief that the more attorneys you have, the more likely victory will be achieved.

As ZeiiMed's army of lawyers sat around the Defendants' counsel table, I waved to Suzanna. She acknowledged with a wink while slightly tilting her head. I guess waving is too primitive a gesture for a lawyer from the arrogant and mighty Tweed, Fox & Fortune.

Both counsel tables were directly in front of the Bench, about six feet apart. The jury box was located along the side wall of the box-shaped room. The wall on the other side of the room across from the jury box consisted mostly of windows. The Bench was, of course, at the front of the room as you entered. The public entrance, at the rear of the room, consisted of two heavy, ten-foot doors that swung unpredictably like the kitchen doors in a busy roadside diner.

On each counsel table were two computer monitors and two microphones. A monitor was also attached to the witness stand, the lectern and the Bench. This permitted electronic distribution of each piece of paper marked as evidence by the clerk, with the document simultaneously projected on a large screen directly in front of the jury box.

I stared at Suzanna. It was probably noticeable, but I figured Mary would kick me under the table if it became too obvious.

Suzanna was wearing a short-sleeved, pink macramé lace dress. Although it was hard to see under the table, she seemed to have matching pink sandals, with black trim and black ankle straps. The very pale shade of her dress accentuated the contrasting colors of her mismatched eyebrows. Her layered, bouffant platinum hairstyle was elegant, professional and appropriately eye-catching for a lead Defendants' counsel. The slight perspiration on her forehead and cheeks was inexplicably appealing.

Mary tapped my arm. Actually, it wasn't a tap–it was a harsh pinch.

"What are you doing?" she asked in a quiet but firm tone.

"What do you mean? I'm not doing anything. Just surveying the opposition," I responded.

"Well, stop doing it so intensely. This isn't a high school mixer."

"Don't worry. Once the jurors arrive, my attention will focus only on the litigation. Until then, it can't hurt for Suzanna to think she has me distracted. Overly confident people tend to make mistakes. I'm counting on it."

"Okay, forget I mentioned it. I agree she probably thinks of herself as a distraction, but if one of ZeiiMed's lawyers stared at me in that manner, I would make sure my displeasure was communicated," Mary said.

"I know–everyone's different. Suzanna wants the attention and enjoys being showered with it," I stated.

"Fine. Do whatever you want. I give up trying to help you."

I actually preferred Mary's dress selection. She was the picture perfect image of a stylish trial counsel. Her shining blond hair complemented the black, long-sleeved Brigette Bailey Torre knit dress, with a bateau neckline. The knee-length hemline was appropriately conservative, but the tight-fitting design emphasized her femininity. I was fortunate to be working with her.

The entrance doors to the Courtroom opened. The Clerk of the Court led about forty people to the wooden benches designated for spectators. The Clerk then randomly selected eight people to sit in the jury box for questioning. Eight prospective jurors took their seats.

As counsel for the Plaintiffs, I proceeded first. The Clerk provided me with a sheet of paper stating the name and occupation of each of the eight. I stood at the counsel table and addressed the jurors in the jury box.

> MR. BRADFORD: Good Morning. I am attorney Brian Bradford and my law firm filed this lawsuit. As you were instructed in the jury training session, this part of the jury process is called *voir dire*. That means I will ask you a few simple questions to determine whether you can be fair and impartial jurors. We all have inclinations and preferences that might mean a particular juror might not qualify for this specific case, but may qualify in another type of case. For example, let's assume Santa Claus was on trial. Some of you may not like Santa–maybe you never got the presents you wanted and just can't get over your ill feelings towards the guy. That's what I am looking to explore. It isn't wrong that you may not like Santa Clause. It simply means you are not the right person for that one particular type of case. The case we have here

today involves a metal-on-metal hip replacement Device that was surgically implanted in my client, Mrs. Dudley. She will tell you all about the suffering she experienced as a result of what we allege was a defective Device. The Defendant made the hip implant Device, which we refer to as the HID, H-I-D. I will inquire as to whether you or anyone in your family had any personal experiences with the HID. So let's begin.

Mr. Lawrence Hartmann, you have been designated Juror #1. Do you believe you can conduct a fair and impartial evaluation of the evidence presented and the law instructed to you by the Judge?

Juror #1 was a middle-aged African-American with slightly greying hair that gave him a look of sophistication and authority. He wore a sports coat and tie. He was tall, yet a little overweight.

JUROR #1: Please refer to me as Dr. Hartmann. I am a practicing pediatrician.

MR. BRADFORD: I apologize. The paper I was given stated only that you were in the medical field. So, Dr. Hartmann, can you answer the question for me?

JUROR #1: Yes, of course. The answer is that I believe I can listen to the testimony and assess whether the law entitles your client to collect damages.

MR. BRADFORD: If you were shown a document that contradicts the testimony of a witness, would you be able to fairly evaluate whether the witness was telling the truth?

MS. NUDBELLO: Objection. You can't ask him that question. There are no such documents and your question implies there are. Please withdraw the question.

MR. BRADFORD: With all due respect, I am going to proceed with the question. I have a right to ask whether a juror believes he or she has the ability to assess truthfulness.

JUROR #1: It's too hot in here for silly questions and silly lawyer repartee. Of course, I'm able to evaluate if the truth is being spoken in the face of contradictory evidence. I listen every day to parents explaining about the sickness or injury suffered by their child. I know when I'm being told a straight story and when I should notify the authorities of possible child abuse. By the way, when is the air conditioning coming on?

MR. BRADFORD: I'm afraid the Courthouse maintenance staff is unable to adjust to global warming and is also apparently unaware of early heat patterns caused by a massive buildup of CO_2 in the air. I'm kidding. The heat and air conditioning monitors are programmed to engage on pre-selected seasonal dates and will not change even if it's so hot all the ice at the North Pole melts and floods downtown with twelve feet of water. By the way, thank you for your candid response to my question. I have no objection to your service as Juror #1 and foreman of the jury.

MS. NUDBELLO: I have no challenge to Juror #1.

MR. BRADFORD: Juror #2, Good Morning. I see your name is Denise Davenport and you are a postal worker. I won't repeat the same questions to save time if you are comfortable providing a response.

Ms. Davenport was dressed in what appeared to be a fashionable running outfit that was green and yellow, with matching sneakers. She was thin, appeared fit and had a tan face, with hair so short it didn't cover her ears.

JUROR #2: Yes, I can answer your inquiries. I believe I will be fair and impartial. But, if a witness is proven to be untruthful, I will certainly disregard whatever story the witness is spinning. I'm a postal worker. I walk hundreds of miles delivering the mail. I work in a world inundated with federal rules and regulations. I comply with them, just as I expect a witness in this Court to abide by his or her sworn promise to tell the truth. And, as an aside, I don't mind the heat because I'm used to carrying a heavy mail bag during the dog days of summer.

MR. BRADFORD: Thank you. That was very informative. I have a couple of follow-up questions. First, have any friends or family members had hip or knee replacement surgery? Second, are any friends or family members practicing lawyers?

JUROR #2: A couple of people in my social circle are lawyers practicing on Long Island. But, that doesn't influence me one way or another. Everyone anticipates that lawyers stretch the truth to zealously or over-zealously pursue their clients' interests. So, I don't focus too much on what lawyers say. I focus instead on the words of the person who actually experienced the events being testified about.

MR. BRADFORD: Okay. I won't take your comment about lawyers personally. Actually, I used to deliver the mail on Long Island as a summer job during college, but the heat still bothers me. Especially, when I'm dressed in a suit and the hot air hangs lifelessly like it does today. No breeze, no movement, no relief. But, forgetting about that for a moment, please respond to my question regarding replacement surgery.

JUROR #2: Don't worry, you still look professional despite the sweat. You have very nice eyelashes.

The other jurors turned and stared at Juror #2, silently communicating the message that such personal comments are not appropriate. The jurors were taking their training session seriously.

JUROR #2: Sorry, I'll keep to the business at hand. As to replacement surgery, I think I had an uncle who had his knee replaced. As far as I know, everything went well.

MR. BRADFORD: I have no challenge to Juror #2.

MS. NUDBELLO: Assuming that Juror #2 makes no more complimentary statements towards Mr. Bradford, I also have no challenge. Mr. Bradford's ego needs no further inflation.

JUROR #2: Ms. Nudbello, I think you are professional and attractive also. I play no favorites.

MS. NUDBELLO: Thank you, let's move on.

Juror #3 was an unemployed, 22-year-old male named Tim Huff. He had unruly hair down to his shoulders and blue jeans.

MR. BRADFORD: Juror #3, Mr. Huff, how are you today?

JUROR #3: Okay, I guess.

MR. BRADFORD: Please provide your responses to the questions I posed to the other jurors.

MR. HUFF: I'm not so good at answering questions, but I can tell you one thing. I hate insurance companies. They screwed my mother by not paying for her medical care and now it's too late because she's dead. I don't know this

ZeiiMed company, but I have a grudge against them all.

MS. NUDBELLO: I challenge Juror #3 and ask that he be dismissed.

MR. BRADFORD: I agree. Mr. Huff, you are dismissed from your duties as a juror.

One of the jurors sitting in the rear of the Courtroom, a Mr. Peter Palmer, became Juror #3 as the replacement for Mr. Huff. Mr. Palmer was a 35-year-old car salesman with oily black hair and acne scars on his face. His button-down shirt was a bright orange, with a couple of coffee stains.

MR. BRADFORD: Mr. Peter Palmer, you are now Juror #3 with the responsibility to fairly and impartially return a verdict. Can you promise to do so?

JUROR #3: Yes, I absolutely assure you I will be fair and even-handed. Now, don't get me wrong. I believe in stretching the truth if necessary to get the deal done. But, I don't believe in lying and I won't stand for it if anyone else does. There are a couple of lawyers on my wife's side of the family, but I avoid them at family parties because they talk and talk and never let me get a word in. It's very annoying.

MR. BRADFORD: Yes, my wife's family seems to act the same way towards me. How about hip or knee replacement surgery? Have any friends or family members had it done?

JUROR #3: No, not that I remember.

MR. BRADFORD: Juror #3 is acceptable.

MS. NUDBELLO: I agree.

The questioning of the remaining jurors was quick and uneventful. All swore to be fair and impartial and none appeared to have an obvious bias. Juror #4 was a veterinarian in her mid-forties. Juror #5, was a residential oil burner serviceman, twenty years old. Juror #6 was a bookkeeper for a grocery store chain for thirty years. She plans to retire in six months to South Carolina with her husband of 40 years.

The jury was set. The Judge scheduled opening statements for Wednesday, March 14, 2012, two days from today.

-35-

Although I enjoy the challenge of presenting a case to a jury in open Court, I usually experience feelings of anxiety the first morning of trial. This time was different. The tension had begun to build as soon as *voir dire* was completed, two days before the trial began.

The Monday evening after jury selection was an uncomfortable situation at home with Kim. I attempted to explain the complexities of the trial and my strategy for cross-examination of the witnesses for ZeiiMed. She was distracted and disinterested. She could have at least pretended to listen, regardless of her level of boredom.

In addition to the usual worries I had about whether the case had been thoroughly and completely prepared for trial, I also had unresolved worries about Dr. Joe and his place in Kim's life. Rather than avoid the sensitive subject until after the trial, I stupidly brought it up once again.

"Are you still spending time with Dr. Joe?" I asked.

"Yes, you know I see him on a regular basis, usually at lunchtime," Kim responded.

"I'm very concerned about how close you two have become. Sooner or later, a man and a woman will start to express their mutual attraction on a physical level. I need to know if this has happened or is about to happen."

"I'm not sure it's any of your business. I love you and we have expressed our love for each other. Why do you need to know about Dr. Joe?" she asked.

"*Why*? How can you ask me that? I'm your husband and we took vows of fidelity and faithfulness, neither of which appears to be a priority of yours at the present time. I have a right to know and I want to know. My only alternative is to hire an investigator to follow you around and take pictures," I said, knowing my comments were inflammatory.

"That's outrageous. You're going to spy on me? Don't bother. I'll tell you. Nothing physical has occurred, although

Joe, I mean Dr. Joe, has asked when I may be ready to advance our relationship."

"So, he wants to know when you will sleep with him. That's great! I get to look forward to coming home from work one night and receiving word that you finally gave in to him. Or, maybe you have no intention of telling me when it happens. Either way, I don't like the result."

"I told you our relationship will remain regardless of what happens with Joe. That's why I don't feel it's necessary to provide you with weekly updates," Kim continued.

"I can't live like that. This isn't the free-love sixties. You can't be involved with him and married to me. It's as simple as that. Think about it and let me know your response. Goodnight. I'm going to bed."

I stormed up the stairs and slammed the door. I guess I made matters worse. Tomorrow, Kim will probably cry in the arms of Dr. Joe while telling him about her mean and insensitive husband. I'm sure he'll suggest they find a private place for an emotional release.

Something else to think about and something else to worry about.

How can I try a lawsuit and juggle personal problems at the same time?

I don't know, but I guess I'm about to find out.

-36-

The next morning, the Tuesday before trial, I arrived at work extra early to complete the outline of my opening statement to the jury. Upon arriving at my desk, I reached into my briefcase to get my note pad. I found something I hadn't put there. It was an envelope. Inside the envelope was a poem in Kim's handwriting.

This can't be good. Why would she write poetry in the middle of a marital disagreement over another man? I'm sure it doesn't contain inspirational words about how she is overwhelmed by an unrelenting passion for her husband. I decided to read the poem anyway. My heart was pounding with dread.

THE CHOICE

We've been feeling things are just not right;
I've been acting cold and tight many, many nights;
Should we try to fix the mix or is the divide too deep?
How can we mend the mess when we no longer agree on what should be?

Love is involved and deeply felt;
Either be with me at the peak or I'll seek others in the street;
There's no discount on having me;
No sale on my love and no bargain for being with no other;

Do you want to make it work or should I work on something else?
Do you agree to always be with me now that 'we' will no longer mean three?
Let me know soon because time is short
and life too tenuous to await the tentative.

I'm not the smartest husband in the world, but I think she's sending me a signal.

It appears she may be willing to go forward as a twosome rather than a threesome.

I guess tonight is the night I find out. Hopefully, I won't say anything stupid.

That will really throw her off guard.

-37-

I arrived home that Tuesday evening at 7 p.m. My opening statement in the trial begins tomorrow at 10 a.m.

I don't know which type of stress is worse–stress in the marriage or stress in anticipation of a trial. What I do know is that living with both at the same time is unbearable. I also know that if I'm able to resolve my marital conflicts, I'm much more capable of handling the professional anxiety.

Based on the content of her poem, I decided to start with an affirmative proclamation of my love and then play the rest by ear. This is a formula that has not worked well in the past, but maybe I'll get lucky this time.

Kim was sitting at the kitchen table in the back of the house. The center hall extends from the living room in the front of the house to the kitchen and family room in the rear of the house.

Kim looked up as I entered the kitchen area. I immediately leaned forward and kissed her lips firmly and enthusiastically.

"That was nice," Kim said.

I sat next to her at the kitchen table. She was wearing a revealing red sun dress that had no buttons or straps. Her shoulders and upper chest were bare, with the stretch material at the top of the dress pressing against the top of her breasts as the only support. The dress clung to the contours of her skin.

"I got your poem."

"Do you mean you found the poem in your brief case or you got the meaning of what I was trying to communicate?" Kim asked, in a quiet, non-aggressive tone.

"Good question. I wasn't clear. I read your poem with great interest and I believe I understand the message being conveyed."

"That's progress. What's your response? I think I implied in the poem that you should be direct and unhesitating."

"Kim, I love you and have always loved you every day of our marriage. I love your looks, your compassion, your caring and your company. It will never change–not on my end. Maybe I'm selfish, maybe I'm narrow-minded, but I don't want to share you mentally or physically with another man. I don't have that capability and I never want to possess that capability. I love you as part of us and I want it to be just us, and no one else. I commit to you and ask that you commit to me just like we did on our wedding day so many years ago."

"That's sweet. I've done a lot of thinking. I believed that on some level I could incorporate Joe into my life and our marriage without hurting or harming anyone. My plan was to continue our life together when we were together, but also have a separate relationship with Joe when you were not around. I was foolish and I apologize. I couldn't go to the next level with Joe because each time he tried to convince me to expand our physical interaction, all I could do was think of you. Plus, I know that you look a lot better naked than he does."

"Thank you for that very candid assessment–except you were kidding about the last part... right? You didn't actually see him naked? You were just imagining that good old Joe can't possibly compare with me on a physical level. I mean, it's an obvious point."

"Stop with the sexual jealousy. I love and want only you. I've made my decision and anything else that happened doesn't matter in the slightest. I will tell Joe our relationship is over and that we can't see each other, even as friends. I'm sure Joe will try to convince me that we can remain friends, but it just won't work. I'll let Joe know face to face at an appropriate time and place."

I leaned forward and kissed her again. First her lips, then her neck. Kim lifted her chin as I made my way affectionately down her neck. Kim put her hands behind my head and slowly guided me downward until I reached the fabric pressing against the top of her breasts. My fingers slid inside the top of the dress and pulled the fabric away from her body, exposing the tender white skin below her tan line. Her hands continued to lower my face into the softness of her figure. Kim arched her back in an instinctive reaction to the stimulation, her large eyes closed as she absorbed the sensations.

"Aren't you being friendly," Kim said.

"It's been a long time. I can't help myself," I responded, as I tilted my head upward to look up at her face.

"I think we would be more comfortable on the couch," Kim said between breaths.

"I agree."

We stood. I placed my hands on the sides of her dress just under each of her arms and pulled the dress down to her waist and then to her knees. Kim stepped out of the dress as she grabbed my shoulder for support.

"Don't you look beautiful," I commented.

"Thank you, but you haven't finished the unwrapping yet. Let's head to the living room."

We walked into the living room hand-in-hand until Kim stretched out along the length of the couch.

"Your turn now. You're a little over-dressed for this party. And please try to hurry," Kim said.

We spoke no more. There was no reason to. Our love was palpable and reciprocal. This is how it was and, hopefully, how it will be from now on.

-38-

At 8:30 a.m. the next morning, March 14, 2012, Mary and I were standing just off Wall Street, hailing a cab to the Courthouse at 60 Centre Street. The twenty boxes of documents needed at trial had been brought to the Courtroom of Judge Douglas Horton Horowitz the previous day.

Mary was professionally attired in a blue two-piece suit with two graduated strands of pearls around her neck, one eighteen inches and the other twenty-four inches in length. It seemed to be her usual Courthouse attire, but it worked well with the contrasting brightness of her blond hair. Mary's hair had been trimmed quite a bit and was now barely shoulder length, rather than extending down her back. It was an appealing look that made her appear younger and better able to endure the heat of the Courtroom.

A cab finally stopped. We climbed into the back.

"How do you feel about today?" Mary asked.

"I feel good. I know I repeat myself, but it's a peak experience to be in a Courtroom presenting a case to a judge, jury, opposing counsel and spectators."

"I know. You've told me. You think it's cool that all those people in the Courtroom are forced to listen to your every word, even when you don't know what you're talking about," Mary responded.

"I said that? I don't think I would say that. Did I say that?"

"Yes, you did. One of your homespun pearls of wisdom. By the way, you look very lawyerly in your navy blue suit and lime green tie," Mary commented.

"Thank you. You are also very appropriately dressed. But, I thought I mentioned that you were not required to wear the same colored suit as I do."

"What you actually said was a sarcastic comment that the Tweed, Fox & Fortune lawyers all look alike in the Courtroom, but luckily I was exempted from such a requirement. You thought you were being funny, but I really didn't think it was comical at the time. Since this conversation is going nowhere, I would like to discuss a new client who has requested the legal services of our firm."

"Okay. What's that all about," I responded.

"First of all," Mary said, "I don't know the name of the client. Only that he is an employee of the federal government as an intelligence operative of some sort. He said he has a secret Department of Justice White Paper dated November 8, 2011 that discusses the White House's position on when the president has the right to kill a U.S. citizen in a foreign country outside an area of active hostilities."

"You mean the White Paper authorizes the President to assassinate American citizens abroad by drone or other means?" I asked.

"Exactly. It's the White House's rationale for the use of lethal force against Americans overseas without a hearing, presentation of evidence, or other due process, whatsoever."

"That sounds like something the government probably doesn't want circulated."

"Of course," Mary said, "That's why our new client wants our help–he intends to someday release the White Paper to the world."

"I got some good advice for him. He better be ready to run far away and stay far away for a long time."

Mary grimaced and continued, "You are missing the point. It's wrong for our government to proclaim a death sentence on Americans overseas without a trial or other opportunity to present evidence demonstrating their innocence."

"I'm not so sure that's correct," I countered. "If some American in the Middle East is actively assisting or engaging in the planning of an attack against us and can't be captured, he should be targeted to go down."

"Maybe so, but you can't give the president sole authority to make that determination as judge and jury. Plus, according to Section 1119(a) of Title 18 of the U.S. Code, it is a crime to kill a national of the United States when the national is outside the United States, but within the jurisdiction of another country. How do you get around that law, duly passed by Congress and signed by the President?" Mary asked.

"My understanding is that Section 1119 does not make it a crime if the killing is justifiable or excusable. That is, Congress did not intend to make it a criminal act to carry out such killings if there was justification."

"That's simply and absolutely wrong," Mary responded." "The government thinks there is an exception for justifiable killings, but the government doesn't know what it's talking about. In 1997, the United States District Court for the Eastern District of California, in the case *United States v. White*, stated that the intent or culpability of the offender of Section 1119 must be evaluated in determining the punishment for its violation. The Federal Court confirmed it was Congressional intent to have the culpability of the offender determined before punishment is imposed under Section 1119. In other words, there must be a factual determination by a judge or jury of the intent or malice of the offender before concluding whether the prohibition on the killing of a U.S. citizen in a foreign country is waived as an excusable killing. The President can't make a determination of guilt on his own and then unilaterally impose a death sentence."

"Of course, what this all means is that the White Paper is very controversial and surely the government will want it back as a top-secret document. Sounds like our lawyers have their work cut out for them. But, one thing is for sure. If our new client discloses the White Paper to the world, his life will never be normal again and he will never live in America again," I said.

"I know, it's sad," Mary said. "But we swore an oath to zealously help and assist him as a client of the firm. I'm going to volunteer to be on the team that represents him."

"That sounds very nice. You inspire me. But, right now, in the next hour, we're going to begin the biggest trial of our lives–let's focus on that for the moment," I suggested.

"No problem–just thought I'd update you on current events at the office. As usual, as long as you're fighting

ZeiiMed in hand-to-hand combat, you're really not interested in anything else."

"That's right. All I care about is defeating ZeiiMed and getting a massive verdict in our client's favor."

"I'm with you," Mary said. "Let's go get 'em."

-39-

The taxi arrived in front of the Courthouse. There was the usual morning congestion at the front entrance, as each visitor is required to pass through an x-ray security checkpoint. As a result, we decided to use the little known and seldom-used rear entrance that is, coincidentally, only a few steps from the entrance to the Federal District Courthouse at 500 Pearl Street.

Also, the rear entrance does not require you to walk up a ton of steps, as does the front entrance. In fact, to reach the rear entrance, you actually walk down a couple of steps that are guarded to the left by a statue depicting Justice and to the right by a statue representing Authority.

Justice and Authority are sculptures designed and created by Philip H. Martony in or around 1901. Each is a five-foot stone statue of a female figure in a sitting position on a throne. Justice has a rolled scroll in her right hand and a round shield in her left, with a sword leaning against her left arm. Authority has five large books under her right leg and also has a rolled scroll, but in her left hand.

Justice and Authority were originally situated in front of the Hall of Records, which later became the Surrogate Court Building on Chambers Street. In 1961, a widening of the street required a change of venue. Authority was moved to a platform in front of the first column at the Courthouse at 60 Centre Street, which is to the left of the entrance door as one enters. Similarly, Justice was placed on an identical platform in front of the last column to the right of the front entrance at 60 Centre Street. In 1997, Justice and Authority were again moved, this time to their current resting place in front of the rear entrance to the Courthouse.

It is interesting to note that the United States Supreme Court Building in Washington, D.C. has two fifty-ton marble statues in the front called "Contemplation of Justice" and "Authority of Law" sculpted by James Earle Fraser in the early 1930's. While Contemplation of Justice is once again a female figure sitting on a throne, Authority of Law is a sitting male figure.

-40-

Once inside the Courthouse, Mary and I walked up two flights of stairs to the Courtroom of Judge Douglas Horton Horowitz.

As we entered the Courtroom, our first reaction, once again, was dismay at the intense heat. There was no breeze and not the slightest circulation of air. Although the abnormally high March temperatures made it warm everywhere, the Courtroom seemed to be a haven for stale air and unbearable humidity.

There were few people in the Courtroom other than New York lawyers. Apparently, no one wanted to be in the heat of the Courtroom, unless required as a participant in the trial.

Suzanna Nudbello was sitting at her counsel table, with only two other attorneys from Tweed, Fox & Fortune. ZeiiMed probably figured that the case was such a sure victory, there was no necessity for the usual army of lawyers.

I waved to Suzanna. She was dressed in black, which worked well with her platinum hair and one dark eyebrow. Once again, her face was moist from the heat. It enhanced her attractiveness. How can I be so easily distracted at such an important time? There must be something wrong with me, but I have no time to figure it out now.

Fred Dudley was sitting at the end of the first spectator's pew. Next to him was Martha Dudley in her wheelchair. I immediately walked over and gave Martha a kiss on the cheek, then shook hands with Fred. I asked Fred to take off his NAVY cap while in the Courtroom.

"A little heat isn't going to hold us back," Martha said with her usual optimism. "Don't worry about losing and don't worry about me. Just present your case in a straightforward fashion using everyday words like you were telling a bedtime story to a young child. You can do it. Go for the jugular."

"Thank you. You pay me to give advice and you're the one dispensing the wisdom and keeping a level head. I should split my fee with you. But all kidding aside, thanks for the pep talk," I responded.

Mary and I sat at our table in front of the Bench. Judge Horowitz quietly walked into the Courtroom through the door next to his Clerk's desk. No announcement of his arrival was made. No bells, whistles or loud bangs of a gavel to command our attention. His black robe made him look particularly uncomfortable in the heat.

The Judge took the Bench and immediately addressed the attorneys.

> JUDGE HOROWITZ: I hope this isn't going to take long. It's so hot in here I'm ready for a swim in the Hudson and I don't care if the water is 52 degrees and contains a toxic level of PCBs. I want both counsel to move this trial along as best you can. No duplication of testimony and no long speeches by counsel. Also, we will not get bogged down identifying, authenticating and admitting into evidence every document in this case. Only the most critical documents should be placed into evidence, and by that I mean a handful. I want this case submitted to the jury in no more than five business days from now.
>
> MS. NUDBELLO: Your Honor, as you may recall, as a result of a series of events that no one fully understands, there are no documents in this case, other than Martha Dudley's medical records. ZeiiMed has no documents. We previously explained to the Court how this occurred. Without any documents, I believe the case can be ready for the jury within the period of time you specified.
>
> MR. BRADFORD: I feel it's necessary to mention that I do have a number of ZeiiMed documents that I intend to place in evidence and show to ZeiiMed witnesses. There are less than ten documents that are critically important, so it

shouldn't delay the progress of the trial significantly.

MS. NUDBELLO: With all due respect, this is an outrage. The ZeiiMed documents were destroyed by a computer worm and it's my understanding none have been retrieved. Mr. Bradford cannot blindside me with documents he is now revealing for the first time at trial.

MR. BRADFORD: The documents I am talking about are emails that were sent to ZeiiMed, so they were received by ZeiiMed and seen by ZeiiMed. Even if Ms. Nudbello doesn't have the documents in front of her now, she nonetheless knows their content. ZeiiMed and their lawyers obviously read them before they were produced to me and then destroyed by the worm. That's probably the reason the worm ate the documents in the first place–ZeiiMed knows how damaging they are. At the appropriate time, I will explain to the Court how I obtained possession of the emails.

JUDGE HOROWITZ: I am not going to resolve this fight now. I did receive the report of the independent, forensic computer expert confirming that a Stuxnet-type worm was released into both parties' computers. However, the expert was unable to confirm how it happened or who was responsible. It doesn't matter now. I want to get started and we'll deal with the issue of documents as we go. The jury is entering the room, so please proceed with opening statements once the jurors are in the jury box. Mr. Bradford, you're up first.

MR. BRADFORD: Good morning, Mr. Foreman and ladies and gentlemen of the jury. The purpose of an opening statement is to describe the evidence you will hear during the trial. Nothing I say is evidence. Evidence consists of the testimony of the witnesses and the contents of documents provided to you.

Before I talk to you about my client, Martha Dudley, I want to discuss the Defendant ZeiiMed for a few moments.

This case is about a device. In fact, it's a case about *the Device*. And what is the Device? The Device is a Medical Device. It's made of various metals. The Device was designed, created, manufactured and sold to the public by ZeiiMed or the subsidiary it controls, MendMed.

The Device isn't something you listen to. It's not something you talk into. It doesn't have Internet access. Why? Because the Device is made to go inside your body. It's put there by a trained and experienced surgeon who cuts open the patient and inserts the Device.

It is common sense that if the Device goes inside your body, the Device should be safe. Certainly, neither you nor I would sell something that becomes a part of a human being, like blood, tissue, and internal organs, unless we were darn sure it not only worked but also wouldn't cause injury. A second grader would agree with us on this point. It's practical everyday sense that the Device should not be sold if it will harm a person once placed inside the body.

Ladies and gentlemen of the jury, that is exactly what ZeiiMed did. The Device was sold regardless of the harm. The evidence will show it. And, even more astounding, or should I say shameful, the evidence will also demonstrate that ZeiiMed knew the Device was defective, yet failed to disclose this knowledge and continued to sell the Device totally aware that you or I would buy the defective Device and have it surgically implanted inside our bodies.

The Device I am talking about is a Hip Implant Device, that I shall refer to as the H-I-D, the HID. The HID is used in a hip replacement operation. It consists of a cup, a ball that inserts in the cup, and a stem about eight inches long that attaches to a short neck on the ball. All are made of metal and the Device is commonly referred to as a metal-on-metal HID.

The uncontested evidence will demonstrate how the HID is implanted. However, I will now provide a short preview of what you will hear during the trial.

A catheter is inserted into the bladder for urination and a tube placed in the windpipe to control breathing. Anesthesia is administered. The surgeon then makes a ten to twelve-inch incision in the hip. Tissue and muscle are pushed aside and separated until the femur, the thigh bone, is exposed. The femur is a thick bone that goes from the hip to the knee. The top of the femur has a ball-shaped head that inserts in a natural cup-shaped socket in the hip. It's the socket and the ball that wear out and need replacement over time.

How does the surgeon do that? Well, a power saw is used to cut through the thigh bone to detach the God-given ball-shaped head from the femur. Once detached, the cup or socket in the hip is drilled out by cutting away the soft tissue, cartilage and muscle. A new metal cup is then cemented, yes, I said cemented, into the hip. Next, a new ball needs to be inserted, but the metal ball must first be attached to the sawed off thigh bone. How is that done you ask? I will tell you. The metal ball has a flexible two-inch metal neck attached to an eight-inch metal rod or stem that is a half-inch thick and tapered to a point at the end. Kind of like a long metal spike with a ball attached at the top. The tapered end of the spike is then jammed deep inside the thighbone and reinforced with a special cement that allows attachment to the body's tissue. It's not unlike a railroad worker using a sledge hammer to pound a metal spike into the tracks. Once done, the metal ball at the top of the spike is inserted into the new metal cup in the hip and the surgeon stitches the incision closed. The HID has now been installed. After a painful recovery and rehabilitation period, the patient should have full movement and flexibility without any more pain.

A miracle it surely is. Unless you were my client, the over sixty Mrs. Martha Dudley. She suffered through surgery and its aftermath based on a promise. A promise that she would walk again pain free. The promise was made by Zeii-Med in the instructional material that came with the HID. The surgeon confirmed the promise to Mrs. Dudley. The promise was not kept. The HID is defective. It's pouring metal poisons in her blood and her internal tissue has turned black due to decay.

She is here today, in the front row, in her wheelchair, next to her husband. Mrs. Dudley is too sick to undergo another operation to remove the defective HID. She is slowly dying and all she wanted was a safe HID so she could walk like everyone else.

I will demonstrate to you that ZeiiMed knew the dangers of the HID and didn't do anything about it. ZeiiMed lied and doesn't care about the consequences to Mrs. Dudley. The malicious and morally depraved ZeiiMed must be made to pay for this horrendous result.

I ask not only for damages to compensate Mrs. Dudley for her pain and suffering, but also billions of dollars in punitive damages to send a message that such abuse will not be tolerated in America by Americans. Thank you for listening.

JUDGE HOROWITZ: I said the openings were to be short. That was informative, but too long. Please proceed in a more concise manner, Ms. Nudbello.

MS. NUDBELLO: Good morning. I am counsel to ZeiiMed. I'm sure you will join me in congratulating Mr. Bradford on a very eloquent and compelling presentation. But, with all due respect, my adversary was not entirely accurate. Yes, Mrs. Dudley is sick. Yes, Mrs. Dudley had her hip replaced with a Device sold by ZeiiMed. Yes, you and I feel very badly that Mrs. Dudley may be suffering. No, it is not ZeiiMed's fault and Mr. Bradford has no evidence to prove it is ZeiiMed's fault. Maybe the surgeon inserted the Device improperly. Maybe the cup was inserted into the hip at the wrong angle. Maybe Mrs. Dudley's previous physical injuries, occupational exposure to toxins and personal habits, like smoking, caused her physical problems. We don't know and this trial will not provide all the answers. However, one thing will be proven–ZeiiMed designed and tested the Device with great care and had no knowledge that it was defective or could cause physical injury to anyone. Thank you. Your Honor, I did my best to keep it short and concise.

After the opening statements, the proceedings were adjourned until the afternoon.

At 2:00 p.m., the Court was again in session.

MR. BRADFORD: I call as my first witness Mrs. Martha Dudley.

Her husband pushed the wheelchair across the floor of the Courtroom to an open area directly in front of the witness stand. The wheelchair was then turned around so Mrs. Dudley could see both the jurors and the attorneys. She was only a couple of feet from the first juror, Jury Foreman

Lawrence Hartmann. Of course, Mrs. Dudley was physically unable to step into the witness stand.

Mrs. Dudley's black hair was again in a bun, and again the Scales of Justice pin was attached to her blouse. Her heavy use of makeup made her face look healthy and radiant from a distance. I forgot to tell Martha to look pale and sickly.

> COURT CLERK: Mrs. Dudley, please raise your right hand. Do you hereby swear to tell the truth, the whole truth, and nothing but the truth.
>
> MRS. DUDLEY: You bet I do.
>
> MR. BRADFORD: Good afternoon. For the record, I note that you are in a wheelchair here today. Is that correct?
>
> MRS. DUDLEY: Yes, it is. I have been in this damn chair ever since that HID they placed in me started saturating my blood with a bunch of poisons.
>
> MR. BRADFORD: That's exactly what I was about to get to. Please explain why you are in the wheelchair.
>
> MS. NUDBELLO: I object. The only way Mrs. Dudley knows anything about the cause of her injuries is because doctors told her. That is hearsay and should not be allowed.
>
> MR. BRADFORD: Your Honor, Mrs. Dudley should be permitted to talk about her physical condition and explain how her physical condition deteriorated over time. Later in the trial, we will call an expert medical witness to testify to the extreme levels of cobalt and chromium in her blood and how this was caused by the grinding of the metal ball against the edges of the metal cup.
>
> JUDGE HOROWITZ: Enough with the long speeches, Mr. Bradford. I will permit the witness to testify as to her injuries and the manner in which the injuries developed over time.

MR. BRADFORD: Please proceed, Mrs. Dudley.

MRS. DUDLEY: It's about time somebody let me talk. I mean no disrespect to the Court, but we all know how lawyers love to talk and talk and talk, my lawyer included. I, on the other hand, will be short and to the point in my testimony. To start with, my hip simply wore out. I didn't need a doctor to confirm that. I knew it. Any movement of my leg, either walking or sitting, caused a sharp pain in my left hip that felt like bone was scraping against bone. So, about five years ago, in 2007, I decided to undergo surgery, with the HID replacing the worn-out God-given cup in my hip bone and the worn-out God-given ball that moves inside the cup. That's when ZeiiMed screwed me and my personal hell began.

MS. NUDBELLO: I object to Mrs. Dudley's use of such crass language.

MRS. DUDLEY: I'm telling it like it is. If you're offended I apologize, but I suspect this isn't the first time you've heard such blunt words.

MR. BRADFORD: Mrs. Dudley, I'll take care of this.

JUDGE HOROWITZ: No, I'll take care of this. The witness is instructed to refrain from overly dramatic characterizations. Just stick to the facts.

MRS. DUDLEY: Yes, Your Honor. After the HID was inserted, I started rehabilitation. Within a month, the hip started making a clicking noise. Then, the condition worsened. I couldn't walk. I couldn't take a step. I heard popping noises and felt like the metal ball had slipped out of the cup. If I lay down and stretched a certain way, I could feel the ball going back into the cup. The pain was extreme. This went on for months. I was hoping my body's tissue would grow around the HID and eventually stabilize the Device. However, by the time my doctor realized the HID was defective and needed to come out, my blood had a dangerously high level of metal contamination nearly ten times higher than normal. My weakened condition, including problems with my kidneys and eyesight due to the blood poisoning, prevented further surgery. I am hopeful that blood transfusions and chelation therapy may help me recover sufficient health to replace the HID. If not, I am stuck in this wheelchair until I die a slow death from this damn Device. I'd like to rip it out myself and wrap it around the neck of the idiot at ZeiiMed who designed the thing.

MR. BRADFORD: Were you ever informed by anyone that there was over a 50% risk that the HID would fail due to its design?

MRS. DUDLEY: No.

MR. BRADFORD: Were you ever told the risk of exposure to toxic metals?

MRS. DUDLEY: No.

MR. BRADFORD: If you had been informed of such risks, would you have still chosen the metal-on-metal HID?

MRS. DUDLEY: I'll tell you one thing for sure–I would not have chosen the metal-on-metal HID manufactured by ZeiiMed.

MS. NUDBELLO: Objection.

JUDGE HOROWITZ: Overruled. Mrs. Dudley's entitled to testify what she would have done or not done if she had been aware of the alleged design defects.

MR. BRADFORD: No further questions.

JUDGE HOROWITZ: Proceed with your cross-examination, Ms. Nudbello.

Ms. Nudbello approached the wheelchair, dragging behind her a wooden chair from her counsel table. She then placed the chair in front of the wheelchair and sat down. Ms.

Nudbello and Mrs. Dudley were now facing each other, with only a couple of feet of space between them.

> MR. BRADFORD: Your Honor, I object to Ms. Nudbello positioning herself directly in the face of my client. I think she should back up and give my client some breathing room.
>
> MS. NUDBELLO: What are you afraid of—that I'll intimidate your client into telling the truth?
>
> MRS. DUDLEY: I can handle it, Brian. If she gets nasty, I'll just push her backwards. There's nothing wrong with my arms. By the way, I love your eyebrows, Ms. Nudbello. Very different.

The jurors grinned and several spectators laughed out loud.

> JUDGE HOROWITZ: In view of the extreme heat, a little levity is welcome. Let's continue in a civilized fashion. Ms. Nudbello can remain seated in front of the witness and shall proceed with her questions in a professional manner. If Mrs. Dudley eventually feels the need for more space, I am sure she will say so loud and clear.
>
> MS. NUDBELLO: Were you ever employed?
>
> MRS. DUDLEY: Yes, I retired about ten years ago. I worked as a receptionist, cashier and bookkeeper at an auto paint and body shop.
>
> MS. NUDBELLO: At an auto body shop where cars were repaired after being in accidents?
>
> MRS. DUDLEY: Yes, of course. Silly question, it seems to me.
>
> MS. NUDBELLO: Is it accurate to say that metal car parts were cut, sanded, scraped and painted at the shop?
>
> MRS. DUDLEY: Yes.
>
> MS. NUDBELLO: Isn't it also true that the reception area where you worked was separated

by only a five-foot partition, so the bodywork was done only a few feet from you?

MRS. DUDLEY: Yes, that's true. The partition separated where I sat from where the body work was done. There was an unobstructed space above the partition.

MS. NUDBELLO: Was there an air filtration system to protect against metal particulates in the air caused by the sanding, cutting and scraping of the car parts?

MRS. DUDLEY: No.

MS. NUDBELLO: How many years did you work there?

MRS. DUDLEY: Twenty years.

MS. NUDBELLO: For twenty years, five days a week, you were exposed to toxic metals and toxic paints in the air, isn't that true?

MR. BRADFORD: Objection. Ms. Nudbello raised her voice and is leaning into the witness. Also, Mrs. Dudley has no personal knowledge of any chemicals in the air at the shop. She didn't conduct an environmental monitoring of the air while she worked there.

JUDGE HOROWITZ: Objection overruled. The witness shall answer based on her years of smelling, tasting and breathing the air at the auto shop. Ms. Nudbello, please don't get any closer to the witness.

MRS. DUDLEY: I didn't conduct a scientific analysis of the air, but I inhaled and exhaled the air in the shop for eight hours a day each business day.

MS. NUDBELLO: Did you smoke cigarettes at work?

MRS. DUDLEY: Yes.

MS. NUDBELLO: How many a day?

MRS. DUDLEY: Ten or fifteen a day.

MS. NUDBELLO: For twenty years?

MRS. DUDLEY: Yes.

MS. NUDBELLO: After you retired, but before the HID was inserted, were you diagnosed with high blood pressure, high cholesterol and hardening of the arteries?

MRS. DUDLEY: Yes, that is generally correct.

MS. NUDBELLO: Isn't it true that your medical records indicated high levels of toxins in your blood before your hip surgery?

MR. BRADFORD: Objection. The medical records speak for themselves. If Ms. Nudbello wants the jury to know what the medical records stated, then get the actual documents and show them to the jury.

JUDGE HOROWITZ: I'll permit the question in so far as it explores Mrs. Dudley's understanding of her medical condition.

MRS. DUDLEY: I'm aware that blood tests prior to my hip surgery revealed some metal toxins resulting from my employment history at the auto repair shop, but I don't know if chromium and cobalt were detected.

MS. NUDBELLO: Both kidney functions and visual acuity can be affected by metal toxins–isn't that correct?

MRS. DUDLEY: I don't know. You'll have to ask my doctors. I simply don't know. All I know is that I can't walk after ZeiiMed's Device was put in me.

MS. NUDBELLO: No further questions.

MRS. DUDLEY: Judge–I'm very tired. Can I have the rest of the day off?

JUDGE HOROWITZ: Any rebuttal questions for Mrs. Dudley?

MR. BRADFORD: I have no further questions for Mrs. Dudley.

JUDGE HOROWITZ: Court is adjourned until tomorrow morning at which time Mr. Bradford will call his next witness.

Mary and I stood as the Judge left the Bench. I grabbed the handles of Mrs. Dudley's wheelchair and pushed it from the front of the Courtroom towards the rear exit. Mrs. Dudley's head seemed to slump to one side, but Mary was walking next to the wheelchair in case she needed assistance.

I leaned towards the front of the wheelchair and quietly spoke into Martha's ear.

"Don't worry about anything. Tomorrow will be our turn. In the next couple of days, we'll have ZeiiMed on the run. I promise you that. We will blow them out of the building. ZeiiMed will beg us to settle."

"Or," Mary said, "ZeiiMed will just kill us all and say it was an accident."

"That's not funny," I responded. "ZeiiMed won't do that– it would show the world that we're telling the truth. Let's not alarm Mrs. Dudley. She just had a very stressful day on the witness stand."

"ZeiiMed doesn't care about the truth, doesn't care about our lives and certainly doesn't want justice to prevail," Mary continued. "You know that all too well. Not only does ZeiiMed inflict suffering on whomever gets in its way, its lawyers show up in Court and try to blame the innocent for the misery that was dispensed. It's nauseating."

"Martha, don't listen to Mary. She's being negative. The trial is stressful on all of us. Everything will be much better tomorrow. I promise."

On the other hand, maybe Mary was right. However, she shouldn't have added to Mrs. Dudley's discomfort by making the point when she did. Mary needs to have better professional judgment, but it's all part of the learning process. I'll talk to her when I get a chance. She must learn that there are times when it is best not to tell the truth to a client. The truth can be too upsetting. Lawyers only tell the truth some of the time, when convenient. I thought everyone knew that.

-41-

At 10 a.m. on the morning of Thursday, March 15, 2012, I called my second witness, Dr. Howard Heeled.

COURT REPORTER: Raise your right hand, please. Do you solemnly swear that the testimony you will give today is the truth, the whole truth and nothing but the truth, so help you God?

DR. HEELED: I do.

MR. BRADFORD: Good Morning, Dr. Heeled. Please state your full name and title for the record.

DR. HEELED: My name is Dr. Howard Heeled and I am the Chief Orthopedic Surgeon at ZeiiMed, as well as the Head Designer of the hip replacement Device, which was implanted in Mrs. Dudley.

Dr. Heeled was confident and relaxed. Why shouldn't he be? He was sure nothing existed that would make his deposition testimony appear inaccurate or untruthful. He didn't know I had the ammunition necessary to expose him as a liar. I intended to conduct a very aggressive examination.

He was dressed in an expensive three-button silk suit from Italy. Since I last saw him at the deposition, the brown birthmarks above each of his eyes appeared larger. Also, his left eye was almost totally concealed by excessive skin hanging below his eyebrow. Gravity caused the drooping skin to function like a window shade over his eye. He was wearing some kind of brace on his wrist. Obviously, I had caused some damage when I deflected his punch during the deposition.

MR. BRADFORD: For the record, we first met when I asked you a series of questions at your deposition. Is that correct?

DR. HEELED: Yes, it is.

MR. BRADFORD: By the way, I notice some kind of brace or bandage. How is your wrist feeling these days? Better, I hope?

DR. HEELED: Yes, it is better. However, Ms. Nudbello told me not to discuss the injury with you and she also asked me not to testify about how the injury occurred.

MS. NUDBELLO: That's correct, Your Honor. I so instructed my client.

MR. BRADFORD: I have no issue with that. I'm not asking any further questions about his wrist. I just wanted to make sure that Dr. Heeled knew how concerned I was about his health–a concern which ZeiiMed apparently doesn't have towards the purchasers of its Device.

MS. NUDBELLO: Objection. There has been no such evidence.

JUDGE HOROWITZ: Sustained. Stick to the evidence and refrain from inflammatory comments. Proceed.

MR. BRADFORD: During your deposition, I made you a promise. A promise to be fulfilled at trial. Do you remember what my promise was?

MS. NUDBELLO: This is highly objectionable. At the deposition, Mr. Bradford wrongfully accused Dr. Heeled of certain conduct that is not relevant or appropriate for the jury to hear.

MR. BRADFORD: Your Honor, I have the right to test the recollection of this witness. If he can't remember what I told him during the deposition, then the jury should be aware of his memory lapse in judging his credibility.

JUDGE HOROWITZ: Proceed with this one question, then I want you to get to the relevant issues surrounding the design of the Device.

DR. HEELED: I remember you told me at the deposition that I was not truthful and you would prove it. I resented your comment and I resented you for saying it. That hasn't changed.

MR. BRADFORD: Did you lie during your deposition?

MS. NUDBELLO: Objection. My client was sworn to tell the truth and that's what he did. It's up to the jury to determine if the witness was untruthful.

MR. BRADFORD: If the witness knows he is a liar and admits to being a liar, then that certainly goes a long way in helping the jury determine the veracity of his testimony.

JUDGE HOROWITZ: The witness will answer the question, but this will be my last warning to you, Mr. Bradford. Stop pursuing side issues and start questioning the witness about the HID and nothing else. If you have documents or prior testimony that demonstrate untruthful responses, then show the evidence to the witness and let the jury decide his veracity.

DR. HEELED: I did not lie during my deposition.

MR. BRADFORD: Will you tell the jury if and when you lie during your testimony today?

DR. HEELED: I am not going to tell a lie today.

MR. BRADFORD: That's not my question. If you do lie today, will you acknowledge the lie to the jury? That's my question.

DR. HEELED: Yes, I will so inform the jury if I make an untrue statement today. Can we get on with this?

MR. BRADFORD: I will ask the questions here. Did you lie when you said you were not going to lie during your testimony today?

DR. HEELED: I don't know what you are asking. If you have a point to make, please make it. Right now, you've got me confused by the question.

MS. NUDBELLO: I'm also confused. Dr. Heeled is a fact witness who is here today to testify to facts. Mr. Bradford's badgering of Dr. Heeled about whether he lied without proof of an untrue statement is unacceptable. Please instruct counsel to go to a new topic or sit down.

MR. BRADFORD: If the witness will answer my last question, I will then switch topics.

JUDGE HOROWITZ: The witness must answer this last question on the truth of his testimony. Then move on, Mr. Bradford.

DR. HEELED: I did not lie when I promised to tell the truth today.

MR. BRADFORD: Remember, you promised this jury you would tell them if you do lie, isn't that correct?

JUDGE HOROWITZ: The witness does not have to answer. His answer is already in the record. One more question like that and I will place you in contempt of Court.

MR. BRADFORD: I apologize, Your Honor. I'm switching gears right now.

ZeiiMed stopped production of the HID in 2010. Was that because ZeiiMed knew the Device was defective based on a high failure rate?

DR. HEELED: No, that is not the reason ZeiiMed ceased production.

MR. BRADFORD: Isn't it a fact that you and other ZeiiMed officials knew since at least 2005 that the cup was too small, too shallow and too thick, thereby preventing the ball from moving freely within the cup during movement?

DR. HEELED: That is not true.

MR. BRADFORD: Isn't it true that defects in the design of the cup forced the ball to scrape against the edges of the cup, causing a release of metal particles?

DR. HEELED: The first part is untrue. As to the second part, there is always some release of metal fragments, but the test model of the HID confirmed time and time again that the exposure was in a safe range.

MR. BRADFORD: Isn't it correct that the cup has a groove on the inside which permits a medical instrument to be inserted inside the cup for assistance in placement of the cup at the correct angle in the hip?

DR. HEELED: That is correct.

MR. BRADFORD: Isn't it also correct that you were informed that the inside groove limited the area within which the ball could rotate during movement, thereby creating metal-on-metal friction between the edges of the groove and the ball?

DR. HEELED: I have no knowledge of that. I was never told it was true and I would have disclosed the problem immediately if I had known.

MR. BRADFORD: Isn't it true that ZeiiMed hired medical doctors as consultants to provide training to other doctors across the nation in the correct surgical implant of the HID?

DR. HEELED: That is correct—ZeiiMed wanted to make sure that hospitals across the nation were performing the surgery efficiently, professionally and with optimum opportunity for a 100% success rate 100% of the time.

MR. BRADFORD: So, these medical consultants are your people, paid ZeiiMed doctors, who recommended the HID to the public and instructed hospital staffs on the correct implantation of the Device.

DR. HEELED: Correct.

MR. BRADFORD: Since the medical consultants dealt with the HID on a daily basis, you must give great credence to any suggestions, comments or opinions of the consultants regarding the everyday implant and functioning of the HID. Isn't that true?

DR. HEELED: That would also be correct. Our consultants provided us with the feedback that confirmed the success of the HID.

MR. BRADFORD: Your Honor, I would like to now adjourn any further questioning of Dr. Heeled until tomorrow. I have quite a few questions still to be asked, but the questions deal with several documents to be presented to the jury and the Court. I will be able to proceed most efficiently if I am provided extra time today to organize both the documents and my questions regarding the documents.

JUDGE HOROWITZ: Any objection, Ms. Nudbello?

MS. NUDBELLO: After the witness intimidation by Mr. Bradford, I think it's a welcome relief to adjourn until tomorrow.

JUDGE HOROWITZ: Court is adjourned until tomorrow, at which time Mr. Bradford will complete his examination of Dr. Heeled, without all the circular and repetitive questions. Mr. Bradford, you are on notice. Further verbal gymnastics with the witness will result in significant sanctions against you and your client. If you've got evidence of the allegations you've asserted against ZeiiMed, then present it to the Court and jury tomorrow or forever hold your peace. Good day.

-42-

The next day, Friday, March 16, 2012, Dr. Heeled returned to the witness stand. The Judge was behind the Bench and all the jurors were present and accounted for. Mary Douglas was with me at our counsel table and Suzanna Nudbello had several young male attorneys assisting her. The public pews in the rear were packed with spectators.

Clearly, word had spread that acrimony was high in the Courtroom. People enjoy watching the vitriol between lawyers and witnesses during a trial. I was certain all would be satisfied customers by the conclusion of today's proceedings. I enjoyed playing to a full house.

> COURT REPORTER: Do you understand that you are still under oath, sworn to tell the truth?
>
> DR. HEELED: I do.
>
> MR. BRADFORD: Good morning. Please explain for the jurors the role of the medical consultants hired by ZeiiMed.
>
> DR. HEELED: ZeiiMed hires the top doctors in the world to test its medical devices and to teach other doctors how to use them. The consultants spread the word and encourage other medical practitioners to add ZeiiMed products to their medical practices.
>
> MR. BRADFORD: Did ZeiiMed hire medical consultants with regard to the HID–the metal-on-metal Device?
>
> DR. HEELED: Yes, of course we did.
>
> MR. BRADFORD: Once the medical consultants had an opportunity to use the HID, was it part of their responsibilities to report to ZeiiMed on the performance of the Device?
>
> DR. HEELED: Yes, we pay close attention to the comments and input of our medical professionals.

MR. BRADFORD: I would like to mark as ZeiiMed Exhibit #1 an email addressed to Dr. Heeled dated March 13, 2006, and admit the document into evidence.

After the document was marked as Exhibit #1, it was scanned and entered into the computer system in the Courtroom. The document immediately appeared on the monitors conveniently installed on the Bench, the counsel tables and the witness stand, as well as the monitors in front of each seat in the jury box and the large video screen facing the jury box.

The Courtroom was silent as ZeiiMed Exhibit #1, dated March 13, 2006, was read by all.

From:Fred Feigelman, MD
Sent:March 13, 2006 3:33 pm
To:Howard Heeled, MD (ZeiiHeeled@medmail.com)
Subject:ZeiiMed's Hip Device ("the Device")

Hope all is well with the family. I'm looking forward to spring after our long winter.

This will confirm our many discussions over the last few months. As you know, I have grave concerns about the design of the metal-on-metal Device and its consistent failure once implanted.

The Cup shape is wrong in a number of ways. The groove exacerbates the problem. There simply isn't enough room inside the surface of the Cup to permit proper movement of the Ball–causing extreme wear on the edges of the Cup. You know what that means. Metallosis has consistently followed implant. The tissue surrounding the Device turns black from necrosis, the Ball snaps out of the Cup and the blood is tainted with chromium and cobalt.

I have been investigating these findings for over a year. I will no longer use the Device at my Hospital. Either redesign or recall immediately.

Sorry to ruin your day, but everything discussed in this email you already know. We've talked about this several times.

Please get back to me as soon as possible.

Regards,

Fred

Fred Feigelman, MD, FACS, FAAOS
Hospital for Special Surgery
535 East 70th Street
New York, NY 10021

Brian Bradford waited. He wanted the Judge and jurors to take plenty of time to read and digest the compelling contents of ZeiiMed Exhibit #1. Brian anticipated that the email would be reviewed multiple times in order to fully understand its impact and implications.

Brian looked at Suzanna as she stared at her monitor with her mouth agape. Her eyes quickly moved from the monitor and locked onto him. Her look of dismay and desperation wasn't simply because the jurors might turn against ZeiiMed, it was because she was certain ZeiiMed would now turn against her in retribution. Brian knew the look–he'd seen it before on the faces of other doomed ZeiiMed lawyers.

MR. BRADFORD: I have now presented Dr. Heeled with a hard copy of the March 13, 2006 email from Fred Feigelman, a Fellow of the American Academy of Orthopaedic Surgeons. Also, everyone has the document, now marked as ZeiiMed Exhibit #1, on their monitors. Dr. Heeled have you reviewed this email?

DR. HEELED: I read it.

MR. BRADFORD: Have you ever seen this email before?

DR. HEELED: I don't remember. It's addressed to me, but that was six years ago. I get hundreds of emails a day. I've received over a million emails since this email was supposedly sent.

MR. BRADFORD: Let's start with a simpler question. Did you receive this email marked as ZeiiMed Exhibit #1? Although this is one of the documents that the computer worm eradicated from ZeiiMed's computers, I caution you that a search of Dr. Feigelman's computer records will confirm that it was in fact sent on March 13, 2006 at 3:33 p.m.

DR. HEELED: I have no reason to believe I didn't receive it. I just don't remember receiving it.

MR. BRADFORD: Who is Dr. Fred Feigelman, the sender of the email?

DR. HEELED: He is a prominent orthopaedic surgeon and at one time was a paid medical consultant of ZeiiMed.

MR. BRADFORD: Isn't it fair to say that Dr. Feigelman is one of the most prominent orthopaedic surgeons in the world? Again, you should be aware that Dr. Feigelman has been served with a subpoena and is scheduled to testify during this trial.

DR. HEELED: Yes, Dr. Feigelman is a well-known and highly skilled surgeon.

MR. BRADFORD: And that's why ZeiiMed hired him as a consultant, isn't that true?

DR. HEELED: Yes, we were proud to have him on our staff.

MR. BRADFORD: And, consistent with Dr. Feigelman's elevated status in the medical community, ZeiiMed held his opinions and evaluations in high regard. Isn't that true?

DR. HEELED: Yes, that is true.

MR. BRADFORD: So, getting back to ZeiiMed Exhibit #1, isn't it also a fact that Dr. Feigelman was telling you that the HID was defective and unsafe to use in any manner? To quote, "Metallosis has consistently followed implant" of the Device. You knew this to be true upon receipt of this email. Isn't that correct?

DR. HEELED: That's what Dr. Feigelman said–but I don't remember reading this email.

MR. BRADFORD: Do you remember Dr. Feigelman orally providing you this same information in 2006? And, please remember, Dr. Feigelman will appear in Court to testify about the conversation.

DR. HEELED: Yes, I do recall Dr. Feigelman speaking to me generally about the issue.

MR. BRADFORD: So, whether it was a result of this email marked as ZeiiMed Exhibit #1 or oral conversations with Dr. Feigelman, you knew it was Dr. Feigelman's opinion that the HID was defectively designed, caused injury and should be recalled?

DR. HEELED: Yes, that was Dr. Feigelman's opinion. He is one of over 600,000 doctors who I communicate with across the country and around the world.

DR. BRADFORD: Isn't it a fact that ZeiiMed made no design changes as a result of the information you received from Dr. Feigelman?

DR. HEELED: We considered it, but in the end made no changes because ZeiiMed didn't agree with Dr. Feigelman's opinion.

MR. BRADFORD: Also, ZeiiMed did not disclose Dr. Feigelman's concerns to the public?

DR. HEELED: It wasn't necessary.

MR. BRADFORD: That's not what I asked you. Please answer the question. Did ZeiiMed disclose Dr. Feigelman's concerns to the public?

DR. HEELED: ZeiiMed did not.

MR. BRADFORD: I have two additional emails from Dr. Feigelman. I would like them marked as ZeiiMed Exhibit #2 and ZeiiMed Exhibit #3 and admitted into evidence.

MS. NUDBELLO: Objection. Your Honor this is an issue that has been previously presented to the Court. I don't know how or where Mr. Bradford obtained these emails. As you are aware, ZeiiMed produced its HID documents, but all documents were then mysteriously destroyed by a computer worm of unknown origins. ZeiiMed is now being blindsided with documents it didn't know existed.

MR. BRADFORD: It is irrelevant that ZeiiMed thought the documents were destroyed. Obviously, ZeiiMed was wrong and it's not my responsibility to inform ZeiiMed of its mis-calculations. First, you would think ZeiiMed would be pleased that suddenly its HID documents are available so we can all learn the truth together. Second, Dr. Feigelman retained copies of all his emails to ZeiiMed as part of his regular business records. Dr. Feigelman will appear in this Courtroom and will testify to the authenticity of these documents. As a result, it doesn't matter if ZeiiMed produced Dr. Feigelman's emails or not. Doctor Feigelman sent the emails to ZeiiMed and will tell the jury about them. That alone is sufficient to have the documents authenticated and entered into evidence. ZeiiMed's mistake was to assume that I would never be able to learn of Dr. Feigelman's involvement with the HID. ZeiiMed was wrong and is now faced with the high cost of that mistake. I got the exhibits from Dr. Feigelman and the same documents were in ZeiiMed's files before the worm was released.

Also, the Court should be aware that months after the worm destroyed all the ZeiiMed documents, a second set of the same HID papers were mysteriously emailed to my colleague Mary Douglas. I don't know who actually sent them, but our investigation revealed it was a Cloud vendor hired by ZeiiMed.

JUDGE HOROWITZ: The objection is overruled. Although the Court never fully understood how or why ZeiiMed's documents were lost, destroyed or eaten by the dog, the fact remains that Dr. Feigelman will presumably verify his emails by his testimony in this Court. Also, Dr. Heeled does not contest that the emails were received by him. As such, Ms. Nudbello, you should not be surprised to see emails that are part of the business records of ZeiiMed. The documents are admitted into evidence, subject to reconsideration if not authenticated by Dr. Feigelman tomorrow.

Mr. Bradford, when you return to your office tonight, please email to Ms. Nudbello all the ZeiiMed HID documents received from the Cloud vendor. After this trial is over, I may conduct a hearing on why ZeiiMed did not disclose that a Cloud vendor retained a copy of the documents destroyed by the worm.

The Court Reporter marked the two emails as ZeiiMed Exhibit #2 and ZeiiMed Exhibit #3. The emails were then posted on all the monitors in the Courtroom.

From:Fred Feigelman, MD
Sent:April 2, 2006 1:00 pm
To:Howard Heeled, MD
(ZeiiHeeled@medmail.com)
Subject:The Device

I haven't heard from you since my email of March 13, 2006. I've polled my colleagues at other hospitals and various ZeiiMed consultants. Everyone agrees. Get the Device off the Market–innocent people are suffering severely. What are you waiting for?

Fred

Fred Feigelman, MD, FACS, FAAOS
Hospital For Special Surgery
535 East 70th Street
New York, NY 10021

From:Fred Feigelman, MD
Sent:April 15, 2006 10:35 am
To:Howard Heeled, MD
(ZeiiHeeled@medmail.com)
Subject:The Device

I am not sending any more emails. This is the last. However, I have instructed all ZeiiMed consultants to stop using the Device. I also told them to send you an email stating that the Device belongs in the trash. You will soon be flooded with emails from ZeiiMed doctors that you hired describing the same defects that ZeiiMed has known for years.

I'm done with ZeiiMed. Feel free to discontinue my monthly consultation fee. A sound sleep is more important than money.

One last thought. Please delete me as a "friend" on your Facebook page. I saw your posting that stated: "the pathetic cripples should stop complaining that they can't immediately walk on water after receiving the Device."

You should be ashamed.

Fred

Fred Feigelman, MD, FACS, FAAOS
Hospital For Special Surgery
535 East 70th Street
New York, NY 10021

MR. BRADFORD: Have you had an opportunity to examine ZeiiMed Exhibits #2 and #3?

DR. HEELED: Yes, I have.

MR. BRADFORD: Do you have any reason to believe that these emails were not received by you?

DR. HEELED: Again, I don't remember reading them in 2006, but I can't say they were not received by me.

MR. BRADFORD: How many paid consultants did ZeiiMed have in 2006 who worked with the Device?

DR. HEELED: About 300 to 400. ZeiiMed wanted to eventually have an orthopedic representative in every major hospital in America.

MR. BRADFORD: According to Dr. Feigelman's email of April 15, 2006 each of these 300 to 400 paid consultants were told to send you a separate email discussing the defects inherent in the metal-on-metal HID. In 2006, did you receive approximately 300 to 400 such emails from ZeiiMed's paid consultants?

DR. HEELED: I don't remember.

MR. BRADFORD: I don't believe you. How dare you have the nerve to tell this jury you don't remember receiving 300 to 400 emails from your own doctors telling you the Device injured people. You don't remember? That is absurd and simply not believable. I have copies of some of these emails and I've served a subpoena on many of the paid consultants to verify they were sent. Do you still insist that you don't remember?

MS. NUDBELLO: Objection. He's screaming at the witness and essentially telling the jurors he's a liar.

JUDGE HOROWITZ: Overruled. The witness brought these problems on himself–Mr. Bradford has the right to question the limited knowledge of the witness.

DR. HEELED: The more I think about it, the clearer my recollection becomes. I do generally remember that some consultants raised the issue of defects in the Device in 2006.

MR. BRADFORD: You promised to tell me when you told a lie. You just told a lie when you said you didn't remember. But, you didn't acknowledge it was a lie. So, you lied twice despite the fact you've sworn to tell the truth. Isn't that true?

DR. HEELED: Stop calling me a liar.

MR. BRADFORD: Why don't you stop lying. I want the truth. In 2006, you learned that ZeiiMed's experts were calling the Device defective and you did nothing. Yes or No?

DR. HEELED: We decided not to redesign or recall after examining the alleged defects.

MR. BRADFORD: ZeiiMed changed nothing and did nothing, correct?

DR. HEELED: We took no affirmative action until 2010 when we discontinued the metal-on-metal Device.

MR. BRADFORD: ZeiiMed did not tell the public that its own doctors, paid by ZeiiMed, confirmed that it caused injury and refused to implant it in their patients. Isn't that true?

DR. HEELED: ZeiiMed made no public announcements I am aware of.

MR. BRADFORD: Your posting on your Facebook page about the "cripples" was taken down by you. Were you worried a lawyer would see it?

DR. HEELED: I don't remember the posting. If I did, then it was simply a bad joke that I decided to delete.

MR. BRADFORD: You are not only untruthful, you are an appalling person who intentionally permitted an unsafe Device to be inserted into human beings. You should be in jail.

Dr. Heeled stood up in the witness stand. He leaned forward and scowled at Brian, showing for the first time his ugly brown teeth as he raised his arm with a clenched fist preparing to throw a punch. Brian instinctively moved closer with both arms extended in an apparent attempt to knock Dr. Heeled out of the witness stand and onto the floor of the Courtroom. Mary moved remarkably fast. She had sensed that Brian was close to his breaking point, so she had prepared herself for immediate action. Before he was able to make contact with Dr. Heeled, Mary lunged towards Brian, hitting his shoulder, deflecting his forward motion and pushing him aside. Several jurors jumped to their feet in alarm.

JUDGE HOROWITZ: I demand order. Order in this Court. Stop now or you will be handcuffed by the police. Dr. Heeled, sit down immediately.

Everyone stopped and stood motionless. Brian knew the Judge was close to declaring a mistrial. That was the last thing he wanted. Dr. Heeled sat down and folded his arms.

> MR. BRADFORD: I apologize to the Court and the jury. I should not have reacted to Dr. Heeled's aggressive action. Thankfully, Ms. Douglas saved me from myself.
>
> JUDGE HOROWITZ: I'm darn close to telling everyone to go home and never come back. That was a disgraceful scene. Counsel, you know better. You'd be in jail if you touched the witness, no matter what Dr. Heeled said or did. However, we have spent a lot of time on this trial in the hope that justice can be done. I don't want to derail that quest. The Court is now adjourned until Monday when clearer heads will prevail, or else.
>
> MR. BRADFORD: Thank you, Your Honor. On Monday, I will call Dr. Feigelman and various other former medical consultants of ZeiiMed to the witness stand to explain in detail the harm caused to Mrs. Dudley by the HID, as well as ZeiiMed's undisclosed knowledge of how defects in the Device caused severe injuries. Also, as a final witness, I will call John Edison, the CEO of ZeiiMed, and the man responsible for all that was done and not done by ZeiiMed with regard to the Device.
>
> JUDGE HOROWITZ: Please clear the Courtroom immediately. I've had enough for one day.

The Judge left the Bench quickly. Mary and I escorted Mr. and Mrs. Dudley out of the Courtroom and into the corridor. I pushed Mrs. Dudley's wheelchair. In the corridor, Mrs. Dudley spotted Dr. Heeled as he mingled with several attorneys from Tweed, Fox & Fortune. I had no idea that Mrs. Dudley felt a personal revulsion to Dr. Heeled, although it was very understandable based on today's testimony.

Mrs. Dudley called in a loud voice, "Dr. Heeled. Yes, you. I have a few words to say to you. How dare you comment about us 'cripples' on Facebook. We don't want to walk on water–we just want to walk. You made the Device–you're the one who crippled me for life. If I could get out of this chair I would slap your face until it turned red."

Dr. Heeled walked over to Mrs. Dudley's wheelchair.

"How dare you speak to me in that fashion," Dr. Heeled said.

"Step back, now," I said. "You get one inch closer to Mrs. Dudley and I will break your nose right here, right now. I may snap your other wrist also, just for good measure."

"You better listen to him. Mr. Bradford is a very violent man capable of extremely irrational behavior," a familiar voice said from behind Dr. Heeled. Dr. Heeled turned to see the person who had spoken. John Edison stepped forward and used his arm to gently push Dr. Heeled out of his way.

"Like I said, Mr. Bradford is like a wild animal. Once he unleashes his anger, he can't be controlled and won't be stopped. He is very dangerous and enjoys seeing the blood of his conquests. Dr. Heeled, you should be very careful when dealing with Mr. Bradford."

"Hello, Mr. Edison. Thank you for the kind and gracious remarks. By the way, you don't look well–your face is horribly sunken. Were you in a car accident?" I asked, with as much sarcasm as possible.

"Actually, I feel quite well. I've been working hard to regain my strength and I'm almost there. Unfortunately, my facial structure will never be the same and my foot will never heal completely. As you are well aware, I curse you everyday of my life for the injuries you inflicted and vow to send you straight to hell."

"Well, before I go to hell, here's a Trial Subpoena requiring your appearance on Monday to testify, " I said to Edison.

Mary quickly pulled the Trial Subpoena from her briefcase and stuffed it into the front pocket of Edison's suit coat.

"I never thought we would be able to serve you with the Subpoena," I continued. "Then you just solved the problem by showing up today. I can't wait to get you on the stand to ask some very uncomfortable questions about the Device. I've got documents that will make you squirm. The truth will be revealed and the world will learn how ZeiiMed does business. See you on Monday."

"You're always so cocky and always so distasteful. I'll be here on Monday because I've been served. However, I'm not sure you will be physically able to attend on Monday. In fact, your wife may be making funeral arrangements on Monday," Edison said, with a crooked smile on his uneven, indented face.

I stepped forward until our noses nearly touched.

"If we weren't in the Courthouse I would pulverize the remaining bones in your jaw," I said, with an intimidating growl. "You're lucky, I have a client to represent and a case to win next week. So, I will control myself today and live to confront you another day. That day is coming and may be here sooner than you think."

Mary pushed herself between us. I backed up.

"For God's sake, let's go, Brian. What's wrong with you? There are reporters around," Mary stated firmly.

Mary put both her hands on my arm and pulled me close to her.

"Walk with me, now. We are leaving," she said.

I relented. We walked together. Mr. Dudley pushed Mrs. Dudley's wheelchair. We headed to the elevators. I didn't look back.

"Do lawyers always act like that?" Mr. Dudley whispered to Mrs. Dudley. "They don't even do that in the movies."

"Keep quiet. Brian's got backbone and I like that," Mrs. Dudley responded to her husband.

-43-

After we left the Courthouse, the Dudleys headed back to Pleasant Pastime. Mary had some errands to do, so I decided to walk back to the office now that the cooler evening air had displaced the unusual March humidity. Before she left, I reminded Mary that Sunday evening we were scheduled to prepare Dr. Feigelman for his trial testimony on Monday.

I was only a few blocks from the Courthouse when I heard my name called. I stopped and turned.

"Brian, I'm glad I caught up with you. I need to talk without any ZeiiMed people around," Suzanna said.

"No problem, I've got a few moments. Actually, I was in no hurry to get back to the office on a Friday evening."

"You did very well today. The Feigelman emails really turned the jurors against ZeiiMed," Suzanna continued.

"Thanks, but it's not necessary..."

"I am getting to something here, so please let me finish," Suzanna said, as she cut me off before I finished my sentence.

"You've created a difficult problem for me," Suzanna continued. "I assured ZeiiMed that we had accomplished our plan and all the documents were gone for good. I knew about the Feigelman emails, but I promised ZeiiMed they would never see the light of day. Of course, I can be disbarred for what I did. However, it no longer matters. The stakes are much larger than simply losing my license to practice law. I'm now concerned about losing my life. I know what ZeiiMed does and I know how ZeiiMed reacts to failure. I'm aware of ZeiiMed's track record with unsuccessful lawyers from Tweed, Fox & Fortune."

"Did anyone ever tell you the story about what actually happened to Charles Wadsworth?" I asked.

"Of course. ZeiiMed had Wadsworth killed because he failed to protect ZeiiMed and failed to carry out the company's instructions," Suzanna responded.

"I always believed that's what happened," I said.

"Next was John Standish Clark and your confrontation with him at the pool. He was forced by ZeiiMed to take you out. ZeiiMed knew his perverse personal habits and blackmailed him into doing as instructed. You're still alive, so Clark will be next. Now I'm likewise expendable. It's only a matter of time before I meet my fate. I anticipate that ZeiiMed will allow me to finish the trial, but after that all bets are off."

"I would love to say your assessment is wrong, but I can't. I know how ZeiiMed works and I know ZeiiMed will hold you responsible for disclosure of the emails, even if by some miracle ZeiiMed wins the case. It's not really your fault, but it happened on your watch. I'm sorry," I said.

"I have a plan though," Suzanna said. "I am relocating to Europe as soon as the trial ends. I don't have a husband or children. I'll do the best I can to change identities and start over, although I'll always live with the haunting thought that each day might be the day ZeiiMed finds me."

"I can help," I offered. "I'll need to talk to Mary, but I think I can buy you some extra time to escape. After the case gets submitted to the jury, I suggest you just walk out of the Courthouse and never come back. I'll inform the Judge that I will be at my law firm awaiting notification from the clerk that a verdict has been reached. You will likewise tell the Court that you are going to your office to await the verdict, when actually you will be on your way to the airport. The Judge is required to wait until both trial counsel are present in the Courtroom before the verdict is announced by the foreman. Of course, several hours will be wasted while the attorneys in your office feverishly attempt to find you so the verdict can be read. Eventually, the Judge will get exasperated and instruct the clerk to read the verdict with another lawyer from your firm present. But, by then you should be flying over the Atlantic Ocean. What do you say – is it a plan?"

"I think it will work. I can't thank you enough. I don't deserve such kindness. I tried to screw you by destroying the documents and then talked with Edison about your demise. Can you ever forgive me?"

"I'm not sure. Planning my death in a conspiracy with Edison is a pretty big sin. Maybe I should reconsider my offer to help you. No, I'm only kidding. Edison is a despicable human being with a talent for luring people into his web of evil. As you said, look how your colleagues were sucked in by Edison and then brutalized."

"I need to go now. You've been a life saver, literally," Suzanna said, as she moved closer and kissed me on the cheek in gratitude.

"You're welcome. Remember, when we're in the Courtroom, we have to act like we still hate each other. No smiles and certainly no more kisses–although if no one is looking feel free to kiss me in the corridor," I said, trying to add a light touch to our new found solidarity.

I don't think Suzanna understood my humor. She just turned and started walking to wherever she was headed, her thoughts now focused on planning her new life somewhere far from here.

-44-

On Saturday afternoon, March 17, 2012, Mr. John Edison convened a meeting with Suzanna Nudbello at the downtown law offices of Tweed, Fox & Fortune located at Two World Financial Center.

"Sorry to drag you in on the weekend," John Edison said to Suzanna. "But, we are in the middle of a trial, so any St. Patrick's Day celebration will just have to wait."

"I'm happy to be here. As a trial attorney, I feel you can never be too prepared–there's always more to do," Suzanna responded.

"As you no doubt surmised, I am not pleased about how the trial has progressed so far," Mr. Edison said.

"I agree with you. I am very disappointed myself. I didn't know Bradford had the Feigelman emails because I believed all the documents had been destroyed by the worm released by ZeiiMed. I wasn't told that ZeiiMed maintained a copy of the HID documents in Cloud storage. Obviously, our adversary knew and somehow figured out a way to gain access to the Cloud. If I had known, I probably would have mentioned there was always the possibility of the Cloud being hacked or compromised."

"It doesn't really matter now, does it," Edison remarked. "I don't care that Bradford knows about the Cloud. I do care that he was able to break into the Cloud. I will find and punish the ZeiiMed executive who permitted his desktop computer or smartphone to be hacked. There are only about ten executives who have the Cloud password and a Cloud accessible computer or phone. I know for sure my phone wasn't used to contact the Cloud because it was never out of my sight. Plus, my desktop computer is shut down when not in use. Even if by some miracle the hackers got my password, they still couldn't access the Cloud documents without a verbal request from my authorized network smartphone. My phone hasn't been used by anyone but me. However, let me return to the point of this discussion. The bottom line is that someone messed up at ZeiiMed and you messed up at trial. You promised that the ZeiiMed documents wouldn't be shown to the jury because they had all been successfully destroyed and you were wrong."

"I am very sorry for that. I'll do everything possible to lessen the impact of the Feigelman emails," Suzanna promised.

"Actually, I have a plan," Edison responded. "I asked you here to tell you about it. Bradford and his trusted associate, Mary something, will not appear in Court on Monday. They are going to encounter quite a few problems over the weekend that will make them unavailable to proceed when the trial resumes. Basically, we are going to take out the 'A Team' in the hope that Tweed, Fox & Fortune will have a better chance of winning against whatever 'B Team' is hastily assembled by Alfonso and Ryan."

"That's wonderful news," Suzanna said. "As your lawyer, I don't want any specifics as to what will happen to them, but I do need to know if Mr. Bradford and Ms. Douglas will encounter this problem in the Courthouse, outside on the street or somewhere else. As you can imagine, I don't want to be in the vicinity when it happens."

"No, you won't be anywhere near what I call 'ground zero,'" Edison answered. "Actually, you will not see them again because they will not make it through the weekend. And, just for good measure, we are also going to arrange some very unfriendly contact with some of Bradford's friends and family just because my hatred of him is so unbounded. Even Dr. Feigelman may not make it past his little prep session with Bradford tomorrow evening. This is going to be the grand finale. My crowning achievement," Edison gloated.

"I wish all my clients disposed of my adversaries so easily," Suzanna said, knowing that any perceived resistance to the plan would lead to harsh consequences.

"Don't think you are out of the woods yet. You will still be held accountable for disclosure of the Feigelman emails regardless of whether it was your fault or not. However, if you correct things and win the trial for ZeiiMed, your punishment will be significantly lessened," Edison said in a casual tone of voice, unaware of the terror felt by Suzanna.

Suzanna knew the chances of winning the trial were slim as a result of the Feigelman emails. Even if Feigelman didn't testify, other medical witnesses who served as ZeiiMed's paid consultants would confirm orally the contents of Feigelman's emails received by them. Her only chance was to appear aligned with Edison, continue the trial and then get the hell out of town once the case was submitted to the jury. With Brian's help, she just might escape.

"I fully intend to succeed at trial. The Feigelman emails were a setback, but not a defeat. We have lined up a number of physicians who will testify that some metal debris in the blood was always anticipated, but Mrs. Dudley's negative health history exacerbated a common side effect into a life-threatening condition. I have all the confidence in the world that the jury will understand and accept our defense," Suzanna stated, with as much false optimism as possible.

"Good," Edison stated. "In that case, I don't need to distract you further from your trial preparation for Monday. I just felt we needed this chat so you wouldn't be thrown off guard when Bradford's replacements appeared in Court on Monday morning. I also wanted you fully prepared in the event Mrs. Dudley's replacement lawyer asks for a mistrial, contending that only Bradford is sufficiently experienced and prepared to properly present the case. I suggest you tell the Judge that Mrs. Dudley's most convincing evidence has already been presented to the jury. The rest of her case is essentially duplicative and does not require a seasoned trial attorney to present it to the jury."

"I greatly appreciate the preview. But I do need to get back to work now. Feel free to use the conference room for as long as you wish. See you Monday in Court," Suzanna said, as she quickly exited the conference room.

Suzanna felt Edison's eyes on her as she walked down the hallway to her office. She hoped her acting performance had fooled him.

Only time would tell.

-45-

On Sunday evening, March 18, 2012, Mary and I were in my office on the 45th floor.

It was about 7:00 p.m. We were preparing the questions to be used in the direct examination of the witnesses scheduled for the next day, including Dr. Feigelman.

Dr. Feigelman was sitting in the reception area on the same floor waiting to be escorted to my office once we were ready to meet with him.

Mary sighed loudly. "This is becoming very tedious. We have been going over this material for hours. I've about had it for the day. I know we still need to devote another hour to our preparation session with Dr. Feigelman, but I'd like to think about something else for a few minutes."

"What do you want to do as a distraction?" I asked, with a slight grin as I remembered Meadhbh's idea of a distraction.

"I know what. I want to talk about the latest office rumor," Mary answered. "Rumor has it that the firm was contacted by a senior manager at Facebook. His name is Mark and he has a legal problem. Apparently, he came to us because of your notoriety in exposing the corporate treachery at ZeiiMed."

"It sounds like a cash rich corporate client–every law firm's dream," I said. "What's his legal problem?"

"It has to do with 'emotional contagion'."

"What the hell is that?"

"It's the transfer of emotional impulses, either good or bad, between or among people, so that the same emotional feeling is experienced without the knowledge or consent of the participants."

"I have no idea what you just said."

"I'll explain. About three months ago, Facebook's Newsfeed Division conducted an experiment on thousands of unsuspecting Facebook users to determine if the emotional impact of the content of the newsfeed could be manipulated to transfer good or bad emotions. That is, emotionally charged information was intentionally transmitted by Facebook to innocent and unknowing users to create an emotional reaction predicted by Facebook. In other words, emotional manipulation. It this making any sense?"

"Yes, we have a zookeeper, in your example it's Facebook, and the zoo animals, which are the Facebook users. The zookeeper is experimenting on the zoo animals by surreptitiously manufacturing a predicted emotional response from the zoo animals. Aren't there animal cruelty laws that criminalize such conduct?" I inquired.

"You're catching on. The actual experiment went like this. The content of the newsfeed was intentionally rearranged to include positive content or negative content to determine if the receivers of the newsfeed content reacted more positively or negatively then a control group," Mary explained.

"Massive emotional contagion on human guinea pigs achieved through data manipulation by a controlling manipulator. It sounds very Orwellian, like the society described in the book *1984*, although I guess it's not fiction in 2012," I commented. "So, what does Mark want us to do for him?"

"I hear that Mark is worried because he knows the public is going to learn of the Facebook experiment sooner or later. While Mark originally thought it was a harmless experiment with socially significant impact, he now realizes that the press will be highly critical. He wants help in deciding how to disclose the experiment in a manner which will minimize the fall out."

"Good luck with that," I said. "I hope I'm not asked to handle the matter. There's no happy ending, as I see it."

"Just letting you know what's going on around the firm," Mary said.

"Thank you. Now let's get back to work. We were scheduled to meet with Dr. Feigelman half an hour ago. He's probably furious with us. Go to reception and get him."

The phone on my desk rang. Mary stopped as she was about to leave.

"Wait a second, Mary. Let's see if this call is important before you get Dr. Feigelman."

"Hello, Brian Bradford here."

"This is Suzanna. Listen carefully. I talked to Edison yesterday. He is about to unleash some murderous scheme on you and maybe those close to you. I don't know what's about to happen, but the consequences will be life threatening. I should have called you sooner, but I think ZeiiMed has all my phones tapped, including my cell. I finally found a pay phone in Penn Station. It will probably happen tonight because Edison said you won't make it through the weekend. I suggest you leave your office now. ZeiiMed knows you're there preparing for tomorrow's trial, so you are probably being pursued at this very moment."

"*WHAT THE HELL IS THAT*?" Mary screeched, as she pointed towards the window behind my desk.

I turned to look as I dropped the phone. Flying towards us was a drone about four feet in length. The white cylindrical fuselage of the device looked like the hull below the saucer of the starship U.S.S. Enterprise. Extending outward about a foot from the hull were four eight-inch spinning rotor blades that faced upward similar to a helicopter's main rotor blade. Two small green headlights attached to the front of the hull stared at me. I immediately recognized a small camera and a mound of grey putty mounted below the hull. The green headlights started to flash. The drone was only a moment from crashing into the window.

"*Run, Mary. Bomb! Go now!*"

Mary quickly moved through the doorway and out of the office. I jumped out of my chair and was halfway across the office when the explosion occurred. Compressed air and shattered glass hit me from behind as I sprinted away from the window towards the doorway. The force lifted me off my feet and threw me into the corridor.

From the floor in the hallway, I looked back. Black smoke saturated the office, with burning flames creating the only illumination. Through the dark haze, I could see a hole in the outside wall of the building twice the size of the window. The drone must have detonated electronically just outside the window. The falling debris caused a storm of dangerous projectiles to rain on the street below.

I slowly managed to stand. My shirt was ripped to shreds and my back had several deep cuts from the glass. I was lucky–extremely lucky.

"Brian, you're bleeding," Mary exclaimed.

"A little. Never mind that. Are you all right?"

"Yes, I am," Mary said. Thanks for your warning. I got out of the office just before the explosion."

Mary grabbed a white scarf from one of the secretary's cubicles and pressed it against my back.

"Mary, give me your phone. Suzanna said something big was about to happen and I think this is just the beginning.

Brian dialed Kim's cell phone.

"Kim, this is Brian. Where are you?"

"I'm sitting in the kitchen at home."

"Are you alone?"

"No. Dr. Joe is here. I was in the process of explaining to him the reasons I can no longer see him when the front door bell rang. He went to answer the door as I answered your call."

"You must leave the house now," I yelled into the phone. "Get in the car and drive away. Go to police headquarters or somewhere with people–lots of people. I believe ZeiiMed is after you and will attempt to kill you. Get Joe and get out of there."

"Oh, God. Will this never end? I love you. I'll get Joe and call you as soon as we're safe."

She dropped the phone and screamed for Joe, but it was too late.

Moments earlier, Dr. Joe had opened the front door to see who rang the bell. There was a large man standing in front of him dressed in a black suit, black tie and a black fedora pulled down to cover his entire forehead. There was a shiny object in his right hand that reflected the brightness of the front door light.

"What can I do for you?" Dr. Joe asked, as he was instantly seized with fear upon realizing that the shiny object was a twelve-inch hunting knife.

Without a word, the stranger in the suit plunged the blade deep into Dr. Joe's soft belly. Dr. Joe's eyes bulged in the frenzied panic of impending doom. He looked incredulously at the blade as it sliced downward through his stomach and into his intestines.

Dr. Joe screamed, "No," as the stranger continued to slice the flesh open down to his scrotum. The heavy, stainless steel blade had cut through his thin leather belt with ease.

Dr. Joe groaned and fell backward into death as he realized his disemboweled organs had fallen to the floor.

The stranger stepped over Dr. Joe. He wiped his shoes on the rug to remove the blood that had formed a pool in the doorway. He headed for the kitchen in the back of the house.

Kim had already fled the house through the back door. When Dr. Joe's dying groans reverberated into the kitchen, Kim knew there was nothing she could do but attempt to escape the same fate. The driveway was next to the house. She jumped in her car as quickly as possible, slammed it in reverse and backed out of the driveway. Her headlights illuminated the pursuing stranger in a dark suit as he exited the kitchen door. A large, blood-soaked knife was clearly visible in his hand.

As Kim backed into the street, she noticed an unfamiliar Mercedes parked near her house. She put her car in "drive" and proceeded as fast as possible towards the end of the road. Only four blocks down the hill and she was at the bottom of busy Main Street, directly in front of the ferry terminal for the Bridgeport-Port Jefferson Steamboat Company.

Kim soon realized that the stranger was now following in the Mercedes. As she approached the bottom of the hill, Kim turned into the ferry terminal. A thirty-foot section of the front hull of the ferry had been lifted upward by hydraulic pumps so that the cars were able to drive directly into the body of the three-hundred-foot vessel. The vehicle deck was ten feet above the water line. The loading of the cars was completed. The ferry's horn blasted a departure signal. A deckhand extended a linked steel chain across the end of the pier as the ferry prepared to pull back from the terminal.

Kim accelerated as she drove up the steep incline of the loading ramp leading to the opened front hull of the ferry. The seaman lifted his arms in a frantic attempt to stop her approaching car. Kim floored the accelerator. The thirty-foot front section of the hull started its slow downward descent to seal the front hull as the ferry slowly inched away from the loading platform.

Kim looked in the rearview mirror. The Mercedes was twenty feet behind her.

Kim kept the accelerator pressed to the floor. The front of her car snapped the linked chain and then lunged forward in an upward direction as she reached the top of the ramp. All four wheels were propelled into the air by the speed of the vehicle. The aerial leap ended quickly as the forward thrust dissipated. The front of the car crashed onto the vehicle deck of the ferry, its rear wheels and axle hanging over the side of the vessel as the ferry inched away from the pier. The front end of the car slowly elevated from the weight of the rear end dangling over the side, like a teetering seesaw. A seaman halted the descent of the thirty-foot front section.

Kim quickly opened the car door and jumped several feet down onto the deck as the front end of the car continued to elevate. She immediately saw the Mercedes accelerating dramatically as it also proceeded up the steep incline of the loading ramp. Reaching the end of the ramp, the Mercedes' front wheels likewise extended into the air as the rear wheels provided the push forward. However, the sedan instantly lost momentum as the rear wheels lost contact with the ramp. The ferry was now six feet from the pier. The front end of the stranger's vehicle crashed into the rear section of Kim's car as it dangled over the outside of the vessel. The Mercedes immediately dropped into the water. Kim's car back-flipped 180 degrees from the rear impact, causing it to fly off the ferry upside down and land on top of the Mercedes. Kim watched as both cars were totally submerged.

The ferry initiated an emergency stop, but was more than forty feet from the pier by the time its movement ceased. A Mayday call was made to the Coast Guard. The vessel's captain left the bridge once the ferry stopped to investigate the incident. Police cars arrived at the ferry terminal. Flood lights illuminated where the cars had disappeared into the water.

There was no sign of life.

-46-

After Brian's call to Kim, he immediately followed with a call to Meadhbh O'Shea.

"Hello, Meadhbh. This is Brian."

"Yes, I know. You don't sound good. Are you sick?"

"No, I'm not sick, but I do have a few cuts and bruises. Another attack by ZeiiMed. A drone detonated a plastic explosive outside the window of my office."

"My God, this sickness never ends. Are you sure you are all right?" Meadhbh asked apprehensively.

"I'll be fine. Actually, it's you I'm worried about. I was warned that Edison had targeted me and those close to me. That would include you, so please be careful leaving work and stay in a public place with plenty of people around. Keep away from your apartment. Call me when you're in a safe place."

"Thanks. I will be cautious and I will be careful. As I told you, I won't be caught defenseless if ZeiiMed's thugs go after me again. So, don't worry about me."

"I do worry about you," I answered.

"Actually, I'm leaving work in a little while," Meadhbh stated. "It's a slow Sunday. I'll keep to crowded streets and take a cab to Judy's apartment. Have a doctor look at those cuts. Love you. Good-bye."

"Love you back," I responded.

I called Kim again. No answer. I notified the Suffolk County Police.

Mary approached. "I think you should go to the Emergency Room. I'll go with you," Mary said.

"Thanks, but no thanks," I said. "I'm heading uptown to make sure nothing happens to Meadhbh. I'll grab my suit jacket from the closet to hide the blood on my shirt. I'm only cut on my back. I'm too far from home to help Kim, so I can only pray the Suffolk Police get to her before ZeiiMed does. But Meadhbh is only uptown, so hopefully I can reach her before ZeiiMed does."

The elevator on the 45th floor opened. Sergeant Melissa Black was the first person off the elevator.

"Are you all right?" the Sergeant asked.

"Yes, I'm living and breathing and nothing is broken. Nice to see you again. What a coincidence that you responded to the explosion," I commented.

"It wasn't a coincidence. I was parked on Wall Street in my patrol car when the explosion occurred. I told you I would keep an eye on you–trouble always seems to find you. By the way, I arrested the guy who was operating the drone. He was a few blocks away. He had a joy stick attached to a GPS device, with a smartphone for detonation of the plastic explosive," the Sergeant stated.

"Good work. But you know, your prisoner will never make it through the night alive. His job was to kill me, and Mary along with me. He failed and his failure will cost him big time."

"These ZeiiMed people are really starting to aggravate me," the Sergeant responded.

"You can help me avoid another attack. I need to get to 84th Street to make sure another possible ZeiiMed target isn't harmed. How about a ride in your squad car?"

"Yes, I can do that. You're not going to get blood on my seats are you?" she asked.

"No, I have a suit jacket to soak up the blood on my shirt," I answered, in no mood for light banter.

"Let's go, then. And, don't forget you agreed to call me Melissa."

As we traveled uptown in the police car, Melissa received a radio message from the Suffolk County Police that Kim was safe, but Dr. Joe was dead from a knife wound.

"This ZeiiMed is one hell of a savage company. I'm sorry for the death of the doctor, but thank goodness your wife is fine."

"Thanks, but the problem with ZeiiMed is that it never ends. Kim survived today, but who knows what will happen the next time. And there is always a next time. It's up to me to take care of the problem once and for all. And today is the day."

A dreaded yet familiar feeling started to percolate within me. I felt the rage slowly start to build. The cranial vault that locked away my genetic predisposition to extreme violent and ruthless savagery opened once again. Out of the recesses of my brain streamed a dark wave of repressed evil predilections like millions of bats simultaneously surging from a cave at the onset of night. I was now focused. I was ready. It was now or never.

Melissa turned her cruiser onto 84th Street. I immediately spotted Meadhbh walking on the sidewalk a couple of blocks from *Très Bien*. There was a sinister-looking man on each side of her, both in dark suits, and each with a fedora. The police car was traveling east on 84th Street and Meadhbh was walking west on the sidewalk on the opposite side of the street.

"Turn around. Meadhbh's on the other sidewalk with two ZeiiMed goons," I said.

Melissa immediately made a u-turn and pulled up next to the sidewalk with the driver's side of the vehicle touching the curb.

She opened her window and leaned her head out of the car, now only a few feet from Meadhbh and the two men on either side of her.

"Police. Stop. Face me and put your hands up," Melissa called out.

The man closest to Melissa pulled his right hand out of his pocket, extended his arm and aimed a Biretta PX4 Storm Sub-Compact 9mm pistol directly at Melissa. Two shots exploded from the muzzle. One of the bullets struck Melissa in the side of the neck. Blood squirted violently from the wound. She fell towards me in the front seat of the squad car. Her head landed on my lap. I pressed both my hands against her neck, desperately attempting to halt the flow of blood as it leaked between my fingers and dripped down my pants. I jammed my finger deep into the wound until the artery stopped bleeding. I was now trapped. I had nowhere to go. If I left the car, Melissa would bleed to death. The suited man stepped closer to the car, the Biretta now pointed directly at me. I waited helplessly, knowing it was over once I saw the smoke from the barrel. I hoped it would be painless.

Three shots fired with an ear-shattering muzzle blast. The man with the Biretta fell against the squad car from the force of the impact, then immediately collapsed into the curb. Behind him, Meadhbh stood motionless. Her FN Five-seven pistol, smoke rising from the barrel, was still pointed at the motionless man now lying on the concrete with three bullet holes in his back. The moment seemed frozen in time.

The second thug suddenly grabbed Meadhbh around her shoulders as he fumbled to find his own weapon. He was too slow. She placed the FN Five-seven directly against his stomach and quickly discharged three more rounds from the semi-automatic. Blood splattered on her face. He released his grip on Meadhbh's shoulder as his arm went limp. He desperately attempted to suck air into his collapsing lungs, a grimace of panic gripping him as he felt death engulfing him. His body fell to the sidewalk.

Meadhbh walked around the squad car and quickly opened the door on the passenger side. She saw Melissa's head on my lap, the massive loss of blood soaking Melissa's hair.

"Don't panic and don't give a second thought to those animals," I spoke firmly. "Listen to me and do exactly as I say. I'm going to release my hold on Melissa's neck and you will take over. You have to insert your finger into her neck or she will bleed to death. But first, put your pistol on the dashboard."

Meadhbh proceeded as instructed. After she placed her weapon on the dashboard, we switched positions and I got out of the car. I then grabbed the FN Five-seven as two police cars with sirens blasting turned the corner on 84th Street.

"Help has arrived. I have to go," I said.

"Go? Go where? What are you going to do?" Meadhbh asked, raising her voice in alarm.

"Stay calm. I've got unfinished business, which I'm going to address right now. You fired six shots, right?"

"Yes, I think so anyway."

"All right," I said. "That gives me fourteen more in the magazine, plus one in the chamber. I love you. I've got to go before the cops stop me. I think Melissa will survive–you've stopped the bleeding."

I bent over and kissed Meadhbh on her lips. We lingered in the fleeting pleasure as long as we could with death and suffering all around us. The blood of her second victim was on her face and dripped into our mouths. Meadhbh didn't seem to mind. Her eyes remained closed as I slowly pulled away.

"Not the best-tasting kiss. I feel like a vampire. But, as you often say, we'll work on perfecting the technique the next time. See you later."

"Now I understand what you're going to do. Go get him, with my blessing. Just be sure to finish Edison off this time," Meadhbh said, as I began running toward *Très Bien*.

-47-

The front door to *Très Bien* is about five feet from the front door of John Edison's building.

I got to Edison's building out of breath, but fearless. I will not be stopped and anyone in my way will be eradicated. I don't care what anyone hears or observes. I don't care if surveillance cameras record my every move. I will be done before the police arrive. I have one goal and nothing will prevent me from achieving my purpose.

Of course, the glass door to Edison's building was locked. A single shot from the pistol shattered it into a million pieces. The recoil was mild, but the muzzle blast was loud and powerful. Several spectators on the street stopped and stared, their alarm expressed by open mouths.

There wasn't much time. Having broken into Edison's apartment once before, I knew it was on the fifth floor and I knew there was a guard watching the elevator. The elevator was about twenty feet from the front door. However, both the entrance to the elevator and the guard next to the elevator cannot be seen from the front lobby because the first section of the lobby ends after twenty feet and then turns sharply to the left about two feet. The elevator is just after the turn.

I walked through the broken glass doorway and quickly moved down the lobby towards the elevator. There was no need to be quiet since everyone had heard the glass explode from the gunshot.

I reached the elevator with the pistol pointed forward in my right hand. I sensed motion inside the elevator and knew that whoever was there had been alerted to my presence. I reached my hand inside the elevator and fired, striking the security guard in the right shoulder. The guard's weapon was in his right hand, but his right arm now dangled limply from the wound.

The guard grabbed his right shoulder with his left hand and screamed in pain. I smashed the side of his head with the base of the metal grip of the FN Five-seven, knocking him unconscious.

I decided to take the stairs. I was sure someone would be waiting upstairs for me to disembark from the elevator. I was exhausted upon reaching the fifth floor. I slowly opened the fire door and looked in the hallway. There were two security guards watching images from the lobby on a video screen attached to the wall. Their weapons were drawn and ready, waiting for the elevator to arrive. I guess it eventually dawned on them that I didn't take the elevator. They turned and looked towards the fire door. I fired four times, two of which hit their targets. The sound caused a piercing pain in my ears, followed by a loud ringing.

Both guards fell to the floor. I leapt out from behind the fire door and kicked the weapons out of their hands. Neither had fatal wounds. They were both conscious. One was holding his shoulder, the other clutching his bloodied knee.

I kneeled next to them. One at a time, I raised the pistol over my head and delivered a blow to the temple of each guard with the full force of a downward swing. I couldn't afford any possibility that they would be able to rejoin the battle.

Apartment 5A was directly in front of me. On the video screen in the hallway, I saw the police entering the lobby of the building. My time was almost up.

I turned the handle to the front door of Apartment 5A. It wasn't locked. I opened the door and stepped in. My right arm was fully extended with the semi-automatic pointed straight ahead.

The first room, the living room, was dark except for one very small lamp with minimal illumination. Sitting on the couch to my left was John Edison. A revolver was next to him on the cushion of the couch, easily within his reach.

"I've been expecting you," Edison said.

"I figured as much," I responded.

"You certainly aren't subtle. First, we spotted you on 84th Street as Meadhbh was shooting everyone in sight. We then kept an eye on you as you blasted your way in here. A real wild west show. You made quite a commotion. The police are on the way up as we speak. So, let's get to the point. What is it you want or is this just a social visit?" Edison asked.

"I'll tell you what this is. It's revenge for trying to kill my wife, revenge for trying to kill Meadhbh and revenge for Dr. Joe," I said, as I turned to my left to face Edison while pointing the pistol directly at him.

"That's a laugh. Dr. Joe was doing your wife, so you're probably happy about his demise. Kim and Meadhbh are unharmed as far as I know. How about a drink," Edison asked, as he started to stand.

"Don't move an inch, you bastard," I said.

"Clearly you are in a bad mood and intend to do something you will regret. As such, you have now forced me to do what I had hoped to avoid in my home," Edison said, as he sat back down.

Two men instantly appeared through the bedroom door to my right. I turned quickly and dove across the room while firing a succession of five 28mm cartridges over a matter of seconds. The men returned fire as they tried to follow my movement across the room, but my barrage of bullets quickly found their marks. The return fire ended. The men fell to the floor.

"Don't even think about that gun on the couch," I warned Edison.

Keeping a close eye on Edison, I walked across the room and fired a single shot into the forehead of each man.

"Nice try, but their little six-shooters were no match to the FN Five-seven. Now it's your turn," I said.

I fired one cartridge into the kneecap of Edison's right leg.

"That leg wasn't much use to you anyway after I put a knife through your foot," I said.

Edison moaned and grabbed his knee. He then extended his left arm to grab the revolver on the couch cushion next to him.

I fired another round into his hip, causing him to fall from the couch, without the gun.

"Looks like you may need hip surgery—I suggest you avoid the metal-on-metal HID made by ZeiiMed."

Edison was now sitting on the floor, his back leaning against the couch, his blood-soaked leg extended in front of him as his hand tried unsuccessfully to stem the flow of blood.

"I'm a mess. Finish the job, you son-of-a-bitch. I'll never walk again and I don't want to be strapped to a wheelchair the rest of my life. Do it. Shoot me now," Edison snarled.

"Sorry, no such luck. I enjoy watching you suffer and I hope it gets worse each remaining day of your miserable life. I'm not cutting short your pain—I want you to wallow in it for years to come."

"Damn you. The police will be here any second. If you don't have the guts to finish this, I'll force your hand. I'm going to pick up my revolver—if you don't shoot, I will kill you without hesitation," Edison declared.

Edison reached for his weapon on the couch. He moaned in pain as he turned slightly to grab it with his blood soaked right hand.

"Don't. Leave it alone. Don't touch that gun," I warned.

Edison took the gun in his hand and lifted it off the couch.

"Okay—you forced me to execute you," I exclaimed.

I pulled the trigger of the FN Five-Seven. It didn't fire. I immediately realized I was out of ammunition.

"The tables have turned. No more bullets. Now you are the one who is about to perish. I may die right here, but I hope to have enough energy for one final task," Edison stated.

Edison's shaking hand could barely hold the revolver as his blood made the metal handle slippery and difficult to control. Edison was frantically attempting to extend his right arm and point the revolver as his eyeballs rolled up into his head. He tried to fire, but his finger momentarily slipped off the trigger, his bodily fluid saturating his hand.

Edison's apartment door flew open. Three uniformed officers entered, their semi-automatic service pistols drawn.

"Put down the guns," yelled the first officer.

I dropped the FN Five-seven. Edison's right arm also dropped. His revolver fell to the floor as he passed out from his wounds. He never fired the shot.

"You're under arrest. Hands behind your back," the officer continued.

I was handcuffed.

"You are under arrest. You have killed and injured enough people for one day. Actually, you're lucky, we almost shot you on sight."

"I shot in self-defense," I responded. "These bastards were trying to kill me. But I was quicker on the trigger. You can see the gun next to this piece of garbage in front of me."

"Tell it to the Judge," I was told.

"Thanks for your help, flatfoot," I said.

"For that, you're going to spend some extra time in our beautiful concrete accommodations. Sometimes, the paperwork gets delayed and the arraignment doesn't get scheduled. It may happen in your case," the officer said, as he chuckled.

Ambulances arrived. Medics were everywhere. The red lights of the police cars made the scene look like a summer carnival. Spotlights were assembled and bathed the street and apartment building in brilliant light.

I was escorted out of the building by two officers, my wrists already starting to ache from the handcuffs. As we walked to the waiting police car, I saw Meadhbh standing on the sidewalk. She was speaking to a uniformed officer who was taking notes. She was crying, her face swollen and pale. She wasn't under arrest, so I guess the officer believed her self-defense alibi. Plus, her lifesaving first aid to Melissa probably helped her cause.

Meadhbh saw me and started to walk closer. The officer grabbed her arm and pulled her back.

I yelled as loud as I could, "Call Mary Douglas. Tell her she's lead counsel in Court tomorrow–the show must go on."

Meadhbh nodded her head and waved good-bye, tears continuing to run down her face. She blew me a kiss.

I was placed in the back seat of the police car and driven to the precinct for booking.

I guess I need a lawyer.

-48-

I was driven to the 19th precinct on East 67th Street. After fingerprinting, a mug shot and removal of personal items, the New York Police Department had an official record of my felony arrest.

This entitled me to a felony arraignment hearing before a Judge in the Criminal Court of the City of New York, where I intend to plead "Not Guilty" and request bail after being informed of my crimes.

While the felony arraignment usually takes place within twenty-four hours of arrest, it was clear to me the police were in no rush. It must have been my attitude. I'll be lucky if the arraignment takes place within seventy-two hours.

After booking, I was put back into the police car. I was told that I would be incarcerated at the Rikers Island correctional institution as a pretrial detainee awaiting arraignment. I seem to recall using several profanities upon being informed of my assignment to Rikers Island. I was told to shut up and take it like a man. I got the feeling that lawyers were given the same amount of consideration as crack dealers and pimps.

There are 11,000 inmates at Rikers Island, most of whom are pretrial detainees or convicted criminals serving a sentence of a year or less. The facility has a number of jail houses run by the New York City Department of Correction. The island on which the correctional complex is located consists of over four hundred acres in the East River.

A golf ball hit with a seven iron from the runways of LaGuardia Airport would land on Rikers Island. The Francis Buono Bridge provides access to the Island from a connecting road in Queens County.

Upon arrival at Rikers Island, I was strip-searched. Standing naked before three male correctional officers, I was told to spread my feet, bend over and cough. As one of the officers conducted a cavity search for drugs on or in my person, I commented that it seemed everyone was enjoying this particular aspect of their job. Shortly thereafter, I was told of my assignment to solitary confinement in the Segregation Unit. I was also informed it was for my own protection because the inmates generally hated lawyers. I knew it was because correction officers don't like detainees with a sassy mouth.

I arrived at the Segregation Unit at about 2:00 a.m. Monday morning, March 19, 2012. I entered a long concrete hallway with about fifty cells, each cell sealed by a solid metal door that had a slight opening at eye level and a smaller opening at the bottom for the food tray.

I entered the cell. The door slammed behind me. The air was fetid. Claustrophobia immediately set in. The stench of urine made me nauseous. The cell was about eight feet by ten feet, with a rusted cot and filthy toilet. The slim cushion on the bed was soiled and torn. The room had no windows and was unbearably hot. A vent above the bed maintained a constant flow of forced air heated to the scalding point.

There was nothing to do except stare at the emptiness of the room. No television, no books, no magazines, and no writing materials. Nothing. The only sounds were the wailing and banging of the other prisoners. I eventually learned that approximately one-third of the detainees in solitary confinement were mentally ill.

I was told the lockdown was for twenty-three hours a day, with one hour of outdoor exposure in a small fenced area. A six-minute phone call was permitted each day.

At 7 p.m. on Monday night, I was permitted my one call. I knew I should have called my wife, but I needed to learn how the trial proceeded during Monday's session.

Luckily, Mary answered her cell phone.

"I'm so happy to hear from you. I was worried sick about you. Meadhbh called and told me everything. After I threw up, I was able to compose myself. I was told earlier today they put you in Rikers."

"Look, Mary, I'm in desperate straits here–but I want to know what happened today," I said.

"The trial went better than I expected. Dr. Feigelman was pretty shaken up after the drone attack and explosion, but he finally got hold of himself by 9:00 this morning. His testimony devastated ZeiiMed's defense. The doctor confirmed everything you told the jury in your opening statement and everything testified to by Mrs. Dudley. Dr. Feigelman personally verified and authenticated his emails to Dr. Heeled. You could hear a pin drop in the Courtroom. Dr. Feigelman's testimony was so credible and so convincing, we don't need any more evidence to win our case. All I need to do is put on a couple of witnesses tomorrow to establish the net worth of ZeiiMed in the event the jury decides to punish ZeiiMed for its malicious acts and award punitive damages."

"That's spectacular. How did Suzanna do on cross-examination," I asked.

"Horribly. It was as if she had given up. Her heart clearly wasn't in it and her questions were lame. She was unable to impeach any of Dr. Feigelman's testimony and actually seemed to reinforce the truth of what he said."

"I'm not surprised. She now understands fully the depravity of ZeiiMed. She is terrified. Once the Judge submits the case to the jury, Suzanna will be on the run from ZeiiMed. She will hopefully be well on her way by the time the jury renders a verdict. But, to maximize her opportunity to get a head start, don't rush back to the Courtroom when you receive verification from the Clerk that the jury has reached a verdict. By the time you belatedly get to the Courtroom and ZeiiMed realizes that Suzanna cannot be found, she'll be long gone."

"No problem," Mary said. "I'll give her as much extra time as I can."

"Yes, we owe her that. Her call Sunday evening saved both our lives," I said. "I'm required to get off the line now. My six minutes are up. Call Kim and tell her I love her. I only get one call a day, but I'll call her tomorrow. See if she needs anything. I'm sure she is mourning the death of Dr. Joe. Most important, please have someone at Alfonso and Ryan get my arraignment scheduled so I can get out of here. I've been in solitary one day and already I feel like I'm losing my mind. I'll call you the day after tomorrow to get an update."

"We're working on it. The prosecutor is dragging his feet. You obviously did something to anger the authorities. But, it doesn't matter. We will get you before a Judge soon and present your application for bail. Please don't get into any fights with the corrections officers. Bye." Mary said, ending the call.

It wasn't fighting with the guards that had me concerned. I was worried about ZeiiMed. The cells in solitary were perfect for staging an apparent suicide. No windows, no cameras, solid metal doors and no contact with anyone for twenty-three continuous hours. It was the ideal location to slash an inmate's wrists and leave the poor soul to bleed out. No one listens or responds to an inmate's screams for medical assistance. Everyone in solitary screams all day for medical attention because it breaks up the monotony. As a result, calls for help are routinely ignored. Blood would need to form a large red pool in the corridor before anyone would respond.

Each hour I am here makes it more likely that ZeiiMed will send a team of guards to set up my death. I have no way to stop it and there is no one to help. I am alone in my cell, anticipating the approaching footsteps of a corrections officer newly added to the payroll of ZeiiMed. I'm sick to my stomach, my head is throbbing and my jumpsuit is soaked with sweat from the extreme heat in the cell. The sense of despair and helplessness is overpowering.

I've got to get out of here.

Somehow, someway.

-49-

On Wednesday, March 21, 2012, the following article appeared on page 6 of the morning edition of the gossip-prone *New York Press*:

MOUTHPIECE MAYHEM IN THE MID-EIGHTIES

Once again, super lawyer Brian Bradford was in a bloody confrontation with Mr. John Edison, the Chief Executive Officer of ZeiiMed, the world's largest health insurance company.

The police at the scene acknowledged that on Sunday night, Mr. Bradford shot and killed two men inside Mr. Edison's apartment at 60 E. 84th Street, in addition to firing two bullets into Mr. Edison himself. Mr. Edison survived and was taken to the hospital.

Three security guards were also found in the corridors of Mr. Edison's building with serious injuries caused by Mr. Bradford's itchy trigger finger. Another two men were found dead by the curb on 84th Street, not far from Edison's apartment building, but no proof has developed that Mr. Bradford killed them. A police sergeant was shot in the neck at the same location. It has been confirmed by reliable sources that Mr. Bradford did not cause the neck wound and actually assisted in stopping the loss of blood so the sergeant was able to survive.

Mr. Bradford told police that ZeiiMed started the mayhem by detonating a bomb carried by a drone outside his office. Independent reports confirmed an explosion at 40 Wall Street.

Mr. Bradford and Mr. Edison previously engaged in a barbarous encounter in the

Central Park Ramble that injured both. What could possibly have caused this savage lawyer to escalate his vendetta against Mr. Edison into another vicious clash that took the lives of several people employed by Mr. Edison or otherwise affiliated with him

Our investigation has not uncovered an answer, but recent events inside the Courtroom at 60 Centre Street may reveal some of the story. For the second time, Mr. Bradford commenced a lawsuit against ZeiiMed. He was actually in Court obtaining testimony from ZeiiMed over the past week. Why Mr. Bradford was unsatisfied with resolving his differences in the Courtroom and proceeded to kill, maim and injure his opponents outside the Courtroom remains a mystery.

Mr. Bradford was arrested by the police on Sunday night after his rampage. He is currently awaiting arraignment at Rikers Island. The criminal trial of Mr. Bradford will hopefully provide more information. However, the more pressing concern of the moment is keeping the violent Mr. Bradford off the streets so his adversaries are no longer subjected to extreme injury or death by the clearly deranged Mr. Bradford.

Most remarkably, it turns out that Mr. Bradford did not need to engage in murder and death to defeat Mr. Edison and ZeiiMed. On Tuesday, the jury returned an enormous verdict against ZeiiMed of compensatory damages in the amount of $250 million and punitive damages in the amount of $3.5 billion.

Since Mr. Bradford was incarcerated Sunday night, he was not present in the Courtroom when the verdict was announced.

His able colleague, Mary Douglas, was present as counsel for the Plaintiff Martha Dudley. Mrs. Dudley had suffered severe injuries due to a faulty hip implant Device.

Mr. Bradford will presumably have little time to enjoy his share of the verdict because his hideous crimes should result in a long-term prison sentence. Another mouthpiece in mothballs. We can only hope this is a new trend. Rather than killing all the lawyers, maybe imprisoning them one by one will prove sufficient.

THE END

EPILOGUE

Mary Douglas

Mary was lead counsel for Martha Dudley in the trial against ZeiiMed when the jury returned a verdict of compensatory damages in the amount of $250 million and punitive damages in the amount of $3.5 billion. After her victory, Mary appeared on several morning shows and was quoted extensively in newspapers across the nation. New clients with the metal-on-metal HID contacted Mary by the hundreds, requesting that she file suit against ZeiiMed.

ZeiiMed filed papers seeking an appeal of the massive verdict, especially the allegedly "excessive" punitive damage award of $3.5 billion. Rather than spend years litigating the appeal, Tweed, Fox & Fortune offered a settlement in the amount of $500 million cash, payable in thirty days. Mary advised Mr. and Mrs. Dudley that it was better to take the cash now rather than go through an extended appeal, which could take years to complete and would probably result in a reduction of the award for punitive damages. The Dudleys agreed and took the cash.

John Standish Clark

His vocal cords never recovered from the injury inflicted by Brian at the pool. He was forced to stop practicing law and is taking classes to learn sign language.

Suzanna Nudbello

Suzanna found an apartment in Palidoro, a town west of Rome. She was fortunate to land a job as an in-house attorney for the Vatican Bank, although not licensed to practice law in Italy.

Suzanna read on the Internet that Brian was arrested and charged with serious crimes. She was confident he would eventually be acquitted—he was a very good lawyer and would somehow figure out how to beat the system.

Once Brian was free, Suzanna planned to contact him to thank him for all his help. She hoped that he would eventually visit her in Italy.

Mrs. Martha Dudley

After agreeing to the $500 million cash settlement, she commenced chelation therapy with intravenous chelating agents to reduce the metallosis to an acceptable level. She then had surgery to remove the metal-on-metal HID and replace it with a state-of-the-art all-ceramic hip joint. The surgery was performed by Dr. Fred Feigelman at the Hospital for Special Surgery. Mrs. Dudley now walks unassisted and donated her wheelchair to the hospital, along with a check for $25 million. Mrs. Dudley no longer lives at Pleasant Pastime.

Dr. Fred Feigelman

As a result of his testimony at trial and his early detection of defects in the Device, Dr. Feigelman became a favorite on the lecture circuit as a motivational speaker. His speeches stressed the importance of sticking with one's beliefs. After Mrs. Dudley's successful surgery, he decided to cease the active practice of medicine. The lecture circuit was lucrative and he received a large advance on a book he was writing about the HID trial against ZeiiMed.

Meadhbh O'Shea

Meadhbh took a two-month leave from work to receive counseling. She was severely traumatized from killing the two strangers on East 84th Street. Her gun permit was revoked because the 20-round magazine in her FN Five-Seven was not permitted under New York law. No mention was made of the illegality of the additional cartridge in the chamber. Also, Meadhbh admitted giving possession of her pistol to Brian, thereby committing another violation of the gun laws.

After her trauma counseling ended, Meadhbh illegally purchased a Springfield XD 40 subcompact semi-automatic handgun that easily fit into her purse. She then returned to her regular shift at *Très Bien*.

Dr. Joe

Dr. Joe's former wife arranged the wake, followed by a Mass at Infant Jesus Roman Catholic Church in Port Jefferson. Kim did not attend the wake because she felt uncomfortable meeting the ex-wife. However, she attended the Mass and sat in the last pew of the Church.

Kim Bradford

The ferry returned her to the terminal after the cars were removed from the water and the body of the Mercedes driver recovered. The police drove Kim home. Dr. Joe's disemboweled body had not yet been removed from the house because it was part of the crime scene. Blood was everywhere. Kim decided to spend a few weeks at her mother's house. She was emotionally traumatized by Dr. Joe's death. She was unable to receive any love or comfort from Brian because he was in jail following his shooting rampage. She didn't know when or if he would be bailed out. Her life was in shambles.

John Edison

The bullet wounds required several surgeries.

Despite intense therapy for months following his surgeries, walking without assistance was still very difficult. He was more comfortable remaining in his wheelchair. A newspaper article in the *New York Press* stated that he may step down as the Chief Executive Officer of ZeiiMed, although ZeiiMed would not confirm the report. ZeiiMed did confirm that Edison resigned from his federal appointment.

The revolver found next to Edison in his apartment was unlicensed. Edison was not charged with a crime. ZeiiMed's many friends in the Police Department expunged all references to his gun from the police report of the incident. The police report also recommended that no charges be made against Edison arising from the shootout at his apartment.

Sergeant Melissa Black

Sergeant Black recovered completely from her wound. She retired with a full disability and moved to the Village of Port Jefferson to raise a family with her husband.

Alfonso and Ryan

The law firm's lease expired. The landlord at 40 Wall Street would not renew. The explosion had caused extensive damage to the building and many lawsuits were commenced as a result of pedestrian injuries from the falling debris. Alfonso and Ryan planned to upgrade to more expensive accommodations now that the firm was flush with cash from its large fee in the settlement with ZeiiMed.

Dr. Howard B. Heeled

After the trial, Dr. Heeled was fired by ZeiiMed. He then took a vacation in Mexico City. He never returned. The police in Mexico City reported that he was accidentally killed during a gun battle between soldiers and the gang members of a drug cartel. Some of Dr. Heeled's family members refused to believe the police report. They believed ZeiiMed paid local gang members to execute him as he walked out of his hotel one morning.

Brian Bradford

Brian was charged with Manslaughter in the Second Degree, a class "C" felony, as a result of the death of the two men inside Edison's apartment. Also added was felony assault with a deadly weapon and reckless endangerment. If convicted, he could receive a lengthy sentence and lose his license to practice law.

His felony arraignment was finally scheduled. Two correction officers from Rikers escorted him to New York County Supreme Court, Criminal Term, located at 100 Centre Street. The handcuffs were taken off once he was in the Courtroom. Brian was dressed in street clothes provided by the authorities, his orange jumpsuit left in his cell.

Mary Douglas appeared as his lawyer.

The young prosecutor argued to the Court that Mr. Bradford might flee the United States if granted bail. He contended that the felony charges and the loss of his career were ample motivation for Bradford to take flight to a foreign jurisdiction.

The prosecution also noted that Suzanna Nudbello apparently left the country before the verdict against ZeiiMed was announced as part of a plan worked out with Mr. Bradford. As such, it was conceivable, even probable, that Mr. Bradford planned to join her. The prosecutor also explained that his investigation, based on the tape recordings of Brian Bradford's phone calls from Rikers, revealed that Mary Douglas likewise assisted Ms. Nudbello in leaving the country. Therefore, she may also assist Mr. Bradford in a rendezvous with Ms. Nudbello outside the jurisdiction of the Court.

The Judge reserved decision on his bail application. The Court did not appear inclined to release Brian before the criminal trial.

Kim was in the Courtroom. Brian waved to her as he was escorted out of the Courtroom. She waved back. She looked stunned.

Brian was returned to the custody of the corrections officers and driven back to his cell at Rikers Island to await the Court's final decision on bail. Brian once again made a profane comment to the officer conducting the strip search. The result was an extended sixty-day assignment to solitary confinement.

Brian was convinced he had little chance of surviving incarceration.

ABOUT THE AUTHOR

Tom Breen has practiced law for many years as a partner in a law firm in downtown New York. He lives with his wife on Long Island. Their two daughters are also practicing attorneys in New York City. Tom's litigation experience was very helpful in creating courtroom and deposition scenes that feature realistic testimony and diverse characters in tense judicial settings. He is also a *Goodreads* author and a member author of International Thriller Writers.

Born in Vincennes, Indiana, he earned his B.A. from the College of the Holy Cross and a Juris Doctor from New England School of Law.

OTHER TITLES BY TOM BREEN

The Complaint

order at www.pegasusbooks.net

www.ingramcontent.com/pod-product-compliance
Lightning Source LLC
Chambersburg PA
CBHW030422310726
48979CB00009B/1575/J

* 9 7 8 1 9 4 1 8 5 9 4 7 6 *